TRAINING SEASON

Leta Blake

ISBN: 978-1494304638
Digital ISBN: 978-1626227194

Cover design © 2013 by Dar Albert at Wicked Smart Designs
www.wickedsmartdesigns.com

Editing by Keira Andrews
keiraandrews.com

Other Books by Leta Blake:

Free Read
Stalking Dreams

Tempting Tales with Keira Andrews
Earthly Desires
Ascending Hearts
Love's Nest

*Dedicated to all Olympic athletes who have given up so much
for their shot at glory and, especially, to all the LGBT citizens of Russia who
have been brutally forced to give up too much. May your efforts be rewarded
with joy, and may your love be returned with love.*

PART ONE

CHAPTER ONE

Early Fall

"Montana? You must be joking."

"It's beautiful there."

"So?"

"And you'll be paid eight thousand dollars a month," Matty's mother replied. "Where else are you going to find that kind of money? To skate at the Olympic level again, you'll need to hire coaches, trainers, and pay for costumes. You'll have to consider the cost of a choreographer, not to mention rink time. You know this."

"Yeah, but do I look like a rugged, plaid-shirt wearing, *Brokeback Mountain* kinda gay? No, I do not." Matty rubbed his lower back. The injury still ached, but it wasn't breathtaking anymore. At least he could skate again and wasn't stuck in bed, sweating in pain every time he moved.

"For eight thousand a month, Matty, you can't afford not to be."

Matty sat down on his bed and looked around the room. Pictures and posters still decorated the walls in a juvenile profusion of color. Gifts from his fans cluttered the vanity and desk, and filled the big trunks lining one wall. Everything from handmade dolls of himself to cross-stitched Christmas stockings featuring him as a skating Santa were in those trunks.

Matty's mother wouldn't let him throw any of it away, and so the gifts collected in the most attractive antique trunks he could find. He loved all of it, of course, but if his dreams of returning to form came true, his mother might need to start renting a storage unit for all of the memorabilia.

At this point, there wasn't much Matty wouldn't do for money. Okay, peddle his ass—*that* he wouldn't do. Theft, drugs, or gambling— *no.* He wouldn't even know where to begin a profitable life of crime, and seeing the inside of a jail cell was a sure way to never skate again. Many had thought his back injury was career ending, and the last thing he needed was to finish his career by being a moron.

He'd looked into getting a job—like, a real one—but nothing paid enough to get him back on the ice, and he was under-qualified by several degrees for anything that would. But...*Montana?*

"Margaret is doing you a giant favor. You'll have to apply for the job, though," his mother said as she paced around his room. Her blouse and slacks hung on her whip-thin form, and she ran her hands through her brown-and-gray bob. "She's on board—she wants to see you skate again. That's the entire reason she contacted me about this. Well, one of the reasons. The other is that they really do want someone to look after the ranch while they're in Europe. Her grandsons used to do it when Margaret and her husband travel, but they're away at college now."

"How do you even know this woman again, Donna?"

"Don't call me by my first name and don't be difficult, Matty. You know she's been a fan of yours for years. She's followed your career and she's come to your competitions and shows. You've met her quite a number of times."

Matty shrugged.

Donna sighed and rolled her eyes. "We email and keep in touch. She's a bit eccentric in the way of old, wealthy people, but she's a good woman, and she's willing to change your life for the price of a few months light work in Montana. Think of it as patronage."

"It's not patronage if she wants more out of me than just my artistry."

"Fine, think of it as a grossly over-paid job and suck it up."

"You realize she just wants me to be her pet, don't you? This could all be some sick tactic to get me alone in the wilderness with her. It could end up like that Stephen King novel. She's going to kidnap me and make me into her own private skater! She'll force me to perform for her pleasure! If I don't, she'll cut off my foot."

"Matty, that's not going to happen."

"You don't know that. It totally could."

Donna puffed out her cheeks and rolled her eyes again. "Do you want to skate again, or don't you?"

Across from his bed, in the place of honor on the wall opposite, was the tattered *Ice Castles* poster, old when he'd gotten it off eBay at the age of ten. It was the movie that had inspired him to skate. He'd wanted to be Lexie so badly, and he'd experienced the first deep stirrings of lust when he imagined being in Nick's arms. He stared at him now, feeling the old thrum of longing.

His eyes skimmed over the photographs of skaters pinned all around the poster. They were a mixture of those he'd admired and some he'd loathed, but all competitors he'd been determined to bury. And he had. Until he hadn't.

He'd spent too much time depressed after his injury. Stuck in his bed with no exercise, and, worse, he'd eaten more food than anyone could justify. He'd never weighed so much or been so out of shape since he'd started skating at the elite level when he was eleven. He was still slim by most standards, but skating had its own rules.

There was so much work to do to get back into fighting form, and sometimes the thought of it exhausted him. Still, if he never made a comeback from his injury, he'd never prove himself. Never make up for his failures. He glanced around at his mementos and sighed.

While his room at his parents' house in Norfolk was comfortable, he still regretted moving out of his much more tastefully decorated apartment in New Jersey. After he got out of the hospital, there'd been no choice but to move back home to Virginia.

Things had been tight for the family since Matty's injury. He'd been out of competition for a whole season, missing out on prize money and also his usual income from ice shows in Japan, Russia, and South Korea. Since he wouldn't be able to compete this season either, he'd lost his funding from the Federation and would have to prove himself all over again.

His father hadn't been able to work since he'd nearly lost his right leg in a car wreck when Matty was nine. The money he'd received from the resulting lawsuit had all gone into Matty's skating career years ago.

Without Matty's income, his mother had taken on a second job. He knew how miserable she was making phone solicitations five nights a week just to make ends meet. Worse, his brother, Joseph, had dipped into his college savings a few times to help with the bills.

If Matty wanted to get life back on track for all of them, he needed the cash this job provided. He gazed thoughtfully at the *Ice Castles* poster again. If Lexie could skate again after losing her sight, then he could come back from this. And he would. Or he wasn't Matty Marcus.

"So, what do I have to do?" he asked his mother, who waited patiently.

She sat beside him on the bed. "Not much. Margaret wants to give you this opportunity. Consider it an extravagant and wonderful gift. But her husband needs a little convincing."

"What does that mean?"

"Basically, he just wants to make sure you're responsible and there won't be any parties, or unwelcome visitors. That kind of thing."

"Unwelcome visitors? You're talking about Elliot."

"I'm talking about Elliot, Joanna—"

"She's my agent!"

"She's not invited to Montana."

"Strict."

"Not just Elliot or Joanna, though. I'm also talking about Heidi, or Zarah, or Franklin, or anyone else. Matty, these people are willing to pay you a lot of money and it's only six months. I think you can do without seeing your friends."

11

"What about my training? After all I've been through, six more months off the ice could be the end of my career. It's already been more than a year, Mom. I'm twenty-one. This is probably my last shot at medaling at the Olympics. It's only two and a half years away."

"There's a rink twenty minutes from the ranch. You could start training again right away. Margaret said she'd ensure you had rink time, and she'd even pay for it in advance if you let her know how many hours a week. This is huge, Matty. This is so much more than eight thousand a month."

"Assuming I get the job," Matty said. "I still have to convince her husband."

"Show up, look your best, demonstrate that you can take care of the horses, be polite, and say 'sir.' I think you'll get the job."

"I have to apply in *person*?" Matty asked.

"I bought your plane ticket this morning. You leave tomorrow." Donna patted his leg and stood up. "Don't pout. It's only Montana, not Moldova."

"If it were Moldova, I'd be able to practice speaking Russian, and, if I was *really* lucky, I could become a victim of human trafficking and get sold into sexual slavery. That could be really hot."

Donna groaned. "Hello, honey? Mouth-brain filter? Engage."

Matty sat up straighter. "Wait. Mama, how did you pay for the ticket?"

Donna patted the door frame. Matty saw her bare ring finger and tears came to his eyes.

"You should start packing for Montana, Matty. If our luck turns around, this time next year you'll be preparing for Cup of Russia."

Matty stared after her, a lump in his throat.

She'd sold her wedding ring—and who knew how much of her other jewelry. Her never-ending faith sometimes made him made him feel deeply ashamed. His parents had already eaten through their retirement accounts, their savings, and given everything they had to his skating. In his estimation, he hadn't paid them back at all. He'd been distracted and irresponsible, and squandered his opportunities.

After his disappointing performance at the last Olympics, and his injury, he was humbled that his mother still believed in him so completely.

Montana it was.

* * *

Matty called his best friend as soon as humanly possible, which, given the short notice afforded by his travel plans, was the moment the plane touched down in Missoula. Elliot was not pleased.

"You're in Montana? What the fuck, bitch?"

Matty told him about the job. "It's in some place called Whitefish."

"Where's *that*?" Elliot asked.

"God only knows. Probably just this side of hell. " He remembered the sight of the snow-dusted mountains as he'd flown in. "A beautiful hell, but hell all the same." Matty paused by an airport kiosk to pull a mirror out of his bag. He checked his carefully tousled brown hair and smoothed out his eyebrows. His brown eyes shone clear in the mid-morning light from the windows, and his full lips were rosy as he touched up his lip gloss. "Just think of what you know about the kind of people who go fly fishing and drive cattle and then put me in the middle of that vision. I'm probably going to experience a hate crime here."

"For sure," Elliot drawled, sounding amazed. "If you get the job I guess you won't be at my unbirthday party this weekend."

"Not unless it's in Montana."

"Sucks. I bought a great Mad Hatter hat for you."

"Mad Hatter? I don't think so Elliot. I was supposed to be Alice."

"You're Alice every year. It's my turn to be Alice, you queen."

"Whatever. You can be Alice all you want because I'm in *Montana*. Kill me now."

"I can't. Your mom would be mad."

Matty snorted.

"So, like, are there gonna be horses and shit?"

"And horse's shit."

"Oh, girl."

"Yeah."

Near the baggage claim, Matty spotted a medium-height, dark-haired woman with liberal gray woven in, wearing a fur coat and big glasses. She held a sign that read *Matthew Christopher Marcus*. She looked about ten years older than his mother, and she started waving her arms like mad trying to get his attention.

"I need to go. I've got to be responsible and charming. Wish me luck."

"Luck," Elliot said with a lack of sincerity that made Matty think Elliot had already lost interest in his situation. Elliot had a short attention span that way. Matty couldn't really blame him. He'd always been distractible since they'd met in third grade and bonded over the box of glitter crayons the art teacher allowed only her favorite and most fabulous students to use.

"Matty, darling," Margaret Page said as she enveloped him in a massive, Dior J'Adore-drenched hug. She was taller than him by an inch at least, and Matty rose on his toes so that his chin fell against her shoulder. "Look at you! Fit as a fiddle now, aren't you? How do you feel? Strong? Ready to train?"

She patted him all over as she talked, grabbing his arms and pulling them out from his sides, examining him like she was a long-lost aunt looking him over to see how much he'd grown.

But Margaret was nice enough, and Matty had no trouble keeping up his end of the conversation during the nearly three-hour drive from Missoula to the ranch. As they drove through miles and miles of farm land with the glorious mountains pulling Matty's attention constantly, she'd interrupt their conversation to wave her hand out the window and say, "This is Kalispell, a good place to look for things you might not find in Whitefish," or "That's Flathead Lake, the biggest freshwater lake west of the Mississippi."

This last she said with great pride in her voice. Matty, overcome by the beauty of the lake, the mountains, and the vast, endless sky, only nodded mutely. It wasn't like him to be left speechless, but the natural beauty around him took his breath away.

During their drive, Margaret asked him some hilarious questions about who was "dating" who in the skating world. The air quotes were Margaret's and she clearly wanted to know who was getting it on. He dished a little dirt to make her happy—and he hoped to get the job—but he kept the biggest insider secrets to himself. He did have a tell-all book to pen one day, assuming he could get back in the game at all.

Whitefish, the closest town to the ranch, was about as quaint as one could imagine, tucked as it was beneath the imposing, impossibly beautiful Big Mountain, and surrounded on all sides by the Rockies. It sort of made Matty want to throw up a little in his mouth. Not because he couldn't appreciate the loveliness of it, but because he was going to end up with a boot in his teeth before this thing was done. He just knew it. Gay boys like him didn't belong in rugged towns like Whitefish.

Margaret drove out of her way to show Matty the ice rink. "It isn't much, darling, but the Stumptown Ice Den is what we've got, and it should do the trick. Time's paid up through March. Twenty hours a week—just schedule in advance when you'll be there, of course. If you need more, you can work that out with management."

"That's too much," Matty said.

"Nonsense, consider it a bonus for doing this for us. Your mom said you could use the money and the time to focus. I want to see you take the gold at Worlds next year, Matty. Make a big comeback. And when you're in the Kiss and Cry, and the camera is on you, it wouldn't be amiss for you to mouth, 'Thank you, Margaret,' all right? I might just wet my pants if you did that."

"Mrs. Page, I sincerely hope I don't deny you that particular dry cleaning bill."

"I think since you'll be living in my house, dusting my trinkets, eating on my plates, and taking care of my horses, you can call me Margaret. In fact, I insist on it."

"Done," Matty agreed. It certainly sounded like he had the job.

The ranch itself was another twenty minutes outside of Whitefish, and Matty's back was starting to ache from sitting before they even got there. He'd need to stretch plenty once he got settled to prevent a setback. He dug around in his bag for ibuprofen and a bottle of water, and downed a few pills.

"I've done my share of traveling," Margaret said. "And I'm getting ready to travel again, but let me tell you, Matty, this land is some of the most beautiful in the world, if I do say so myself."

Matty had done his share of traveling, too, and he had to agree with her.

"George and I moved here after his heart attack. He was only forty-two at the time and I somehow just knew that living here, in the fresh mountain air, he'd heal up just fine. That was twenty years ago now. He's strong as an ox, Matty. That's what Montana does for a person." She patted his knee and smiled at the road ahead of them. "I hope it works its healing magic on you too."

When they pulled up alongside two long driveways that seemed to stretch back into forever, Margaret got out and opened the blue mailbox. Before getting back behind the wheel, she knocked the snow off the red one next to it.

"Rob's box," she said, as though that explained a lot.

Matty just nodded.

As she drove up the pine-lined drive toward the house, she muttered, "Bills, bills, I swear that's all we get. I've got giant, pre-addressed and metered envelopes in a file in the desk in the library. I'll show you when we get inside. Just dump the bills in there every week and send them to our accountant. There's another file with envelopes for the other mail—except for junk mail, which I trust you to sort out—and you can just send that along to my sister every week. She'll handle it from there."

"I'm inspired by your organizational skills," he said, feeling warm and fuzzy toward her. "I'm kind of a freak about that kind of thing myself."

Margaret looked pleased. "Listen, you've got the job, okay, hon?

So long as you don't offend George, and I'm sure you won't. But, just...well, be yourself."

Matty smiled. "I can't be anything else."

George Page met them in the driveway in front of the two-story, log and stone ranch house, wearing a cowboy hat, a white button-up shirt, and carrying a rifle. He was not smiling, and he eyed Matty like he was John Wayne about to challenge him to a gun fight.

"So, you're the skater."

"I am, Mr. Page. Sir," Matty said, shivering in the cold air. He pulled his coat around him a little tighter and smiled, willing the man to love him like every good and righteous human being in the world ought. "I also love horses."

The man's eyes became less narrow. He rested the butt of the shotgun on his foot as he said, "Horses?"

"Yes, sir. In fact, I had a horse as a kid. I adored him. His name was Butterscotch Brier." Matty smiled fondly. He'd had a soft yellow-ish mane and a smooth caramel-colored coat. Matty had loved standing on a stool to brush him down. The methodical work had soothed him. He'd also loved how the wind had rushed over his skin as he rode, digging his heels into Butterscotch to go faster. The sensation of flying through air was something he loved about skating too.

"What happened to him?"

"Well, I had to sell him once I started my figure skating career. He wasn't getting enough attention."

"Hmmph." George looked unimpressed.

"But I grew up in the country. Before my dad hurt his leg, we had a small farm in Virginia," Matty went on, forcing likeability into every molecule of his body. "I'm excited to get some time away from the city. I've missed the countryside. Though this," he motioned toward the mountains and the piney brush that fell away into beautiful strips of land, "is so different from where I'm from. It's stunning."

George's face registered something that appeared to be interest, so Matty forged ahead. "Oh, and I love mucking out stalls. It's satisfying to get them fresh again. Makes me feel like I've really accomplished something."

George said, "You got the job when you said you were familiar with horses. Don't go lying about liking to muck out stalls. Blowing smoke up my ass isn't gonna win you any points."

Matty could see why this guy was rich. He didn't tolerate any nonsense. Still, Matty hadn't been lying. He'd never been exactly normal in his fetish for cleanliness, but his horse had always appreciated it.

"I'm a clean freak," Matty said. "I really do like cleaning horse stalls."

George was speculative, but he finally said, "Okay, then. Margaret wants it to be you, and I don't have time to deal with this, so I'll let her have you as her little pet project. Let me tell you the rules, son. No parties. No friends from *wherever* to keep you company. I'm taking a risk on *you*, not your boyfriend or your best girlfriend, got it? If you need help with the horses, Rob Lovely's ranch is next door, and he's trustworthy. Bought this land offa him after his daddy died. You can rely on him if you have any problems. You agree to that and you've got eight thousand dollars a month in your bank account, a car to drive for the next six months, and a place to live. Do we have a deal?"

"Yes, sir," Matty said, sticking out his hand to shake on it. "We most certainly do."

CHAPTER TWO

He had to live here for six months. He didn't know if he could bear it.

The Pages' ranch house was well-appointed, if you liked country-chic crossed with rancher-tough, and dashed liberally with a world traveler's beloved trinkets. But it made Matty want to cry and start ripping quilts from the walls, or slash the patchwork patterned sofa, and take a sledge hammer to the faux-brick tiles in the kitchen.

The only items Matty didn't want to get rid of or destroy in the Pages' house-from-interior-decorator-hell were the bear skin rugs in front of each fireplace, the deer skins that hung on the den's walls, and the mink throw pillows on Matty's guest room bed. Everything else *had to go.*

Even the view from the house wasn't all that spectacular. Given how breathless he'd been at every turn on the drive in, he found it unfair and disappointing. Situated at the base of a mountain, the house's back porch looked onto ascending pines, thus the mountain itself was blocked from view by virtue of being much too close.

The view from the front porch wasn't terrible. It was all lovely hills that rolled out to flat strips of land dotted with the neighbor's cattle and smaller animals that looked like goats.

All in all, Matty felt like he was an alien plopped down in the middle of a beautiful, but utterly foreign landscape. He'd never felt so isolated from everything and everyone that shaped Matty Marcus into the rare creature he knew himself to be—not even Japan had seemed so insurmountably strange to him.

The Pages settled Matty into the house, showing him around the ranch, explaining his duties several times over, and introducing him to the horses, Daisy and Maple Syrup.

"Maple Syrup is the sweetie. He's my darling," Margaret said, feeding the horse in question a sugar cube. "Daisy? She's more of a diva, I guess you might say. She likes to have her own way. Headstrong is a better word for it, I suppose. I wouldn't try to ride her, if you take the notion."

Matty had mixed feelings about whether or not he should ride the horses. George made it clear that he *could,* but he'd rather that Matty *didn't.* The horses would get plenty of exercise in the fields and along the trails up into the base of the mountains.

"They'll wander back home at dinner time and you can put them in their stalls if the weather is too bad," George added. "They're accustomed to that."

"Yes," Margaret agreed. "Now that we're old, they aren't ridden much anymore. We should probably look for a new home for them. But our grandsons still ride when they visit in the summer, and it's not like the horses are *unhappy* here. They do have each other."

Given that Matty's injury was still freshly healed, a fall from a horse could be a disaster. He didn't think he'd risk it.

He was told if there was a big snow, the horses needed to be kept in the smaller fields closer to the barn or in the barn itself until the worst of the weather had passed.

"If they do get caught up in a snowstorm later in the winter, let Rob Lovely know and either he or one of his ranch hands will go out and fetch 'em." George then very pointedly put Rob Lovely's phone number on the refrigerator door under a rooster magnet.

"But don't worry," Margaret said. "The first big snow shouldn't come until November at the very earliest."

As Matty's luck would have it, the weather had been unseasonably cold for October, with lows in the mid-twenties at night, and not getting much above forty during the day. In fact, an intense cold front was due this weekend and temperatures might drop into the teens or below.

To make it worse, they were calling for freezing rain. George warned that the pine trees shading the long drive made it icy and dangerous, especially near the house where it curved around a few trees and sloped uphill. Matty had to be sure to salt the drive and get snow tires put on the car the second week of October, or as soon as he heard a snowstorm being forecast, whichever came sooner.

If the ice did come as predicted, Matty figured he could count out making it in to the skating rink until next week. He'd have to salt the drive and, given how long it was, that'd take all day and would probably aggravate his back injury. The thought pissed him off. He *had* to get back into some kind of reasonable shape if he was going to be able to return to competitive skating and start with a new coach in April after the end of the current skating season. There was no time to lose.

Matty still couldn't believe that Denise, his former coach, had really retired after his injury. She was only fifty-six, but she'd had enough of the politics, if not the sport. Matty blamed himself for her decision. If he'd been easier to work with, if he'd followed Denise's instructions instead of fighting her every step of the way, maybe she would have found her job more rewarding. But after it was clear he was out last season, she'd given up her other students and moved to California with her girlfriend. Donna got the occasional postcard or email from her, and from all reports, they seemed quite happy.

Matty vacuumed and cleaned the entire house immediately after dropping the Pages at the airport, and was disturbed to find that all of the little trinkets strewn about were fuzzy with a film of dust, as though Margaret hadn't really cleaned them in months—if ever.

Matty set about thoroughly and methodically washing each item in warm water, scrubbing with a toothbrush until every last one was clean, all the while marveling at what would make a woman buy a shot glass from every city she'd ever been to, and collect ceramic figurines of children in lamb outfits.

Still, when he was done, it was sparkling and fresh in the living room. He thought Margaret would be pleased—if she weren't on her way to Australia, at that very moment, probably getting all geared up to pick out a shot glass in Sydney.

The house was big, but the rooms available to Matty were few. Upstairs was locked off, since really everything he needed was downstairs. They'd given him their best guest room, Margaret had said, and she'd hoped he'd be comfortable in it. He lied and said he would be.

On the phone with Elliot as he scrubbed down the kitchen and analyzed the cookware, he said, "It's horrible. The scenery is amazing, but completely not my kind of place. I don't hike, or fish, or ski, and the town is the size of my shoe. Elliot, everything in this house is so ugly I can feel it killing my soul. And I'm already lonely."

"I could fly out next week to keep you company for a while," Elliot offered, kind of reluctantly.

"Alas, Mr. Page told me my best girlfriend was absolutely not invited."

"Would you love me more if I pretended to feel at all sorry about that?"

Matty couldn't blame Elliot. They both liked a faster pace of life. His dream was to move to Manhattan and merge into that world. He adored the people rushing to work, hailing taxis, walking their dogs, and never looking his way twice. It inspired him and filled him with passion for life.

From what he could tell, Whitefish was not going to provide him with any kind of inspiration. In fact, based on his trip to the Safeway in Whitefish it was clear no one in the town knew what to do with a man wearing a touch of lip gloss or carrying a handbag. He heard some unflattering remarks from fellow shoppers as he walked the paltry aisles.

It wasn't a big deal, really—nothing he hadn't heard before—but he was already upset by the discovery that they had very little that was organic or fresh, so it was insult to injury. He wanted to cry as he paid the cashier eighty dollars for inferior food, but instead he smiled prettily and said thank you. Then he took the bags to the car himself, declining help from the obviously confused and pimply teenage boy who called him "ma'am."

Oh, Whitefish. What additional horrors did the town have in store for him?

* * *

A week later, Matty opened the six boxes of his belongings his mother had mailed, trying to find where she'd packed the fur coats, his make-up, and his underwear. It was as though she'd run from one corner of his room to another, randomly adding things to the boxes, with little rhyme or reason. They'd all been marked *Matty's room* as though that described the contents in any helpful way.

He found his make-up in a small cardboard box beneath his gym socks and a gold, sequined vest he'd worn for a competition when he was fifteen. He had no idea why his mother had included it, but he put it on, because, aside from Flathead Lake and the glint of the sun on the mountains, it was the sparkliest thing he'd seen since arriving in Montana. It lifted his spirits in an unexpected and very necessary way.

Matty sighed as he took his make-up into the bathroom and began organizing it on the vanity. Looking through the products, he opened one of the small jars of blue, glittery eye shadow, and applied a little to his eyelids absentmindedly. He thought about how he was going to survive the next six months, and wondered if he'd be able to train himself enough to lure in a renowned coach.

His heart was set on Valentina Chapayeva from the Ukraine, and he swallowed hard and sent up a small prayer that by April he'd have what it took to gain her interest and join her rink in New York. Even though he was a national champion, he was afraid he'd been out of sight so long that he'd be out of mind in the skating world.

He sorted through the body glitter, lipsticks, and rouge, finding a few things that he'd nearly forgotten about. He looked in the mirror, puckered his lips, and ran his hands through his hair.

Music. Yes, he needed some music—something fast to get his body moving. He fiddled with the stereo in the living room and figured out how to dock his iPod

Eight songs later, he had glitter body paint smeared on his chest, his eyes done up in brilliant blues and greens, and bright, cotton-candy pink lipstick on his lips. Wearing only his track pants and the gold sequined vest, he was far from fierce, but still shiny, and that made him feel almost as good. He danced across the room, easily keeping the rhythm with no one's judging gaze to throw him off. He gave his body over to it, and spun around madly, jumping, kicking, and leaping.

He paused in the middle of the room, feeling a little flushed, but not winded. He was glad his workouts back home had increased his stamina. His current plan was to get up every day, have a small breakfast, get the horses settled and then work out, either in a gym, on the ice, or both.

Matty recognized how bratty it was to complain about the ranch house. After all, it had amazing amenities. Margaret's exercise room beside his bedroom had a treadmill and Bowflex. He supposed on days he couldn't get into Kalispell for a proper workout in the Athletic Club (something else arranged for him by Margaret) it would do to help keep him strong. He also had a plan for skating when he couldn't get into Whitefish's rink.

He'd discovered his plan B when George had walked him around the ranch, pointing out various areas that the horses sometimes lingered. As they'd walked, Matty had noticed two men on horses, riding among the cattle on the hill below.

"Rob's ranch hands," George explained. "He's got four employees over there now. Rob's expanding his operation. He's finally making a bit of a profit, I reckon. First time since his old man died, I think."

Matty nodded absently, his eyes fixed on something else entirely. To the left of where George pointed, there was a very large, seemingly shallow, mostly circular pond. It was situated in the shadow of the mountain on one side and sheltered on the other by a large, fat pine. Though the temperature had climbed to almost forty that morning, Matty could see the glitter of ice over the shaded top of the pond.

He'd studied it carefully as George talked on and on about horses and the neighbor's cattle, and ranch hands and profits, finally interrupting him to ask, "Does that ever freeze over?"

"Sure. It's halfway to frozen over now. Give it two more days of temperatures like this and it'll be frozen half through."

"How deep is it?"

"Not that deep." George had smirked like he was amused by something private. "That's Margaret's little personal Flathead Pond. Built it for her when I bought the place from Rob. She wasn't too happy because she wanted land on the lake. I couldn't pass up the good deal Rob offered me, so I told her I'd *build* her a damn lake." George chuckled, a sound Matty hadn't heard him make before. "Oh yes, she was fit to be tied over this here pond. First she was mad and then she laughed until she cried." He grinned. "Yep, Rob's ranch manager, Bing Lozar, dug this out for her and had it lined."

"Has anyone ever skated on it?" Matty had asked.

"The boys do it all the time. Used to pretend to be Wayne Gretzky and Mark Messier out there."

Matty had smiled, thinking that George might not have liked it if his grandsons had pretended to be Matty Marcus out there. "Mind if I skate on it, sir?"

"Fine by me. Just don't bust your head." George had pointed his finger at him. "If you do, don't even think about suing me."

With that in mind, Matty had gone out to the pond already that morning and found it was definitely frozen several inches down. It wasn't the best surface, but in an emergency it would do.

Another song came on, and Matty ran a hand through his hair. He twirled a bit more, the room flashing by, and he allowed himself to sink into the spin, the dizzy familiar feeling of the world going into a precarious balance.

A loud crash brought him front and center.

He stood panting, listening for something more. A rolling crunch rattled through the room. Clutching his chest, he jumped. The noise seemed to come from the front porch.

Matty grabbed a coat from the box next to him—his mink from his last trip to Russia—and slipped it on. His heart raced as he tiptoed toward the living room window.

Was it a bear? Did bears live in Montana? And why had he never thought to investigate that possibility before now? What if it was an elk? Were they dangerous? Maybe it was a coyote, or a wolf, or just a really big, scary person.

He peered out the front window. He squinted into the sun and saw nothing but pine trees and cows like always. The knock on the door, a heavy, hard thudding, made his heart race like he was sitting in the Kiss and Cry waiting for scores to come in.

Matty glanced in the mirror by the front door, smoothed his hair, wiped a stray bit of eyeliner away, and threw his chest out and his chin up. Matty Marcus was rocking the glittery glory on a ranch in Montana. *Never let it be said that rural locales took any shine away from this bitch.* He opened the door.

The man on the front porch, with his hand raised to knock again, was blond, and he might as well have been Montana personified—tall, strong, and heart-stoppingly handsome. He was also probably not a day over thirty.

"Uh..." The man cleared his throat and flung his thumb over his shoulder toward the hill. "Hi. I'm the neighbor. Thought I'd bring some...ah..."

He didn't seem to know where to look. His eyes slid down to Matty's bare chest peeking out from the fur coat and gold sequined vest, and then down over Matty's track pants to his bare feet. The man swallowed and looked away. He kept talking, though.

"I brought some firewood up from the barn. Thought you might need it...or want it. It's supposed to get pretty cold tonight. I figured you didn't have any close to the house yet. George doesn't bring it up unless he needs it. So I brought some. Up. For you."

Matty felt his practiced "now we're talking to the media" smile settle on his face. He stuck out his hand. "Thank you. That's very kind of you. I appreciate you thinking of me."

The man shook firmly. "Rob Lovely," he said. "I live over the hill and a few acres over."

The name was definitely fitting, Matty thought.

He supposed since he was dressed up in glitter and blue eye shadow, he should be glad the guy wasn't running away to alert any local homophobic hicks with baseball bats that the Pages had a flamer living in their house for the winter.

Matty pulled his coat around himself a little tighter when Rob released his hand. "Matty Marcus. Nice to meet you."

"So, are you from Missoula?" Rob said, his face revealed how much he doubted that.

"What makes you think I'm not from Polebridge?" Matty asked a little coyly, bring up a town Margaret had mentioned located almost due north of Whitefish with less than 30 residents.

He waited for the guy to stammer through an answer that could be summed up as Matty failing the good ol', pussy-loving, ranch-raised country boy looks test.

"Margaret said she was bringing in a friend's kid from the city," Rob said, rubbing his hands together, and keeping his eyes focused out toward the pastures.

"Oh," Matty said, amazed at how sweetly the guy had side-stepped an awkward moment. He even felt a little guilty for trying to set him up to begin with. "Well, I think by 'the city', she actually meant The City, as in New York. She seems to think I've lived there, even though I haven't. I'd like to, though. I will one day." His nipples ached from the cold, so he pulled the fur completely around his torso.

"I've never been, but I'm sure it's exciting," Rob said, his eyes moving to where Matty had covered up his exposed skin. "Is that a mink?"

"As a matter of fact, it is," Matty said, running a hand down its softness.

"My ex-wife's mother had one of a similar style, but it didn't look nearly so..." Rob flushed. "I mean...uh, it looks better on you. Well, um, I mean..."

"Thank you," Matty said, putting him out of his misery.

"You're welcome." Rob said, stuffing his hands in the pockets of his coat. "It's been a strangely cold October. Probably not the best of weather. Have you been able to get out and explore at all?"

"I'm still settling in," Matty said.

"Right." There was a silence as Rob swallowed hard and rubbed a hand over his forehead like he had a sudden headache. "Well, I piled the logs over there." He nodded toward the side of the porch. "I, uh, should let you get back to..." He smiled and used his head to indicate Matty's state of dress and state of being. "That. Or whatever."

"Thank you. I'd invite you in, but I'm sort of in the middle of *this*, so..." Matty paused and Rob flushed again, looked away and cleared his throat.

Matty retreated into the house, closing the door partway as he spoke. "Thanks again for the firewood. It was very thoughtful of you."

"Anytime," Rob said, backing away a few steps. "Just give me a call if you need anything. Help with the horses. Or whatever you need help with." He looked embarrassed for a moment, but then he offered Matty a fantastic smile. His teeth were white and straight and his eyes glowed. Matty noticed that they were green and very kind.

"I might take you up on that," Matty said, putting one bare foot on top of the other.

The movement seemed to catch Rob's eye. He looked at Matty's feet again before clearing his throat again. "Please do. I'm the neighborly sort and I'm happy to help."

Rob lifted his eyes again and a small wave of attraction washed over Matty. God, he needed to get laid if he was getting turned on by stammering Montana ranchers.

Rob nodded and lifted his hand and let it drop. Then he turned and trudged back through the front yard. Matty watched him walk, noting the sure, easy swing of his step as he crossed the lawn and then mounted the foot of the hill.

When Rob was a dark smudge against the sky, Matty shut the door and leaned against it. He glanced at himself again in the mirror and imagined being Rob Lovely from Montana. What had it been like to find *this* fabulous creature on the other side of a neighbor's door? It must have been like stumbling across The Man Who Fell to Montana. He laughed softly at the thought, threw off his coat, and sashayed to the kitchen for a mid-morning cup of piping hot water with bitters to trick his still-hungry stomach.

* * *

Maple Syrup made pleased nickering sounds as Matty patted his nose after putting him in his stall. Daisy was indeed a diva, but seemed to understand that she'd found a kindred spirit in him. She was incredibly obedient and listened carefully when Matty spent some extra time brushing her down and talking to her softly in Russian.

He hoped to be fluent enough by April to converse with Valentina Chapayeva, in her own language, should she agree to take him on. Besides, Russian was great, full of history and passion, and learning it felt amazing. Matty *always* strove to be amazing.

After taking a shower later that evening, Matty called his mother. He told her about Rob Lovely stopping by to bring wood up to the porch, and how he'd answered the door dressed like, well, himself.

"Honey, just remember Montana isn't New York City, and it isn't even New Jersey. People there might not be as…accepting."

"You've told me all of my life to speak my mind and be my own person," Matty said absently, studying his fingernails. He'd have to find a place in town to get a manicure because his nails looked like trailer trash.

"I'm just saying be careful."

"Careful is as careful does, Mama," Matty said, refusing to let the fear reach him. He'd spent his life with it, and he hadn't been careful yet. He wasn't going to start now. "And what careful does is boring. Can I talk to Dad?"

"Matty," his mother chided, but Matty knew she'd let it go. She had to—he was how she'd raised him to be. "Okay, hold on. Randy! Matty's on the phone and wants to talk to you."

His father's gruff hello filled Matty with a warm, safe feeling, and he clutched the phone a little tighter to his ear.

"Dad, how do you build a fire?"

Matty smiled at his father's confused, inarticulate snort, and he clarified, "I'm sitting here next to a fireplace, and thanks to the handsome neighbor, I've got firewood. Now how do I make them work together without burning down the Pages' house, singeing the bear rug, or setting myself aflame?"

He almost wished his father would have taken that bait and made a joke about how Matty was already flaming, like his brother Joey would have, but it also touched Matty's heart that it would never in a million years occur to his father to say that.

Soon he had a dinner of hot water with bitters, a plate of cut-up fruit and vegetables, and a small piece of lean meat eaten before a blazing fire. He flipped through several books on the Cyrillic alphabet his mother had packed in with his shoes before slamming the books shut. Bored, he went to wash the dishes.

As it turned out, the television only got the four main networks, and the computer only had dial-up. It would do for checking his email, but not much else. He typed like a chicken pecking for seed, but had thought that if he got really bored, he might take the time to learn more about Flathead County, do a vanity search or two, and definitely look at porn.

Thank god for the Pages' landline, since the reception on Matty's cell was spotty at best. At least they had 4G service in Kalispell and Whitefish itself, but it didn't reach into the hinterland. Matty supposed it was for the best. Cold turkey was the only way to break his addiction to Instagram and Tumblr, not to mention Facebook. And Twitter, and Snapchat, and—yes. This was a good thing.

Matty supposed he shouldn't be surprised about the dearth of technology since he'd moved into the home of people old enough to be his grandparents. Still, it was clear that he'd need to make a trip to town for some books, because he couldn't keep Elliot on the phone with him twenty-four seven.

Sighing, Matty gazed at the lattice of frost working its way up the den's windows and the strange, wild darkness beyond it. It had been over a week now since he'd even been on the ice. Too long. He wondered if he'd be able to get to Whitefish tomorrow, or if he'd have to spend the day salting the driveway and getting snow tires put on.

He missed the ice. The feel of it, the sound of it, the way he felt when he moved on it. It was a passion, but also his escape, a place where his emotions turned into movement. Where he was able to show the world his journey and express himself, and not in some cliché, New Age way.

At this time two years ago, he'd been training and competing, preparing for Nationals, and then the Olympics, and Worlds. He'd been unfocused and undisciplined, refusing to let Denise train him the way he needed. He'd been distracted, and maybe a little lovesick. He hadn't handled the thing with Cody and Vance very well.

It had been terrible and humiliating being dumped like that and replaced so quickly. Everyone around them knew, even if no one said anything publicly, and it had sucked in every way. Competing against

Vance and seeing Cody in the stands cheering for his opponent blew his cool. He'd succumbed to those emotions, yes, but more importantly when it came to his skating performance, he'd just been an entitled brat.

He'd never admit it to anyone, but the truth was he was lazy. He'd been given a gift but he'd never developed proper discipline. Skating had been so easy for him in so many ways, or at least easier than it was for other people, and he'd been a slacker when it came to really putting in the time.

To make it worse, Denise couldn't rein him in. She was too nice and couldn't command his respect and fear. Matty knew if he was going to buckle down and work, and really achieve his potential as a skater, he needed a coach who could whip him into submission.

Fuck, if he was being honest, he wouldn't mind that in a boyfriend either.

He'd taken his talent and success for granted, and he'd paid the price. The injury had been the icing on top of the shit cake. He still had the terrible taste in his mouth from it. Nothing like being bedridden for months on end to make you appreciate the things you *do* have in your life.

Matty sat on the sofa, watching the glimmer of the now-dying coals. He wondered if it was possible to skate the way he had when he was starting out. Fresh. Pure. Like a bird soaring. Or was he too mucked up now to fly? Bogged down with too much shit to lift into the air? There was only one way to know.

Under an ocean of stars, beneath a Montana sky, he tested his wings.

George had been right about the pond. After a week of odd October coldness, it was frozen over now. The ice was rough, and Matty felt the jitter of it under his feet as he stepped out. At first he just allowed himself to move slowly, to feel the rush of the winter wind in his face and ruffling his hair, and his breath coming in cold, white puffs.

And then in his mind, the sky opened to him.

The footwork and the twirls came like a current of air pouring over him, and he took a jump with a smile on his face, landing it easily, arms out, hands perfect, and so he moved into the next one, his eyes closed, trusting his feet to find the ice without him.

The slam of the ice against his ass was perfect, and he laughed, slapping his gloved hands together, hearing it echo over the hills. He stood up, his arms at his sides, and he began again as joy spun out from him for the first time in too long.

He was a bird and he flew.

CHAPTER THREE

The next morning Matty woke up to two and a half inches of snow and patches of ice on the driveway. He considered the salt George had shown him, thought about the time it would take to lay it out, and though he knew it would be the smart thing to do, he felt resistant. He didn't want to waste his day or irritate his injury. The falls from the night before had required some ice and ibuprofen as it was.

Matty decided to head directly to the pond after caring for the horses, leaving the Whitefish rink, the problem of the driveway, and the promises he'd made to George for another day. It was such a beautiful morning with the sun sparkling on the fresh snow that he didn't even feel much regret.

As he approached the pond, he scratched at his unshaven face and surveyed the area. It was breathtaking. He put in his earbuds and pressed play on his iPod, making sure that it was clipped on securely before setting out on the ice. He wasn't tentative this time. No, he was fast and ready to work his body in ways that he hadn't in a while.

His smile stretched his cheeks as he landed the first jump. An easy one, sure, but it felt good all the same. He flew through some footwork and then laughed when the music for an exhibition piece he'd done a few years ago began on shuffle play. He fell into the program, surprised at how much he remembered. At the end of the song, he closed his eyes and did some improvisations, opening himself up to the music, and moving with it as it spoke to him. A long skid on his knees across the ice left him laughing and happy.

When he stood up and brushed off his pants, he grabbed his chest and *screamed*.

Rob stood by the edge of the pond with one hand on a blond boy's shoulder and the other raised in a gesture of apology.

Matty tore out his earbuds and bent over, hands on his knees. "Holy shit, you scared the crap out of me!"

"Sorry!" Rob said, his face twisting with guilt. "We called out, but I guess you didn't hear us."

"Yeah," Matty said, gesturing at his iPod. "Music."

"Sorry," Rob said again. "We'll, uh, just go."

"But Dad," the kid started, turning blue, pleading eyes up at his father. Rob just shook his head and indicated that they should move along. The kid looked disappointed, and Matty saw the skates hanging over his shoulders.

"Wait," Matty called out. "Did you want to skate?"

The boy tugged on his father's hand, and Rob turned back around, He shrugged. "Yeah. George lets Ben skate. So long as I won't sue if he busts his head open."

Matty laughed. "I got the same warning." He waved Ben over. "Go ahead. I'm finished here."

"We don't want to interrupt," Rob said.

"I should do weights now anyway. Or *Bowflex*, rather. Gotta love me some Bowflex," Matty said.

Rob smiled, a soft chuckle escaping his lips. "Margaret claims it makes her ass look like a forty-year-old's."

They both laughed as Ben jumped up and down impatiently.

Matty said, "So, go on. Skate!"

Ben broke free from his father with a grin on his face. "Awesome! Thank you!"

Matty wiped his forehead with his arm and watched the kid pull on his very beat up, very second-hand skates. Rob took off one of his gloves, shook it out, and put it back on. Matty watched, his eyes lingering a little on Rob's large, well-shaped fingers. Then he smiled and met Rob's soft, green eyes. "I didn't mean to scream like that. It wasn't very ladylike of me."

Rob's smile quivered like he was about to laugh, but he just nodded and shoved his gloved hands in the pockets of his coat. "Sorry for surprising you. We didn't expect to find you here."

Matty pushed his sweaty, cold hair away from his face, and shrugged. "I don't imagine you would." He watched Ben launch himself out onto the rough ice and straight into a single Axel. "Not with a perfectly good rink in town..." Matty trailed off.

Ben fell but stood up again. He pushed around the pond forcefully, determination on his face and in his movements.

"He's pretty good at this," Matty said, crossing his arms over his chest and watching Ben try another jump.

"Well, thanks," Rob said.

Matty glanced back at Rob and noticed that his smile was a little crooked, but in a charming kind of way.

Rob went on. "When he's with his mom he goes to the rink a lot, but I can't afford to take him in to town all the time. By the way, you're not bad at it yourself."

Matty burst out laughing. "Thanks."

Rob shrugged. "You're welcome."

Matty waited a moment to see if Rob was joking. "I'm a figure skater. Two time U.S. national champion, actually. I competed at the last Olympics."

"Wow. Congratulations. That's impressive. What brings you here? Are you through with skating? I'd have thought you'd train year round?"

"Unfortunately, an injury kept me out of the current season. And last season as well."

Matty didn't want to mention the skating politics, or his poor performances, or the money problems, since that all seemed crass. Not that he had a problem with being crass, but right now, in front of Rob Lovely, didn't feel like the right time to indulge.

Rob crinkled his brow in polite sympathy. "Sorry to hear about that. You're okay now?"

"I'm good, actually, and I'm working toward being amazing again. Hopefully I'll be able to start serious training in April for next season."

"What did you hurt? If you don't mind me asking, that is."

Matty put his hand on his lower back, but before he could answer Rob's eyes were drawn to something just over Matty's shoulder.

He frowned, shouting, "Hey! Be careful, son. If you bust your head, your mom will kill me!"

"And Cowboy George will panic that you'll sue." Matty looked over his shoulder to see Ben flinging himself into another attempt at an Axel, and slamming down hard. "Pull your stomach in tighter, and keep your head up," Matty said, skating over to pull the kid from the ice. "Are you okay?"

Ben shrugged. "Yeah. I've fallen harder than that."

"We should have a contest sometime." Matty smiled. "Who can fall the hardest and keep on going." Rob made a noise that sounded like discouragement and Matty glanced up at him. "You have to fall to skate."

Rob looked uncomfortable, and it occurred to Matty that maybe Rob didn't really want his son to skate. It probably didn't fit in with the manly ideals that a rancher held for his kid.

"My dad told me something similar about riding bulls."

Matty blinked at Rob. "You ride bulls?"

Ben's boyish laugh bounced off the quiet hills as he skated in circles. "Hell no. He hated his dad."

"Hate is a strong word, Ben," Rob said.

Matty glanced up at Rob, surprised that the "hell" was left unaddressed. "So, you don't hate your dad or bulls," Matty said.

"Bulls are all right," Rob replied. "So long as they mount my cows, earn their keep, and keep their horns the hell away from my ass."

Laughing, Matty sat down on the ground by the pond to take off his skates. He watched Ben. He was a strong skater, though unrefined and rough. "How long has he been taking lessons?" Matty asked.

"He doesn't really," Rob said. "He just likes to skate."

Matty watched the kid leap and land before losing it and crashing down on his side. He seemed fearless. Matty put his chin in his hand and watched him get up to try again. "Well, he's got some talent and, more importantly—and trust me on this one—a lot of drive."

"You think?"

"Definitely." Matty stood up and kicked his boots in the snow. "How long has he liked to skate?"

Rob shrugged. "A couple of years? I don't know for sure. He's always enjoyed taking a turn around the pond, but these tries at jumps and things are kind of new."

"Would he *like* lessons?" Matty asked.

"I'm not sure. He lives most of the time with his mom. I only get him on the weekends, and a few weeks here and there when she goes away on business trips."

"Well, he's welcome to talk to me about skating any time."

"Thanks. I'll let him know." Rob glanced down at his watch. "Ben, ten more minutes. I've got to get back to Lila before too long. She doesn't like to wait for dinner."

"Yeah, Dad. Okay."

"Well, good to see you." Matty started to walk away backwards, watching Ben skate. "Oh, and thanks for the firewood," he called. "I made my first fire last night and I didn't even set myself aflame! It was fantastic!"

"If you need more, there's plenty where that came from."

"Sure, I'll take your wood anytime!" Matty fought the smile that threatened to engulf his face, and he coughed, using it for a cover of his laugh.

But Rob laughed outright. "Consider me at your service. Though, technically, it wasn't my wood. So maybe it's more accurate to say that you'll take George's wood anytime."

Matty cracked up. "No, definitely not. I'm sure it's aged and gnarled."

Rob smiled, and his teeth were bright, reflecting the sun and snow, his eyes crinkling at the edges. He glanced toward Ben. "I'm sure."

Matty felt his cheeks warm, and he laughed again, still walking backwards.

Ben yelled, "See ya!"

"Bye!" Matty bounced a little as he headed back to the house thinking that back in the day Denise would have killed to get her hands on that kid.

* * *

The next morning Matty woke to what looked like four inches of snow, but after a two-hour Bowflex and treadmill session, he looked out to find the driveway was completely clear. Closer inspection when he trekked down to the mailbox showed that it had been plowed and thoroughly salted. The snow was piled by the side of the drive and the main road was entirely clear. Now that he felt okay about getting the car off the property, he could go into town, take care of the snow tire situation, and head over to the Stumptown Ice Den.

Matty didn't see any indication of who he should thank for his miraculously salted driveway, but he had a pretty good idea who was responsible. Mr. Handsome Neighborly Guy with a son named Ben and a girlfriend named Lila, and a warm, friendly demeanor. Really, Matty thought he should find that all so quaint to the point of having crossed over into disgusting, but instead he just thought Rob was super hot and super charming in a hunky kind of way.

Maple Sugar and Daisy were irked when Matty took less time with them, but Matty spoke to them in Russian, explaining that he'd be back in the evening to load them into their comfy stalls. As it was, he had a place to be, and some ice to kill...or die on. Depending on how he looked at it.

The Whitefish Stumptown Ice Den wasn't too awful...relatively. Matty had seen worse rinks in his years, and he was glad the ice was at least regulation size. He'd have plenty of room to move. It was the middle of a weekday, and he was pleased to find the place mostly empty.

Matty got a lot of attention from the owner, so he smiled a lot, joked, and shook hands all around. Everyone refrained from mentioning his actual performance at the Olympics, instead congratulated him on making it onto the team to begin with. A few older ladies who were there for seniors skating asked him about his travels, and he was happy to talk with them about the amazing places he'd been.

Questions about his rivalry with the uptight, annoying, "give it your all and all will be yours" current Olympic gold medalist, Alex Hampton, were to be expected. He played the answers wonderfully, he thought. In fact, he kind of wished there had been a camera there to capture his performance.

He struck just the right notes of real resentment and humorous faux-support, followed by a flash of genuine good-guy sweetness, and some kind words that seemed like he was opting to take the high road rather than reveal anything truly nasty. Matty loved when he played those moments like the answer was an art-form, a word sculpture built with grace, created to be strong with subtle and unsubtle meaning. Making digs at his rivals didn't have to be tacky—it could be yet another way to make life beautiful.

As Matty skated, he thought about Alex Hampton and Vance Jones, and the upcoming batch of rivals he'd have to overcome. A few months ago, those thoughts wore him out and tore him down. He'd found himself deflating on the ice, slowing and wincing, going home early to complain to his mother that his back hurt, when really, it was his pride that ached the most.

Now, stuck on a ranch in Montana for six months, his options for how to spend his time were limited. He could harass Elliot by phone, but that grew boring once he'd told Elliot everything there was to tell about the horrors of his current position, and grew hurtful when Elliot told him of the fabulous fun he was having with his new roommates in Greenwich Village.

So, Matty could work on his Russian, talk to the horses, and feel miserably sorry for himself. Or he could work out obsessively and plan his comeback.

The scenarios he entertained included standing on the top of the podium while the announcers were forced to eat their previously nasty predictions and cruel innuendos. In his more immature moments, he indulged in fantasies of Alex Hampton crying miserably, streaky tears marring his ugly face, as Matty accepted untold gold medals. Okay, so it was unlikely to happen, but it was Matty's imagination and he could make Alex cry in it if he wanted.

In his *most* immature fantasies, Cody ran onto the ice, shoving Vance aside to grab Matty's free hand—the one not clutching giant masses of roses fans had tossed down— and begged Matty to come back to him. Of course, Matty declined because he had so many better options now that he'd won every gold he could ever win.

Matty sighed. Really, he still thought it wouldn't have hurt so badly if he'd been the one to end it. But it was horrible to feel like he hadn't been worthy of *Cody's* affection. What did that even say about him if he couldn't even keep the heart of someone so needy?

But not loyal—Cody was anything but loyal, as it turned out. And loyalty was everything to Matty when it came to matters of the heart. Maybe Vance wouldn't find Cody so fickle, and maybe he would. Vance could just wait and see if Matty extended any empathy when Cody once again moved on to bigger and better things.

He snapped around the ice with clean, quick strokes, and sure jumps, more realistic fantasies of winning feeding his workout—except for when he would fall and the fantasy crashed down with him. But the falls only made him angrier and more determined. Each time he'd dig deep, stand up, and start again.

After conquering Alex and Vance on the ice several times over in his mind, Matty was ready to tackle the small grocery store near the ranch again. He walked in with his sunglasses on, his iPod set to his favorite playlist, and his head held in its most regal pose.

Matty took his time in the fruit and vegetable section. He was contemplating the ripeness of several mangos from Argentina when someone interrupted Christina's "Dirrty" by tugging on his arm.

"Hey," Rob Lovely said, giving him a sky-wide smile.

Matty pulled the buds from his ears and took hold of Rob's outstretched, large, well-shaped hand. He tried to ignore the flare of desire that shot through him. "Oh, hi."

"I, uh, wanted to say hello, and thank you again for letting Ben skate yesterday."

Matty pushed his sunglasses up onto his head. "Of course. It wasn't a problem. George's pond *es su* pond and all that. Thank *you* for plowing my drive."

Rob caught the eye of someone to Matty's left. Rob jerked his chin up in greeting. "Hi, Mrs. Kellerman."

Matty glanced over and gave a tight-lipped smile to the old biddy who was blatantly staring at him as if he was an escaped circus freak. She blinked in return, but didn't look away. Matty sighed and turned back to Rob. "It was really incredibly nice."

"No problem." Rob smiled toward a man who was hovering near the lettuce and obviously listening to their conversation.

"I suppose that a penchant for gossip is almost like opinions and assholes," Matty said. "Everyone in a small town has one."

Rob laughed softly.

"Christ, am I *really* that interesting, though?" His voice was defiant and he glared at the old man who grabbed a head of lettuce and had the decency to look embarrassed before hustling away.

Rob cleared his throat and waved a dismissal toward the onlookers. "Don't let them bother you. Like you said, it's a small town. Curiosity is in the well water."

Matty shrugged. "Not bothered. It would take a lot more than *this* to bother me. Anyway, yeah, thanks for—"

"Forget it. But I guess I had a few questions. About skating. For Ben. If you don't mind? I mean, I know that the middle of the grocery store is…"

Matty thought Rob seemed kind of nervous. "No, it's fine. Really. Go right ahead." Matty half-turned his attention to the mangoes again. "I said you could ask any time, and I don't say things I don't mean."

Rob sighed, rolled his eyes a little, and nodded at yet another older woman who was also watching them closely. "Mrs. Guthries," he said in greeting. "Mrs. Guthries, would you like an introduction?"

Mrs. Guthries waved. "Oh no, dear. It seems you have something to discuss. I can meet the boy another day." She smiled and Matty didn't know what to make of her expression. She looked as though Matty was edible. It was unnerving. "Have you warned him about the snow, Rob? I hear there is a lot more coming, quite early this year."

"I'll be sure to tell him." He looked at Matty again and said in a bit of a sarcastic tone, "There's an early snow forecast."

"Thanks."

His expression changed to genuine concern, though, when he added, "By the way, you need to put snow tires on the car. Did you already take care of that?"

Matty frowned and nodded. He didn't need anyone babysitting him, much less his handsome neighbor.

"And don't worry about the driveway. I'll have the hands keep it plowed when they do mine."

"I can handle it," Matty said.

"I know you can, but why should you? I'm happy to have them do it. It's not a problem."

Mrs. Guthries' expression was nearly giddy. Her wrinkles creased deeply with her wide smile.

Rob cleared his throat. "Sure you don't want that introduction, Mrs. Guthries?"

She shook her head, grabbed her onions and moved on, darting mischievous glances back.

"What was that about?"

"She was my first grade teacher."

"I hope she's retired now. She looks a million years old, and seems to have lost all sense of decorum," Matty said, watching as she teetered her way down the aisle. "But, back to Ben."

"Right, well, he's pretty interested in it, I guess. Skating. I was wondering, is it really worth it? Isn't it kind of late to get started at his age? Everything I've ever heard during the Olympics is that everyone starts when they're three or something. I know he's small for his age, so you might think he's younger, but Ben's twelve."

"Twelve is a fairly advanced age to start serious figure skating, true. But that's only a year older than me when I began," Matty said. He remembered the expression of shock and awe on Denise's face the first time he skated for her. "So, obviously, it can be done. The real question is how badly he wants to do it, and if he's prepared to sacrifice for it."

"He's *twelve*," Rob repeated. "How can he even know that?"

Matty shrugged. "Some five year olds know it. If you're passionate about something, age doesn't make much of a difference."

Rob lifted his chin toward Mrs. Guthries, who'd circled back around and was now pretending to look at tomatoes across the aisle from them. Matty sighed when the man who had been listening earlier came back by to study the peaches.

"Ladies and gentlemen," Matty said tightly, gaining their attention. "I swear on my darling mother's soul that it isn't catching. Okay? Your friend here is safe from me. So you can go back to your own business now."

Mrs. Guthries and the older man both stared at him open-mouthed, but before they could say anything, Rob coughed softly and flicked his head. The both looked ashamed and then convened together over the apples, furtively whispering to each other.

Rob sighed. "I'm sorry. They can't help it. You're new—"

"And not exactly the picture of Montana ruggedness they're accustomed to seeing at the store. I understand."

"Sorry," Rob repeated, looking embarrassed.

"Forget about it. Anyway, the only way to know with Ben is to give it a try. If he isn't interested, you'll know pretty quickly. And if he is, then you'll know that too. Talent is a given, but whether or not he can learn everything in time to be a competitor, I don't know. And maybe he wouldn't want that. Not everyone has to go to the Olympics to be satisfied with their accomplishments in the sport."

Rob nodded, his brows crinkling thoughtfully. He touched Matty's arm. "Thank you for talking to me about this. It's a lot to consider. I don't want him to get hurt. Emotionally or physically."

"He's a good boy," Mrs. Guthries piped up.

Rob's eyes rolled in exasperation. "Mrs. Guthries, *please*, I don't mean to be rude, but this is a private conversation."

Mrs. Guthries looked unrepentant but moved on, dragging the gentleman with her, and waving her small, wrinkled hand at Matty as she walked away.

Matty cleared his throat. "Well, if you have other questions just call or—"

"Sure, of course," Rob said, distracted and pushing his shopping cart away. "Thanks. I should go. Good to see you."

"You too." Matty watched as Rob headed toward the checkout lane. He lowered his sunglasses.

After finally choosing a mango, Matty put the earbuds back in, and bobbed his head as he carefully picked through the store's cheese selection. After swinging through the baking aisle, he headed toward the eggs, dairy, and meat sections. At the cash register he removed his headphones and stuffed the iPod in his bag.

"Oh my God. You're Matty Marcus," the checkout girl said, a new one from the last time he'd been in. The girl was probably twenty years old max, and smiled like sunshine had been poured into her by God himself. "I *love* you. I've been a fan since forever."

Matty grinned and pushed his sunglasses up on his head again. He put his hand out. "Thank you so much! That is so nice. You just made my day!"

She shook his hand and snapped her gum, grinning and laughing. "Man, I can't believe you're here at my store."

"I can't believe it either," Matty said, pulling his wallet out of his bag as she started scanning items.

"This is a lot of stuff. Are you staying around here?"

Matty smiled enigmatically. "I'm doing some training in the area, preparing to compete next season."

"Really? That's awesome! I'm so excited! I was afraid after you lost your U.S. title and bombed at the Olympics, you were done with skating. How's your back?"

Matty smiled prettily as the wave of humiliation splashed over him. His ninth place finish was an albatross around his neck. "It's much better now. As long as I have the fire and the drive to compete, then I'm going to keep fighting for it. I love to skate."

One of the worst things about competing in the public arena was that his failures were public as well. It made Matty feel terribly vulnerable to have some of his most painful and embarrassing memories shared by everyone.

He also hated that in a moment of loss he was an open book. The photos of his expressions immediately following a disappointing performance showed everything— his hurt, his embarrassment, his *failure*. He hated that more than anything. He wished he could hide his emotions from everyone, and keep them bottled up inside until he could be alone. Like Alex "no nonsense, all practice, no fun" Hampton.

"I can't wait to tell my mom I met you. She used to skate when she was a teenager, and we follow the sport together." She finished scanning the final item. "That's ninety-three-ten. Paper or plastic?"

Matty pulled out a few small, collapsible bags. "I brought my own." He debited the groceries with his card and looked at her name tag as she bagged. "Thank you, Rebecca. It was nice to meet you."

"No, thank *you*. How long are you staying? Do you think you'll be back in the store?"

"I'll be here about six months, and I'll be back, yes." Matty picked up the bags and paused before walking away. "I wish the store carried more organic items. Do you know where I can find that sort of thing?"

"There's a farmer's market but it ends in September, so you're a little late for that. Let me think. There's Third Street Market, and some specialty stores in Kalispell and Missoula."

"Fantastic. Thanks for everything, Rebecca." He waved to the glowing girl. "Tell your mom Matty Marcus said hi."

He left the store grinning. In the end, it had been a good day— even if he did have a ton of people staring at him in the fruit aisle, and even if he wasn't with Elliot tripping through Greenwich Village, and even if he wasn't anywhere close to where he wanted to be on the ice. He was skating again, and he had a handsome, neighborly man who shoveled the driveway for him. Not to mention he had a little fangirl at the grocery store.

It could be worse. It could be so much worse.

CHAPTER FOUR

Around noon the next day, Matty set off on a hike across the freshly snow-covered pastures to get some fresh air. Just as Mrs. Guthries had predicted, the skies had let loose with another early, surprisingly heavy October snowfall. It transformed the land overnight, making it even more beautiful.

Matty had settled the horses, worked out in Margaret's gym, and spent some time plodding through changes in his contract with his agent, Joanna. Given that legalese might as well have been Chinese, it was slow going. He'd promised his mother years ago to never take anyone's word—not even hers—on signing a contract, and that he would always, always read it himself first.

Now he needed to get out before his brain exploded from boredom. The sun sparkled on the snow and glinted off the white mountaintops. The air itself seemed effervescent, and danced over Matty's skin.

As he rounded the hill that separated the Pages' land from Rob's, he noticed he wasn't alone. Cows and a single horse dotted the hill across the way, behind a loosely held-together fence. There was a new sound too—and it wasn't mooing.

There in the middle of a pasture of cows, Rob—bundled in a winter jacket and thick gloves, golden head bare in the sunlight—spun around in a circle, arms stretched wide, singing "The Sound of Music" earnestly at the top of his voice.

Matty pressed his lips together, trying to hold in the laugh, undecided if he wanted to leave Rob Lovely to his musical moment, or sneak closer to startle him with a round of applause when he was done. It'd be good payback for scaring the pants off him the other day at the pond. But Rob had already more than made up for that by salting and plowing the drive for him, hadn't he? Matty should turn back and not embarrass the guy.

Matty decided to keep walking toward him, making no attempt to disguise his approach. But Rob was oblivious, singing on in a hearty tenor, his eyes squeezed shut as he swung around and around. Chewing cud, the cows watched him—a rather indifferent audience.

Matty couldn't stop himself. He was close enough now to truly startle Rob. He joined in when Rob reached the middle of the bridge.

Rob jerked and stumbled mid-twirl, falling to the ground with an exclamation. By the time Matty finished out the bridge, he stood over Rob, who sat on his ass in the snow beside a tired-looking cow. His face was red, and his eyes were dark with what must have been embarrassment.

"I know singing isn't my talent," Matty said, reaching a hand down to help pull Rob up. "But I'm not so bad that my contribution to the moment knocked you over, right?"

"What? No. I just... I was—how can I explain this?" He laughed.

Matty cocked his head and waited, curious.

"It's such a beautiful day...and, well, Ben and I watched that movie the other day, so I...." Rob looked like he wanted to find a way to reverse time. "I guess I don't have an excuse," he said. "I was singing 'The Sound of Music' and pretending to be Julie Andrews. Case closed."

"I see. Well, given that I don figure skates and glittery costumes to skate around dramatically pretending to be any number of campy things, I really don't have room to judge. However, you have a very nice voice. I can judge that."

Rob brushed the snow off his jeans. "Thanks."

"I'm terrible. I can barely carry a tune."

"You sing with a lot of enthusiasm, though."

Matty chuckled. "You're not even going to pretend it was good?" He wanted to be offended, but Rob seemed so good-natured in his honesty, like he didn't mean any harm by it at all. "You're not going to be on *The Voice* anytime either."

Rob laughed whole-heartedly, his face splitting wide with a sweet grin. "No, that's for sure. Thank God."

The cow beside them made a soft noise, and Rob patted her side. Matty studied his handsome profile edged by the gleam of sunshine off the snow. Rob's full mouth was beautiful, and his strong nose and chin cut a nice line. Matty noticed the shimmery gold of Rob's lashes, lowered to his still slightly pink cheek as he gazed down at the ground.

Rob cleared his throat and looked up at Matty, catching his gaze. "So, is there something I can help you with? Need any more wood carried up to the house?"

"No, no, thank you. I can carry it myself, and you've done so much for me as it is."

Rob shrugged. "Just being neighborly."

"Of course."

The sound of horse hooves caught his attention and they both turned to see two men on horseback riding toward them. Two working dogs trotted behind them, tails up, and their eye on the cattle.

Rob sighed. "That'll be Charlie and Terry. Ranch hands."

"Ah." Matty didn't really want to meet them. He figured they wouldn't take too well to him. After all, he was wearing a silver and pink coat and a bright orange scarf. He basically screamed "queer, here, get used it." But he didn't really *want* to stick around today and make rough, rural ranch hands get used to him. He'd rather go back at the Pages' house and toast his toes in front of a fire.

"I told them about you," Rob said. "They'll be happy to meet you."

Matty smiled but it felt false.

Though the riders were bundled up against the cold weather, Matty could see that they were both slim, young, and handsome. Neither could have been older than twenty-five. Charlie was dark and appeared to have Native American heritage, and Terry was a redhead with freckles that nearly ate up the paleness of his skin. They were friendly enough, swinging down from their horses to greet Matty man-to-man with firm handshakes and hat tips. It kind of blew Matty's mind that they both wore actual cowboy hats. He wondered where Rob's hat was and why he wasn't wearing one.

"This the new neighbor?" Charlie asked.

"Yes, this is Mr. Marcus," Rob said, indicating Matty.

After exchanging some pleasantries and everyone telling Matty yet again that this cold and snow was unusual weather for early October, Charlie turned to Rob.

"Bing sent us out to fetch you. He's ready to show off the changes he made to the goats' winter housing."

Rob's expression wasn't eager, but he smiled at Charlie. "Great. Can't wait to see it."

"When I first arrived I saw the goats mixed in with the cows," Matty said. "Where are they now? In their winter housing?"

"Yes," Rob said. "They need to be sheltered from the winds. Usually, though, I wouldn't have to put them in until November."

Terry said in a deep, rough voice that was surprising given the baby-roundness of his face, "The little boogers are going to be cooped up a whole extra month this year."

Rob shoved his gloved hands in his coat pockets and looked to Matty. "Goats are my latest money-making endeavor. We'll see if my investment pays off this spring."

"Cool." Matty had no opinion of goats other than a certainty that he probably wouldn't like them. Rumor had it that they ate shoes and coat sleeves, and he liked his shoes and coats very much. More than he liked most humans, and definitely more than he liked goats.

"Halal meat, especially chevon, brings in a bundle at Ramadan and other Muslim holidays."

"Are you Muslim?" It seemed unlikely given Rob's blond hair and green eyes, but Matty knew better than to stereotype. He'd traveled the world and seen all types.

"No," he said, laughing softly. "My father just turned over in his grave and said 'I told you so, Robert!'"

Terry and Charlie snorted knowingly. They both patted the same cow who'd approached Rob earlier. She seemed an especially affectionate one for some reason.

"Raising cattle and goats to meet the requirements for Muslims, and Jews for that matter, fetches a higher price at market near their holidays," Rob explained.

"And they said I wouldn't learn anything new in Montana."

Rob grinned. "Did they now?"

"Bing's a little impatient, Rob," Terry said. "He wants to get over to the school for Candace's Parents' Day lunch, remember?"

"That's right." Rob looked at Matty with hesitation in his eyes.

Matty jerked his thumb over his shoulder. "I need to get back now. I was just getting some fresh air. It was great meeting you guys," he said to Terry and Charlie.

"You too, kid," Charlie said.

He couldn't be much younger than Charlie, but he let it go. He didn't think it was wise to pick a fight with a real, live cowboy over something like that. His mother would be so pleased with his discretion. He almost thought he should call her and say, "See, I've learned a thing or two since I offended the entire U.S. Skating Federation with my big mouth, I swear."

"Mr. Marcus," Rob corrected.

Charlie looked abashed. "Sorry, Mr. Marcus, no offense intended."

"Not much taken," Matty said, and Charlie smiled at him. It was a wide grin, and he was missing a tooth on the bottom. Matty wondered how that had happened.

"You really should come around sometime," Terry said. "We'll teach you more than you ever cared to know about goats."

"Sure," Matty replied.

He was certain his terror showed in his eyes because Terry chuckled. "They don't bite. Much."

Rob headed toward his horse, which was now rubbing haunches with the same affectionate cow. He called over his shoulder, "Feel free to stop by any time. If you need help with anything or just want some company, the Lovely household has an open door policy for that sort of thing."

"I wouldn't want to interrupt your work," Matty said. "I'm sure you're awfully busy with—whatever it is you do. You know, with ranching."

Terry and Charlie snorted their laughter again.

Rob frowned at them, and took his horse's reins to swing up. He looked almost regal on the horse with white puffs of his breath wreathing his head. "What do you think I hired these smartasses for?" he asked, winking at his employees.

Terry and Charlie waved and grinned at Matty.

"But really, it's fine to drop in. I'm usually cooped up in my office at the house working on the finances. Bing, Terry, Charlie, and Dino do the dirty work these days."

"He's a pretty boy rancher," Terry said, teasing. "Only likes to get his hands in the muck when he feels like it."

"Terry," Rob said, a note of warning behind his laughter. "I worked this ranch from the time I was eight years old. I've done plenty of dirty work, and until I hired you and Charlie last year, I did both of your current duties."

Terry held his hands up in surrender. "Just teasing, boss."

"So, like I said," Rob went on, turning his attention back to Matty. "Stop by anytime. If I don't answer the door of the house, try the big barn—the loud one, with the goats. I'll be there, most likely, or Bing will be there. Someone will know where I am, and if you need help, someone will be happy to help you."

"Thanks. Will do." He couldn't resist teasing Rob a little. "Hey, thanks for sharing the spotlight with me. I bet Julie would've been enraged to have someone cut in on her like that."

Terry and Charlie glanced at each other in confusion, but Rob didn't bother to explain, and neither did Matty.

"Ms. Andrews is a classy broad. I bet she would've handled it with grace." Rob chuckled and indicated where his now-wet ass sat in the leather saddle. "More grace than me anyway."

"I don't know, that fall was pretty graceful." Matty turned and headed back across the field, calling over his shoulder. "Have a great day."

The cows mooed and seemed sorry to see him go, but Matty didn't look back. He knew that Rob wasn't going to be watching him walk away, but he didn't want to give any indication of his own urge to turn and look at Rob's strong figure on horseback, framed by the sun. Especially not with an audience.

The sound of the horses' hooves faded and Matty finally glanced back. Charlie remained behind with the cattle and seemed to be checking a line of fencing. But Rob was out of sight, and Matty headed back to the Pages' house filled with a strange disappointment that Terry and Charlie had turned up at all.

* * *

Baking was something Matty was good at, even if it got a little messy at times. But that's why he had cleaning supplies and a vacuum cleaner, and Margaret's vacuum cleaner was divine. He sometimes thought it might actually suction up dirt through the carpet, padding, boards, and the cellar under the house, because it was just that strong. Such a powerful vacuum cleaner almost made up for not having cable television and for only having dial-up internet. Almost.

A batch of brownies later, the house smelled heavenly, and he stood over the cooling pan breathing in the scent. Carefully, he cut them into three by three inch squares, and stacked them attractively on one of Margaret's plates.

It was late afternoon on a Thursday, and he'd taken care of the horses and had a good session at the rink. He'd returned to the ranch, iced his back down, and grown bored out of his mind. It was then he'd decided to bake brownies. He'd realized as he stirred the batter that he must have known he'd need this excuse to visit Rob, because it wasn't as if he could eat the brownies himself—yet he'd bought the ingredients for them.

Matty had showered at the gym, but he washed his face again, and pondered his make-up as he sat in front of the vanity mirror in the guest bathroom. Choosing the concealer, he evened out his skin tone, and then picked up the eyelash curler, making his clear brown eyes look more open and pretty. He thought they were his best feature, and he did his best to make them stand out.

He tapped his finger over the various glitter eye shadows, but those were for fun, and this was more along the lines of business. He took a neutral shade and applied it sparingly, bringing his eyes out a little more, but nothing too extreme. A touch of barely there rouge and some not-too-shiny lip gloss, and he looked fresh and lovely, if he did say so himself.

He put on a pair of jeans that made his skater's ass look slightly less gargantuan, and chose a blue roundneck sweater with gold accent flecks throughout—something just a little shiny, but not screamingly gay. Not that he cared about looking gay, because he happened to *like* looking gay. Or at least he liked wearing things that others said made him look gay. And if the appearance of homosexuality, at least according to the conservative establishment, came out of wearing what he liked, then so be it.

But today he wasn't trying to make a statement, just deliver some brownies and hopefully get the hell away from the Pages' hideous trinkets for a while.

Back in the kitchen, Matty leaned close to smell the brownies again. He was still about nine pounds over where he wanted and needed to be to train effectively, but he gave into temptation, taking the first brownie off the pyramid, and putting it on a little plate, smack dab in the middle of the decorative country cock. With a sharp knife, he carefully cut one-sixth off the brownie, and then placed the larger portion back on the top of the pyramid. He sliced the sliver into three bits, and ate them slowly, letting the chocolate dissolve on his tongue. He closed his eyes. Heaven.

Rob Lovely's ranch was picturesque. Matty imagined his grandmother would happily buy a painting of it and hang it over her fireplace. The mountains rose majestically behind red, vibrant barns that shone against the fading fall landscape. The two-story house, complete with a quaint wrap-around porch, was white with green shutters.

From the direction of the barns, Matty could hear the bleating of goats, and he wondered if the evil rooster also resided there. He removed his glove to knock on the door, glancing over his shoulder at the cows roaming over the hills and in the pasture he'd walked through. He'd barely avoided the patties they left behind. He glanced down at the boots he'd designated as stylish but okay to destroy, and it appeared they would survive to fulfill their function another day.

The door opened and Rob stood solidly in the entry way, his wide shoulders filling out a green T-shirt, and his smile bright. He rubbed a white kitchen towel over his hands, and the scent of something delicious drifted out from the house.

"Well, hey there," Rob said, opening the door wider. "Come on in. Excuse the mess. I wasn't expecting anyone."

Matty held out the plate. "I come bearing gifts of thanks."

"They look delicious." Rob took the brownies from him.

"They are." Matty smiled. "I just wanted to give you a better thank you for the firewood and the driveway. You really didn't have to do that. Also, I wanted to make up for embarrassing you with the 'Sound of Music' thing. *And* I wanted thank you for apologizing for everyone at the grocery store the other day. That was above and beyond."

"Wow, you had a lot of reasons to come." Rob said, smiling. "But really, as soon as you started singing, too, the embarrassment was worth it."

Matty feigned bashfulness. "P'shaw." He waved a hand. He hadn't mentioned another reason—that Rob was exceedingly attractive.

What was the harm in looking?

"Please, come in. To tell you the truth, I've only had Lila and the ranch hands to talk to since the Pages left. I get tired of talking about cows, goats, and hay, and Lila's never been chatty." Rob grinned. "I could use the company."

Matty glanced back toward the cow pasture he'd traversed and the hill that blocked his view of the Pages' ranch house, and pretended to consider. "If you insist."

As he stepped into the small foyer he put his hand to his heart in surprise. The house was gorgeous. Decorated with antiques, yes, but understatedly so. He followed Rob down the hallway toward the kitchen and glanced into the neat living room featuring a comfortable but attractive sofa, a television of tasteful size, and a beautiful upright piano.

"Do you play?" Matty asked as they passed the room and entered the kitchen. He couldn't envision Rob bringing Mozart forth with his wide, rancher's hands.

"The piano? A little," Rob replied, setting Matty's plate of brownies on the spotless kitchen counter. "I'm self-taught. I can pick out a thing or two. 'The Sound of Music,' for example." His face flushed slightly but he smiled winningly at Matty. "And I've written some little ditties of my own, but nothing truly proficient."

Proficient. Matty blinked slowly. That had been strangely hot. Who knew he had a kink for ranchers with good vocabularies? Rob indicated the stools around the bar in the kitchen, and Matty sat down.

"Brownies are Ben's favorite. It's too bad he's gone back to his mother's. I'll have to save one for him for next weekend."

"I hope you and Lila enjoy the rest," Matty said, perching on the stool with his hands clasped on the counter. He held his back very straight, feeling a twinge from the injury, but he breathed through it.

Rob looked at him strangely. " I'm sure I'll love them, but chocolate isn't really good for dogs."

"Dogs?"

Rob looked even more confused. "Lila. My dog. You said you hoped she'd enjoy the brownies? Am I missing something?"

Matty laughed, shaking his head. "No, you're not missing anything. *I* was missing something. I assumed Lila was your girlfriend or wife."

Rob's lips quirked a little. "You should have your gaydar assessed, Mr. Marcus. It appears to be malfunctioning."

Matty swallowed hard. Oh God, and the man was gay—and he looked like *that*. Christ, Matty was going to be violating his own body for hours tonight if the heat curling in his abdomen was any indication.

"Please, call me Matty. And tell your ranch hands too."

"All right."

"It's just that no one calls me Mr. Marcus except for doctors, so I associate it with needles, which I'm a little squeamish about. I don't enjoy things being poked into me." Matty heard his own words as they left his mouth, and he glanced through his lashes at Rob, who was looking at him without attempting to conceal his amusement.

"Strange, I got a rather different impression."

Matty's lips twitched. "Now, now, making some assumptions there, aren't we?"

"Have I made an ass out me in front of you?"

"They aren't wrong assumptions, mind you. Just assumptions."

Rob laughed.

Matty propped his chin on his palm, watching as Rob lifted the lid of the stew pot on his stove and stirred. "That smells amazing."

"My mother's recipe—Southwestern Chili Burger and Bean Soup. Care to share a bowl with me?"

Matty hesitated, not only because his stomach made an impressive gurgling noise of enthusiasm as soon as Rob lifted the lid, but also because he knew that declining proffered food was considered in most countries to be a slight of nearly unforgivable, and definitely unforgettable proportions.

"I just ate before I came, but a very small bowl would be fantastic!" Matty took a deep breath through his nose, sniffing for dramatic effect. "It smells amazing."

Rob stirred the soup again. "It's ready enough. Would you grab some spoons? They're in that drawer. We can eat at the table."

Matty slid open the drawer and blinked in awe and appreciation of the organization therein. Elliot's silverware drawer was a disaster and collected weird crumbs and stuff in the bottom. It grossed him out. But Rob's drawer was spotless, and his spoons were like little bowls hooked onto a sweetly shaped stem. They made Matty want to fill them with things just to use them. If he had one of them for his very own, he'd drink his hot water with bitters with it, and he was certain that he would feel fuller.

"So, you skate," Rob said as they sat down at the table.

"So, *you* have a lot of cows."

"I do! And goats. But they aren't very interesting."

"I admit I've never had a very great appreciation for cows, aside from the fact that they are precursors to some fabulous accessories. Alas, I think my experience with actual cows has only cemented my opinion of them."

"I'll be sure to tell them you said that," Rob said.

"Great. They'll be chasing me around the pastures, bent on my destruction, mooing, 'You will not wear *me*, Matty Marcus. Prepare to die!' before trampling me."

Rob chuckled. "You have a vivid imagination."

"I've heard that before, actually. It comes in handy on long, lonely nights in Montana. Sometimes, when I'm done vacuuming, I make shadow figures on the walls with my hands. I have deep, emotionally satisfying conversations with them."

"You're funny...and interesting." He took a mouthful of stew.

Matty noticed Rob ate his soup without slurping. Manners had always been a little bit of a kink. After all, it was only fun to buck standards if you actually knew how to comply with them to begin with.

Matty dipped the bowl-shaped spoon into the soup, and blew on it lightly. "I've heard that before, too, though usually it's phrased as 'flamboyant,' 'over the top,' 'outspoken,' and 'controversial.' You know, less neutral terms."

"I have to admit, after we talked the other day, and you told me that you were at the Olympics, I Googled your name. Hoo boy."

Matty laughed. "You can say that again."

"Yeah, I thought I'd find a write up or two, and instead I found a veritable universe of links. There are entire forums dedicated to the analysis and worship of you! In multiple languages! That must be a little strange."

"It is, but I'm kind of used to it. I mean, I don't take it for granted. I've always worked very hard to keep the people who support me happy and invested in me. If they aren't, who else will go on my skating journeys with me?"

"Your finger shadow friends?"

"Exactly! A figure skater needs an audience. Besides, it isn't as though I'm Britney Spears and can't go for a soda without the paparazzi in my face. Since I've been in Whitefish, I've been recognized by exactly one person, and she was, like most of my fans, really nice."

"Fans," Rob said, his soup half gone in the time it had taken Matty to reply. "Again, I can't even imagine."

Matty hadn't even moved beyond the smelling and blowing stage yet. "Like you've never had a fan? Look at you! There must have been a dozen girls and a few boys hanging on you at school, and don't tell me you didn't play football? With those shoulders? Please."

"I didn't play football."

"I bet you did!" Matty laughed. "You are so totally the type.

Admit it."

"I was in the marching band. Played the bass drum. I was far from cool."

Matty blinked at him and put his spoon back in his bowl. "You were in the marching band?"

Rob nodded.

Matty took his napkin from his lap and stood up. "I'm sorry, but I just remembered that I've got a really important date with my vacuum cleaner."

Rob started laughing and Matty sat back down.

"Yeah, that was pretty much my relationship with girls in high school, which, hey, worked well for me. It's easier to be in the closet when no one wants you anyway. I've been out for a long time now though."

Matty didn't know anything about being in the closet. Sure he'd never said the words, "I'm gay," in front of a camera or to a reporter, but he lived out every day, and had introduced a guy from his class as his boyfriend to his mother when he was only nine. Of course the kid had slugged him, and refused to secretly hold his hand when the teacher turned the lights out for a video from that point forward, but Matty had never been closeted as far as he was concerned.

"But some of the girls must have liked you. You were *married* even." Matty was kind of amazed at the idea of a gay man going that far, even though he understood it and knew the reasons some men did it.

"Actually, I wasn't," Rob said. "Or rather, I was only married in the most technical sense of the word."

"What does that mean, exactly?"

"Ben's mother and I...we were best friends for a long time. We met in grade school, and she was the first person I ever told about being gay. That was when I was fifteen. Then, one night in college, we were drinking, and I have no idea what happened, but Ben came out of it. I guess it was some tiny bit of bi showing through. I don't have a clue, but I don't mind the outcome." Rob glanced up from his chili. "And, yes, I'm sure he's mine."

"I *never*—" Matty was flabbergasted.

"I know. But you'd be surprised how often I hear that question. Even Margaret asked me once." Rob finished his soup and his spoon clanked against the empty bowl. "I would have trusted Anja no matter what, but she insisted on a paternity test to prove it to my parents." Rob stood up, sighing heavily. "The marriage was for my parents, too, but that's another story."

Matty lowered his soup spoon without tasting it, and blew on a fresh spoonful. The mention of Rob's parents seemed to have brought the mood down, and Matty wanted to lighten it again. "Speaking of ridiculous questions, you won't believe what I'm asked in every interview I give. Ever."

"Oh yeah?" Rob asked.

"*Everyone* asks me if I'm gay, either directly or in some round about, gay-baiting way."

Rob rinsed his bowl, and turned to him, chuckling. "Why would they ask that?"

Matty waved a hand over himself. "I know, right? I mean, what's not to understand, bitches? I think I make it pretty clear. I don't see why I have to spell it out. For Liberace's sake, I've been spelling it out since I could pick out my own clothes!"

"Well, for what it's worth, I knew you were gay the moment I saw you."

Matty sighed. "*Thank you.*"

"I'm kind of surprised you didn't know the same about me, actually," Rob said, leaning against the counter and studying Matty with a sweetly serious expression. "I mean, surely straight guys don't look at you like that."

"Actually, *everyone* looks at me like that. Grandmothers, mothers, gay guys, straight guys—hell, even *babies* look at me like that. Okay, not babies." Matty stood up and handed his untouched bowl to Rob. "Sometimes the lines are hard to distinguish between 'you've got a hot bod,' and 'you make me so uncomfortable that I don't know where to look,' and 'I want to kick your faggy ass.' At first, I wasn't sure which of the latter two you fell under, though when you smiled at me, I figured it was uncomfortable and not violent."

"No, it was the first option." Rob handed the bowl back to Matty. "Aren't you even going to taste it?"

Matty bit his lip. He'd hoped that Rob wasn't paying close enough attention to notice that the blowing had never translated into eating. And wait, Rob thought he had a hot bod? He tried to focus. "The thing is, if I have a taste, I won't be able to stop with just one. Then I'll eat the whole bowl, and who knows how many calories that might be?"

Rob's eyes narrowed as he took in Matty's body. "I think you could stand a few more calories."

"Yet you'd be wrong. I have to lose at least nine pounds to even be in good training condition, and then another three to six to actually compete."

Rob blinked slowly, looking Matty up and down. "You're talking about losing as much as fifteen pounds. What would be left on your body for a person to bite?"

Matty's breath felt warmth in his chest, and he tingled all over as his eyes met Rob's. He swallowed. "My ass. There's always plenty of ass for that."

Rob's eyes were hot like fire, and Matty had to take a step back because he couldn't breathe quite right. He didn't think snatching the soup bowl from Rob's hands, dashing it to the ground, and kissing him madly was the right way to end this conversation. *Or was it?*

"I should go. The soup smelled amazing. I feel completely full just from that," Matty said, backing away and grabbing his coat from the kitchen bar stool.

Rob sat the bowl down and came around the bar, his hands extended as though to calm or placate, but Matty walked quickly down the hallway, past the room with the piano, and past the coat rack lined with masculine, sexy hats, to the front door.

"If you're not interested," Rob said from behind him, "I can take the rejection. I enjoy your company, or what I've known of it so far. I didn't mean to run you off."

Matty pulled on his coat. "Interest isn't the problem. Or no, it is the problem. I think I'm a little nervous, maybe, because I like you, and having sex with you right this second seems like a brilliant idea on one hand, and a terrible idea on another, so I'm going to leave, and we can reconvene when I'm...less..."

Rob grabbed Matty's hand. "But—"

Matty moved onto tiptoes and kissed Rob hard, half-hoping it would be nothing—a lifeless, boring moment that he could walk away from. But no, the kiss was lightning and butter—hot, striking, and Sunday-morning-pancakes right.

He pulled away, his lips wet and his hands shaking as he let go of Rob's shoulders. He brought the back of his hand up to wipe his mouth, staring at the fucking perfect oriental carpet lining the hallway floor. He whispered, "Shit. That is *not* good."

"Not good?" Rob asked, his voice sounding a little gruff and dazed.

He didn't need a distraction from training. He wanted to go back to having a handsome neighbor who plowed his drive for him. Oh God, *plowed his drive*. Fuck. That sounded so *dirty*. In the very best way.

"Um, I mean, I have to go," Matty said, flinging the door open before he could change his mind. "Enjoy the brownies!"

* * *

That evening Matty spoke in English to Daisy as he hosed off his boots. He'd stepped in half a dozen cow patties in his distraction as he'd raced back over the pastures and hills to the Pages' house.

"It's incredibly out of character for me," Matty told the horse. She nickered softly and bent her head down to brush against his shoulder. "I pretend to be a whore, I know, but I'm a bit too much of a tsarina in reality. Cleanliness is a virtue after all, and I do like to keep myself as clean as possible."

Matty sighed. "Besides, as fun as it might sound in theory, letting just anyone touch my dirty bits isn't very appealing. I don't know this guy from Adam, or Roy, or Frank, or Bill, or anyone really. Christ, though, when he looked at me? Daisy, I thought I was gonna yank off all my clothes and get on my elbows and knees for him right there on the kitchen floor."

Daisy made a sighing sound.

"I know. It's the loneliness. It's getting to me. And the celibacy. It's been way too long."

He wasn't into short-term flings, though he'd had a few before. Before Cody, there'd been a run of hot nights during which he enjoyed himself a lot, and left the other guy wanting more. Given what a pain in the ass he was, that might be the best way to do it. Enjoy and walk. He didn't imagine there was anyone out there who could really handle him long term anyway. The thing with Cody had pretty much proven that, hadn't it?

He thought about Rob's big hands, his green eyes, and his warm, relaxed energy.

"Daisy, it's not as though it's out of the question. He's very attractive, there's no denying that. He's good looking, nice company, and a fantastic kisser, even when taken by surprise, so I think that I could maybe break off a piece. Enjoy it for a while."

Daisy snorted and Matty sat his boots aside to dry.

"I know, I know...it's not really my style and sluttiness is so out of fashion."

He patted Daisy's nose and blew a kiss to Maple Syrup before heading back to the warm house for a phone appointment with his mother. The thought of talking to his mom should have killed any lingering desire, but he found himself still turning Rob's lips and smile over and over in his mind.

CHAPTER FIVE

After two painful days of skating like crap and thinking of Rob's mouth, Matty was in the middle of preparing a salad for dinner when a knock on the door fell heavy and hard. It could only be one person, since he didn't know anyone else in Montana.

"Hi," Matty said, opening the door to find Rob on the doorstep holding a covered bowl.

"Hey. I had leftovers. I thought I'd bring this over in hopes that you might actually eat it."

Matty stood back and let Rob inside, taking the bowl from him. "Thank you." Matty watched Rob take his coat off. "Um, are you staying?"

"Yes, I am," Rob said, a laugh rumbling in his chest. "I think we should talk don't you?"

Matty didn't know if he wanted to talk, actually. Mostly, he wanted to kiss Rob again. He looked amazing in a light blue sweater and jeans, and his hair a blond mess. Still, if Rob wanted to talk, then he supposed he should do that. The main thing was to take control of the situation, Matty thought.

Taking a deep breath, Matty balanced the bowl carefully between his palms. "Rob, I should apologize. Honestly, I don't usually kiss and run."

"It was a surprise, sure, but not an unpleasant one. The kiss, I mean." Rob said, making his way toward the kitchen.

He'd obviously been in the Pages' house quite a few times and seemed entirely comfortable. Matty set the bowl on the kitchen counter as Rob pulled out a chair at the table.

"Still." Rob went on. "I wasn't sure where it came from. I mean, there was some flirting, yeah, but we were just having soup. Or, well, I was. You were smelling soup."

Matty felt his cheeks grow warm and he brought one hand up to his eyes. Oh God. He was such an idiot. He hadn't even opened himself up to the guy and he could already read the writing on the wall. Starting with an "r" and ending with an "n"—rejection. Matty was about to be on the receiving end of the "let's just be friends" talk. He could feel it.

"I'm sorry. Kissing you was out of line. I can't imagine that being more than friends would ever be a good idea in this situation. I think I was just lonely," Matty said quickly, hoping to get in a preemptive strike.

"It's no problem. The kiss was great. I find you incredibly attractive. I won't deny that." Rob smiled. "And who said anything about only being friends? It's just that, in general, I do prefer to be a little more familiar with someone before I get intimate with them."

Oh God, how embarrassing. Rob *did* think he was a slut. If only he knew just how few men there had actually been.

"Wow. Talk about not the impression I'd hoped to make." Matty's stomach felt like rocks had been dumped into it. "That wasn't my usual *modus operandi.*"

"Don't worry about it," Rob said again before pointing at the bowl. "If you zap it for about ninety seconds that should do the trick. I'd really like to see what you think of my mother's recipe."

Matty reluctantly put the bowl of soup in the microwave since he didn't see how he could politely get out of eating it. It was clearly a peace offering, or a test, or both somehow all at once, and to decline would be insulting.

"It smells amazing," Matty said as the microwave spun the bowl around. "It reminds me of when I was a kid and my mom would make Hamburger Helper. It smelled kind of like this."

"I promise, it will taste *so* much better."

When it was ready, Matty sat down across from Rob with the bowl, his head bent over it, taking in the wonderful smell.

Rob went to the second drawer next to the dishwasher and got out a spoon. "You'll need this," he said. "Unlike scent, which finds your nose without any effort on your part, you must use this ingenious utensil to bring the soup to your mouth in order to taste it."

Matty laughed. Rob's fingernails were surprisingly well-tended for a rancher, Matty noticed as he took the spoon from Rob's hand. There was a brief stand-off as Matty sat with the spoon poised over the bowl, and Rob sat opposite him observing intently. Finally, Matty dipped the spoon into the thick liquid.

The first taste was unreal. He heard himself make an ungodly moan, and his eyes rolled back. There had to be a pound of fat in this bowl alone, but, Jesus, it was so good he wanted to fill a bathtub with it and get a straw. He forced himself to put the spoon down after realizing that he'd gobbled up at least ten mouthfuls. He felt satisfied and warm in a way he couldn't remember feeling for quite some time.

"Good?" Rob asked, his voice soft and gruff, like he was holding back.

Matty glanced up to see Rob watching him with that same lustful expression that had led to Matty fleeing Rob's kitchen. His cock grew half hard, and he cleared his throat. "Yes. Thank you. It's very good."

Matty was definitely going to need to add an extra workout tomorrow if he ate the entire bowl, but he could feel Rob's eyes on him. He took another bite, and another, closing his own eyes and letting himself go with the pleasure, releasing himself, giving in.

"I never realized watching a figure skater eat would be such a sexy experience," Rob said. "I can't explain this, but I am so turned on right now."

Matty dropped the spoon in the empty bowl with a clatter and met Rob's eyes. His cock was hard, and he felt hot all over, inside and out. "I am too."

"Just tell me, yes or no."

Matty swallowed hard, and he turned sideways in the chair, spreading his legs a little. "Yes. God yes. Please."

Rob was on the floor between his thighs before Matty could say another word. He pushed Matty's track pants down, and Matty gasped and hunched over Rob's head when he sucked Matty's cock into his mouth. It was hot and wet, and so fucking good. Rob sucked even better than he kissed, and the kiss had been pretty amazing.

It had been so long since someone's mouth had been on Matty's cock. Legs splayed, he gave himself over to the sensations. God, he was not going to last. His hands fell to Rob's hair, tangling into it. He made a soft sound and whispered, "Coming soon...now."

Rob dove down, taking in as much of Matty's cock as he could, rubbing his tongue along the shaft as he went. Matty's feet skidded as he wrapped his ankles around the legs of the chair, trying to hold on, wanting it to last a little longer. He bit his lip, his eyes rolled back again, and he jerked his hips, thrusting up and into Rob's mouth.

"Now," he repeated, pulling at Rob's hair, but Rob only opened wider, taking him deeper. Then he shot off, trembling, and it felt gorgeous and stunning, sweet and really fucking needed.

"Oh," Matty whimpered as Rob lifted off his cock. A smear of come decorated Rob's lower lip and Matty leaned forward to lick it off.

Rob ran a tongue over the place Matty had licked. The intimacy of that warmed him, and he brought his hands up to Rob's face, lifting it for a kiss. Matty fell into it, delicious, sweet, hungry, and good.

He slid from the chair to kneel next to Rob, both of them tumbling to the hardwood kitchen floor. Matty tried to find the button of Rob's jeans while Rob's hands grasped his ass and shoved his track pants further down around his knees. Both of them were kissing, licking, humping, and rolling.

The wood dug into Matty's sharp edges—his hips, elbows, even his spine, but it was good, it was okay, because he didn't want to give up the contact to move to someplace soft. It had been too fucking long since he'd done this with anyone, too fucking long since he'd pushed a man's jeans around his hips and slithered down his body to suck his dick in, licking and working it hard and fast.

Rob moaned above him, hand going first to cover his eyes, and then down to cup the back of Matty's head. His fingers twined into Matty's hair, playing with it, not pushing or shoving, just touching so fucking sweetly that Matty wanted to grab Rob's hand and force it down harder, make him take control. When Matty pulled off Rob's cock, he gasped with joy when Rob grabbed his hair and moved him back down. God, that was it. That was what he wanted.

Rob's fingers loosened again when Matty was back on his cock, and he rubbed his fingers through Matty's hair, eliciting shivers and moans. When Rob was ready, he pulled Matty's hair again until Matty came off his cock. Then he jerked him up to his mouth. Rob rolled him over, the weight of his still-half dressed body pressing Matty against the wood. Matty was going to have bruises from this. He knew it. He just knew it. He fucking *loved* it.

They rutted against each other madly, shoving each other's shirts up to get skin on skin, and Rob grabbed Matty's ass, pulling him against him tightly. Matty buried his face against Rob's neck, the scratch of stubble along his forehead rough and sweet. Matty was hard again, and when Rob's finger tapped against his asshole, he jerked and spread his legs as wide as he could in his track pants.

"Got a condom?" Rob asked, gruffly.

"No. Yes. Um, fuck. In my wallet." Matty wanted to cry because he had no idea where his wallet was at that moment.

"Do you want to?"

"God, I want to, but don't move off me. Just keep on…please…I don't want to have time to think."

Rob sucked on Matty's ear lobe, and Matty whimpered, moving faster, feeling Rob's dick rub alongside his own. The pain of his spine and hips digging against the hard floor was good, and when Rob kissed him, sucked on his chin, and mouthed his neck, it just all got so much better.

As Rob thrust faster, with more determination, Matty pulled his legs up and wrapped them around Rob's back and brought his head up to Rob's shoulder. Then Rob grunted as he shot hot and wet between them. Matty bit Rob's jaw and came, too, trembling and jerking in Rob's arms.

Matty panted, releasing Rob to lie limply on the floor. "Holy Mary Mother of God."

Rob lifted up and rolled off Matty, lying next to him, gasping and looking up at the ceiling. Matty closed his eyes and started to shiver.

"Wow. I, uh..." Matty couldn't really think at all, much less think of any words that might express how he felt. He supposed he could say that it had been stunning, because that was true in multiple ways. Stunning that it happened. Stunning how it happened. Stunning that it was so fucking good. Stunningly good.

Rob stood, and Matty watched him move carefully across the kitchen to grab a few paper towels, wiping at his stomach with them before buttoning his jeans. He came back to Matty with another paper towel, and Matty noticed that as Rob wiped the come away from Matty's stomach, he didn't meet Matty's gaze.

"Hey."

Rob looked at him. Instead of the insecurity that Matty was expecting, he found warm amusement and calm satisfaction.

"That was hot."

"You're hot." Rob tucked Matty's cock away, and pulled up his track pants for him.

Rob helped Matty up. "So, I guess my comments earlier about wanting to know someone a little better before getting intimate seem pretty ridiculous right about now."

"And did I really say something about just being friends?" Matty said, shaking his head at his own stupidity.

"Well, I don't think you really meant that," Rob said, picking up the empty soup bowl and rinsing it out.

"You think?" Matty said, laughing as he stood watching Rob wipe the bowl dry.

Rob put the bowl on the counter and turned to him seriously. "Are we going to do this again?"

Matty blinked. "Is there a reason why we shouldn't?"

Now that he'd done this once, he didn't think he could handle living the whole winter in Montana next to a handsome, sexy neighbor who *didn't* make him come.

Rob studied him a moment before smiling slyly. "I can't think of one."

* * *

"You are such a prude," Elliot said.

Matty could practically hear Elliot's eye roll over the phone. "I just had sex with what basically amounts to a complete stranger on the kitchen floor of my employer's house and you're calling me a prude?"

"I'm calling you a prude because you ran away from his place like a little faggoty baby bitch to begin with, made him chase after you, and now you're all like, 'I had sex with him on the kitchen floor like a bad ass,' but I can tell you're freaked out by it."

"No, I'm not. I just like to, you know, *make the choice* to let someone lay me, not just find myself in the middle of hot sex not knowing how I got there. And that's what it felt like to me. I mean, he didn't force me or anything. But you know what I mean."

"I'll tell you how you got there, Matty. You took a job in Montana, met a hot rancher, and did the smart thing by letting him make you come. Twice?"

"Twice."

"Now, the important question: was it good?"

Matty flopped back onto the pillows on his bed, gripped the phone tighter, and whispered, "Oh my God, Elliot. Good doesn't even begin to cover it. More like—"

"Nuclear," Elliot supplied.

"Supernova," Matty said, though that was perhaps hyperbole, because while it had indeed been fantastically hot, he imagined that fucking would've been even hotter. His eyes rolled up, his breathing went wonky, and he got half hard just imagining Rob holding him down and fucking him. Jesus, fuck, dammit, he wondered if he could make it across the cow field at night and demand that Rob make good on the unspoken promise to fuck him senseless.

"Gonna cue up Mr Hudson and Kanye now?" Elliot said.

"Oh, fuck you, Elliot. You just wish a hot rancher had sucked you and blown your mind tonight."

"Actually, I got some too. A little piece of rock-n-roll goodness. Yeah, I'm a star fucker, baby. You only wish you had the hotness that was up on top of me tonight."

"Who?" Matty rolled his eyes for even asking. "Oh, please. You lie, bitch."

"Fine, so maybe it was in my dreams, but it was a hot one."

"One day, I'm going to smother you in your sleep. Just you wait and see. I'll do it with a teddy bear. Not even a cute teddy bear. I'm going to find the ugliest one ever and smother you with *that*. Wait and see."

"Promises, promises."

CHAPTER SIX

The next afternoon Matty returned from practicing at the rink, pleased with himself and exhausted. He groomed the horses, put them in their stalls, and showered before making dinner. He'd thought about the sex with Rob pretty much all day, and he'd been surprised at how smoothly he'd skated. He always heard that sex interfered with training, but today he'd been like a dream on the ice, landing nearly every jump.

Matty picked up the receiver from the phone on the kitchen wall and listened to the dial tone before hanging it up. The next time he dialed the first three digits of Rob's phone number, which, yes, he'd memorized already. He hung up again and sighed.

He hadn't really done this kind of thing before. He didn't know the rules. Could he call tonight? Would it be rude to ask Rob to come over? A booty call of sorts? How did Montanans handle this sort of thing? And if it was just sex, why not? Why was he hesitating to push the button?

He stared at the phone, trying to think of an excuse to call—something that wouldn't sound too desperate—when it rang. Matty's heart beat double time, and as he said hello, he thought he sounded oddly squeaky.

"Hey."

Rob's voice sounded like sunshine—warm and bright. Matty's stomach flip-flopped.

"I just wanted to call. I, uh, have Ben tonight. All weekend, actually. But I wanted to touch base."

"Which base?" Matty asked, lowering his lashes even though Rob wasn't there to see his flirtation.

"All of them. Multiple times," Rob said.

"Gorgeous answer."

"Gorgeous you," Rob replied, tossing out the words like he was saying something incredibly unremarkable, but they made Matty's knees a little weak. "Tomorrow morning, Terry and I have to ride out with Bing to look into an injured elk Charlie thinks he saw up on my back forty. If we can find him, we'll call out the wildlife rehabilitation specialist, and that could take a while."

"That sounds like quite an adventure."

"Just a day on the ranch, really. Not as romantic as it seems, I promise."

"Romantic sounds nice," Matty said with some innuendo in his tone.

"It really does. Soon, I hope. But, in the meantime, Ben and I were wondering if you'd join us for dinner tomorrow night."

Matty hesitated. Dinner with the kid. That seemed like maybe a little much. God, though, he was lonely, and Rob was so fucking nice and funny, and the kid had seemed pretty cool too. What could it hurt? It wasn't like Rob was asking him for his hand in marriage, for fuck's sake.

"I'd love that. I'll bring dessert."

"More brownies?"

"Did you eat them all already?" Matty asked, kind of amazed and filled with envy.

"I didn't even manage to save one for Ben."

"Greedy," Matty murmured.

"Delicious."

By the end of the conversation, which was too short and yet laden with additional innuendo, Matty was so fucking horny he didn't know what to do with himself.

He went to his room, stripped off his clothes, and climbed into bed. He was hard, and his hands were shaking he wanted it so fucking badly. He stroked his cock for a while, thinking of Rob's mouth, his tongue flicking on his cock. Groaning, he rolled onto his stomach to thrust against the mattress, circling his hips.

When he couldn't take it anymore, he got up on his hands and knees, the soft mattress giving a little under him, to jerk off fast and hard. He fell flat on his face at the last moment, and covered his dick with his other hand to catch the come.

After panting into the sheets, he rolled over onto his back, staring up at the ceiling. Fucking hell, it was ridiculous. He didn't even really know the guy. It occurred to him that maybe once he did know Rob better, this crazed lust would vanish. The idea was a relief. He wasn't accustomed to fits of uncontrollable desire and need. It felt too messy, and he breathed easier thinking that it would probably pass soon.

* * *

Matty arrived at Rob's house wearing his favorite jeans and a tight red sweater under his heavy fur-lined winter coat, a little lip gloss, and a touch of blush. He'd also decided to drive over rather than walk the pasture because he'd worn his favorite shoes instead of boots. It was silly to drive down the Pages' driveway, only to make a U-turn into Rob's, but his shoes were amazing. That was much more important in the scheme of things.

Down by the barns and outbuildings, two trucks remained. A third truck, green and muddy along the bottom with one of the working dogs in the back, drove up from the barns to the main driveway and slowed as Matty stepped out of the car. The driver side window rolled down.

"Evening," a rumbling voice said, kindly. "You must be Matty."

The voice belonged to a man old enough to be his father— probably old enough to be Rob's father too. He realized this must be Rob's ranch manager. His weathered face and strong hands gripping the steering wheel spoke to years of hard work. Another of the working dogs Matty had seen around the ranch sat on the seat beside him.

"And you must be Bing," Matty said, winningly. He didn't know Rob's relationship with his ranch manager, but he didn't want to piss the man off. He didn't want to embarrass Rob either, and he didn't know if Rob was out to his crew or not. Though it seemed likely.

"Rob's been riding herd on me all day so he could get home in time to make dinner for you tonight," Bing said with a sly smile.

So, Rob was out to Bing at least. That much was obvious. A curl of pleasure unfolded in Matty's gut to hear that Rob had been eager for their dinner tonight and not shy about expressing it.

"I hope he wasn't a slave driver," Matty said.

Bing shrugged his strong shoulders, pulling the dark, wool ranch coat tight. "Rob works hard. He's a good kid."

"He seems like it."

Bing narrowed his eyes, taking Matty in before nodding his head slowly. "Well, enjoy your dinner. Tell Rob that Charlie and Dino are finishing up with the goats and then they'll be gone for the night too. The ranch is all his."

"I'll let him know."

Bing stuck his hand out and Matty shook it, feeling the gnarled calluses rub against his own smooth skin. He felt suddenly very young and out of his element.

"Good meeting you, son."

Matty got the impression he wanted to say more, but he just touched his forehead like he was still wearing a cowboy hat, and was on his way.

Matty lingered a moment before walking up to the front porch. Night was falling fast around him, and the stars filled the big Montana sky in a way that left him reeling when he gazed up. Finally, chilled from the cold and eager to see Rob again, he grabbed the plate from the passenger seat of his car and strode up to Rob's front door.

"Hi!" Ben answered the door, his blond hair a tousled mess, football jersey dirty and a little torn, and a massive grin on his face. "Guess what I did? Guess!"

Matty chuckled. "I have no idea. What did you do?"

"Landed an Axel! I did! I totally did! Do you want to see? I can show you. On the pond! Do you want to?"

Matty did want to see, actually, but…his shoes. Matty looked at them and considered driving back to the Pages' house for boots to wear out to the pond.

"Leave it for now, Ben. I'm sure Matty isn't up for trekking through the pasture tonight." Rob walked down the hallway toward them, his hands outstretched for the brownies.

Matty's breath caught in his throat. Rob looked amazing. God, beyond amazing. Like shockingly hot. How had he not noticed it the first time they met? He was like a fucking man-mountain of sexiness. It hit him that Rob had never said Matty's name out loud before. At least Matty didn't think he had, and it sounded really good coming out of his mouth, like it should always come out of it, over and over, especially when he was coming.

Matty was only half-aware of the boy next to him now that Rob was standing there looking like *that*. Matty cleared his throat, focusing on Ben again. "How about in the morning? After I feed the horses I don't have much going on, and we could work on it together if you wanted."

"You don't have to—" Rob started.

"No, I want to," Matty said. "I love kids and I'm good at teaching, or so my agent tells me." Matty smiled at Ben. "Really, I'd like to see it, but in the morning."

"Cool!" Ben jumped up and down a little.

"Come on in," Rob said. "Ben, help Matty with his coat."

Ben took the coat from Matty and hung it on the coat rack next to Rob's things. "Want to play X-box with me? Or—"

"Ben," Rob said. "Go take a shower, please. I need Matty's help in the kitchen. There will be plenty of time for his attention later."

Ben sighed and then, ignoring his father, smiled brightly at Matty. "Have you ever played Halo? It's really cool—"

"Ben." Rob's voice took on the parental tone that Matty still heard really quite frequently from his own mother. It made him kind of want to laugh. "Shower."

Ben departed without protest after that, but he did look over his shoulder at Matty to grin again as he started up the stairs.

Rob called after him. "Put on some fresh clothes. Don't just put those back on. Okay?" He waited with an ear toward the stairs and then called again, more loudly, "*Okay?*"

Ben yelled down, "Okay, Dad."

Rob relaxed and turned to Matty, putting the brownies on the hallway sideboard before taking his gloves from him and stuffing them into the pockets of Matty's coat.

"You look great," Rob said.

In that moment, Matty realized—though why it hadn't occurred to him before he didn't know—that this was a date. A date with a kid along, yeah, but a date.

"Thank you." Matty brushed his hand over his hair. He looked up through his lashes and smiled. He couldn't help but smirk at the heated expression on Rob's face. It warmed Matty's skin and he pulled a little at the collar of his sweater. The lust was mutual, that was for sure.

"I was instructed to tell you that once Charlie and Dino leave, the ranch is all yours."

"You met Bing." Rob led Matty past the living room with the piano.

He'd have to get Rob to play something for him tonight before he went home. He knew just what he would suggest. "I did. He was nice."

"He's great. He's the reason the ranch is finally pulling a profit. Unlike my father, Bing listens to me, implements my ideas, and doesn't tell me all the reasons it can't or shouldn't be done. Tea, soda, water?"

"Water, please." Matty sat on one of the stools in the kitchen, taking an ice water from Rob, who went back to the preparation of the main course. Chicken, apparently. Off to the side sat some sweet potatoes, which made Matty happy and grumpy at the same time. He loved sweet potatoes, and there was no way he could allow himself to eat one in its entirety.

"Raising Halal-certified cattle was an idea I had in college to increase our profits," Rob went on. "The ranch has always struggled. It's not always easy to maintain this far north. I even backed Bing's suggestion of goats years ago, but my father dismissed our ideas. Said he wasn't going to raise meat for terrorists."

"Wow."

"Yeah."

Rob turned away and washed his hands again. He smiled at Matty, "Sorry, I don't mean to sound bitter, and I shouldn't speak ill of the dead. Something came up today that reminded me of some bad times with my father. I try, but I guess I haven't really let it go. I'm loyal that way I guess."

His laugh was tight and not like the assured chuckles Matty had heard from him before.

"This isn't exactly an ideal opening conversation for our evening together. I'm sorry."

"Don't worry about it. There are tons of bad times I haven't let go of either," Matty said. "Like every bad skate I've ever had. If you wanted to see me cry with rage, I could recount every mortifying second of what went wrong and how. And don't think I've forgotten the name of every single judge who's ever unfairly dinged me. Politics. It's a thing in figure skating."

"You're generous to let me get away with starting the evening off on a negative note."

"Oh, I beg to differ. I'm a selfish brat, I promise."

"A sexy brat, maybe."

Matty watched in horror as Rob smothered several pieces of chicken with cheese, and rubbed butter all over some sweet potatoes. "Before we go any further, I need to ask you a really important question."

Rob glanced up, concern in his eyes. "All right."

"Are you actually a Hampton fan or something?" Matty asked, sipping his ice water and trying to prevent the heart attack he was going to have just watching Rob cook.

"Who?" Rob continued to assault the sweet potatoes.

"My arch rival. My nemesis, so to speak," Matty's mouth watered in betrayal when Rob opened the oven and the amazing scent of some kind of cheesy casserole wafted out. "Alex Hampton."

"I've never heard of him," Rob said, setting the timer. "Is he good?"

"Yes," Matty admitted grudgingly.

"Why?"

"Because he practices twenty hours a day and gives it a hundred and fifty percent!" Matty said in a cheerful automaton voice. His smile disappeared and he grumbled. "He's probably gearing up for Skate America right now. The Federation always assigns him to Skate America. They would have given me Skate Timbuktu if they could have."

Rob threw him an amused glance. "No, I meant why did you ask if I was his fan?"

"With the dinner you've prepared, I can only imagine that you want to make me gain a hundred pounds to ensure I never skate competitively again." Matty added, "Though I'm sure it's delicious and it will be worth extra calor—"

Rob pulled a plate from the oven. He showed Matty its contents: a plain, non-cheese-smothered chicken breast. "I've been keeping this warm for you. Four ounces, low fat, and certified organic. I know because I raised her and slaughtered her myself."

"You killed a chicken for me?" Matty asked, kind of grossed out and somehow crazy flattered.

"Well, not for you, silly." Rob put the plate back in the over. "For dinner. For a couple of dinners, actually. I'm making chicken casserole for tomorrow night, and I made some soup. We'll make good use of her."

"I feel strangely deflated. Though, I suppose that murdering a cow in my honor and using its hide to make hand-tooled accessories for me would be the ultimate expression of an intent to woo, don't you think?"

Rob laughed. "As it is, a chicken will have to do."

Ben leaped into the kitchen, landing in an exaggerated pose. "Ben Lovely, five-time Olympic Champion—"

"Five time, huh?" Rob said. "So, you'd be in competitive condition for twenty years? You'd be, what? Forty?"

"It could happen!" Ben shoved up the long sleeves he wore under his clean football jersey. "Lots of things can happen, Dad."

"True," Rob replied, absently, fiddling with the position of the items in the oven.

"Dad made special food for you," Ben said. "He says you have to be basically anorexic to skate like you do. Is that true?"

Matty paused for a moment, sorting through the slam of feelings buzzing through him. "Well, your dad is amazingly sweet to make something special for me, although saying that I have an eating disorder is a bit of a turn-off. But yes, I skate very well, which is helped by keeping a lower body weight." A glance at Rob showed that he was embarrassed.

Rob said, "Ben, could you get some fresh thyme from the window garden?"

Ben made a sound of frustration at being sent out of the room again, but he did as he was told.

Rob wiped his hands and came around the counter to stand over Matty, peering down at him in the stool. Then he said, very softly, "You can't imagine how hot I find your body. Don't even try to make that into something it wasn't. I'm having trouble keeping my hands to myself as it is." He grabbed Matty's hair and pulled his head back, kissing his neck and licking his ear. "Blisteringly hot."

Matty was still catching his breath with his eyes closed, wondering where Rob went, when he felt something pressed into his hand. It was a piece of paper listing rink times, and Ben was standing in front of him, his eyes on said paper.

"What do you think?" Ben said.

"About what?" Matty asked, dazed. He glanced toward Rob, who was picking apart the thyme that Ben had brought back like he hadn't just blown Matty's mind.

"Should I try out?" Ben asked.

Matty looked at the paper again and saw that it was actually practice times, and the list was for something called *Holidays on Ice*. Apparently, it was a Christmas show held at a Missoula ice rink. It was holding open auditions for a Nutcracker-themed performance.

"Sure, why not? What do you have to lose?"

"I dunno," Ben said, looking down at his feet and sighing heavily. "Not much, I guess. The guys at school already call me a fag."

"Wait, what?" Matty put the list down on the counter. He glanced at Rob, who had stopped cooking and was staring at Ben.

"Yeah," Ben shrugged. "It's no biggie. I just wish they'd shut up. The girls are starting to believe it, I think."

"Who's calling you names?" Rob asked, his voice tight and restrained.

"And *why*?" Matty asked.

The kid wasn't gay. At least, Matty was pretty sure he wasn't gay, and it wasn't just the football jersey, but the complete lack of ping on Matty's gaydar. Though, he supposed, given his gaydar's failure to pick up Rob, he might not want to put so much faith in it.

"Because I'm always talking about skating lately, and because…well, because."

"Because your dad is gay," Rob said.

"It's okay, Dad. They're stupid. That's all."

"They *are* stupid," Matty agreed. "Listen, Ben, someone is always going to find a reason to try to tear you down, or keep you from doing what you want to do. Take it from me. But the best thing you can do is be strong in yourself. The girls who matter won't make assumptions or believe the douchey bullshit these jerks are spouting."

"Yeah," Ben said, the uncertainty heavy in his voice. "So, I'll try out then." He picked up the schedule, not meeting his father's eye. "But it looks like I'd have to miss some of our times together, Dad."

Ben sounded thoughtful and sad about not seeing his dad. Matty wondered about the divorce, and the marriage Rob had said was for his parents.

"Let me see." Rob took the sheet from him. "I could come down to spend a half day with you on those weekends. Bing could handle the ranch."

"Maybe," Ben said, and took the paper back. "I don't know. I like being here with you. I'll have to think about it."

"Whatever you want, Ben." Rob squeezed his shoulder.

Dinner was good, though Matty envied Ben and Rob a great deal, because *their* dinner looked and smelled fanfuckingtastic. But the chicken Rob had made for him was very nice, and he ate it slowly, knowing it would make him feel fuller if he took his time with it.

It was also during dinner that Ben asked, "So, do you have a boyfriend? You know, back home? Where you're from?"

Matty glanced at Rob, and wondered momentarily if Ben was asking at his father's behest, but Matty could tell by Rob's face that he wasn't.

"Well, in a way, I do." Matty felt, rather than saw, the stillness from Rob's side of the small kitchen table. "It's a pretty intense relationship." Matty paused for effect, but the cold, uncomfortable feeling drifting from Rob made him come to a quick conclusion. "His name is Figure Skating."

"At first I thought it was a real boyfriend, man," Ben said, chuckling around his brownie, his eyes scrunched up adorably. "I was all like, 'Dad is gonna be *so* disappointed.'"

Rob cleared his throat. "Ben, you wonder why I don't bring the men I go out with home to meet you? This is why." But his tone was amused, and Matty was thrilled by Ben's honest revelation and Rob's low-key acceptance of it. Rob acted as though the idea that he'd be disappointed if Matty had a boyfriend back home was so incredibly obvious that it wasn't even necessary to be embarrassed about it.

"So, are you guys dating now?" asked Ben.

Rob said, "I don't know. I'll have to ask Figure Skating if he's willing to share."

Matty laughed so hard that he almost had to put his head down on the table to try to catch his breath.

Ben added, "Matty, why don't you call Figure Skating and find out?"

"Yeah, Matty," Rob said, his pretty-as-Montana face glowing with amusement. "I killed a chicken for you, after all. What's Figure Skating done for you lately?"

"Not much," Matty said, wiping at his eyes, and trying to recover, but he couldn't stop laughing. "Nothing that I can repeat in front of a child. It's far too graphic. And not in the good way."

"Are you saying Figure Skating screwed you in the ass without any lube?" Ben asked.

This set Matty off again. He was laughing so hard that he barely heard Rob's soft admonishment, and Ben's garbled defense.

Right around the time Matty finally calmed down, the phone rang. Ben pushed his chair back. "Can I get it? It's probably Mom."

Rob nodded his agreement that Ben could be excused. "Tell her to call me later. Tell her I miss her."

Ben trotted from the room with the cordless phone, his greeting to his mother drifting back to them, "Hey! There's a really famous figure skater here having dinner with us. I think Dad likes him. Like, a *lot*."

Rob rolled his eyes and continued to eat as though nothing untoward had been said. Matty chewed another bite of chicken and swallowed. "If you don't mind me asking, what's the deal there? Do you get along and all?"

"Yeah," Rob frowned a little. "We've been friends our whole life, and we're lucky enough to share Ben."

"*But...*" Matty supplied.

"We have our disagreements."

"About how to raise him?"

"About the way I live my life, mainly." Rob chuckled under his breath, and watched Matty eat the last few bites of his food as he seemed to think about what he wanted to say. "She thinks I should give up the business here and move to the city."

"To Missoula to be closer to Ben," Matty surmised.

"Well, yes, but no. See, we grew up here. Rancher's kids, both of us. Growing up, all we could talk about was getting out of here. Going someplace better than this."

Rob's smile grew wistful. "We used to play out in the cow pasture, and Anja was the grand actress. She'd stand on a big rock over where the Pages' house is now and act out these scenes. She wanted to get to New York. She had big dreams." Rob lowered his voice. "That night in college? It changed a lot of things for her. For both of us."

"What about you?" Matty asked. "When Anja was playing the Broadway lead, what were you doing?"

Rob's ears turned a little red, but his voice was steady. "I made up the songs she sang. I wanted to write Broadway musicals."

"Yeah?"

"Yeah, but I figured out from a young age that music wasn't my talent."

"You sounded pretty good out in the field."

Rob chuckled. "Thank you, but I realized I just didn't have the creativity, well, *musical* creativity that is, to become a composer, which is what I wanted to be as a little kid."

Matty was just about to say that he was sorry when Rob waved it off.

"Don't worry. Eventually I figured out what I really wanted to do. Or so I thought. I wanted to go into medicine. Maybe become a doctor. I considered nursing at one point, or physical therapy. I even looked into audiology. But none of that was in the cards."

"Why?"

Rob shrugged. "My dad. He was pretty insistent that I take over the ranch, and he kept me busy most of my adolescence with work around here. He'd only agree to help send me to college if I majored in farm and ranch management. We struck a compromise when I went with large animal veterinary medicine and animal husbandry. You'd think he would have been pleased, but he was kind of a control freak."

Matty nodded and said nothing. His dad was pretty much entirely the opposite of what Rob was describing. He always felt safe just *thinking* about his dad. Hearing Rob's story made Matty want to call his dad and thank him over and over for being so awesome. His father might not *get him* but he loved him, and that was so much more than enough.

Matty recalled a night when he still lived at home. He'd gone into his mother's bathroom to apply some make-up because she had better lighting in there. When he'd come out, his dad was lying in bed massaging some lotion into the scars on his leg. He'd looked Matty up and down, taking in the shoes, the tight jeans, the gauzy blouse, and the make-up Matty was wearing.

He'd said, "What are you up to, son?" in that weary voice Matty was accustomed to hearing at such times.

"I'm going out with Elliot. Do I look pretty?" Sometimes Matty just *had* to push his father's buttons just a little bit. It was only fair.

"You look like you might get your ass kicked, so keep your eyes open and stay safe."

"Sure, Dad." He'd given his dad a hug.

"Love you, son," his dad said, all gruff in Matty's ear.

That was the kind of man Matty had as a father. He might not like everything that Matty did. He might even have his doubts about skating, but he loved Matty, and he would never hold him back from what he wanted in life.

"In the end, though, I did switch majors to Farm and Ranch Management, after Anja got pregnant with Ben."

"I see. So, the marching band? Was that the last hurrah of your childhood musical aspirations?"

Rob laughed. "No, I'd let them go long before that. Sadly, that was my form of rebellion. The bass drum made a lot of noise and it rattled the animals, which upset my dad. Thinking about that aspect of it, it was kind of a dick move for me to make. Still, kids are kids. Good choices aren't exactly the biggest motivation during that period of our lives."

"And you make good choices now?"

Rob sighed. "You get right to the heart of it, don't you? Anja says this is a cop out. I think it's a nice life for my kid. There's a lot to offer in the country, especially for a boy. But Anja says I'm avoiding reality out here."

Matty stood up and followed Rob to the sink, bringing dishes along with him. Rob began to clean up and Matty helped, rinsing off the dirty dishes and handing them to Rob to load into the dishwasher.

"How did your folks pass away?" Matty asked, pitching his voice to a tender note, hoping that he didn't sound as callous as he feared.

"Car accident when Ben was six. As soon as the estate was settled, Anja and I divorced, and she went to Missoula. I stayed here."

"You said the other day that the marriage was for your parents."

Rob's mouth twisted bitterly. "The paternity test, the marriage—it was all to get Ben his due. This ranch was worth quite a lot. I wanted to make sure he got his inheritance. I didn't care if they left anything to me. Okay, yeah, this place is my home, and I love it. But if they'd cut me off, it probably would've been the best thing that could have happened to me."

Rob banged the dishes around and he took a deep breath, turning away from the dishwasher and from Matty. He seemed to physically shake it off. "Sorry, talking about my parents tends to send me over the edge a little. Anja says I haven't processed my grief. I think the problem is that I still want to punch my dad and shake my mother and scream *why* at them. Anja says that proves her point."

Rob faced him. Matty wrapped his arms around him, saying nothing, just pressing against Rob's body, rubbing his back and taking deep breaths.

After only a moment, Rob's arms came up around him and Matty felt the heavy weight of Rob leaning against him. It wasn't sexual, even though he found Rob incredibly hot. Instead, it just felt really warm and friendly. Matty liked it.

"Are you going to make out with him now?" Ben's voice came from the door. "Or do you have a minute to talk to Mom?"

Rob pulled away. He shot Matty a grateful glance and Ben an exasperated one. He took the phone and walked out of the room.

"You like my dad?" Ben asked, leaning against the counter.

"Seems like he's a pretty great guy."

71

"He is." Ben narrowed his eyes. "He dated someone last year and I *hated* him. He talked to me like I was a kid or something."

Matty laughed. "Was he at least nice looking?"

"I dunno. Maybe. I guess." Ben pulled out a bar stool and sat down. "Tell me about the Olympics. Can you really speak Russian? One of the sites Dad and I looked at said you could. Did you really sleep with that Cody guy? He looked kinda like Dad, don't you think? Only not as handsome."

"I can really speak Russian. A little. Do you want me to teach you something cool to say?"

"Don't think I didn't notice that you avoided the other questions, but, yeah, teach me something. Girls will think it's awesome."

Matty tried to teach Ben to say, "You are beautiful and I am at your service."

Ben was slow at it, but Matty continued to persevere until Ben finally managed the whole phrase—even if it was with horrible pronunciation. But they were both having so much fun and laughing so hard Matty didn't care.

* * *

Once Ben was in bed, Rob brought out a bottle of red wine and two glasses. "Join me?" He sat at the table.

His voice was so sweet that Matty wanted to comply with anything he requested. "A fourth of a glass," Matty replied. "I don't mean to be ridiculous, but I'm an elite athlete. Part of the territory is being very serious about what I put into my body."

Rob poured and passed the glass to Matty. "The double entendre there is killing me, but I'll just leave it on the table for now." His eyes were hot and very green when they met Matty's gaze. "So, I've spilled my guts about me tonight. Let's even the score a little. Tell me about your family."

Matty took a sip of the wine, feeling the woody-spicy taste of it roll on his tongue. "Well, my family isn't my trial. My mother is the most amazing, supportive woman in the universe. She goes all over the world with me when I skate, and she's done everything that she can to make my dream happen for me. In fact, she's the one who arranged this job with the Pages. It's great money. Skating is an expensive sport."

Matty found that Rob was a good listener. He asked all the right questions to keep the conversation moving ever deeper. Because of that, Matty soon found himself standing at an emotional precipice. He was good at talking, good at expressing important concepts and emotions, but he wasn't good at cutting through that final bit of protection and laying himself bare. He kept a little armor up with most people nearly all of the time.

But Rob deftly moved them both into a position where Matty was on the verge of exposing more than he felt comfortable with. Worse, Matty could sense the temptation to leap into it, to believe in Rob. He hoped he wouldn't smash on the rocks below.

"It's broken your heart," Rob said. "Skating and the recent failures, the kicks in the nuts when you were already down. It's pretty much left you a mess, hasn't it?"

Matty could feel the pull of gravity. He drew back and he let his public mask slip down. He could answer truthfully hidden behind it, but it wouldn't be so scary, and it wouldn't hurt so much.

"Yeah, of course. It's always disappointing to be treated like a second-class citizen because I don't fit the Federation's profile. It hurts and I feel sad, but I have to focus and move on. I have to prove to them that they can't beat me down."

Rob studied him and nodded a little. There was something about Rob's expression that let Matty know he'd seen his retreat from vulnerability. His face all but said, "I saw what you did there." But Rob didn't call him out on it, and Matty was grateful, though he also felt kind of like a dick. Rob had shared something of his soul, and Matty had backed out at the last moment and put up the wall.

The night ended when Rob said, "Ben's here, and while there is a very large part of me that would kill to get back to what we started the other night, this isn't the time."

Matty plastered an understanding smile on his face, because *of course* they couldn't fuck with Ben in the house. Matty was *very loud* after all. But it was still intensely disappointing. *Is a quick mutual jerk off out of the question?* But he knew that it was, at least tonight, so he gathered up his things. "Remind Ben to be at the pond at nine-thirty tomorrow morning. I'll be waiting for him."

"Sure thing." Rob walked Matty to the door.

Matty pulled on his coat and stepped out into the dark of the porch. He turned around to say goodbye, but Rob stepped out, too, closing the door behind him.

"Come here," Rob said.

The kiss was hot and overwhelming. Matty gripped Rob's hard, strong arms, and Rob wrapped his hands around the small of Matty's back, pulling him close and tight. Matty closed his eyes as Rob pressed hot, wet, kisses over his face and down his neck, and he was hard, already so fucking hard. He pushed against Rob, trying to get some leverage.

When Rob maneuvered him a little down the porch, he was confused until he felt the solid wall against his back. Pressed firmly between the wall and Rob, Matty pushed his hard cock against Rob's thigh. Rob's own thrusts seemed to hit Matty mid-stomach, until Rob reached down, grabbed Matty's ass, and hauled him up, using the wall for support. Then it was easier. The kiss was smoother, and yet harder, too, because they were rocking against each other, and Matty could feel the bruises from the floor sex the other night pressing against the hard wood slats of the house. He whimpered. Rob wrapped his arms around Matty's back, cradling him closer, cushioning him from the house.

Matty grasped Rob's waist with his thighs, and groaned, trying to find what he needed. Rob grunted and shook.

Matty whimpered, kissing Rob's mouth, his chin, and his ear, whispering, "Come on, yeah, that's it."

Rob kissed him gently, and then lowered him down. Matty was about to register a complaint to let Rob know that he had not yet achieved his objective, when Rob unbuttoned Matty's jeans and pushed his hand inside. Matty held on to Rob's biceps, his back against the wall, sheltered from the world by Rob's body. He closed his eyes, whimpering as Rob jerked his cock and kissed him. It was dark, and Matty knew that Rob couldn't see, but at the last moment, he ducked his head and hid his face against Rob's chest, overcome from his orgasm, gulping in air, and holding back a cry.

"Shh," Rob breathed in his ear. "God. You are so hot."

Matty made noises but they were mainly just whimpers. He thought he should tell Rob he was hot, too, but he couldn't speak at the moment. He stood shaking in the shelter of Rob's arms as Rob used a handkerchief to clean them both up.

"I feel like a teenager making out on the front porch hoping my parents won't catch us," Rob whispered.

Matty trembled as zipped himself up. He was still so close to Rob that he could smell his sweat and their come mixed together.

"Though I never really did that, so I guess this is my belated adolescence or something."

"I should be insulted, I think. But I'm not. I'm quite thrilled to be the one you're fulfilling adolescent fantasies with."

Rob ran a thumb over Matty's lips and tilted his face up to kiss him again. "Is that strawberry lip gloss?"

"Yes," Matty said. He'd reapplied it in the bathroom earlier. "Do you like it?"

Rob laughed. "Sure, sweetheart. It's adorable."

"I was going for pretty." The term "sweetheart" had not gone unnoticed and he waited for some kind of panic to drop in. Instead he just felt really well cared for, and kind of adored. He liked that.

"Well, you're always pretty, aren't you?" Rob said. "At least as far as I've seen."

"Not in the morning with bags under my eyes and no concealer." Matty moved out of Rob's arms. "I have to go since I'm teaching your son a thing or two in the morning. Are you going to come watch?"

"I wish I could, but I have things I have to take care of." Rob said as Matty stepped from the porch.

"Rancherly things, I assume."

Rob laughed. "Yes. Exactly. Drive safely."

"It's a perilous journey down these two driveways. I might need a cup of coffee for the long trip."

Rob waved at him when he reached his car. Matty could see Rob in his rearview mirror, standing on the porch, watching him drive away.

Matty picked up the phone as soon as he returned to the Pages'. He wanted to call his mother and tell her all about Rob, but it was far too late on the east coast for that. He thought about calling Elliot, but he figured Elliot would just make fun of him, and while he normally welcomed that, he didn't want hear it just yet. So, he called his little brother. Surely a college freshman would still be awake.

When Joseph answered the phone groggy and kind of worried, Matty breathed, "Oh my God, Joey-Joe, I've met this amazing guy!"

CHAPTER SEVEN

The next morning, Maple Syrup was grumpy with him, which Matty attributed to his relationship with Daisy. He thought Maple Syrup was a little jealous of the time Matty spent talking to Daisy in Russian, brushing her down, and giving her special treats. He supposed he should be more attentive to Margaret's sweetie, and so he gave Maple Syrup some sugar and talked to *him* in Russian for a while. Maple Syrup just snorted. Clearly, the horse disapproved of anything except for English.

The sky was a brilliant, wide-open blue as Matty headed to the pond. He'd decked himself out for training Ben, and he was pretty excited to get started. Unfortunately, he had to wait. And wait. Finally when Ben showed up, Matty pointed a stick he'd picked up, and said with a thick Russian accent, "Young man, if training with me, then on time! You think Oksana Baiul was late to practice? Or Evgeni Plushenko? Well?"

Ben cracked up and couldn't seem to catch his breath. "Oh my God? What are you wearing?"

Matty pulled at his long, red wig and adjusted his glasses. "I am Yuliya Yasneyeva. I am called Yuliya. Is there problem?"

Ben was wide-eyed as laughter continued to shake his body.

"You skater! I coach! My appearance is not on ice. You worry how *you* look, young man. Understand?"

"Are you crazy?" Ben asked, still laughing, and not really sounding all that judgmental about the issue.

"Yes," Matty replied. "Crazy for ice. Now, show Yuliya what you can do."

Ben laughed a little more and then sat down to pull on his skates. Matty bent to help him, taking the opportunity to study the leather and blades. If Ben was any good, and if he had any desire to really skate, then he would absolutely need new ones.

When Ben fell down, Matty encouraged him, and then scolded as necessary, working him through some basics. His costume and accent, though, seemed to keep the tone light, because even when Matty chastised Ben for not listening or for making the same mistake fifteen times in a row, Ben laughed at him and never grew defensive.

"All right," Matty called out after a few hours. "I call day. Ben, go home. Eat good food. Build strong body. Come back next weekend. We work again."

Ben skated over to Matty. He grabbed him around the waist and hugged him hard. "Thank you. You're amazing."

"This they say much in my home country. But here, in America, my amazing is not understood."

Ben plopped down on the snow-covered bank beside the pond. "So, next weekend, do we skate here again? What happens if the pond melts?"

Matty studied him. "If in one month you still skate with me, we go to rink."

"Will you wear this get-up at the rink too?"

Matty narrowed his eyes and adjusted the glasses. "This 'get-up' is Yuliya Yasneyeva. There is problem?"

"No, but I'd pay money to see you wear this in public."

"You wish to see your friend, Mr. Matty Marcus, get his ass kicked, no?"

"Nah, of course not." Ben grew serious. "Do you really worry about that?"

"Mr. Marcus worry about many thing. *Yuliya* worry about teaching you skate."

"You're crazy."

"This I have heard before," Matty said.

After Ben trudged over the hill, occasionally turning around to wave, Matty pulled off the wig and the glasses, dug around in his bag, and brought out his own skates. He had his own training to do.

* * *

"Wait, this guy has a *kid*?" Elliot gasped over the phone. "What hot mess have you gotten yourself into, girl?"

"Shut up, Elliot. Like you haven't slept with a load of hairy daddies in your time."

"But they weren't, like, *actual* daddies."

"Rob's only thirty, tops—"

"You don't really know how old he is, do you, bitch? He's probably forty and just looks good for his age."

"And Rob isn't hairy. He's incredibly smooth, and well-built, and, oh my God, Elliot, *his hands*."

Matty drifted a little on the thought of Rob's hands. When he'd talked to Joseph the other night, he hadn't really gotten to dwell on these kinds of details, because he'd been all, "Ugh, shut up. I'm sleeping. Call Mom! Or Elliot! Just…God, you're a dick."

It hadn't stopped Matty from keeping Joey on the line for a good thirty minutes, telling him about Rob, and Ben, and dinner, and how Rob had made a plate just for him, and how he was so fucking funny.

"Did I tell you he's super sweet and really funny?"

"Yes, three times already. Jesus, are you in love with him or what?"

"What? I barely know him."

"You sound in love. The last time you got this way it was over Cody and his big hungry bottom."

Matty sighed. "Which was the whole problem. Not that I don't top very well, mind you."

"Blow that load up someone else's ass, baby. I know you like it on your hands and knees, just like any good girl should."

Matty didn't dispute it, though he could be very toppy sometimes. If he felt like it. It was just, God, so much *effort* to be toppy, and he felt like he had plenty of effort going on in the rest of his life. Sometimes it was awesome to sit back and let another person take control. So long as they did really good, dirty, hot things to him. He thought about Rob and his big, strong arms. Rob could do a lot with those. He could hold him down, fuck him wild with a dildo—there were all kinds of nice things he could do with those strong arm muscles.

"Are you listening?" Elliot was asking.

"No. I'm trying not to come in my pants," Matty said. Thinking about Rob and a dildo had taken him to DEFCON 1 levels of arousal.

"I'm your best friend because that doesn't make me uncomfortable." Elliot sighed. "Maybe this will help: *Don't. Fall. In. Love. With. Him.* It will only bring you pain. And, more importantly, it will only bring *me* pain."

Matty covered his eyes with his hands. Elliot was right. But he could control his emotions. He wasn't in love, just completely aroused by Rob. Okay, maybe he was in like. He could be in like, couldn't he? He had that right. Skating and the fucking Federation couldn't take *everything* away from him.

"That's all I have to say for now," Elliot said. "I'm hanging up because your tortured, horny breathing is grossing me out."

Matty was about to say something brilliant in reply, though he didn't know what, because all of his blood was in his dick. Then Elliot *did* hang up.

"Bitch," Matty said to the dial tone.

* * *

Rob called Sunday night. It was directly after Matty had taken care of the insistent problem that had arisen during his phone call with Elliot, and then vacuumed the entire Page ranch house. Well, at least the downstairs, since the upstairs was inaccessible. Matty shuddered to think of the dust accumulating up there.

"Hi," Rob said, his voice warm and easy. "Anja came to pick up Ben a few minutes ago. I was wondering if you'd like to come over?"

"You didn't waste any time, did you?" Matty laughed.

"No. I didn't."

He didn't sound at all ashamed or tentative, as if he knew Matty would be completely okay with that. Matty liked his confidence. It made him feel warm and secure. Rob might not know what he wanted with his entire life, but he wanted Matty right this minute, and that felt really damn right.

"Okay, um, give me forty-five minutes."

"That long?"

"I know, right? But I look like hell and I need a shower."

Rob made a sound of frustration and Matty was instantly hard.

"Hurry," Rob said.

"I will," Matty promised, trying to sound soothing, but it just came out breathy and wanting instead.

When he was showered and fresh, Matty stood outside Rob's house, his hands shaking in anticipation. He had been extra thorough in his ministrations, and he was ready for whatever Rob wanted to do with him. He rang the doorbell again, a weird tension in his stomach building as he wondered if it was going to be awkward now. He always hated the pre-sex moments when everyone just kind of giggled and felt uncomfortable.

Rob opened the door, reached out, and grabbed Matty by the coat, kissing him before the door was even shut. Rob yanked at Matty's coat, throwing it on the floor, and then pushed his hands under Matty's shirt. They were cold and a little rough, but not unpleasantly so.

Matty arched into the touch, lifting his arms for Rob to pull the sweater over his head, leaving him bare on top and exposed. Rob dove in to suck his neck and bite his shoulder. Matty whimpered, lifting up on his toes to clutch at Rob's head, holding him fast as Matty squirmed to get more. So much for awkward beginnings. Nothing was awkward about this at all. It was hectic and greedy, and kind of rough, but really fucking good.

Rob pulled Matty along, both of them stumbling up the stairs as Rob kissed, licked, and nibbled at Matty's torso, stopping to suck his nipples, and then struggling to get Matty's pants undone before they were even on the top stair. Rob hoisted him up then, kissing him as Matty wrapped his legs around Rob's waist and was carried down the hall.

Rob's bed was soft. Matty clutched at the comforter as Rob pushed his legs apart and fell between them, their hard cocks colliding and rubbing against each other with their thrusts. Matty wrapped his legs around him again, and clung as Rob rocked against him, jolting them both with his force.

"I want to fuck you," Rob ground out.

"That's a good idea. Yes, um, yeah. Please." The words tumbled out of him.

When Rob pulled away to get the condom and lube, Matty reached for him, eager to have him back against him. "I don't need a lot of prep. I like it rough."

Rob shoved Matty's legs back, lunging down to kiss him again. "I'll take care of you. Let me decide what you need."

Matty arched at the words. His cock flexed and his ass squeezed reflexively. He half wanted to crawl out of his skin because he was so turned on. It was nearly too much, and every brush of Rob's flesh against him made his cock twitch and ache so much he didn't know if he could handle it.

Rob pushed against Matty's legs. "Hold yourself open for me."

Matty pulled his legs high, gripping behind his knees. Rob kept a hand on Matty's thigh, touching him, keeping it intimate between them. He met Matty's gaze.

"Relax," he said like a tender order.

Matty's eyes rolled up as two fingers, slick with lube, pressed into his ass. Not too rough, but not gentle either. Matty rocked on them, biting his lip, and whimpering.

"That's good. You're so fucking sexy."

Matty's toes curled as Rob hit his prostate with his fingers, and then his cock jerked as Rob did it again. "I'm so turned on," Matty panted. "I've been turned on for days. Please, come on and do this."

Rob pulled his fingers free and Matty lifted his ass, begging with his body, wanting to be fucked so badly he felt like he might gag on his desire. Then he stuffed his fist into his mouth to keep from yelling, because Rob was pretty fucking big and it hurt. Matty bit his hand, whimpering and gasping around it.

"Okay?" Rob asked.

Matty nodded and breathed around his knuckles, his ass clenching and releasing, as Rob slid deeper into him, thick and long.

"God..." Rob bowed his head, taking a slow, shuddering breath. Matty felt Rob's cock jerk inside him, and knew Rob was on the edge. He held as still as possible, trying not to even breath, afraid of sending Rob over before they'd even started.

"Fuck." Rob slammed into Matty's ass.

Clawing at Rob's arms, Matty threw his head back.

He made crazy noises as Rob fucked him, his moans warbling with the rapid-fire pace of Rob's thrusts. He pulled his own hair, trying to take it, trying to make it last. He lifted his hips up and held them, biting his lip, feeling like he was about to come apart in a thousand-million pieces.

Then, like flying over ice, he hit the blissful moment that went on so gorgeously long, like infinity opening to grab him up. Rob's hand moved on Matty's cock at the same pace as his thrusts, and Matty reached down to slow it, because he wasn't going to be able to hold off, not when this moment of infinity dropped down on him, and then he arched, grunting and crying out as hot come shot out of him in staccato bursts, painting his own chest and neck.

"Fuck!" Rob muttered, pounding into him. "Holy fuck!"

Rob's body quivered and his face went soft and slack as he shook through his orgasm. Matty felt his own cock jerk again in a small sympathetic aftershock, watching how Rob's orgasm wracked through him. Rob collapsed onto Matty as he shook through several reverberations.

"Fucking hell," he panted against Matty's neck, his cock still quivering in Matty's ass. "Goddamn it."

"Yeah," Matty murmured, almost speechless in his own post-orgasmic haze.

After Rob pulled out and disposed of the condom, they lay curled together in the bed. Rob was already half hard again, Matty noticed, as he ran his hands over Matty's body, touching every line of his abs, and tracing his arms with gentle fingers.

"You're pretty flexible," Rob said, his mouth pressed tenderly to Matty's neck.

"Yoga. It's great. I miss my yoga instructor." He moved a little to the left and shifted his hips. His back was bothering him. He was flexible, yeah, but he needed to be careful not to aggravate his injury. "You're..." Matty ran his hands over Rob's chest and shoulders. "So built."

"Ranch work. Pushing cattle around, riding horses, and building fences. It's all *Brokeback Mountain* hotness here, you know."

Matty grinned, running his hands over Rob's jaw and moving up to kiss him. "My cowboy."

Rob stilled before brushing Matty's lips.

"You don't like that?"

"No, I do. I like the idea of being your anything."

Matty murmured soft sounds as he took Rob's nipple into his

mouth. "So, can I ride, Cowboy?"

"Giddy up," Rob said so incredibly seriously that Matty had to laugh.

Riding Rob's cock a few minutes later, he laughed again—joyful laughter as he told Rob how good it felt, how amazing fucking him was. He shot his load on Rob's chest with a huge smile on his face. Why had he ever resisted coming here? He fucking loved Montana.

PART TWO

CHAPTER EIGHT

Matty woke up the next morning to snuffly wetness on his hand, and he opened his eyes to find a brown and white, shaggy dog on the bed, sniffing his fingers eagerly. Matty sat up. He was alone, except for the Australian shepherd mix, which came at his face next, tail wagging, and tongue ready.

Matty held the dog off. "Hey, hey now. Wait a minute. No tongue kisses. I don't even know you."

"That's Lila." Rob's voice came from the bathroom. Then, in a higher pitch, "Lila, come here, girl. Come here."

Lila jumped off the bed and trotted to her master as Rob said, "That's a good dog. Leave Matty alone. He needs his rest."

Rob came out fully dressed in blue jeans, T-shirt, and a thick flannel shirt over it. Very rancher-chic. Morning sun seeped lightly into the room from the window, and Rob sat down on the bed next to Matty. He gestured at a tray on the bedside table. It held yogurt, honey, and some granola in a separate bowls.

"I wish I could stay and eat with you, but we're testing the herd for brucellosis today. If you want, I could have one of the hands run over and take care of the Pages' horses too. You could go back to sleep. You've got to be tired."

Matty leaned his head into Rob's palm as Rob touched his hair tenderly. Part of him wanted to play the part, roll down into the bed, bat his lashes at Rob and claim that he was so entirely exhausted from their activities that he simply couldn't move. Somehow he knew that if he did that, Rob would lean over him, kiss him tenderly, and brush his hair out of his eyes before leaving to do his work. It would be amazing to be babied like that. He missed that kind of thing so much.

Instead, he sat up straighter. "This looks great, and I'll eat the yogurt, but let me take care of the horses."

"Are you sure? I could do it myself if you don't want Terry or Dino to do it for you."

"No, it's all good. Besides, I've got to get into town to skate today. I'm going to record myself to see if I can figure out the issue with the triple Salchow landing I keep tripping on."

Rob ran his hands down Matty's neck, stopping to draw a small spiral in the hollow of his throat. "Can I see you tonight?"

"I'm sure you *can*. The question is if you *will*."

Rob grabbed his hair and pulled him close, laying a kiss on his lips. "Smartass."

"Yeah," Matty said. "I'd like to see you tonight too. I'll call you when I get back in from town."

"Or, I could meet you in town. I should be done with the testing in time to meet you for dinner and I could show you around a little."

"That sounds great."

"Take your time leaving. I'll see you later." Rob kissed him. Then, indicating the tray, "Eat something."

"I'm not anorexic, you realize."

"I know," Rob said, winking. He left the room whistling under his breath.

As soon as he was out the door, Lila hopped up on the bed again, her brown and white spotted face in Matty's personal space, panting and begging for him to pet her. Matty scratched her ear and she plopped down with her head on his leg. Her big brown eyes went from him to the tray beside the bed.

"Oh, I see what this is about." He moved the tray onto his lap, eating almost all the yogurt under Lila's hopeful eyes.

* * *

Back at the Pages', Matty's eager acceptance to go out later left him with some worries. He wouldn't call them regrets, *but* there was no doubt he'd been hoping they'd fuck their brains out again tonight. What if going out somewhere interfered with that?

On top of those concerns, he was worried about the *implications* of going out. Was it another date? A public one? What did that say about Rob's expectations? Matty knew that was something he needed to address sooner rather than later, but he really wanted to get more amazing sex out of this whole deal before he did. Just in case the well dried up when Rob understood that no matter how good they were together, they had no future.

Matty paused in mucking out Daisy's stall and really let himself feel the truth of that last thought. It made him deeply sad—inexplicably given how little he actually knew Rob. He left the stall to go stare at the horizon, the hills and mountains rolling away into the distance.

If he took everything out of the equation—skating, New York, Moscow, Hong Kong, Seoul, the Olympics—this wasn't a bad life in Montana. He could even say that so far he'd been pretty happy here, except for the dearth of fashionable people, and the terrible food options at the local grocery store, and the boredom, and the ungodly furniture he had to gaze at day in and day out. But other than that, life had a nice regularity to it, something that his OCD nature could find pleasure in.

Even if he still wanted to feel the teeming streets of New York City around him, or party in Moscow, or go to a boutique and buy some fabulous item that would make his brother confused and his friends envious—he felt good here. Other than everything he was missing, this place was all right. At least he wasn't distracted from his skating.

After mucking the stalls, Matty headed into the house for a shower and to grab his skating equipment. He was getting a late start, but if it cut into his practice time, or he had to share the ice with the post-school crowd as his punishment for not having mucked the stalls over the weekend, then so be it.

It turned out he had plenty of room to skate and, aside from a young girl practicing shooting a puck into a net, he was alone on the ice. The skating went well, despite the hours he'd spent pursuing pleasure the night before. Once the public free-skate time began, he drove into Kalispell to work out in the gym. It was a good effort, and he quit only a little earlier than normal to hit the showers. Between all the sex the night before, mucking the stalls that morning, skating, and lifting weights, he felt boneless and exhausted.

He stayed under the hot water for a long time thinking of Rob. They'd fucked three times, and Matty would've taken it again if Rob could've given it to him. It'd been amazing. After riding Rob, Matty had taken his dick on elbows and knees, and he was still a little sore from that one. He turned into the water, and tried to slow his breaths as he remembered Rob moaning, *"Your ass is great. You're gonna make me come."*

His dick fattened up at the memory, so he finished quickly, and grabbed a towel.

It was late afternoon when Matty texted Rob to ask if Rob had finished testing the herd for…Bucephalus, or whatever it was called. He kind of hoped Rob would suggest they meet up at the ranch, because while his ass was definitely feeling the effects of the prior night's activities, he was very willing to brave it again. The orgasms had been literally incredible. As in, hard to believe. As in, if he hadn't had them himself, he would not have found a description of them to be plausible.

He had his jeans and sweater on, and his hair half blow-dried when his phone buzzed.

Finished for day a few hours ago. Am at Bill's Place. On left on way out of town. Can't miss it. Join me?

Matty read the message twice. Bill's Place? Wasn't that the run-down shack of a bar just after Kalispell and before Whitefish, smack in the middle of nothing but ranchland? Okay. He looked in the mirror, applied a gloss to his lips, put on some concealer to cover the places where his skin tone was uneven, and considered. This was Rob and he was at this Bill's Place joint. So, okay. Matty would go.

He texted back:

Be there in twenty.

* * *

From the outside the bar looked as though it might tumble down at any moment, and the wooden structure appeared to have never seen the wet side of a paint brush. Yet the inside was tidy—for a bar—and smelled lemony fresh, like someone had just Pledged every table and chair, and possibly the entire old-fashioned wood bar.

Rob sat at said bar, drinking what looked like a cola, and laughing about something the barkeep had just said. The joint was empty except for the two of them, and Matty stood in the half-open doorway, the dust motes circling in the air around him, until the bartender nodded in his direction.

"That him?" He rolled his eyes. "Yeah, obviously that's him." The dark-haired man wore a plaid shirt and jeans, and a cowboy hat hanging on a hook behind the bar likely belonged to him. He looked in his thirties, although his skin was craggy.

Rob stood up, a big grin splitting his face, and motioned for Matty to join him. "Hey! Come on in! Matty, this is Bill. Bill, this is Matty Marcus. He's staying at the Pages' place this winter."

Now that Matty thought about it, it was strange to be introduced like that. He was used to more of a star-fucker approach, he supposed. He remembered how often his friends, and even some of his family members would say, "This is Matty. He's on the U.S. figure skating team. He'll be competing at the Olympics." Or after the Olympics, "This is my friend Matty Marcus. You might recognize him from the Olympics?"

Matty would then be obligated to poo-poo and play down the introduction, or possibly play it up to look like a diva bitch, depending on the situation. But here he was just the guy taking care of the Pages' ranch while they were away. It was a trip, and yet he also wanted to pipe up and explain who he *really* was, because that introduction failed to encompass the reality of him.

Matty shook Bill's hand at the bar. "Nice to meet you. Is this your place?"

"Since Grandpa Bill died, yep. Sure is."

Rob pulled out the stool beside him, and Matty sat down, wincing a little because his back hurt. But by Rob's expression it was clear he'd misinterpreted the source of his pain. A mix of concern, lust, and pride flashed over his face.

As amusing as it was to Matty to see Rob taking credit for his discomfort, he still disillusioned him. "I hurt my back a little today on the ice. I'll need to ice it down later, and maybe take it easy tomorrow." He adjusted his posture, sitting very straight since it hurt less that way. "Quadruple Axel. The nightmare."

"Figure skating?" Bill asked, cleaning his glasses with a very white rag.

"Uh-huh."

"Get you a drink?"

"Thanks. I'll have water for now."

Bill, with his tough guy face, and his deep, cigarette-trashed voice, asked, "Sparkling or tap?"

Matty's lips quivered as he fought back a laugh. People kept on not being what he expected, and it never stopped amusing him. "Sparkling, but of course." He lowered his lashes.

"Done," Bill said.

"Matty's a competitive figure skater," Rob supplied.

"Ah, explains the ass," Bill muttered, handing Matty an ice-cold Perrier, the bottle beaded with water droplets.

Matty blinked. For real? He glanced around the room again. It looked like a honky-tonk out of a movie.

Bill evaluated him closely. "Pretty, too. You sure can pick 'em, Rob. I gotta give you that."

Matty found himself uncharacteristically speechless, and he opened his bottle of water, taking too big of a swig. The bubbles exploded into his nose, and coughed and sneezed, covering his mouth and nose with his elbow.

Rob laughed. "I think he's in shock or something. He normally rattles on like you wouldn't believe."

"About what?" Bill asked.

"Oh, himself, or whatever. He's very amusing."

Matty was still coughing, and he glared at Rob, who seemed to take pity on him.

"Okay, this is Bill. He's been my good friend since high school. The only other gay guy in my graduating class—"

"*Out* gay guy," Bill said. "There are a few guys who are married with kids, but totally never objected to me blowing them back in the day. Or even now." Bill covered his mouth and coughed, but it sounded like he said, "Eric Brown."

Rob rolled his eyes. "Whatever. Anyway, yeah, Bill and I go back."

"Popped his cherry," Bill added with a gleam in his eye.

Rob snorted. "If you call a quick handjob in the back of the school bus when we were fifteen popping my cherry, fine."

"He's not really my type," Bill said. "I like 'em a lot more—"

"Straight," Rob said. "A lot more straight and a lot more likely to punch him in the face for even trying."

Bill turned his head and showed his profile. "See my pretty nose?"

Matty said, "It's a very lovely nose. Soft and flat. Nice."

Bill laughed. "Yeah, that's what comes of the kind of guy I like. What can I say? My psychologist says I've internalized the oppressor. I just say I like it rough."

Matty winked. "There's nothing wrong with liking it rough."

Bill's smile twitched with mischief. "Well, Rob. Very pretty—and kinky too? This one is the works, ain't he though?"

Matty took a moment to reconcile the use of the word "ain't" by the same man who had just discussed internalizing the oppressor.

Bill slapped his towel down on the counter. "So, how long will you be around? For good?"

Matty slipped easily into talking about his sport, explaining the competition season, the training periods, and the traveling exhibition shows. Bill listened and asked smart questions, and Rob did as well. Although it was clear, to Matty's touched amusement, that Rob had been researching on his own. He had some questions about the sport and Matty's competitors that he could only have asked if he'd been reading up on it.

Bill even noticed. "Well, if that's not evidence of smit, I don't know what is."

Matty raised an eyebrow. "Smit?"

"Smit, being smitten, possessing smit," Bill went on.

Rob said, "Well, I think my smit is pretty obvious, so I won't pretend it doesn't exist, but I was actually looking into it with Ben. He's very interested in the sport, and we both wanted to know more about how it all works. I was hoping to dissuade him, actually. It seems like a hard life in a lot of ways." He glanced toward Matty like he was apologizing for what he was saying. "I don't know that I want him giving up so much and maybe not getting anything in return."

"Did it work?" Matty asked a little defensively, thinking of the determination and passion that Ben had thrown into their work together the prior weekend. The kid had something special, but if he didn't want to put in the time and effort...Matty understood, but it was still kind of disappointing.

"Nope. It just convinced him even more that he wanted to pursue it. I'm leaving it to him to break it to his mom. I don't know where we'll find the money..." Rob trailed off, his eyes growing distant. "Maybe we'll have more to spare this summer after the goats kid and we sell them for Eid al-Fitr."

"It's expensive," Matty agreed. That was, after all, why he was even here in Montana to begin with. "It's probably $90,000 a year at this point for me. There's my coach, my choreographer, the costumes, the skates, travel costs, the help I give my folks, sending my brother to school...there's a lot of money behind it."

Rob rubbed his eyes. "I don't know that we can afford that. I don't make a lot off the ranch right now. The improvements I made after my dad died cost me."

"Maybe Anja's right," Bill said, and then held up his hands. "Whoa, just sayin.'"

Rob glared at Bill for a moment. "Maybe, but if I sell now..."

"You lose. I know."

Matty had to admit he was pretty clueless about business, and even more clueless about ranching. "I don't understand. I thought you said the ranch was worth something, and that was why you'd married Anja and stuff. To secure your son's future."

"It *was* worth a lot." Rob sighed. "A fortune, really. But then the real estate bubble burst right after my parents died. I had to sell off part of the land to the Pages and take out a lot of loans to get by over the past nine years. That's how long it's taken me to transition the ranch from my father's way of doing things to mine. Now the land's barely worth what I owe on it. If it hadn't been for my folks' insurance money, we'd be destitute. The estate taxes would have wiped us out."

"If he sold now," Bill said, "he wouldn't get any money out of it, but if he holds on, and the market recovers, then he could be looking at having a good fortune on his hands again. A nest egg for himself, and an inheritance for Ben."

"Right. Or if I build up the goat side of the business, continue to raise the cattle for the Halal market, and make the ranch more profitable, then I'll have an operation someone's willing to pay for, if I ever choose to go that route."

"But," Bill went on. "Anja's point is, what's the good in having money *one day* if you're not living your dream *now*."

"And I suppose Anja knows just what my dream is, too, doesn't she?"

Bill held his hands up again. "Listen, I'm just explaining to your new friend Matty here. I'll shut up."

"Thank you kindly," Rob bit out before looking away.

"See now, if this were me and my best friend Elliot, I'd call you a bitch," Matty said, gesturing at Bill. "And you'd call me a bitch, and then I'd threaten to kill you in your sleep—probably with a stuffed toy, because that's my M.O.—and then you'd say that you *like* breath play, and we'd laugh. So, Bill, on the count of three…one, two, three."

"I'll kill you in your sleep with a buzz saw. Because that's *my* M.O.," Bill said.

"Bitch," Rob said.

Laughter broke the tension, and Matty lifted his bottle of sparkling water, clanking it against Rob's head gently. "Cheers!"

"How did your testing for bovine brain-eating illness go?" Matty asked.

Rob chuckled. "Brucellosis. It's a bacteria that causes spontaneous abortions in cows."

"Ew."

"And it didn't go so well. Dino showed up this morning with a bred-heifer in poor condition he'd bought off a ne're-do-well, wanna-be farmer in Beaver Creek. We spent the morning getting her checked out by the vet, dewormed, and then figuring out how adding her will affect our hay supply."

"You'll have to test for the bacteria tomorrow?"

"Yes." Rob sighed. "I'm still a little worried about the winter feeding situation. It's hay supply in the winter that will make or break a rancher, and the addition of even one head of cattle more than expected can hit us hard, especially a lactating cow with a calf to feed."

"Will it be okay?"

"Probably. Like with anything to do with ranching, we'll have to wait and see. I'd have liked a little notice, but Dino saw a chance to save her life and he took it. Can't blame him for that. If it all works out, that's one more calf for the market and another milk cow for the ranch, which Bing's been wanting for a while now."

"Is he still hoping to make soap?" Bill asked.

"Yep."

"You'd think he was a queer with his obsession with wanting to make that fancy-schmancy soap."

"He's straight but not narrow." Rob chuckled. "He smells damn good, so whatever he bathes with, I think we could make a killing if we can replicate it the way he wants."

Matty didn't have much to say about the ranching—or soap— business. It seemed so real in a way, especially when compared to the ephemeral nature of his own career. Everything Rob talked about came down to flesh and blood, food and water, and the problems of life itself.

An hour later, Rob smiled. "What do you say we head out?"

Matty reached for his bag to pull out some cash, but Bill waved him off. "Forget it. It's on Rob's tab. That he never pays."

Rob shrugged. "Send the gay mafia to collect and I'll pony up."

"I've got my request for assistance in already, but they're kind of busy fighting for our right to join the heteros in the misery of marriage at the moment."

"Ah well. I'll be waiting when they finally get freed up."

"Evening customers will be here soon. Time for the mood lights." Bill flipped a switch and some additional lights came on in the room, not bright or intense, but yellow and dark. It kind of made the place look a little dirty. If Matty hadn't seen how spotless it was before, he would've been afraid to touch anything. Bill turned on the stereo next, and an old country song from before Matty was even born filled the room.

Rob lips quirked up. "My mom danced in the kitchen to this once. I remember the curtains billowing out from the window. She wore a yellow dress. She'd just made cookies. Chocolate chip."

For the first time, Rob looked fond when mentioning his parents.

He turned to Matty. "Dance with me before we go. Just this song. I know it's corny, but I'd really like it." He tugged Matty off the stool. "Come on."

If questioned about it, Matty would have to admit it was nice being held tight, his face turned into Rob's chest, smelling his detergent and cologne while the music played. If he didn't think about it, he could pretend it was a Christina Aguilera ballad they were dancing to, slow and close, circling in one spot again and again. But when it came down to it, he didn't want to pretend anything to be different from the way it was at all. The country song suited the moment just fine.

Rob hummed a little in his ear and his voice was nice. Matty's heart slowed, his eyes closed, and he relaxed, moving slowly to the music.

"Not bad," Rob whispered softly.

The song was over before Matty knew it, and he smiled goofily.

"Now, if that wasn't the most darlin' thing I ever did see."

"Shut it, Bill," Rob said, also smiling.

Matty said nothing at all. It kind of freaked him out, but he pretty much felt exactly the same way.

* * *

On the way home they stopped by the Safeway to get some fresh salad fixings for dinner. Matty was incredibly relieved and happy they were going back to Rob's place. That meant he was going to get laid again, laid again, *laid again*. It was like a song in his head, and he could have skipped around the store to the beat of it.

Rebecca was working the register, and Matty could feel her eyes following them as they chose the vegetables and Matty spent some time picking out the perfect dessert.

"This is dessert?" Rob asked. "Are you sure? It looks oddly like a pineapple to me."

"It's good for dessert. You'll see. Trust me."

Rob took the basket from Matty's hands at the checkout line.

"What are you doing?" Matty asked.

"Buying dinner."

"Oh no. I'm buying dinner." Matty fished in his handbag for his wallet. "Don't even. I'm serious, Rob. Don't."

"Hi, Mr. Lovely," Rebecca said, scanning the items and weighing the fruit. "Mr. Marcus."

"Hi," they both said, jostling each other trying to get closest to the register.

"That's twenty-three-thirteen," Rebecca said, popping her gum.

"Here." Matty thrust a fifty at her, just as Rob stuck out a twenty and a five.

"We don't take anything higher than a twenty dollar bill." Rebecca watched them with interest. "Sorry."

"What kind of backwoods, ridiculous store doesn't take a fifty dollar bill?" Matty muttered, looking through his wallet, but not finding anything smaller.

"Next time." Rob smiled in a way that was super annoying.

"You know, I *can* pay my own way, and I *will*, because I am not a damsel in fucking distress. Do you understand?"

Rob looked vaguely surprised. "I was under no illusion that you were a damsel of any nature, my good sir."

Matty narrowed his eyes, shoved his wallet in his purse, and turned his back on Rob.

"So, um, do you have your bag, Mr. Marcus?" Rebecca asked. "Or do you want me to use one of ours?"

"Fuck the environment. Use plastic."

He didn't really know what had flipped his switch. He was always a moody and sensitive sort of guy. He *knew* that. He could spin from playful to bitchy in two seconds flat, but he'd been in a good mood when they came in. What was the big deal if Rob wanted to pay? Matty gritted his teeth. He might be smaller than Rob, he might even be prettier in his own way, what with his delicate features and all, but he was *not* less of a man for it, and he could buy his own goddamn food.

"So, like, are you guys on a date?" Rebecca asked, tentatively.

"No," Matty said, and walked away, wrapping his scarf a little tighter, and putting his nose in the cold Montana winter air.

Rob exited less than a minute later, his brow furrowed, and his arms gripping two *paper* bags firmly.

"I thought I said plastic," Matty said.

"I prefer paper. I can put it in the compost or use it to wrap a present. That sort of thing."

"Very earth-conscious of you."

Rob opened his door and got in. Matty climbed into his own car and started the engine. He waited for Rob to pull out, not sure if he was going to follow him to his place or go be lonely and miserable at the Pages' in protest. It took a few minutes for Matty to realize that Rob hadn't started the truck and that he was just sitting there staring out the windshield.

Matty waited, trying to decide what to do. What to say. He finally got out of his car and opened Rob's passenger side door. "What is up with you?"

Rob just shrugged.

Eyes narrowed, Matty climbed into the truck. He might have given in by switching cars, but he was going to make Rob talk first, that was for sure. Rob could make this or break this with the next words out of his mouth, and Matty had a crazy, terrifying hope that Rob would break it. Then he could somehow escape this sudden intense entanglement, even at the expense of great sex, because…fuck, he could already tell he was going to get hurt. Better now than later.

Rob stared out the windshield. He didn't move, and barely seemed to be breathing. When Matty turned to dart a look out of the corner of his eye, he saw that Rob had his eyes closed, and his head back on the head rest. Matty waited. He waited some more. Rob's breaths started to come in even, slow measures, like…like he was…

"Are you *asleep*?" Matty asked, incredulous.

Rob shook himself, and sat up, yawning. "It's been a long few days. Sorry." He rubbed at his eyes in a way that was oddly endearing.

Matty's fingers itched to smooth through Rob's hair, but he clasped his hands together instead.

"You know, I only wanted to pay because I know you're saving money for your career," Rob said, starting the truck.

"And I just listened to you talk about how your ranch is barely turning a profit and you can't afford skating lessons for Ben."

"That's true."

"So, I don't need you to decide for me what—"

"Matty, look. I'm not the kind of guy who's going to tell you what to do with your life, okay? Or with your money. I might tell you what to do in bed, but you always have the right to say you don't want to do it."

Rob turned and looked at him, his face and eyes barely visible in the dark of the truck, but Matty could feel his intensity.

"You're amazing, driven, and inspiring. I wouldn't change a damn thing about you. I even like that you threw a bratty fit just now over paying for the food, because for some reason everything about you makes me a little crazy in the good way. But I don't ever want you to look back and think to yourself, *that was a waste*. I mean that in every way, from the time you're with me to the money you spend around me. Do you get what I'm saying?"

Matty nodded, speechless.

"Are you sure?"

"I'm sure."

"Good."

Matty climbed over the gear shift, crawling onto Rob's lap. His ass hit the steering wheel as he kissed Rob hard. The honking was loud, and he pulled away, tumbling back into his own seat. Rob leaned over, and Matty grabbed Rob's hair to pull him down, kissing his mouth and his chin, and then nuzzling his neck.

Rob kissed him gently on the lips, nose, and forehead before pulling back. "I'm glad we understand each other." He ducked his head a little and looked out the window, and laughed under his breath. "I'm pretty sure that Rebecca knows we're on a date now."

Rebecca stood in the doorway of the grocery store watching. Matty gave her a little wave and blew a kiss. "That, or she thinks I'm a giant slut. Come to think of it, she wouldn't be that far off."

"Somehow I think you're all blah-blah-blah with that and not nearly enough action." Rob smiled slyly.

"I'll have you know that I've been incredibly sexually depraved during my relatively short life."

Rob smiled. "When we get back, you'll have to show me. I'd love to see how dirty you can be."

CHAPTER NINE

The rest of the week went by in a wonderful haze of horses, skating, workouts, and sex. Matty had never felt so physically sated in his life. He went to bed every night wanting for nothing, except maybe more food. Still, his dietary needs were being met to a T with the guidelines from his nutritionist back home. Rob had photocopied them and whenever Matty was skeptical of a meal Rob had prepared, Rob would pull out the guidelines and go through them, showing how he'd taken Matty's requirements absolutely into account.

Sex…well, sex was fucking amazing.

Matty could lose time remembering the naked hours he spent on Rob's bed, pinned under his strong body, or held down with Rob's amazing arms, or held open and licked until he was squirming and trembling and begging. He had never been so free as he was on Rob's ranch in Montana, away from everything but his body, lifted from the restrictions of society, coaches, family, and the world. Just him and Rob and the endless hours of the night that stretched on and on—sweaty, sticky, and filthy hot—that left him satisfied, aching, boneless, and terrifyingly happy.

Rob was commanding in bed. He moved Matty where he wanted him, held him just so, and placed pillows under his knees or hips to make him more comfortable. Matty loved sucking Rob's cock on his hands and knees, while Rob rubbed Matty's back and gave instructions, holding his hair in a tight fist, keeping him on his cock when he came down his throat.

He loved being on Rob's bed, his torso and arms wrapped tight in a thick blanket, like a cocoon while his legs were thrust up to his ears, and Rob pounded into him. Matty had left claw marks on his own arms the first time they did it that way. He'd adored it—the sense of being contained and confined, wrapped up and swaddled while Rob rode him hard, fucking him until he'd lost control completely and come all over Rob's stomach and the blanket.

It had been even better after when Rob had held him, rolling them both into the blanket together, kissing Matty's mouth and hair, and each eyelid, telling him how good it had been. How good *he* had been.

When Friday night rolled around, and Ben arrived at his father's house, Matty felt like an addict forced to go cold turkey. His hands literally shook as he cut up the cheese and fruit for dinner. He sat at the Pages' kitchen table, staring at the walls, trying to remember what he had done to entertain himself before being with Rob had become his favorite pastime.

As he ate the last of his fruit, he remembered he had quite a few messages from Elliot and his mother that he hadn't returned during the week. The last one from his mom had sounded vaguely panicked even. God, he was a terrible son, an awful, ungrateful boy to have not called her back by now. She was probably going to give him a ton of crap about it.

"Where have you been? I was going to call the Flathead County police department if I hadn't heard from you by tomorrow."

"Sorry, Mama." Matty lowered his voice to a pitch that sounded genuine. He *was* sorry she was worried. He was, however, not at all sorry that he'd been so distracted by amazing sex and the amusing company of a handsome man.

"So...?"

"Well, Mama, I have met a man."

"A man. What kind of man?"

"A rancher."

"A rancher," she repeated, as though that meant nothing at all to her.

"Yes, and he has beautiful hands. His hands are like an opera."

"*Oh*. You've met a *man*. I thought you meant you'd met a man *and*...and something else was going to be said after that. Something big."

"Oh, he's big."

"*Matty!*"

"He's a rancher, Mother! Of course he's big! He's tall, like a mountain, and strong like...a mountain, and funny—"

"Like a mountain?"

"No, just listen, Donna," he said.

"Matty, you know my first name is off limits."

"He's like *Montana* in man form, and he even tastes like Montana. Like pure white snow on majestic mountains. He smells like clean water—"

"Probably because he showers."

"You aren't going to let me rhapsodize here, are you?"

"The bad poetry is killing me, honey. It's got to stop."

"Donna."

"Matty."

"Fine, okay, I'm stopping with the poetry, but you wanted to know where I'd been, and that's where I've been. With the man."

"Does this man have a name?"

"Rob Lovely."

His mother started laughing. "You're not kidding, are you?"

"No. It's a delightful name for a delightful person."

"Matty, you're not getting distracted are you?"

Sighing, he flopped down on the patchwork sofa. "No, Mama, I'm not. I'm working my ass off every day at the rink, and I'm doing additional training at the gym, and I'm having amazing, acrobatic sex every night. I've written the appropriate people for the coaching situation, and I've taken all my vitamins, and I'm eating well, and I've still found some time, though very little, to study Russian. The horses are being fed, and I'm doing my job—though I've vacuumed a little less, but something had to give—and the acrobatic sex seemed worth the loss, at least for now."

"Honey, are you being safe?"

"I wear my seat belt, yes."

"Does this Rob Lovely wear a seat belt too?"

Matty sighed. "Mother, seat belts should be worn at all times when in a moving vehicle. Didn't you teach me that?"

"So long as we're both talking about condoms here, then I'll leave it."

"Consider it left."

"And what about your heart? Are you being careful with it too?"

"I'm living very heart healthy. I swear."

Matty heard his mother's worry loud and clear. It was in the way she hesitated, looking for the words that wouldn't make him pissy and hang up the phone. It was in the slow intake of breath and the subtle sighs. He didn't know what else to do about it, though. He was kind of worried himself, though not at all willing to walk away. Not yet, anyway. Not until he had to.

"I should go, Mom. I've got to get up early and train Rob's kid on the Pages' pond. He's learning to skate. He's got a lot of talent."

"Wait. Rob has a *child*? And you're training him? Just how old is this Rob anyway?"

"You know, I've never asked him." He waited a few beats, feeling his mother's ire raise over the line, but cutting her off before she could speak. "I'd guess he was twenty-nine or thirty. I don't really know for sure. Maybe a little older or younger. I don't see why it matters."

"But he's got a child?"

"A son. Ben. And, no, he's not married, and, yes, I'm sure, and Mama, if you met him, you'd love him. I swear. On my soul and chocolate pudding."

The conversation dragged on a bit more after that, with Matty forced to fill in a bit more information about Rob. Who, where, when, how, and why. As his mother, Matty figured it was her prerogative to push the questions.

"So, he's a good guy."

"Yeah, honestly. If it were a different time in my life, I might think he was *the* guy."

"But he's not. Because of skating?"

"Because I have to do this, Mama. I only get one shot at being the best athlete I can be. This is my time."

Matty waited for her response. What she said stayed with him for hours after he hung up.

"Matty, you do what you have to do, and I'll support you one hundred percent. All of us take risks, whether we know it or not. Every day, we walk away from once-in-a-lifetime opportunities chasing after other once-in-a-lifetime opportunities. We just have to hope we're choosing the right thing to chase."

* * *

The next morning Yuliya Yasneyeva met Ben Lovely on the ice at eight-thirty sharp. Ben was not late, and Yuliya was not unhappy with his performance on the ice, even going so far as to applaud him and offer him hot cocoa as a reward.

"This very special in my homeland. You warm inside when drink, yes?"

Ben asked, "Is it spiked? Like with cognac or something? Or vodka?"

"You accuse Yuliya Yasneyeva of corrupting youth? No more hot cocoa for you! Only skate!"

Ben laughed and pushed off onto the ice. Matty glanced up to see three cows and a big, tall man walking over the hill toward the pond. Standing, he pushed Yuliya's glasses up his nose, and adjusted the wig. "Big man, take your future handbags and get away from pond. This is time for coach and boy. Go! In my country, arrest you for trespass! Take your terrible moo-beasts and leave."

Cackling, Rob paused by the opposite end of the pond. "Ben told me you dressed up as a Russian lady. I believed him—I mean, who would make that up? But, wow, this is pretty fucking hysterical."

"You mock? You mock coach of son? Foolish! You must leave now. We must work!"

"The other night you asked if I was going to come watch."

"Not Yuliya, sir. Mr. Marcus. Now things change. You deal with, yes? And never to mock technique, mister cow man!"

Rob raised his hands and backed away, pausing to pat the rump of one of the cows that had followed him. "I'm leaving. No mocking intended. Continue with your work."

"If father of boy wish to be laid, he will learn place. When coach is with skater, father is not to be interfere. Yes?"

Ben laughed and stuck a finger in his mouth, pretending to gag. "Too much information!" he called.

"Too much? Yuliya will give you too much. Another double toe loop and then another and another, and we will see too much!"

"Dad, go on! Before she kills me!"

Matty held his head high and made his tone as imperious as possible. "If only kill you, you are lucky boy. Now get back to work! Both of you!"

* * *

After dinner, sitting side by side on Rob's couch, Ben showed Matty the schedule for the Missoula rink's production of *Holidays on Ice*.

"I'm a soldier. Will you come?"

Matty put his arm around Ben and squeezed him. "I wouldn't miss it!" He paused. "But what about your coach? Would you rather Yuliya Yasneyeva come, or me?"

Ben flushed. "Um, will you be offended if I'd rather it be you? I kind of want to keep Yuliya away from Missoula. I don't want the kids there to…get the wrong idea and think that my dad's boyfriend…I mean, you know. I already have enough trouble there."

"Of course." Matty gave him another squeeze. "You know you can talk to me about that, right? Believe me, I understand all about being different."

Ben frowned, and pushed stray hair off his face. "The thing is, I'm not really different, you know? I like the same girls they like, I listen to the same music, and I wear the same clothes. I don't get why they pick on me."

"They'll always find a reason to pick on you, Ben. If there's anything in you that's special, something that makes you shine, they'll try to tear you down. And you're special. You're talented and amazing. They might not know exactly how you're special, but they sense it. It's like an atmospheric disturbance surrounds you or something."

"I'm not special. I'm just a dork. I'm not different at all."

"Do you think Yuliya Yasneyeva coaches you for shits and giggles? You're amazing on the ice, Ben. You inspire me with how fearless you are. You make *me* want to be better. I want to be like you with an endless future in front of me. For me, the clock is ticking. But you? You've got *it*, Ben. If you want it—and you have to want it. That's what all of this has been about."

Matty looked up when Rob cleared his throat from the doorway. Rob met his gaze, and Matty was overwhelmed by the expression he found there—gratitude, affection, and sadness combined.

"Dessert," Rob said. "In the kitchen."

Ben hopped up. "Awesome. What is it?"

"Sliced pears." Rob clapped his hands together with false enthusiasm.

"*What?*"

"You can blame Matty for that." Rob smiled.

"Come on now," Matty said. "They're really good and a lot healthier than the brownies I put in the refrigerator for the two of you earlier."

Ben whooped and took off for the kitchen while Rob shook his head, laughing under his breath.

Matty pointed a finger at him. "Just remember this the next time I have a bitch attack over something ridiculous. I can be really sweet sometimes." He shoved Rob aside on his way into the kitchen. "Besides, I think I've earned a third of one, so it wasn't entirely selfless."

"Of course not," Rob murmured, slapping Matty's ass as he followed close behind.

* * *

"Go as a fairy," Matty said, annoyed, flipping through his sweaters, looking for the gray one that was extra warm, even if it didn't flatter his eyes.

"Um, can you say *obvious*?" Elliot said. "It's a post-Halloween, November-madness costume party and I have to look amazing."

"You'd look amazing as a fairy."

"You think?"

"Sparkling wings, glittery make-up—what's not to like? And you'd get laid." Matty pulled on the sweater and tugged it into place with a glance in the mirror. He sat down at the vanity table, and put the phone on speaker beside him. A little concealer, a little rouge—the usual. Since he was going out he added some longer fake lashes, only to change his mind and take them off again.

"For sure," Elliot agreed. "Like, probably all night long by all kinds of guys. What are you doing tonight? Hanging out and sniffing glue? Or boinking your rancher again?"

"I'm going to a corn maze."

"Oh, bitch. You've lost your ever-loving mind. This thing with the rancher has officially passed over from worrisome into terrifying."

"It's a corn maze, Elliot, not the apocalypse."

"Have you *seen* that movie? *Children of the Corn*? I don't think you have, or you wouldn't be going anywhere near the cornfields."

"If Malachi is going to get me, I'll look pretty while he does it. Besides, it's been snowing here for weeks now. The maze will be white and sparkling. It should be very cool."

"Bitch. I don't even."

"Elliot, has it occurred to you that calling me 'bitch' is totally misogynistic?"

"Yeah, but you know you like it."

"True." Matty posed in front of the mirror, thrusting out a hip, checking himself from all angles. He grabbed a stole and wrapped it around his neck. "Stole or scarf?"

"Stole."

Matty hung the stole back up carefully and chose a gray and green-flecked scarf he'd picked up in Hong Kong one year. "I've got to go or I'll be late."

"Matty, wait," Elliot said, in a voice soft and earnest. "Is this, what you're doing...you know, for real? Or are you just playing around?"

Matty paused. He didn't lie to Elliot often, but sometimes it had to be done. "What do you think? I still have my priorities in line. Don't worry so much. You sound like my mother. Elliot, I always thought you'd be the one in the jail cell with me, not on the outside giving me sorrowful looks as you paid my bail." He pulled on a warm, non-fur coat, and double-checked his face in the mirror. "What kind of best friend are you turning out to be? I don't need coddling."

"This just seems different." Elliot's tone was earnest and baby sweet. "I can't pick up the pieces if you fall apart. I never can. You're the best figure skater out there. Or you could be. You just need to get it together—and keep it together. I can't help but wonder if this isn't going to end with you losing it."

"Stop worrying. It's all fun and games."

"Until someone breaks their own heart," Elliot murmured before bidding him goodnight and hanging up.

Matty pulled on the boots designated for destruction. He leaned against the bedroom doorway for a moment, gazing down the hall into the Pages' country-chic living room. He couldn't remember the last time a conversation with Elliot had ended on such a serious note.

Was he going to break his own heart? Matty sighed, and put his hand to his chest, feeling his heart thumping in a regular, steady way. So far, so good.

CHAPTER TEN

Climbing out of the car in the half-full parking lot of Bill's Place, Matty took a fortifying breath. Rob swore that Bill made the best burgers in town, and Matty swore that he would bring his own bag of salad, because just a bite of a burger would be more calories than he could possibly justify. Between his training, taking care of the horses, and the massive amounts of sex, Matty was almost down to fighting weight. He only had two pounds to go.

He recalled the night before when Rob had run his hands over Matty's body, feeling every muscle and tendon, and then followed his fingers with his lips. *"The way you're put together is beautiful."*

Matty leaned back against the car door for a moment, orienting himself after the rush of feeling that swelled in him thinking of Rob's voice, his eyes, and how sincere he'd been, so sweet and ridiculously earnest.

The bar was crowded, and at first all Matty could see was a bunch of shoulders, backs, and asses, in different brands and colors of blue jeans and plaid shirts. Then, like Moses parting the sea, Rob moved through the crowd and put his arm around Matty. Matty nearly knocked Rob's arm away.

He wasn't accustomed to living his life as anything but an out man, even if he never said the apparently all-important three little words to the media, but rural Montana wasn't New York City, and announcing his gayness in a room of big, burly ranchers seemed like a bad idea.

Matty took a closer look. The room was full of men, yeah, but many of them were touching, and some were kissing. "What the shit is going on?"

Rob laughed. "It's a gay bar. Men come all the way up from Missoula on the weekends. It's one of the oldest in Montana."

"I...oh. Okay, um. Unexpected, but okay," Matty said. "When we were here before, I guess it was just us and Bill, so I didn't realize." As his eyes adjusted to the lower light, he saw there were all types of men there, and even a trans* person or two, unless Bill's Place was also sponsoring a post-Halloween, November-madness costume party. Matty didn't think so.

"There's a little drag show later." Rob motioned toward a small stage erected in the corner. "The corn maze is just northeast of Kalispell, so we could come back after to watch if you'd like."

Matty could feel eyes all over him and he felt a strange impulse to wave and blow kisses like he was greeting fans or something. "Let's start with dinner and save decisions about shenanigans until later."

"Shenanigans," Rob echoed, guiding Matty to a booth in the back of the room, away from prying eyes. Bill merely lifted his chin in acknowledgment as they walked by.

Matty sat down, surprised when Rob scooted in beside him, rather than across from him.

Rob said, "Staking a claim. Do you care?"

Matty leaned around Rob and gave everyone in the room a once over, especially the guys who were checking him out. "I don't see anyone else I want to fuck, so sure. Stake away."

Rob put his arm around Matty and waved a short, balding waiter in his late twenties over to the table. Matty smiled and gave his order for an empty bowl.

Rob rolled his eyes when Matty brought a plastic bag of salad contents from his handbag. "You thought I wouldn't do it?" Matty asked.

"I was pretty sure you would, actually, but it looks even more ridiculous than my imagination had supplied."

"It bugs you."

Rob turned in the booth until he was facing Matty. He ran his hand up Matty's leg and gently cupped his crotch. "No. Your eccentricities turn me on."

"In that case." Matty spread his legs so Rob could get a better feel. He pulled a small flask from his bag and poured a little of its contents on the salad. "Olive oil. Good for salad dressing, and *other* things. You know, when on the go."

Bill approached with Rob's burger, and Matty nodded toward him. "Your delicious stack of meaty calories is here."

"Hey, Matty. How's it going?" His eyes focused on Matty's salad. "Just so you know, I do have salad on the menu."

"I noticed, but I'm a control freak. In case that wasn't completely clear."

Bill chuckled. "Oh, it's clear." He winked at Rob and then changed the topic. "You guys should stay for the drag contest. If it's anything like last year, it should be pretty amusing. And I promise Empress Kathleen will not win again. Ebony Cakes was *robbed*."

"I hate that feeling," Matty said. "Tell Ebony Cakes that Matty Marcus wishes her lots of luck."

Bill blew him a kiss as he walked away.

When Rob took a bite of his hamburger, Matty watched in envy as a glob of mayonnaise and ketchup fell to his plate. It had been a really long time since Matty had just dug into a big, yummy burger and eaten it without concern for his weight. Even when he'd been laid up with his injury, every time he ate anything off of his diet, he felt guilty. Like he was letting not only himself down, but other people, too, because if he didn't skate well, they suffered. Not just his immediate family, but his friends, his coaches—everyone he knew.

Scores from biased judges were out of his control. Even his health, to some extent, was out of his control. Things like the conditions of the ice, or his competitors' performances were completely out of his control. But his weight and diet he could rule with an iron fist. No one could say he wasn't doing a good enough job of it. That was one reason he hated eating in front of his competitors. Even the food became a competition.

"What are you thinking about?" Rob asked.

"Oh, you know, the usual."

"Sex?"

Matty laughed. "Skating, actually, but I'm sure that sex would have come into the mix eventually. Why?"

"Your forehead was kind of scrunched up and you looked sad and serious at the same time."

"Sad and serious—and you thought I was thinking about *sex*?"

Rob smiled. "No, I just wanted to lighten your mood. I knew you were thinking about skating. Care to share?"

"It's going to sound strange, but I was thinking about how I don't like to eat in front of other skaters."

"Yeah? Why not?"

"I guess because I feel like they judge me. It makes me feel unsafe or something."

"I can see that."

"Really? Most people think I'm being crazy or have an eating disorder."

"I haven't ruled that last bit out," Rob said, easily, like he was saying he hadn't ruled out the possibility that the sky was blue, or Matty was hot, or water was wet. "But, historically, meals have always been considered a time of vulnerability. Kings had tasters to make sure they weren't being poisoned. Attacks planned during meal time are more successful, because people are relaxed. They've let their guard down."

Rob leaned back in the booth, his hamburger with a single bite taken from it resting on the plate. He kicked his feet up to the opposite bench, and continued. "Generally, when you sit down to eat, it's kind of

106

like sex in a way, because you're opening your body up to receive something. Your soul, too, I guess. You're taking something in and trusting that it's good for you. That it's sufficient. Having an enemy watch us eat brings us, at an instinctual level, to a very vulnerable place. So we feel we have to keep our guard up."

Rob paused, looking thoughtful. "I wonder if we would even absorb the nutrients as well in those situations, or if our body is prepared for the possibility that the food itself is the enemy as well."

Matty sat with his salad-laden fork, listening to Rob with a mouth full of half-chewed spinach, and a weird, hot, open feeling in his chest. Even his mother thought his issues with eating in front of the other skaters was a ridiculous eccentricity.

He looked around. The room was full of people, most of them men Matty wouldn't *really* want to meet or talk to on his most friendly of days, and the place itself was a bit of a horror in that side-show kind of way that he and Elliot would normally enjoy making fun of. But right now, being there with Rob, feeling understood and cared for, Matty couldn't think of a single place he'd rather be. Which was *insane.*

"Now what are you thinking about?" Rob asked, taking another bite of his burger.

Matty finished chewing and swallowed. He kept his tone light, pushing away the unsettling feelings. "This isn't exactly my kind of scene. I'm more into posh and elegant rather than rural and *Deliverance.*"

"That was Appalachia. This is Montana. Big difference."

Matty was unconvinced. True, most of the men in the room looked like the kind of rugged adults that one would expect to grow out of the stereotypical Montanan boy, but the fact that the only thing Bill's Place had going for it, besides being incredibly clean, was that it didn't have straw or peanuts on the floor, didn't really mean Matty was not currently ensconced in the very definition of "hick."

Rob added, "But, yeah, I usually only stop by when there's no one else around. Bill and I go back, but this isn't my scene."

"What is your scene?" Matty asked, suddenly curious.

He couldn't really imagine Rob outside of Montana. He tried to picture him in New York City, at any decent gay club, and while he was sure Rob would be a popular piece of meat, he'd also be entirely out of place.

"I guess I don't have one."

"Then how do you meet guys?"

"I manage it."

"Rob," Matty said, concern for the man beside him overriding his other thoughts. "You live on a ranch in the middle of nowhere. You *must* get lonely. Don't you ever wish you had someone?"

Rob looked at him strangely, and then took a bite of his burger. Matty ate a bit more of his salad to stuff his mouth with something before he could say something else that made both of them uncomfortable.

Rob finally said, "You sound like Anja. That's another reason she wants me to move to Missoula. She wants me to meet someone and settle down."

"You seem like the type who'd enjoy settling down." A small wave of nausea washed over him, and he put his fork down. He didn't feel like eating anymore.

Rob studied him. "So do you, actually."

Matty scoffed. "First, I can't imagine anyone putting up with me for an extended length of time, and second, I'm hard to pin down. It's impossible to even think like that when you don't know where you're going to end up."

"Birds like a nest to come home to."

Matty rolled his eyes. "Great. In your eyes, I'm a bird."

"Why is that a bad thing?"

"Usually people say that when they're going to call me flighty or irresponsible."

"I was thinking more along the lines of beautiful and breathtaking."

Matty glanced up coyly.

Rob persisted. "Don't pretend I'm wrong. You're one of those birds who collects shiny things for their nests, aren't you?"

"What color am I, then?"

"Hmm. Blue."

Matty was pleased to have steered the conversation in a lighter direction. He was starting to feel like Rob saw way too much. Vanity and beauty he could deal with, but the rest was too deep—too close to home. "Why not brown to go with my eyes?"

"I think blue so that when you fly you'll be like grace itself and nearly blend with the sky."

Matty felt too satisfied with that answer to even laugh. He added, "With a red scarf to make me really pop."

"Absolutely."

He shook his head when Rob offered him the final bite of his burger. Rob polished it off easily.

"Maybe you'd be better as a blackbird instead, with red, heart-shaped feathers on your wings."

Matty's pulse began to pound, and his hand drew up to his chest, covering the betraying organ.

"And you'd fly with a different kind of grace. Wounded, less innocent." He wiped his mouth with his napkin. "Are you ready to go?"

In the parking lot, Matty climbed into the passenger seat of Rob's truck after agreeing they'd pick up his car at Bill's Place on the way home later.

"Yeah, I think a blackbird," Rob said, still musing. "You'd never blend with the sky."

"Too dirty to fly clean," Matty murmured.

He didn't climb over the gear shift and make out with Rob like he had in the grocery store lot, but how was it that Rob kept doing things that made a crazy buzzed-calmness descend upon him? The terror and wonder pinned him in place as the night sky outside of the truck started to move, and Rob's warm hand fell to his knee.

* * *

Before they went into the maze itself, they were able to follow other people's progress by watching the reflected light of their lanterns. A few times lanterns blinked out and didn't come back on. Matty asked about it.

The guy who took their money for tickets said, "Another make-out session. It's amazing how being lost makes people want to have sex."

"We won't get lost," Matty said to Rob as they entered the maze. "I have a great sense of direction. If I can navigate Hong Kong, I can navigate a corn maze."

Rob put his hand in Matty's hair, grabbing hold and pulling a little.

"Ow." Matty batted his hand away. "Stop that."

Rob laughed and gave Matty a hot look before breaking into a jog and then a near-sprint, essentially forcing Matty to follow or be left in the dark without a lantern. When Rob finally let Matty catch up, they were both panting, and, as far as Matty could tell, completely lost. In his dash to keep up, he hadn't been able to pay any attention to which turns they'd taken, or even which direction they were facing. Matty stamped his feet against the ground, pissed off. He couldn't believe his plans at maze domination had been utterly undone by a runaway boyfriend.

Boyfriend. If that's what Rob was. He really didn't know.

"I wanted to beat the best time," Matty grumbled, punching Rob in the chest half-heartedly. "Jerk."

Rob turned the lantern off and grabbed Matty by the front of his coat. "Funny, I was much more interested in finding a good place to suck your dick."

Matty glanced around, shaking in anticipation as Rob, took off his gloves, sank to his knees and tugged at Matty's zipper. "Oh, well, that's a good idea too...ah, God."

His cock was engulfed in hot, wet, wonderful heat, and he thrust experimentally, loving the sweet pull and tug. He closed his eyes when Rob took him deep, getting his cock wet all over. Matty whimpered when Rob suddenly stood up. He kept his hand on Matty's now slick dick, jerking it steadily.

"Thought you were gonna suck me," Matty whispered.

Rob didn't respond, but it was all good again when he kissed Matty's mouth hard. Matty fell into that, moving his hips in a soft circle with Rob's hand. He groaned as Rob's lips trailed over his cheek to his earlobe.

Rob whispered in his ear, "Do you trust me?"

Shivering, Matty nodded.

"I want to hear you say it."

"I trust you," Matty said, breathless. Rob's hand on his cock was strong, and he squeezed a little tighter than was entirely comfortable, but Matty kind of liked it.

"Good. Now take off your left glove and put it in your pocket."

"Why?"

"Do it."

Matty complied.

"Now, if you want me to stop, then snap your fingers three times, okay?"

"Why wouldn't I just—mmph—" Matty's words were cut off by Rob's hand on his mouth, and he swallowed a little air in surprise.

Rob moved behind him and pulled Matty's body against his own. Keeping one hand on Matty's mouth, Rob reached into the pocket of his coat and pulled out the little flask that Matty recognized as his own.

"Pour some into my hand," Rob said.

Matty managed to open the flask and pour olive oil into Rob's palm. He capped the flask again and stuck it into his own coat pocket. All the while Rob held his hand over Matty's mouth. It was kind of hot.

Slippery with the oil, Rob's hand felt amazing as it closed over Matty's dick. He moved it fast and rough, pumping him without a lot of the finesse Matty knew he was capable of, but with a ton of intent. Matty leaned back against Rob's body, shifting his legs. He stared up at the night sky as Rob worked his dick. His small moans were muffled by

Rob's hand, and his body was wracked with shivers from the cold and the hot, sweet surrender of giving himself over to Rob's control.

Rob's thumb swirled over the head of his cock, pressing against the slit. He ducked his head to Matty's ear and whispered, "Remember, if you snap three times. I'll hear it, and I'll stop."

Matty was confused by the reminder until Rob's hand shifted. He not only covered Matty's mouth, but also pinched his nose shut so he couldn't breathe. Matty's body jerked and squirmed against the loss of air.

Rob spoke softly in his ear. "Shh, I've got you. Trust me. I'd never hurt you."

Panic rose, and Matty yelled, the sound muffled against Rob's palm. When Rob released his nose and Matty sucked air in hard, he snorted and started shaking all over. Rob's hand was still over his mouth, so Matty couldn't say what he was feeling. His mind shouted, though. *Oh God, oh God, oh God, oh motherfucking God.*

"Now again," Rob whispered, hot and damp breath against Matty's ear contrasting with the cold of the night. Rob pinched Matty's nose again. "Shh, relax. Focus on my hand and how good it feels. Look at the sky."

Matty quaked in Rob's arms. He could pull away if he wanted. He knew he could. His arms weren't even restrained, and Rob had given him a safe out. Yet he felt completely taken over, under Rob's command. He obeyed, striving to do as Rob asked. He focused on the slip and slide of Rob's hand on his cock, the tight pull, the rhythm of it, and he thrust into Rob's fist. As the need for air became intense, his body jerked against his will. He shook his head, his throat working and gagging for it. Puffs of exhales broke through Rob's fingers, but his mouth was held fast by Rob's big, strong hand. He couldn't suck any air in to replace what he let out.

"That's good. Like that. Come on sweetheart, let go, let go," Rob cooed in his ear.

Matty's cock *ached*, throbbing with every touch of Rob's hand. His hips jerked in rhythm with the strokes, desperate to reach climax. His vision swam and his throat stung with the fruitless search for oxygen. When Rob released his nose, Matty sucked in air so loudly that it was all he could hear, huffing through his nostrils like a race horse.

"Good boy." Then the air was gone again.

Matty flung his head back on Rob's shoulder, his entire body shaking and his heart pounding so hard that it resounded in his fingertips and toes. Rob's whispers came through to him, words of encouragement and affection. "So good...so fucking beautiful and sweet...come on. Good boy, let go, there...like that. Let go."

Matty groaned deep in his throat, and he grabbed hold of Rob's hand on his cock, jerking fast and hard with him. He brought his other hand up to cover Rob's on his mouth. He held it pressed there, showing Rob how much he wanted this—how much he needed it. Rob gripped his face even tighter, not allowing a sip of air in or out.

The world spun around him, and Matty gave into it, descending into the sensations—the pain and the pleasure—as desperation focused his mind. He was so close, so close, *so close.*

Rob let him breathe, and Matty sucked in air, the approaching orgasm ripped away while oxygen filled his burning lungs. He moaned again, and tapped Rob's hand, begging with the whimpers in his throat, with the touch of his fingers, and the way he moved his hips. He wanted more. He was ready.

Rob pinched his nose again, and Matty's body betrayed him, squirming and seeking a breath. Matty tried to master his own reactions. He arched, desperate noises vibrating in his throat, and Rob's voice was in his ear again, hot and humid.

"Sweetheart, relax. Trust me to take care of you. Let go."

Matty fought his bucking body for control, and finally succeeded, going limp in Rob's arms. He dissolved into the pleasure in his groin, which was rapidly gaining on the pain of his burning lungs. He was a mess of want, a disaster of desire, and he convulsed one more time. Then he waited, still and mentally begging as his orgasm barreled toward him. He opened himself up, ready to be torn apart by it. He felt a hot wash of tears in his eyes, but they didn't fall.

Rob's voice was intense, almost as desperate as Matty felt. "Do you see the North Star? Wherever you are, whenever you see that, you'll think of this. You'll think of me here with you, taking care of you, and you'll never forget. Do you understand?"

Matty stared at the star, his heart trip hammering, orgasm sounding like a train whistle in his ear, and he shook, shattered, and groaned, shooting hard, over and over. He twitched in Rob's arms as dots swirled in his vision, completely overcome.

When Rob moved his hand away from Matty's mouth and nose, Matty came again, a strange, dry orgasm, full of trembling and moaning as he gulped in air. The ecstasy of release filled him from head to foot, and Rob's strong arms held him tight.

"So, Blackbird, was it good?" Rob asked, wiping off Matty's dick with a handkerchief before tucking his cock away and zipping him back up.

Matty nearly burst into tears, but he held them back as he turned. He buried his face in Rob's jacket, wrapped his arms around Rob tightly, and found he was still shaking. He couldn't even say how much he'd needed that, and how much it had meant to trust Rob that way. How good it had been to let go.

Rob stroked Matty's hair. "I know, sweetheart. I know."

* * *

On the drive back to Whitefish, Matty watched the night flicker by outside his window. Rob was quiet, too, eventually putting the radio on a station that played classical music interspersed with a disc jockey who talked briefly about the pieces in a baritone whisper.

Eventually, Rob reached over to slide his hand over Matty's hair. "Doing okay?"

Matty sighed and nodded, taking Rob's hand in his and kissing the knuckles. "Yes. Just thinking."

"About?"

"Things. About what happened in the corn field. About sex with you. About us."

Rob pulled his hand back to change gears and then put it Matty's thigh, stroking lightly. "Okay. Are they thoughts I should know about?"

"I guess I was wondering how you knew I'd be into that. Into being kinky like that. It's like you've known from the beginning. Do I just scream kink monster, or did you know some other way?"

"I didn't know until we were in the middle of it, I guess."

"Have you ever done something like that before?"

"Yes."

"When?"

Rob rubbed Matty's thigh and seemed to be gathering his words. Finally, he said, "After my folks died, it was the first time I really felt free to explore who I was sexually. My dad wasn't thrilled that I was gay, but he didn't deny it either. My mom cried when I first came out to her. But in the end, the argument between us was over how I wasn't what they wanted me to be. In general. The fact that I was gay was only one aspect of how I disappointed them both."

"But you're amazing."

"They didn't think so."

"How could they not?"

"I can think of lots of reasons why they didn't. After they died, I was determined that I wasn't going to let them dictate my life anymore. I explored new ways of ranching, sold the land to the Pages, and experimented sexually with a group of people out of Missoula."

"Oh." For some reason this surprised Matty. He didn't imagine Rob as the kind of person who played with other people. Not in a sexual way. He was intense, and he was defiantly out of the closet for living in such a small town, but when it came to what they did together, it always seemed intensely personal, and always about just the two of them.

"The group I joined was into dominance and submission, and I tried out both sides of that. Submission was not my forte." He chuckled. "I enjoyed experimenting with domination, obviously, but it never felt entirely right with any of the guys I was with."

Matty felt an unexpected surge of jealousy. He didn't like the idea of Rob being with anyone else the way he was with him.

"But with you, it just came up from somewhere deep inside me, and it feels...really right. Seeing how you react, hearing the sounds you make, feeling how you respond to me, how you want me to take control—it's intoxicating."

Matty's skin grew warm, flushing his face, and his cock fattened up with a quick rush of blood. "Yeah?"

"Yeah. It's exciting in a way I've never felt before. When I'm with you, I know what to do, what you need. It's intense for me. The most intense thing I've experienced, honestly."

"Me too," Matty murmured. "I've never done any of this before, though. My last real boyfriend was more submissive than me."

Rob made a soft sound that could have been surprise or encouragement to continue, or possibly both.

Matty bit his lip and then whispered, like it was a terrible secret, "Cody was a bottom."

Rob was quiet for a moment. "I can see how that would be a deal breaker for you."

Matty laughed so hard he had to wave a hand in front of his face to catch a breath.

"What?" Rob asked, laughing, too, though he obviously didn't know why.

"It's just...it wasn't. I was in love with him and I was willing to work it out."

"Wow."

"It seems ridiculous now, doesn't it? But at the time, I was crazy about him."

"I admit I'm feeling a little jealous." Rob sounded surprised by this.

Matty flushed under the heat of how smug he felt about that. "You shouldn't. Obviously, we weren't meant to be. He dumped me for Vance Jones—another figure skater. He's a bit of a starfucker, I guess."

Rob chuckled. "His loss."

"Tell me about it. My ass is fine."

"So fine."

Matty grinned and caressed Rob's hand where it rested on his thigh. "I didn't really love topping. I mean, I was good at it, but it was exhausting trying to figure out what he wanted and how he liked it."

"You're more of a switch than me, then. I wasn't even good at being submissive. I was bored by it, and sometimes found it funny. Or maybe I just never really respected the tops I worked with. I'm not sure."

Matty smiled. "I think you just know your place—and it's not on your knees."

"Unless I want it to be."

"Touché."

Matty stroked Rob's knuckles, admiring the calluses. After a few moments of comfortable quiet, he said, "We never really talked about HIV status and sexually transmitted diseases. I know we're using condoms, but I think maybe we should discuss it."

"All right."

"Well, this will be fast. To sum up, I'm negative and don't have any diseases."

"Ditto."

"For what it's worth, it's been over twelve months since my last sexual encounter."

"Let's see, almost three months since hand jobs and blow jobs were exchanged. Over a year since I last fucked a guy. Another thing I learned from my ventures into the BDSM group in Missoula is that I'm picky."

"Selective," Matty corrected.

"Quality over quantity."

"So, when's the last time you were tested?"

"Three weeks before you arrived for some life insurance I took out. All negative."

Matty nodded. "Good. My mom will be pleased that we talked about this."

"You're going to tell your mom about this conversation?" Rob raised an eyebrow.

"Hell no."

"Oh, okay. Good."

Matty grinned and took Rob's hand, leaning his head back against the headrest. "I don't want to go back to Bill's Place for the drag show." He twined their fingers together. "I want to go back to your place."

"Tired?"

"Nope." He grinned again.

Rob's eyes gleamed, and he stepped on the gas.

CHAPTER ELEVEN

"How far is this place?"

"We're almost there, Dad."

It was Thanksgiving morning, and it turned out even rural Montana had holiday traffic. The drive from the airport seemed to be taking forever, and Matty's father shifted uncomfortably in the passenger seat. If his own back was hurting, then he knew his dad's leg had to be causing him a lot of pain. In an attempt to reduce the stress in the car, he told his family all about the house.

"The plaid couch makes me want to vomit," he said. "But the workout room is nice when it's too snowy to get into the gym."

"Who cares what the couch looks like?" Joey—or *Joseph* as he was calling himself now—asked.

Matty squeaked in outrage. "Do I even need to dignify that, *Joseph*?" He tried to accept the name change only because his brother had to accept so many things about Matty over the years. Which, in the scheme of things, were probably a lot more ridiculous than insisting on being called by his full given name.

The week before, Matty had gotten permission from Margaret to open the upstairs rooms for his family to use during one of her rare phone calls to check in. It seemed that traveling the world was very distracting, and Margaret trusted him so completely that she didn't feel the need to micromanage from their current location in South Korea, which Matty appreciated.

Matty had spent the better part of three evenings dusting, vacuuming, and scrubbing the bathrooms upstairs. There wasn't much he could do about the décor, though. It was going to be patchwork quilts and duck figurines no matter what, but he kind of thought his mom and dad might actually like it. It was more their style than his, that was for sure.

"I want to see the pond," Donna said. "The one where you've been teaching your neighbor's son. What's his name again?"

"Ben." A shot of adrenaline rushed through Matty. His mom was going to meet Rob and Ben. He hoped she thought they were as amazing as he did. He couldn't imagine that she wouldn't. Rob was smart, and kind, and funny. He was hard working, and warm. He was thoughtful. He was basically everything a mom could want for her son.

Matty cleared his throat. That was why he was so nervous. His mom would absolutely see that and she'd know what Matty no longer wanted to admit to himself— that there was no way this was going to work. At least at this point in his life. Maybe one day, if Rob could wait...oh God, when had he started to think like *that*?

"I bought all the stuff that we'll need for dinner, Mama." Matty glanced at her in the rearview mirror. "Rob's going to supply the turkey."

"From his ranch?" Donna asked.

"No, I think he bought this one." His cell phone was vibrating and he glanced down to see an incoming text.

Valentina's yours. Contract information to follow.

Matty dropped the phone, clutched his chest, and screamed. He danced in his seat, and started laughing like crazy.

"Watch it!" Joey yelled from the back seat.

Matty swerved back over the line to his side of the road, still jumping up and down, shaking the whole car. His foot was unsteady on the gas, making them lurch like the car was drunk.

"Oh my God, Mama! We got Valentina!"

Pandemonium broke out between Matty and his mother as his father took hold of the wheel.

"Son, I didn't come to Montana to die. I came for turkey."

They all laughed at that, and Matty finally got a hold of himself.

"He nearly killed us," Joey said to Rob almost an hour later on the Pages' front porch.

Matty's father greeted Rob with his usual gruff politeness. Rob took his hand and smiled in his sweet, wide-open way, and Matty's heart fluttered. Matty's dad patted Rob's arm.

"Nice to meet you, son. Now if you'll all excuse me, I need to get settled." He disappeared inside with Donna and Joey, who carried in their bags and waved off Rob's offer of help.

It had been brief, but Matty felt ridiculously pleased by the interaction between Rob and his dad. "Sorry if that seemed rude. 'Get settled' means he has to take pain meds and rest his leg."

"Not at all. I know they've had a long day of traveling. Don't you want to show them around the house?"

Matty shrugged. "They'll figure it out. Their bedrooms are the ones without the glittery make-up in the adjoining bathroom." He bounced on his toes, and was about to blurt out his news when Donna and Joey returned, ready for their ranch tour.

With grand gestures, Matty pointed out the barn where Maple Syrup and Daisy were eating hay, and the direction of the Pages' pond. His mother squinted into the setting sun, nodding and patting his arm.

"Calm down, honey. I know you're excited, but—"

Matty threw his arms wide and twirled in a circle. "But I can't

118

calm down, Mama! You're here!" Between the news about Valentina, and Rob meeting his family, he couldn't hold still.

Joey, now taller than Matty remembered, and already charmed by Rob given how uncharacteristically chatty he was being, repeated, "He nearly killed us. I mean, he almost ran head-on into a massive truck. I would have died before getting anywhere with Reese Connelly."

"Or anyone at all ever," Matty noted.

"Which only makes it worse," Joey replied, a little darkly.

Matty rolled his eyes and waved his hand, indicating that Joey was being a drama queen, which was rather hilarious.

Rob nodded and winked at Matty before asking Joey, "So, what was the excitement that led to this near-death experience?"

"He got Valentina." Joey pushed his fine dark hair behind his ears. He'd grown it out long enough to look like a scruffy '70s throwback. Matty wondered if he could convince his brother to go to the barber in town with him before he left. Did barbers even work the day after Thanksgiving?

Joey went on. "He finally landed the girl of his dreams." Joey wiped a fake tear from his cheek. "A Russian girl. That's my brother. So proud."

Rob's eyebrows lifted. "A Russian girl?"

"A coach. She'll kick him into shape, I bet. And he'll like it."

Matty sighed and walked up to the porch. "You're telling this all wrong, my little Joey-monster. This is how it goes: 'Once upon a time, Princess Matty was looking for the right person to mold him into something better than he could achieve on his own. Someone who could inspire him, whip him into submission—"

"I thought you weren't going to give me details about your sex life anymore," Joey said.

"Joey!" Donna scolded uselessly, but she was laughing too.

Matty smirked. "Touché, Joseph." He gave up on his story and turned to Rob. "Valentina Chapayeva is a Ukrainian coach. She's coached four Olympic gold medalists in her time, and now..." He paused for dramatic flair. "*Now* she's going to coach *me*!"

"It's a dream come true," Donna added. "Matty needs someone like her. His last coach had a hard time making him focus."

Rob grinned, and Matty's heart flipped from the cuteness. Rob put his arm around him and shook him a little. "That's fantastic!"

"It is! It means everything will change for me."

When Rob let go, Matty jumped up and down, spastic and unable to stop until Donna came over and grabbed him in a hug.

Rob chuckled. "I know you've talked about a new coach, but I guess I didn't understand how important this was to you."

"It's the only way to get medals. I can't do it on my own or with coaches that can't keep me in line." Matty cleared his throat. "I can be a little hard to control."

He couldn't help but look at Rob, as though pulled to acknowledge him and the fact that Rob knew what Matty was talking about in a very intimate way. The look that passed between them brought a rush of heat into his cheeks, and Joey made a strangled sound.

"I'm going inside," Joey said. "It's getting gross out here."

But Matty noticed that Joey stayed put.

Donna rolled her eyes and put her arm around Matty's waist, tipping her head to his shoulder. Matty pressed his head to hers, overcome by happiness that she was there, and that he had a future in skating still, and this was going to be a great Thanksgiving after all. He threw his arms around Donna again, and when he squealed with happiness, she did too.

"I've missed you, Mama," Matty murmured.

"Missed you too."

She kissed his ear, and then whispered, "He's very handsome."

"Isn't he?" Matty agreed, *sotto voce*, glancing over to where Rob was talking more with Joey about Matty's questionable driving skills, which was very annoying because Matty was a gifted driver. Okay, so he was terrible, but Joey needed to shut up about it. "I can't get enough of him."

Matty could feel Donna's evaluating gaze, but he kept his focus on Rob.

She let go of Matty. "Let's head inside and see what you've bought. God help you, we'd better not be eating lettuce for Thanksgiving."

* * *

"Like a canon shot, or something," Rob said. "After all that pushing and pushing and pushing, he just—boom—shot out all at once. It was amazing. Kind of shocking. Anja cried. I almost did. Partly because I was afraid she'd broken my hand after gripping it for ten hours."

Donna chuckled as she rolled the pie dough flat. "The miracle of birth. Although Matty didn't take long at all. Couldn't wait to get out in the world and start squawking."

"I'm going to stop you right there, Mother. No baby stories. Or kid stories. No stories of any kind." Matty cut pecans into tiny pieces for the

120

filling. "How many more?"

She glanced over. "That's enough. Start on the apples for the stuffing now. Cut up six of them."

"Are you sure I can't help?" Rob asked.

"You'll just get in the way. If you're sure you don't want to go watch football with Joey and Randy, just keep talking. I like to have something to listen to while I cook. I suppose a ranch doesn't just stop for a holiday. Did you have to put in some work this morning?"

"A little. I gave the men the day off. I fed the goats, horses, and working dogs, and spread hay for the cattle. Luckily there weren't any surprises today, and it all went smoothly. Day-to-day on a ranch, you never know just what you're going to get."

"Oh my God, knock on wood," Matty exclaimed, rapping his fist on a cabinet. "There will be no escaped cows on Thanksgiving! The tsarina has spoken, and so it shall be!"

Rob smiled. "Yes, ma'am."

Donna asked, "When's Ben getting here?"

Rob looked at his watch. "Not for a few hours. He's probably having a blast with his cousins and Anja's family."

"Not that we aren't happy for your company, and not to be nosy—"

"Uh-oh," Matty said. "She's about to be spectacularly nosy."

"Shh. I'm just wondering if you normally share Thanksgiving with Ben's mother's family? Has your invitation to eat with us interrupted your usual activities?"

"No, I'm always invited, but I never go. Something about sitting at a table with the man who's never apologized for calling me 'the faggot who ruined my daughter's life,' or for trying to convince Anja to have an abortion because 'it might turn out like *him*' has never really appealed to me. I generally try to avoid him."

"I can see why," Donna said. "That's terrible."

"In fact, I usually spend Thanksgiving with the Pages since my folks died. So this feels a lot like the same old, same old." He shot a look at Matty. "Don't tell George or Margaret I said this, but the company is better this year."

"Isn't he cute, Mama?"

"Yes, very cute. Now where did I put the condensed milk?"

Matty shoved it her way. "Donna, you would lose your butt if it wasn't attached."

"Now it's my turn to be nosy," Rob said. "What's with the Donna thing? Sometimes it's Donna, sometimes it's Mama. I always called my mother 'Mom' and was done with it."

Matty put his arm around his mother's shoulders. "I call her Donna when she's Donna, Mama when she's Mama, and Mother when I'm being a brat."

"And Mom when he's distracted," Donna said.

"So the thing about losing her butt...that wasn't being a brat?" Rob asked.

Matty snorted. "No. That's me being a stand-up comedian."

"There's a huge difference." Donna rolled her eyes.

"Keep your day job, sweetheart." Rob laughed.

Matty thrilled at the use of the endearment Rob used mainly in intimate moments, and he felt his mother go still underneath his arm. He moved away from her, and started chopping the celery for the stuffing.

"I intend to," Matty said. "In fact, practice has been going great. It's almost to the point that I can't go much further alone now. My stamina is back up, and my strength is good. I need a professional."

"That's what Valentina will do for you," his mother said, stirring the pecan pie filling in a big mixing bowl. "Luckily for us one of her skaters is retiring at the end of the season and she'll have an open slot."

"Oh my God, Anton should have retired forever ago. He's like, almost thirty."

"That old, huh?" Rob whistled. "Surprised he can still walk, let alone skate."

"Ha, ha. You know what I mean. Skating isn't like real life. Almost thirty is ancient in singles. He's only hanging on because Worlds is in his hometown this year. St. Petersburg. Such an amazing city." Matty swallowed down the petulant flare of resentment that he wouldn't be there.

"Do you know where you'll have to go to work with the new coach?" Rob asked.

Matty swallowed and glanced at Rob, who was watching him chop. "Her training center's in New York City." He looked down at the apples, unable to meet Rob's gaze. "Mama, rumor is Julien's even considering working with her."

"Julien Alban? You've always liked him. That'll be a good match for you on the ice. He's a real doll."

"Uh-huh." He forced himself to look at Rob, and Matty's heart dropped into his stomach.

Rob took a deep breath and stood up. "I think I'll go see what the score is."

Matty's gut tightened, and he bit his lip. This wasn't what he'd wanted. Not in a million years. The look of hurt in Rob's eyes made him feel sick, and he sat the knife down on the cutting block, pressing the back of his hand against his mouth.

"He took it pretty well, don't you think?"

"What?" Matty asked, softly.

"You leaving. He took it well."

"He's known that I'm leaving. He's always known." Matty's throat ached.

"Well, that's good. You're both on the same page."

Matty looked at her, and Donna's face softened. She pushed the bowl aside. "Oh, honey." She wrapped her arms around him. "You're in love with him."

Matty nodded against her shoulder, tears coming to his eyes. He snuffled a little against her neck before taking a long, cleansing breath. He pulled away and looked at the ceiling, batting away the tears so they wouldn't mess his make-up.

He could feel Donna's eyes on him, but he couldn't look at her now. He turned back to the chopping board and started in on the celery. "I knew better. It just happened. I guess I'll survive it somehow. I always do."

Donna sighed behind him, and he kept his eyes on the celery, obliterating it into tiny pieces. Much smaller than necessary, but he didn't care. It made him feel better.

* * *

Ben showed up right after the longest dinner of Matty's life. At least Donna and Joey had kept up a constant patter of conversation, and Rob, Randy, and Matty had only had to nod and murmur. Matty needed to get Rob alone to talk, but right now he was glad for the distraction of Ben, who threw his arms around his dad, and then hugged Matty too.

"I brought my skates. If you have time tomorrow."

Matty grinned. "How about tonight?"

"An impromptu ice show?" Donna asked. "For us?"

"Why not?" Though he felt so full from eating his feelings at dinner that he wasn't sure he could lift himself off the ice for even the easiest jump. He hadn't eaten so much in months. Regardless, he wanted to show Ben off, and let Donna see what a special kid he was, and how he was doing under Matty's tutelage.

The night was clear, and everyone, including Randy, bundled up to come out and watch. Matty whispered to Ben as they walked, using his arms to demonstrate. "Do you think you can do it like that?" Matty asked.

"Sure," Ben said, grabbing Matty's arm and holding on tight with a grin on his face. "I can totally do that."

The pond had a dusting of snow on it and Joey was helpful in his own way. He threw himself on the ice, pretending to be a human snowplow as he used his body, arms, and legs to push off the snow.

"I told you that he didn't need a third glass of wine," Matty said as they all laughed.

The pond was jittery and rough, but Ben grinned from ear to ear as he threw himself into it with his usual fire. Matty positioned himself on the other side of the pond and counted off a beat. On four they began to move, both of them doing small modified jumps in the little routine Matty was working out for Ben.

Claps and whoops filled the frosty air, and then Matty left the ice to Ben. His face aching from smiling so hard, he watched the boy land two double toe loops in a row. Matty clapped as Ben pumped the air with his fist.

"Yeah!" Ben yelled. It echoed in the night air, bouncing off the hills.

"Yuliya Yasneyeva will be sorry she missed that!" Matty called.

Ben cracked up, which made him fall on his Lutz. He sprawled there on the ice, laughing. "You are such a freak! I love you!"

Matty skated out and pulled him up to hug him. Whispering in Ben's ear, Matty suggested they try a death spiral with Ben as the girl. They both cracked up when they failed miserably, and Ben fell on his head.

"Good thing George isn't here, or he'd be warning you not to sue, Rob!" Matty laughed.

Rob smiled genuinely. "Good thing."

Ben was tough and he was up again immediately, racing around the pond, zooming at Matty and swerving at the last minute in game of ice skating chicken. Matty chased him a bit, picking up some speed for a spin. The world blurred and whirled, and when he pulled out of it, he saw Ben skating around him in the opposite direction.

He felt like the cog of a gear, the center that pulled this together. Ben, his family, Rob, Montana, New York City, Valentina, skating, the Olympics, the world—he just didn't know how to make it all keep moving without his career aspirations gumming up the works.

Ben skated alone while Matty stood on the side of the pond and issued commands in Russian. Matty nodded when he landed a jump well, and his chest swelled with joy and pride when a glance toward his mother proved she was impressed and excited by Ben's performance too. Matty grinned. That was his kid out there, and he adored him.

After the audience patted them both on the back, Matty stood in front of Rob, smiling up at him. "Do you think Yuliya Yasneyeva's done a good job with him?"

Rob's mouth was set in a strange, sad line, and Matty's heart fluttered down from the heights to which it had risen. Rob visibly shook himself, and pulled Matty into a hug.

"Thanks for taking the time with him. You're amazing."

"He's pretty amazing too."

"Yeah, he is."

"You're not so bad yourself."

Smiling, Rob brushed their noses together, and Matty felt the lingering tension between them lift.

* * *

Later, Ben fell asleep on the bear rug in front of the fire listening to Matty and Donna talk about the time they'd spent in Russia together for various competitions. Joey and Randy had gone to bed earlier, citing exhaustion, which Matty believed when it came to his dad. But he suspected Joey felt a little sick after drinking another half a bottle of wine. He'd need to check on him later.

On the couch, Matty listened to his mom talk with Rob beside him as he watched Ben sleep on the rug. He looked so small there, his face relaxed and innocent. Matty was really going to miss him. Who'd have thought he'd ever get so attached to a kid? Not to mention the kid's dad.

"You look sad," Donna said.

Matty shook himself out of his reverie and lied, "Oh, just thinking about quads and the likelihood that I'll ever consistently land them."

Donna looked unconvinced but she left it, and turned her attention to talking Rob into allowing Ben to stay the night. "We'll send him over tomorrow after breakfast. Don't disturb him. Growing kids need a lot of sleep."

"Funny, she didn't take that line when she was waking me up at three in the morning to get to the rink on time when I was only a little older than him."

"You would have killed me if I hadn't." Donna ruffled Matty's hair.

Matty followed Rob out to the front porch after Rob said goodbye to Donna. Matty pulled on a coat, but he was still cold. He rubbed his hands over his arms. "Thanks for coming over tonight. I wanted my family to meet you, and they all think you're great. I can tell."

Rob drew Matty into his warm arms and held on tightly, his face in Matty's hair, unsteady breath against his scalp. Matty pulled back. "What's wrong?"

Rob shook his head. "I love your family. They're all great. I love *you* with your family."

"And...?"

Rob sighed. "It's going to be hard to let you go, that's all."

Matty's stomach twisted. "Yeah. It's going to be hard to go."

"No it won't. You'll be back where you want to be. Where you belong. You'll skate and you'll win, and you'll remember this time with a fondness, maybe. That's all I expect."

"Well, that's shitty." Matty punched Rob's arm kind of hard. "Don't you know that I've fallen in love with you?"

Rob stared down at him, his arms tightening to prevent Matty from succeeding in his half-hearted struggle to get away. "I love you too. It doesn't change things."

Matty couldn't breathe. He'd avoided this conversation for so long that he didn't know how to hold back his emotions now that Rob was just *having it.* He rubbed his face against Rob's coat, wiping away the surprise tears.

"You'll go train with this Valentina and you'll win. And I'll always love you. But we'll move on. That's how it works. That's the way things go. I'm a grown-up, Matty. Don't think I ever had any illusions about how this ends."

Matty grabbed Rob's coat and clung tightly, his face buried against Rob's chest. He stood there for a long time, warm in Rob's arms in the cold November night.

* * *

At the airport Sunday morning, after the hustle and bustle of getting his father checked in and assisted, and Joey being freakishly affectionate in his goodbye, Matty clung to his mother. "I'm not gonna let you go home."

"I've got to work, Matty. I haven't won the Power Ball yet."

"I want to be your Power Ball. I want to make it so you won't have to work anymore."

"I'm the parent here, Matty. It's my responsibility to take care of you, not the other way around."

Matty nodded, and thought about the lost money from the shows and competitions he'd missed. No matter what she said, the money was important. He had a responsibility to them and Joey, and he wasn't going to let them down. He'd do his best to make all the years they gave up worth it. Reluctantly, Matty released her.

She brushed his hair out of his eyes. "I love Rob. We all do. And Ben is terrific." She studied Matty's face. "If he's the one, honey, it will work out. Believe me."

Matty swallowed hard and put on his best smile for her. "I love you."

"I love you too." Donna grabbed her carry-on bag and set off toward the security check, looking back a few times and waving. Matty waited until she was taking off her shoes and putting them in a bin.

He only cried for ten minutes on the way back, and he wasn't sure what the tears were about—his family leaving for home, or Rob and their lack of future. He thought it was more the latter, but he couldn't think about it anymore. Thinking about it made him start to shake.

That night on Rob's bed, swaddled tightly in the blankets again with his arms trapped against his chest, Matty's knees were by his ears and his ass was spread open by Rob's big hands. He jerked as Rob's tongue flicked his asshole and pushed against Rob's shoulder with one foot, shoving away from how good it was.

Rob grabbed Matty's hips and pulled him back to the center of the bed. Matty's head bumped over the mattress limply, and his breath came in a mix of whimpers and small cries as Rob pushed his legs up again and went back to his ass. Matty had lost track of time and his sanity. It seemed like it had gone on for hours, but he didn't know anymore. It was so good—so overwhelming that it could have been days for all he knew.

He hadn't been rimmed too often in the past, and most of the time it'd been done tentatively. But this was strong, fast, and hard, and he went higher and higher, landing only when he managed to get a foot onto Rob's shoulder and push him away. It was too good, so fucking good, that he wanted to crawl out of his own skin before he just *couldn't* take it anymore.

When Rob gave him a break, Matty panted, his eyes fluttering as he tried to get his bearings. He blinked at the ceiling, the little plaster spatter-stars making swirling patterns, and then, oh, oh *God*, Rob was back, biting small, maddening nips to the skin around Matty's anus, his finger slipping teasingly over it, making Matty arch and beg.

It was so much more intense when he couldn't move like this, when he couldn't help but give in to Rob's mouth and hands. Matty's thighs shook and he clenched his fists against his chest, wishing the sheets weren't wrapped so tightly he couldn't reach his own nipples. But he didn't have room to think about it, not when Rob's tongue was pressing into him, his teeth were scraping against him, and Matty was so hard it hurt. His tender cock rubbed against the soft blanket holding him securely.

Rob lifted up, met Matty's eyes and then chills rushed through Matty, prickling at his skin as his ass stretched to accommodate Rob's cock. "God, God, oh...fuck, yeah. I...please..." Matty whispered in a ragged staccato rhythm as Rob pushed and held. Matty's ass opened and tensed, pulling Rob in slowly—too slowly. Matty begged. "Just fuck me."

Rob rubbed his hands along Matty's legs and kissed his feet, holding Matty's gaze but not saying anything. Controlled, so in control, and Matty's face twisted up. He felt his body go slack, and then like that, just like *that* Rob was in. So fucking *in*, and hard, and Matty wanted to grab his own cock. But he was trapped at Rob's mercy, and he closed his eyes, cursing under his breath and aching for Rob to move. So close to begging for it again, and then—

Fuck.

The noise Matty made was loud, and it was long, and he couldn't stop it from coming out of his mouth. The way Rob was fucking him— so fast, hard, and without any breaks, just strong, continuous motion that rocked him back and forth, his cock jerking with every thrust—was so fucking amazing, so intense and crazy, that he couldn't keep quiet if he tried.

Matty's teeth banged against each other, and he clenched his jaw. Sweat prickled on his forehead, and a combination of lube and sweat ran down his ass crack, so each of Rob's thrusts resounded with a wet smack. It was dirty and hot, and somehow fucking sweet because Rob was so *present*, showing how important this was with his body, with the care he took to make it good, and the way he was giving Matty everything he had now.

Just like in the corn maze, he had to give up and take it. He had to *feel* things, real things and not just sex things, as Rob plowed him. His emotions were wild when he was vulnerable like this, and he was shocked by the harsh flow of them, more intense than the fuck. Some were absolutely terrifying to him. His heart clenched with sorrow, and he rode through the stomach-dropping sensation of fear. His chest ached as Matty grappled to hold on to the last vestiges of the deepest emotions he always tried to hide.

Then it broke, and he was aching, bursting, coming apart at the seams. Rob's gentle touch on his cheek wiped a tear away, and Matty moved his face to kiss Rob's palm, whimpers and half-sobs all he could get out.

"Let it all go. That's good."

Matty closed his eyes again, and he was so close, so fucking close.

He needed a hand on his cock, because he had to come. His body and heart couldn't take much more without release. Rob seemed to understand, and he pulled out of Matty's ass, leaving Matty groaning. Then he shoved back in, hard, and jerked Matty's cock.

Matty thought he levitated, and the bed had given way beneath him because he was gone, gone, gone—coming so hard he couldn't see. He was nothing but a ball of jerking pleasure, and then he slammed down again into his still-convulsing body. He was freaked out because he was crying, fucking *crying*, and that was too weird, and Rob hadn't come yet.

Rob rocked into him quickly, kissing Matty's mouth, whispering things that Matty couldn't process. Then Rob's body stiffened and his cock throbbed in Matty's ass. Rob muffled his cry against the wad of blankets wrapped over Matty's chest.

Matty wanted to wipe off his face, but his hands were trapped by the blankets and Rob's weight. He was still shaking, and he could even feel his feet trembling. He was completely tapped of all emotion and strength, like he'd just landed fifty quads in a row and he had absolutely nothing left to give.

Rob pulled out of him, unswaddled the blankets, and turned away to pull his condom off. Matty wiped his hot hands over his face and shivered. Rob pulled Matty close, and tucked his head under his chin. Listening to Rob's heartbeat, his mind was like a snowy television screen until he fell asleep.

* * *

"Oh fuck!" He sat bolt upright. "I forgot the horses. I have to go."

Rob pulled him down again. "Shh. It's the middle of the night. I took care of them while you were taking your folks to the airport."

Matty sank down into the warmth and kissed Rob's neck. He whispered, "How are you so amazing?"

"I'm not. You kind of make me want to be, though."

"Oh my God, I think that might be one of the sweetest things anyone's ever said to me, even if it is complete and utter bullshit."

"I'm not bullshitting you, but you already know that."

Matty knew it all too well, and it scared the crap out of him. Where on Earth was he going to ever find *this* again? Someone who made him feel this way—accepted, loved, appreciated, admired—and could also fuck him blind, and knew just what to do to blow his defenses up completely like carefully laid mines along his boundaries.

He still felt shaken by the sex they'd had earlier, like Rob had reached inside and rearranged his soul. It wasn't anything he'd ever experienced before, and it felt so precious. He didn't know what to say, or what to do. Fuck, he couldn't even tell Elliot about this because Elliot would never understand. Or if he did, he'd pity him, and this was too sacred for that. How could Matty explain anyway? It was all too personal and intimate to break it into words.

Rob wrapped his arm around Matty, holding him close, and whispered, "Did it scare you away?"

Matty turned his face into the curve of Rob's neck, kissing softly. "It scared me, but I'm still here."

"Good. Because I'm not ready for you to go yet."

Matty swallowed hard, crawled on top of Rob, and held on tight. He was suddenly acutely aware that he wasn't sure either of them would ever be ready for that. Yet what choice did he have? Skating was his life, and so many people depended on him. It wasn't just about what he wanted. He wasn't sure it ever had been.

CHAPTER TWELVE

"Come on, Matty. It's a small thing, yeah, but it will get your name out there again. You are your brand."

Matty gripped Rob's cordless phone. "Joanna, please, I'm the one who told you that. Don't start spouting it back at me now just to get your way. How did you even get this number?"

"What kind of agent would I be if I couldn't? Listen, you're going to do it. You're great with kids, and you're a good teacher. It's on your calendar, and you're *going* to do it."

"Fine, but I really don't see how teaching a children's seminar in Missoula is 'getting my name back out there.' Get me on Oprah, woman. What do you think I'm paying you for?"

"Matty, to get interviews you have to have something to say. They've already heard about your injury. What they need is a comeback story, so we'll hit them when you've actually, you know, come back. In the meantime you can create the material for a heartwarming story of how you mentored youth in the sticks."

Matty was sitting on Rob's back porch next to the wood-burning outdoor fireplace, throwing a stick for Lila. Up in the pastures, he could see the outlines of Dino and Terry on horseback, and two of the work dogs moving in and out of the herd.

"Fine. Later." He hung up on Joanna before she could say something else to annoy him, because he was in *that* kind of mood. He was trying to spare her. Or that's what he told himself.

Rob was in the house making hot chocolate for himself, and a cup of hot water with six drops of bitters for Matty. "It's like Christmas in a cup, I'm telling you," Matty had said earlier. "It will warm you up inside and take all the Grinch away!"

Rob had laughed. "Then why are you such a bitch lately?"

Matty deflected. "You try landing a triple Axel in combination with a triple toe—not just once, but consistently, because your life completely depends on it."

"I'm a very observant boyfriend and I haven't noticed the tell-tale red dot on your head from the hit-man's laser."

Matty had just stared at him then, the word *boyfriend* thrown into the space between them without any warning or reaction from Rob. He'd been thinking of Rob as his boyfriend for a while now. What else would he call the guy who had confessed his love to him, and bossed him around in the near-nightly Naked Olympics held in Rob's bed?

But he'd been very careful to never say it. People thought he had no filter, but he did. The most important things, the things that scared him, were kept incredibly close. The fact that Rob was his boyfriend was apparently one of those things, even if it was extremely obvious.

So obvious that Rob hadn't even seemed to think Matty's stunned reaction was due to the term, but instead to his making fun of Matty's life-or-death feelings about triple Axel combinations.

Rob had chuckled. "Come on, sweetheart, assassins aren't hanging out at the rink, okay? It's not so dire as all that."

"It's dire," Matty had said, and vacated to the porch, demanding his hot water be delivered to him there.

Instead he'd been handed the phone, and now was roped into a small-time seminar with some pre-teen kids at a rink in Missoula. It wasn't that he wouldn't enjoy it, because he would, but he was starting to feel washed up.

God, if only he had the money *now*. He could be training with a serious coach instead of trying to convince himself that the drills he was doing were moving him toward his full potential. He knew he was too big of a baby to push himself all the way. Every day he walked away from the rink thinking that if he had proper motivation he could have done more.

Then there was Rob, and how fucking in love with him Matty had fallen. It was killing him to feel this way. It was like an endless bipolar mess, swinging between ecstasy and misery and back again in seconds. The idea of leaving Rob behind made him feel like he was in physical pain, and he was angry about it. Fuck Rob for making him feel this way. Fuck him for bringing wood and getting all of this started.

Fuck him for plowing the drive, and for having a son that skates, and for being amazing in bed, and for making Matty come like that's all his body was built to do. Fuck him, fuck him, *fuck him*.

The back door opened, and Rob handed him the hot mug. Matty cradled it close, smelling the steam and hating everything.

"Everything okay?" Rob asked.

Matty didn't answer, distracted by his churning stomach and the taste of bile in his mouth.

"Who was that on the phone?" Rob sounded concerned.

"Joanna. My agent." His sigh was epic, and he felt a furious weight pressing down on his shoulders. "Everything's fine."

Rob didn't say anything for several minutes, and Matty was grateful. If he had, Matty wasn't sure that Rob would like whatever was said in return.

Rob finally sighed too. "I'm going inside."

Matty nodded, his eyes on the horizon, and his hair whipping in the cold wind. "Yeah. Do that."

Just before he shut the door, Rob said, "It's okay that you're anxious to go now that you've lined up your new coach. You don't have to pretend you're not."

Matty's lip curled into a snarl, and his hands tightened on the mug. He turned around just as the door closed completely.

That was the problem, wasn't it? He wanted to go, but he wanted to stay, and he couldn't have it both ways. He threw the mug on the concrete patio, a mixture of satisfaction and annoyance flooding him when it broke into five chunky pieces. He stared at the mess a few moments, and then knelt down and carefully cleaned it up, knocking Lila away as she tried to lap up the spilled water.

He only cut himself once.

* * *

Rob's attention to his finger was sweet. Medicine, Band-Aid, kisses, and now Matty was on the bed, face down in a pillow, being fucked so hard he was grunting, sweating, and breaking out into chills with each stroke. It was better than the hysterics he'd been so close to earlier. Easier to let himself go in bed—and less humiliating.

Rob seemed to be working out something too. His grip was rough, and he kept pulling Matty back into place, slapping his ass hard and making him yelp. It was hot, but it wasn't Rob's usual behavior. While he was always commanding, he was also emotionally focused. Now he felt absent, that he was fucking to fuck, not fucking to communicate something deeper than that.

If it hadn't been Rob he was in bed with, Matty might have been scared. As it was, he just felt like he probably deserved it.

Rob grabbed a handful of Matty's hair and held his head down against the pillow, and then jerked his head back up again. "Ready for more?"

"Yeah. Always," Matty said, hoping he sounded casual and brave, and not needy and broken.

"Don't bullshit me." Rob tugged on his hair again.

Matty whimpered and closed his eyes. "Okay," he said. "I'm sorry."

"Don't bullshit me ever, but definitely not in bed." Rob smacked his ass so hard Matty clamped down on Rob's cock and simultaneously scrambled at the bed to get away.

Rob rubbed the place he'd smacked, soothing the pain, and Matty relaxed enough to pull off Rob's cock and roll onto his back, tears smarting in his eyes.

"That fucking hurt."

"You've got a safeword. Use it."

Matty covered his face with his hands. His ass was twitching, and he wanted to get back on his hands and knees, but he wasn't sure if he could take whatever it was Rob was offering. His clothes were on the chair across the room. He could get dressed and go home.

"Are you ready for more?" Rob asked again.

"No," Matty said, the word breaking a little.

"That's better. That's at least fucking honest, which is more than you've been with me all day."

Matty stared at Rob's flushed face, his green eyes hurt and angry at the same time. He started to say something but Rob just shook his head, and Matty closed his mouth.

"You talk a lot, but lately you're not telling me everything, and it's got to come out."

Matty cleared his throat. "Can you please just fuck me?"

Anger cracked Rob's expression, and Matty felt strangely like laughing when Rob flipped him onto his stomach and pushed his legs apart. He thrust into him hard, fast, and deep. Matty arched his back, pushing his ass up. Rob grabbed a handful of his hair and shoved his face in the pillow again, fucking him with rapid, strong thrusts until Matty was kicking and digging his fingers into the sheets.

Rob pulled Matty up to his knees, released his head enough for Matty to catch a breath, and then pulled his cock out of Matty's ass. Matty keened, pushing back for it, begging with his body, and Rob shoved his shoulders down, shoving his face back to the mattress. Matty could feel his ass clenching on air, and he whispered, "Please."

At the same moment, Rob pushed his dick all the way in with one long, smooth stroke, and then all the way out again. Matty frantically reached back, trying to grab hold of Rob, but Rob caught his hands and forced them down, holding Matty still as he pushed his cock in and out again.

"Rob, please, for fuck's sake—"

Rob punched his cock in again, and pulled it free. Matty fought Rob's grip on his wrists, trying to get loose so he could change his position, or stop, or go faster—just *anything* that meant Rob's cock stayed in his ass for longer than three second intervals.

But Rob took his time, holding Matty in place and jamming his cock in fast and pulling it out slow, or thrusting in slow and jerking it out fast. Matty felt like he was going nuts, twisting and bucking, trying to get free, but Rob was heavy and strong, and he was clearly determined to make Matty lose it.

He was going to. Matty was going to lose his fucking mind.

After screaming and biting the pillow, Matty got his hand free and threw an elbow at Rob. Rob caught it and brought it back to the mattress, holding him in place and fucking him hard for several long, almost perfect strokes. Then he was out again.

"Fuck me, you bastard." Matty's throat was raw, and his heart pounded with rage and lust. Rob pushed Matty's hands harder into the mattress, and used his other leg to hold Matty down as he rubbed his cock along Matty's ass crack and didn't push in at all. Matty squirmed and fought, struggling to get more. Fuck Rob. Fuck him for teasing him, and for making him want to cry.

"Goddammit," Matty yelled. "I hate you. I fucking hate you."

Rob pressed into him slowly, and Matty stopped fighting. His heart ached as he whispered, "I hate you. I hate you. I hate you," over and over as Rob finally, *finally* started fucking him with long strokes.

Rob released his hands, and held him tight now, whispering in his ear, "There. That wasn't so hard. There you go. There, sweetheart."

Matty rocked his hips in time with Rob's thrusts, and rubbed his face in the pillow, his chest tight with sobs he couldn't release. He didn't know when his chant changed from "I hate you" to "I love you," but it was all the same, and Rob knew that.

Rob knew exactly what he needed, and Matty wanted to hate him for it. But somehow it got twisted into this—into love, and sex, and being fucked while he begged and sometimes cried. It was fucked up, and it scared the shit out of him to think about leaving it behind.

He barely recognized his own voice. "I'm scared of losing." He meant so much more than competitions.

Moving together now, they reached for the edge, crying out softly as they tumbled over. Afterward, Rob pressed tender kisses to Matty's flushed skin, like he was made of the most precious stuff in the world. It all left Matty feeling like he'd been taken apart and put back together again. He almost wanted to ask if the seams were visible. Would anyone else know?

Could they take one look at him and see he'd been remade?

CHAPTER THIRTEEN

"And Elliot is going to be in New York City, and I swore I'd *never* miss a New Year's Eve in New York," Matty whined, stretched out across Rob on the sofa.

Rob held the agricultural journal he was reading a bit higher, trying to see it over Matty's body. "I'm devastated on your behalf."

Matty narrowed his eyes. "I thought you liked my family."

"I do. I'm sorry they can't come for Christmas. I was ridiculing your vow to always be in New York for New Year's Eve."

"You're heartless."

"Uh-huh." Rob flipped a page and yawned widely.

The day before Rob had helped Terry, Dino, and Bing wrangle some cattle that had trampled a fence and gotten into the woods near the national park. It'd been exhausting since three of the cows had decided they were not going to budge from the apparently delicious patch of dry, brown winter grass they'd discovered under a tree. To make it worse, once they'd driven the adventurers back onto Rob's land, a bunch of snow had dumped on them as they'd mended the fence.

Rob had dawdled over breakfast, and was lazing around with Matty. He'd mentioned something about getting caught up on the books, but he hadn't moved from the sofa yet, and it was verging on nine o'clock. Matty shifted on Rob's body and made himself more comfortable.

"I'm trying to read about the possible advantages of adding a milk goat operation to the ranch, sweetheart. You're kind of in my way."

"The advantages of a milk goat operation. Did I truly just hear those words?"

"Goat milk soap is all Bing talks about."

"I feel like I'm in some kind of insane alternate universe where if I look out the window I'll find Amish buggies. I will, won't I?"

"If you're lucky. Otherwise it means you're stuck in Montana getting fucked by some crazy sadist rancher."

"God, that sounds like a really bad sex book you'd pick up to read on an airplane." Matty scooted a bit on Rob's body, making him grunt. Matty spread out his hands to demonstrate the title of the book, knocking the journal away. "*'Big Sky of Desire'* by M. O. Lester. The story of young, lithe figure skater, Bobby Barker, trapped for the winter in a small Montana town and robbed of his innocence by the lecherous attentions of his sadistic neighbor, Mark Beauty. Tied down against his will and struck with leather horse whips, Bobby realizes his own inner strength and love for rough sex—"

"I have leather horse whips, actually," Rob said.

"You do?" Matty sat up, nearly smacking his forehead against Rob's chin.

"Of course. Have you seen my ranch?"

"Oh my God, go get them!"

Rob laughed, pushed Matty off, and stood up slowly, stretching. "Actually, I was thinking we should head into Missoula to do some shopping. Most of the shops stay open late this time of year. I have some things I need to get for Ben. Last I checked, you need to pick up a few things for your folks."

Matty blinked. "You're passing up *whips* for *shopping*?"

"You're bitching about *shopping*?" Rob countered.

"I feel so torn!" Matty pulled at his hair. "Oh my God. You suck."

"Go on, take care of the horses and get ready. I'll pick you up in an hour."

"Two. I have to look my best if we're going into the city. Someone might actually *see* me in the city."

"People see you here."

"Yeah, but they don't even look twice now. My fashion goes to waste. It's like I've become boring to them or something."

Rob kissed him and rubbed his thumb over Matty's lower lip. "Never. Impossible. And I'll pick you up in one hour."

"If I say yes, can I have whips later?" Matty asked a little breathlessly.

Rob frowned. "I'll think about it. I don't like the idea of marking your skin."

"Don't turn into a prude on me now," Matty whined.

Rob kissed him again. "Don't push me. Or you might find there's a price."

Matty clasped his hands together over his heart and called out as Rob left the room, "Would that price be leather horse whips?"

"Go home!" Rob yelled back.

Matty flopped on Rob's sofa and stared up at the ceiling. "Oh my God, *horse whips*," he whispered to himself, trying to figure out how he was going to lose his erection.

* * *

Downtown Missoula wasn't New York City, but Matty was able to find a few items for his mother, Elliot, and Joey. His father was impossible to shop for, but he'd find something or die trying. He said that every year and still lived, so the declaration had worked so far.

Rob bought Ben's gifts, and then took Matty into a place called Butterfly Herbs. The store was annoyingly beautiful on the outside, and the inside was no better. Stocked with delicious-smelling teas, bulk herbs and spices, and featuring a lunch counter and a few booths at which people were eating amazing-looking sandwiches and drinking decadent smelling coffee, the store was a nightmare to Matty.

His stomach rumbled. He felt a little faint with hunger and an irrational irritation that Rob brought him to a place where everything smelled so good and there was nothing he dared to eat.

But Rob headed toward the knickknacks and handmade jewelry. Matty had to admit that much of it was beautiful and there were a few pieces he lingered over, thinking they'd look amazing on him, but there was certainly nothing in the store for his father.

Rob lifted up a beautiful necklace and handed it to the salesperson.

"For Anja," he said to Matty.

Oh, yes, Anja. The mother of Rob's kid. Whom Matty had yet to meet. He knew Anja was aware of his presence in Rob's life because Ben had mentioned a few times that Rob and Anja sometimes talked about Matty. While Matty wasn't quite above pumping a twelve-year-old for information, he hadn't stooped to it *yet*. Still, he wondered quite often what Rob said to Anja about him, and what her opinion was of the situation. Rob was still with him, so Matty supposed he shouldn't worry. Yet he did.

What if the reason he hadn't met her was because she disapproved? Or what if Rob told her things, like concerns he had, but he didn't share them with Matty? And did it ever occur to Rob that maybe Matty *should* meet Anja? After all, Matty was coaching their kid, kind of, and usually the parents wanted to meet the coach, right? Or did Anja trust Rob's opinion so completely?

What about the fact that she was Rob's best friend? If Elliot was anywhere remotely near Montana, like even in Kansas, for example, Matty would have found a way to introduce him to Rob. For one thing, he'd like to gloat about the incredibly hot rancher he was getting down and dirty with, but for another, Elliot was like his family and he'd want them to know each other.

"Does she like that sort of thing?" Matty asked as the clerk wrapped the necklace in tissue paper.

"No, I'm buying it because I think she'll hate it." Rob took the bag from the shopkeeper's hand and thanked him.

"Oh," Matty replied. It was only a little snooty, but he couldn't keep his nose from going up in the air. It wasn't even that he didn't like the necklace, because he did, but now that he'd thought about it, the whole Anja thing was pissing him off.

They stepped out onto the street. The holiday decorations were so cool and laid-back that Matty wanted to grab a giant glitter pen and bitterly deface the entire downtown to add some over-the-top drama and glitz.

"What's up?" Rob asked.

"Nothing. I'm just thinking about the seminar I have to do next week. It's a lot of kids."

"You love kids."

"When they're smart and funny, sure, but when they're bratty, coughing, snot-nosed germ-factories, I don't really love them so much."

Rob pressed his lips together and seemed to be fighting a laugh. "If this is a bratty attempt to get me to use those whips—"

"I don't think I'm in the mood anymore anyway," Matty said. "I just want to go home. This city has exactly zero decent stores. It's sucked the spirit of Shopmas right out of me."

Rob stopped walking. "Out with it. This has nothing to do with any of that, and you can tell me now, or you can tell me later, but don't choose later, because I'm not in the mood for that tonight."

Matty swallowed. He didn't like being cornered and part of him wanted to fly into an attack of his own, because he could. He also knew it would leave a metaphorical mess of entrails all over the street if he went that route. But the weight of knowing that in a matter of months he'd be gone, and this tryst, or whatever it was, would be over pressed on him. He didn't want to waste the time left.

"Okay. It just occurred to me that I've never met Anja and I started to wonder why."

After several long beats, Rob said, "And you thought that bitching about the seminar, the town, and declaring yourself sexually unavailable for the evening would get that question answered for you?"

"Listen, if you're going to be a bitch, then I'll be a bitch too. I promise there will be blood in the streets." Matty crossed his arms over his chest, glaring.

"Jesus, you know if you just talked to me, we could maybe get somewhere that didn't include this kind of bullshit." Rob sighed, but when he spoke again, his voice was serious and even. "Listen—I haven't introduced you to Anja because I know you're leaving. I'm already too invested in this thing, and I figured keeping that little bit of separation, keeping you from having complete access to my family and my life might make it not hurt so damn much when you go. Is that fair?

Am I allowed that?"

Matty felt like the biggest cunt in the universe and he didn't know what to say. He forgot sometimes that Rob was going to hurt too. Matty was so often caught up in his own pain that he just let that slip, needing Rob to be the solid one. The touchstone.

"As it turns out," Rob went on, not waiting for Matty to reply, "I was going to invite you to Christmas with me and Ben. Obviously Anja will be there, and I thought it would be a nice time for you two to meet."

"But what about keeping me separate?"

"It was a stupid idea. You're in. Pretending that you aren't won't make it less true. Besides, she wants to meet you. And Yuliya Yasneyeva, apparently. I keep hearing about that."

"I'm a bitch." Matty dropped his hands to his side, wanting to move in for a hug, but wondering if that would be selfish.

"Yeah, well, it's cute. Sometimes. Not now. But sometimes." Rob smiled and pulled him in. He wrapped his arms around Matty and squeezed.

"Have I earned a whipping?" Matty whispered, half teasing and half serious.

Rob laughed. "No. You haven't. And don't try for one either because it will just piss me off at this point."

Matty considered pushing it, but his stomach twisted when he thought of Rob angry with him. "Any good places for espresso around here?"

"We just left the best place, but let's get a real meal. I know you're not a fan, but you're getting so thin I'm starting to see your bones."

"Perfect," Matty said, falling into step beside Rob. "I'm close, then. A pound and a half and I'll be home free!"

"Or too fucking skinny."

"You'll still want me, though," Matty said, quite sure of it.

"Food, now. You'll eat some too. Looking at it and smelling it will not suffice."

Matty put his arm around him. "Yes, well, if that's my punishment..."

Rob rolled his eyes. "Yes, whatever. That's your punishment. Jesus, sometimes I'm sure that a shit-load of counseling is in your future."

"Or you could just keep fucking me sane."

"Is that what you think I'm doing? I thought I was making love to you."

"That's some kinky love you've got. Not that I'm complaining."

Matty had felt a physical jolt at Rob's words, but he kept walking, kept talking, and yet didn't say anything at all. Rob had told him he loved him, and it had meant the world at the time, but hearing him describe what they did together as more than kinky sex made Matty want to take off running.

It wasn't like Matty didn't *know*. It wasn't like he hadn't *felt* it. But hearing it said out loud, like it was just any old thing that someone said, like it was a given, made his heart thump, and his ears rush with the beat of his blood. It was a relief. It was terrifying. It was everything.

And now he had to go eat actual food. He just might throw up.

CHAPTER FOURTEEN

It was a few days later that Matty and Rob returned to Missoula for Ben's show. Matty had to admit the hotel room was nice. Not as high class as some he'd stayed in, but quality all the same. The window looked out on a snowy Missoula street twinkling with Christmas lights.

Rob was quiet, and Matty filled in the space with stories about his old coach, Denise, and a trip to South Korea. When Rob remained distant and distracted, Matty even talked about the fiasco of the Olympics, which usually made him nauseous to even think about, but he was searching for a way into Rob, and making himself vulnerable sometimes did the trick.

Truthfully, the Olympics had been one of his most humiliating failures. He sat on the white comforter, spilling his guts about it while Rob looked out the window.

Matty's stomach hurt, and his hands were shaking. "I was late and almost missed my event. I'd been throwing up the entire morning. I told Denise it was food poisoning, but it wasn't. It was nerves. So, I was in the bathroom puking when I should've been catching the bus. I had to take a taxi."

Rob turned from the window, gazing at Matty.

"I was so angry with myself. My head felt like it was missing. I mean, there I was on the ice, and my head seemed disconnected from my body, like it was somewhere else, and my body was there on its own. Then the music started."

Rob cleared his throat, and his shoulders tensed.

"I did horribly. It was like a really bad dream where I was watching someone kick down the most elaborate and beautiful sand castle. Something it had taken me years to build, but it was me doing the kicking. I hated myself. I hated Denise. I even hated my fans for still loving me."

Rob crossed his arms over his chest and stared at Matty with a strange, appraising expression.

"What?"

Rob shook his head, and sighed. "When did you decide you weren't worth it?"

"I don't—"

"It's like you're two people, Matty. The one who wants it, who fights for it, and the one who doesn't think he deserves it anyway. The one who decides you'll just fall instead of making a bad landing. I've seen you do it. Like that's what you deserve."

"I—"

Rob interrupted again. "What I want to know is when did this happen? Because your parents are behind you, and your friends support you, and you want it so badly that you're changing your life for it, but I see it in you. The person who wants to be told no, who wants the performance to fail. I see the man who wants them to slap him with low scores because it wouldn't feel right if they didn't."

Matty's face felt hot, and he narrowed his eyes. "You—"

"Stop."

"I don't—"

Rob stepped forward and put his hand over Matty's mouth.

Matty pushed Rob's hand away and said, "No."

"Safeword," Rob said.

Matty thought about the safeword, rolled it around in his head, and licked his lips, his heart pounding. His mind surfed through ten thousand retorts to everything Rob had said. Cruel rejoinders raced through his brain, all of them just waiting to fly off his tongue. Matty shut his mouth.

"Take your clothes off," Rob said. He opened the bag he'd packed and pulled out lube and some very long velvet ties.

"Are you going to make love to me now?" Matty asked, trying to sound angry and sarcastic, referencing their conversation from days before, but his voice sounded unsteady, uncertain, and even needy.

"I'm going to give you what you want," Rob replied, tersely. "Maybe if *I* do it, you'll stop asking the judges for it. Maybe you'll stop trying to do it to yourself."

Before long, Matty was on his back, his wrists bound to the bed frame with the long velvet ties, limiting his range of movement to a few sliding inches. His knees were bent and ankles hooked behind his elbows, leaving his ass open to Rob's mouth and hands. Matty writhed as Rob landed another hard smack across his ass cheeks before diving back in to lick and bite at his hole. Matty tugged at the ropes, and curled his toes, trying to hold completely still as Rob tongue-fucked him, chills racing up his back, the head of his cock wet with pre-come.

Matty's ass cheeks stung from the hard slaps Rob kept giving him, slaps that made him yelp and took his breath away, but were soothed by Rob's tongue on his hole, or his fingers pressing inside. Then Rob took his cock into his mouth, sucking away the pre-come, and probing at his slit, slurping as he swallowed Matty's cock deep, swallowing around him, and shoving his fingers inside.

Matty was loud. During sex he made noises that would be embarrassing if he wasn't so fucking shameless about what he wanted.

He tugged at the ropes, wanting to grab Rob's head when he pulled off and push him back onto his cock, but was helpless to do anything but whine.

Rob brought Matty's legs down and rubbed his hips, then pressed down on his thighs to ease the tension. "No condom tonight? Like we talked about?"

Matty's hips jerked at the words, and a drop of pre-come slid down his cock.

"Yeah, okay."

His mother would kill him if she knew. She'd made him promise a long time ago that there would be no exceptions to the seat-belt rule, and now...God, he felt his lust dying out a little. Thinking about his mother during sex was so fucking wrong.

"Are you sure?" Rob asked, reaching for the lube he'd put by the bed. "I have some in the suitcase. You can change your mind."

Matty shook his head. "I'm sure. Very sure. I want to do it. Like that. With you. I trust you."

God, he wanted that. He wanted it so fucking badly he started to shake, his legs jerking like he was cold, and his cock jumping rock hard against his stomach. They'd talked about it and they both wanted it. They were negative, disease-free, and both of them had never had anal sex without a condom before. Matty's pulse raced just imagining Rob shooting his load into him, and the sloppy slick of it sliding out.

"Okay," Rob said, his breath warm on Matty's face. His lips were soft, and he tasted vaguely musky from Matty's ass, which was hot and weird. Matty fucking loved it. He moaned, sliding his tongue into Rob's mouth, tasting himself and Rob's toothpaste. Matty jerked at the ropes, wanting to touch, wanting to hold Rob close as they did this.

"Please." Matty pulled at the ropes, making his eyes big and pretty. "I want to hold you."

Rob kissed him again, tongue hot and slick, his teeth sharp and insistent on his mouth, and Matty shivered as Rob's hands ran up his arms, pulled at the ropes, and made them slightly tighter.

"No. We'll do this my way."

Matty shivered. They would, and he would *love it*. He felt slick all over, wet with Rob's spit on his ass and cock, sweat running down the side of his face, collecting in his hair and beading on his chest and stomach. Rob's hand on Matty's cock, covered in lube, was a shock, and Matty's eyes were wide with surprise, a question frozen on his lips as Rob positioned himself, and...oh God, oh God!

Matty squeezed his eyes shut, and took a shuddering breath that came out in a desperate, needy whimper. He fought hard not to buck—

LETA BLAKE

not to mess this moment up by thrusting too soon. Rob's legs and weight held Matty down, and Rob used his hands to hold Matty's hips steady. He was fucking *tight*, and Matty's cock ached from friction as Rob's asshole squeezed around the head, and then, *fuck*, opened and swallowed his cockhead.

Matty cried out, tugging at the ropes again, his eyes rolled so far up into his head that it hurt. He skidded his feet on the bed, trying to keep from thrusting up, trying to hold still and let Rob do this—let Rob take him this way.

"Shh," Rob whispered holding Matty's hips so tightly there might be bruises later.

But Matty didn't care. He was rushing hot and cold, trembling and somehow scared shitless. He was inside Rob's body, fucking his ass for the first time, and he was bare, so fucking bare. It was raw and hot, and so good that he didn't know what to do, or what to say, or if he could even breathe right now. His cock was swallowed by sweet convulsing heat, and Rob was holding him down, taking him in, and Matty was gonna freak out any second.

He could feel it in his gut—the urge to either thrust or scream or come, or all three, combining into something he couldn't control.

"Oh God, I can't—" Matty muttered. His hips jerked up, and he was all the way in. It was tight, hot, good, and fuck, fuck, fuck...oh, fuck. He pushed up and ground his hips against Rob's ass. He had to open his eyes because he wanted to look at Rob's face. Rob looked fucking glorious with lust and slack mouthed with want, and Matty jerked at the ropes fiercely, wanting free, wanting to roll Rob over and fuck him like mad.

Rob shushed him and ran soothing hands down Matty's arms, and then bent to kiss his lips, rubbing his mouth against Matty's stubble and biting his jaw, licking a line down to Matty's neck. He kissed him there, murmuring about Matty's cock, and God, he needed to shut up or Matty was going to come.

Fuck, it was hot, so amazingly hot how much Rob wanted him, wanted this, and Rob was talking about it, telling him he loved him, that his cock was hot inside him, that he was a good boy to fuck him like this. Matty tucked his feet up for leverage and slammed into Rob's ass, rough and mindless, working hard and fast.

Rob flung his head back and straightened up, taking Matty's thrusts and riding him like he did it all the fucking time, like his ass was pounded like this every day. Matty groaned, biting his lip, wanting to make it last, but wanting to come and feel his cock slip and slide in his mess in Rob's ass.

145

Suddenly, Rob pulled off, and Matty's cock was thrusting into cold dry air, and he gasped in shocked denial. His heart beat wildly. His hips, unable to hold still, jerked up into nothing. Then Rob shoved Matty's legs up and spit on his hole, and it was rough, fucking rough, because the lube from earlier wasn't so slick anymore, but the spit helped.

His ass burned, but Rob reached for the lube and poured some over his cock as it pushed in. It felt so hot—flesh on flesh—though Matty's body felt confused. His cock was still wet with Rob's ass, and he was shaking from the fuck, and now he was being plowed hard and fast, Rob grunting and cursing under his breath, pulling out again to slap Matty's ass and then pushing back in, muttering about how tight and hot it was, how different, how fucking good.

He pushed Matty's legs up and rutted hard into Matty's ass, his mouth at Matty's ear saying dirty things and calling him sweetheart. Then he shuddered, and Matty gasped, feeling Rob's cock jerk inside him. Oh God...fuck. Rob's spunk was in his ass. Rob moved experimentally, thrusting into his come-filled hole. He grabbed Matty's arms, clenched hard, and shook some more, as though another orgasm had taken him.

Then he was pulling out, pulling up, and he kissed Matty hard and then tender, touching his cheek with one hand, before pushing Matty's legs up farther to look at his ass.

"Fucking hot," he whispered.

Matty felt it, the hot, slick wetness that slipped from his convulsing hole and slid down his crack.

Rob groaned and kissed the insides of Matty's thighs, staring as Matty's ass clenched and unclenched, and come pushed out of him, trailing a tickling, hot path to the sheets. Rob bit his hipbone lightly and grabbed Matty's cock, positioning himself again. He slid down, his body taking Matty much more easily this time.

"Fuck," Rob muttered. His ass clenched, and his cock jerked some more. "Do it. Come in me now."

Matty tugged at the ropes again and whispered, "Please?"

Rob gently ran his fingers down Matty's stomach and reached behind himself to feel where Matty entered him. He quickly untied the ropes and rubbed Matty's wrists before kissing him. "Come in me," Rob commanded.

Matty wrapped his arms around Rob's back, feeling the muscles flex He pulled his feet up, got the purchase he needed, and fucked Rob's ass, kissing and biting Rob's lips, whimpering and holding him so tight against his body that it almost made it hard to fuck him. But he needed him close, needed him tight up against him like that, and he dug his nails in as it came rushing toward him, breathless and fast. He cried out, biting down on Rob's shoulder as he hit orgasm, endless rushing shivers taking over, and the deep, soul-aching jerks of his cock spurting into Rob's ass.

"Mmm," Rob said in his ear. "Move a little. Feel that?"

Matty thrust and it was good, fucking good in there, slick and easy. Rob pulled off and kissed Matty's mouth. He rolled onto his back and pulled Matty in beside him. Matty kissed Rob's neck and whispered, "I want to see."

Rob took his chin and kissed him before spreading his legs for Matty to move down between them. It *was* hot. Rob's asshole was red and a little tender looking, but the white, gorgeous jizz that slipped from his hole was *Matty's*, and Matty's cock was still slick with it too.

"Oh my God."

"Touch it," Rob said.

Matty reached out a finger and ran it through the come collecting in Rob's ass crack. He carefully fingered Rob's asshole and pushed it back in. "I want to—" and he stopped because it was weird, and kind of gross, and he didn't know what Rob would think.

"Go on then," Rob said, taking hold of his head and pushing him toward his ass. "Do it."

Matty swallowed hard and tentatively put out his tongue, tasting the come on Rob's anus. He moaned as Rob's hole twitched, pulling at his tongue.

"God," Rob barked and tugged Matty in closer. "Eat it."

Matty closed his eyes and ate Rob's ass, licking and biting, tasting the come and feeling the wrinkled hole shiver against his mouth. It was weirdly hot, and he loved how the come smeared against his cheeks as he worked. He finally felt Rob pull hard at his hair. Matty opened his eyes to see Rob's stomach quivering, his breath coming in hard, fast waves, and his eyes burning and green.

"Come here." Rob pulled him up, wiping the come off his cheeks before kissing his lips. "You are such a dirty girl," he murmured.

"Thank you." Matty was still shaking and freaking out that he wanted to go back down there and lick Rob's hole more. Wanted to make him hard, and get fucked again.

Rob pulled him close, grabbed a fistful of his hair, and kissed his mouth. Matty jerked in shock as Rob smacked his ass again. Then again, and again, rough and without any soothing rubs between. Rob put his mouth to Matty's ear.

"So you don't need it from the judges. I love you, Matty."

Rob spanked his ass so hard tears came to Matty's eyes, and it was glorious.

* * *

"Why are you so upset? You were almost late to the Olympics, and this isn't even close to as important," Rob said.

"Don't throw the Olympics in my face, bitch."

"I'm not your bitch," Rob countered as he stepped on the gas. "I'm pretty sure you're *my* bitch."

"Sure, eat some come from a guy's ass, and he's all, 'you're my bitch now.' Wouldn't my mother be proud?" He shifted uncomfortably.

"You sure you're okay?" Rob's brow furrowed.

"Yes. I told you, I get far worse bruises every day on the ice. My ass can take a lot."

Rob grinned. "Yeah, I know."

Matty crossed his legs and held onto his knees, letting the swerve of the truck throw him into the door a bit. "I don't want to be late, but could you drive less like an insane person?"

Rob smirked. "See, I never failed *my* driver's test. Not even once. You however—"

"I should never have told you that. Is this why relationships fail? People use shit against each other?"

"I don't know. I think our relationship is going to fail because you're in love with someone else, and I can't compete with him."

The flare of unexpected pain was so shocking and strong that Matty's hand flew to his chest. He stared out at the city flashing by in devil-may-care Christmas cheer as his gut twisted with a vital, deep, and hurtful anger.

"Figure Skating is all that and a bag of chips," Rob went on. "You can't get enough of him. A little bit of hot sex and some good conversation isn't enough to—"

"Shut up." Matty crossed his arms over his chest.

"I—hey, I was just...Matty, sweetheart, I was kidding."

Matty gave Rob a what-the-fuck look. "In what way is that supposed to be funny? I'm in love with you. And I hate you for it. I hate *myself* for it. The worst thing is that skating *is* all consuming. So please, go on and tell me how the hell that's supposed to be fucking funny?"

"Well—"

"No." Matty put up his hand. "See, here's the thing. I'm fucked up. No, this is fucked up. I'm on my hands and knees for you, taking it however you give it to me, and I don't want it to ever stop, and it's *fucked up.* We're fucked up."

A glance from the corner of his eye showed that Rob's fingers were tight on the wheel, and that he was nodding slowly, swallowing hard.

"Funny, but I feel the same way. Like I'm the one on my hands and knees, taking what I can get."

Matty's stomach twisted at the frayed ends to Rob's voice—the desperate sadness. He felt a strong, crazy urge to unbuckle his seat belt and crawl into Rob's lap, even though they were driving.

Matty cleared his throat. "I don't want this to be over." And how was it they could go from scorching, soul-quaking sex, to playful tenderness afterward—to fighting like this in the blink of an eye?

"It's not." Rob reached out and squeezed his hand. "You're right, though. It is fucked up. For both of us. It's gone beyond what it was supposed to be, and I can't say that I'm ready to walk away."

"Maybe when skating isn't—"

"I can't live for that faint possibility and neither can you. Frankly, Matty, I can't even let myself entertain the thought." Rob turned into a parking garage. "This is the place."

Matty said nothing as they got out of the truck, and the tweet of the automatic lock sounded behind them. Rob put his arm around Matty's shoulders and tucked him close, and they walked together into the night air. There in the sky was the North Star, low on the horizon. He swallowed hard. Snow, mountains, and complete surrender filled his mind.

Surrender. It was the only option available to him, and yet somehow it was so fucking hard to do. He wrapped his arm around Rob's waist and they held each other tightly as they entered the arena.

"Matty!" Ben's voice cut through the crowded area.

"Sure, give life to a kid, feed him, clothe him, support him in every way, and who does he care about the most? The pretty guy I'm with. Fantastic," Rob said, as Ben pushed through the gaggle of teenagers and little kids with their mothers.

"Matty, you came!" Ben raised his arms to hug Matty but suddenly glanced to his left and skidded to a halt. "Hey," he said, lifting his hand and waving from about three feet away.

Matty followed Ben's nervous glances and saw a tall kid in a soldier's costume. The sneer and narrowed eyes focused on Ben were familiar. Matty had been the recipient of similar looks off and on throughout his whole life.

Matty waved back. "You look great, Ben! Very...vermin-y."

"Really ratty," Rob chimed in.

Ben stuck out his tongue. "I was supposed to be a soldier, but..." He glanced again at the guy across the room. "Things change."

Matty felt Rob start to move away, understood that he was going to hug Ben, and quickly grabbed Rob's arm and held him fast.

Rob frowned down at Matty, but simply said to Ben, "You look great. You're not nervous are you?"

Ben rolled his eyes and sighed. "Not any more nervous than I was the last three nights, Dad."

"So, pretty nervous," Matty said.

Ben grinned. "Yeah."

Rob said, "Too bad your mom isn't here tonight. I'm sorry I couldn't make it before, honey. But—"

"Dad, don't call me that here," Ben muttered under his breath. "Just call me Ben. Okay?"

Rob blinked and seemed to finally clue in to the guy who was still taking the time out of his busy prepubescent life to glare at Ben. "Oh. I—I can do that. Sure."

"I know about Lila being sick, Dad, and I understand why you couldn't come the other nights. She's your baby—"

"No, she's my dog. You're my—"

Matty elbowed Rob hard.

"Ow." Rob cleared his throat. "That doesn't mean I didn't want to be here. It's just with the emergency vet visits, and the medicines that were making her puke...well, I wanted to make sure she was out of the woods."

"Poor Lila," Ben said.

"Yes, and my poor blue Louis Vuitton purse," Matty murmured. Lila had vomited into it by some cruel trick of fate shortly after her first dose of medicine.

"Oh no," Ben said, trying to keep the laughter out of his voice. "I'm not sure what's the bigger tragedy here."

Matty and Rob spoke in unison.

"Lila," Matty said.

"The bag," Rob said.

"What?" Matty rolled his eyes. "You don't think I'd absolutely sacrifice my bag for your dog? Of course Lila's more important."

"Based on the tears and horror-stricken expressions, I'm not sure I believe you."

Matty playfully put his hand under Rob's chin to try to shut him up. Rob grinned, and for a brief, horrible moment Matty thought Rob was going to kiss him, and the guy in the corner would have an even better reason to make Ben's life hell. Instead, the lights started to blink, and the scramble began for the skaters to take their places, and the audience their seats in the bleachers.

As they settled in, Rob wrapped his scarf around his neck even tighter. "It's freezing in here."

Matty thought of the feel of the ice on his fingers, and the beautiful feeling of racing over it on blades. "I've spent ten years in rinks like this. Sometimes, it feels like it's the only place I'm really home, and other times I hate it so much I want to murder the ice. Stab it to death. Sometimes it feels like the ice is a living thing and it hates me." He sighed. "I sound like an insane person."

Rob nodded. "Therapy. Loads of it."

Matty tried to smile, but he wasn't sure Rob was joking. In fact, he kind of thought he wasn't. "What about you?"

Rob took his hand and twined their fingers together gently. He pressed a quick kiss to the back of Matty's hand. "Oh, believe me, I need therapy too."

The lights went out, the music began, and Clara and her friends began to shake the presents under the tree set up at the far end of the rink. Matty gripped Rob's fingers and rested his head on Rob's shoulder for a moment. He could smell Rob's soap, shampoo, and the warm scent of his skin. He bit his lip, wondering how long he'd be able to remember the way Rob smelled.

* * *

"It's too bad Anja had to miss it." Rob fell back on the hotel bed.

"Uh-huh." Matty climbed on top of Rob.

"What are you…"

"There's this special thing Elliot's dad taught him when he was a kid in order to charm the woman he was surely going to marry one day. Being his best friend, of course, he shared it with me." Matty held Rob's arms down on the mattress and straddled his waist.

Rob lifted his eyebrows and grinned, not struggling at all, which Matty aimed to change.

"It's called whuffling."

Rob didn't seem intimidated, but Matty knew that wouldn't last. From now on, he suspected the word "whuffle" would bring terror to Rob's eyes.

"It's when you breathe really fast against someone's ear," Matty explained. "Like this."

Rob bucked up, laughing and struggling and twisting underneath Matty's body. "Stop, oh my God, stop!"

"Safeword," Matty said, laughing and holding Rob down pretty easily. Sometimes he forgot how strong he was off the ice.

"Oh fuck you."

"Then I'll whuffle you," Matty murmured.

Rob's body convulsed under him hysterically as Matty breathed rapidly in his ear. "Oh God, stop." Rob laughed.

Matty could feel Rob's pounding heart against his chest. He whispered, "Safe. Word."

Rob squirmed and fought. Finally, he cried, "Cowbell! Fucking cowbell!"

"Needs more cowbell." Matty rolled to the side, laughing and smirking. "You do realize that wasn't even a minute. I've never safeworded. You're a total wuss."

Rob rolled his eyes. "You're missing the point of the exercise, sweetheart, if you think it's a competition."

"I won," Matty said.

"It's not about winning or losing."

"It's how you play the game, and I *won*."

Rob flipped over and pinned him down. "Then let me deliver your gold medal to you, Mr. Marcus. How do you want it?"

"Um, like this is good," Matty said, already breathless. "And no condom. I…I really like that."

His eyes rolled up and his toes curled as Rob took over, melting away any lingering frustration and fear into seamless union and hot, intense orgasm.

CHAPTER FIFTEEN

Rob seemed a little nervous as they pulled into the parking lot of Anja's apartment complex on Christmas Eve. Matty reached out and touched Rob's hand, feeling the tension in the way Rob gripped the gear shift. His own nerves made his stomach tremulous.

"So, when she hates me, are you going to stop fucking me?" Matty said, faking a light-hearted tone and looking out the window at the beige and white apartments.

"Seriously, does anyone who meets you ever hate you?"

Matty considered. "Eventually most people hate me."

"Well, tonight is not 'eventually.' Tonight is, 'Matty shines like a million twinkling stars.' I'm sure hearts will spring from Anja's eyes."

"Then you agree that eventually everyone hates me."

Rob looked suspiciously like he might laugh. "Wait, first you said 'most people,' and now you're saying 'everyone,' and that's a big difference. I need clarity before I can voice my opinion."

"Are you trying to make me even more nervous before meeting the woman in your life? Because it's working." Matty looked down at his shoes, wishing he'd chosen the silver pair. "God, these shoes are hideous. Why did I wear them? They're not…festive. It's Christmas. I should look festive."

Rob tapped at Matty's seat belt. "Time to get out. I think the glitter lip gloss makes up for the lack of festive shoes, sweetheart."

"Don't patronize me."

"Get out of the truck."

"*You* get out."

Rob did just that and Matty was left with nothing to do but follow. His unfestive shoes and his sparkle—*not* glitter—lip gloss would hopefully be enough to distract Anja from how much she would shortly hate him.

As though he read Matty's mind, Rob asked, "Besides, why would she hate you?"

Matty rolled his eyes. "I'm not a nice person."

"Sure. I forgot."

Matty took Rob's hand and didn't say the rest. She'd hate him because Matty was leaving, and Rob and Ben were going to get hurt. He was stupid. He should have stayed at home. He shouldn't have made brownies for the guy who plowed and salted his drive. He should've stayed at the Pages' house alone all winter and never talked to or fucked anyone. It would have been the safest thing to do. The smartest.

"C'mon," Rob said, wrapping his arm around Matty's shoulder. "You look beautiful, and she's gonna love you."

Matty leaned against Rob's warm frame. She'd like him, maybe. For now. Really, why did he care? He was just a blip on the radar of their lives. But it was starting to kind of scare him, the idea that he'd be just a surreal memory. *Do you remember that one Christmas when that ice skater was Dad's boyfriend?*

Unfairly, he wanted to be more than that.

Anja looked a lot like Ben, and a lot like Rob for that matter. Blonde, blue-eyed, medium-boned with a white, wide grin. Based on the fine lines around her eyes, she smiled a lot. She took Matty's coat, complimented his outfit, and freed him of his contribution of brownies.

"I've heard about these!"

She was stylish and smart, which Matty could appreciate. She laughed at almost everything Matty said, which seemed promising. Dinner was a disaster of calories, but Matty sucked it up and ate his food like a good guest. It was really fucking delicious, so he didn't mind too much.

As soon as Matty put down his fork and collapsed back in his seat, completely stuffed, Ben clapped his hands.

"Presents!" he declared.

"Let's wait until our food digests," Rob said, but his eyes twinkled. "We don't need to rush off from the table. Matty has some more potatoes left to eat."

Ben's eyes bugged out, and he looked like he might have a seizure until Anja started laughing and stood up from the table, gesturing with her wine glass toward the living room.

"C'mon, kiddo, let's see what you got."

The living room was cozy, with a low, wide sofa and a matching loveseat angled toward the large television screen. The Christmas tree was set up in the corner, and the ambient glow of its small colored lights filled the room. The presents under it were small for the most part and covered with a hodge-podge of different wrapping papers. There were several with shiny foil paper featuring dancing snowmen and frolicking reindeer, which must have been Anja and Ben's choice.

There was one bigger box and several smaller ones in a classy poinsettia motif that Matty pegged as being from Anja's folks. Rob's five gifts were wrapped in red, green, and gold plaid, and the three boxes wrapped in gold-stars on a nice cream background were Matty's contribution to the small pile.

"Have a seat," Anja said, brushing a friendly hand over his shoulder as she passed by. "Wherever you're most comfortable."

Matty chose the place next to Rob on the loveseat. Their thighs pressed together, and Rob swung his arm around Matty's shoulders. Warm anticipation rose in him, and he leaned into Rob's body, feeling comfortable and accepted.

"So far, so good, huh?" Rob whispered.

"I didn't see hearts come out of her eyes."

"Give her time. Not everyone can fall in love with you at first sight like I did."

Matty's smile tugged at his lips, and he looked up at Rob through his lashes. He was surprised when Rob gave him a soft, lingering kiss before clearing his throat and turning his attention to where Anja was fiddling with the stereo system on a table by the window.

"It's the round button," he said, like he'd told her that before. "Beside the big green letters that say 'power.'"

"Har, har, jerkface. I know that. I'm trying to figure out which disc to listen to first."

Ben had crashed down in front of the tree and started sorting through the presents, making a pile for each of them.

"This one's for me, and this one's for me, and this one's for me." Ben's voice rose excitedly. "This one's for Dad." He sounded disappointed every time he came to a present for someone else. Matty laughed, and Rob rolled his eyes.

"Here!" Anja announced, pulling out a CD and putting it in the player. "Rob burned this for me when Ben was two, and he actually had to use an old-school CD burner to manage it. Remember, Rob?"

"Sure do."

The beginning of Bing Crosby and David Bowie's "Little Drummer Boy" began as Anja sat on the sofa, swirling her wine, and laughing at Ben. The song reminded Matty of his mother. It was one of her favorites. This was the first Christmas he'd spent away from her, and suddenly, as the music tapped into that place inside him where all his love for her was stored, he missed her terribly.

He leaned his head against Rob's shoulder, thinking about how every Christmas for as long as he could remember his mom had worn a Santa hat and handed out the gifts, while his dad sat in his easy chair with an elf hat plopped crookedly on his head, and a small glass of whiskey to celebrate.

Matty wondered whether now he was grown-up if Christmas traditions were something he was going to miss every year. At what point would he be adult enough to make traditions of his own? Here with Rob it was nice. Beautiful even. But it wasn't going to happen again.

He glanced at the wooden clock hanging on the wall over the TV. It was already after nine. Donna was undoubtedly already in bed by now and Joseph was probably out with friends. He remembered when Joey had still believed in Santa Claus, and how it had been his responsibility to make sure his little brother didn't get out of bed while his parents were setting up the goods. Things changed so fast. It didn't seem all that long ago, but *Joseph* was far too old for Santa these days.

His family's money problems definitely put a damper on this year's Christmas. Matty's only present from them was the Thanksgiving visit and a cheery phone call from his mother that morning before he'd headed out to feed the horses. He knew Joseph's only gifts were going to be a few new outfits for school, and some tickets to a basketball game. Things were just that tight—and it was all because of him.

Matty's responsibility to his family pressed down on him. He felt more than saw Rob's eyes on him, and he smiled up at him to dismiss the worry.

"Here it is!" Ben exclaimed. His voice pitched to a frequency of excitement Matty had never heard him reach before. "I found it! It was at the very bottom!"

Anja smiled knowingly. "Oh yes. I've heard a lot about this."

"What is it?" Matty asked. "Something he's been pining for? Let me guess, the latest add-on to that video game he's been telling me about?"

"Nope," Ben said, standing up from the small piles of presents and grinning at Matty. His face was flushed as he rushed over to the loveseat. "It's not for me. It's for you."

"For me?"

"Yeah." Ben thrust a tiny gift wrapped in foil snowmen into his hands.

Matty tried to shrug off the weight of his previous thoughts. He smiled at Ben and shook the present gamely. There was a small rattle.

"Sounds like…" Matty shook it some more. "Paperclips! How did you know? I love paperclips! Thank you!"

Ben laughed. "No, open it. It's from me. I made it for you myself."

Matty didn't know what to make of Ben wanting him to open the present before he opened any of his own. Rob was quiet beside him, and Anja leaned forward in anticipation, her wine glass dangling between her fingers, and her blue eyes warm and soft.

"Okay." Matty ripped into the present to make a show of looking eager. "Let's see what you've made here."

He was speechless as he lifted a rough silver chain covered with tiny metal tabs that clanged together. It was a necklace, but he wasn't sure if it was beautiful or ugly. It was unique, that was certain. "Ben it's—"

He'd planned to say amazing, but Ben jumped forward nearly into his lap to point at each tab. "See? High scores. I know they replaced the six-point-oh system a while ago, but the new system is too hard to put on a necklace. This tab is a five-point-eight, and this one says five-point-nine, and that one's a six-point-oh. I'm giving you all the scores you need between now and the next Olympics. See?"

"You made this?" Matty asked, his throat feeling extraordinarily tight as he fingered through each tab and read the marks there.

"Yeah. My Grandpa's got this cool machine that lets you etch on tin, and he had a bunch of these tabs left over from when he was making something for my mom."

"Ben...I don't know what to say."

But Ben wasn't done talking. "Isn't it cool? I got the idea when I was looking at some old figure skating stuff on YouTube. All those older scores, you know?" Ben's blue eyes were shiny as he explained. "One guy was talking about his good luck charms and I was like, that's what Matty needs! Then I thought you needed good scores more than good luck, and I realized I could make both for you."

Ben wrapped his hand around Matty's to close it around the chain. "So here. Between you and your ambition, and how much my dad and I believe in you, this necklace has all the luck you'll ever need."

Matty couldn't speak. He realized his hand was shaking as he lifted the necklace to slip it over his neck. There was no clasp, but it was long enough to simply drop down over his head.

Rob leaned over and fingered the tabs, looking at each one closely. "Why not six-point-oh on all of them?"

"Because Matty's awesome, but he's not perfect," Ben said, with a "duh" in his tone. "Well, not always perfect."

Rob made a soft sound, and then whispered, "Isn't that the truth?"

"Perfection lies in the imperfection," Anja said, lifting her glass in a toast. "To Matty. May he always feel our friendship and support wherever he goes, and may success always find him."

"Hear, hear," Rob agreed, and kissed the side of Matty's head.

Matty hugged Ben tightly. "Thank you. No one has ever given me a present that means as much to me. I'll wear it all the time. I promise."

"Really? You don't have to."

"I want to."

Ben released him. "Awesome. Now? My presents! Dad, come help me get the big one from Grandma and Grandpa out from behind the tree?"

Training Season

The loveseat lurched as Rob stood to help Ben, but Matty didn't glance up from the necklace. He looked at each tab, the numbers etched in Ben's shaky hand, each personal and so imperfect, and each one made just for him. His chest hurt as he stared at the six-point-oh on the next-to-last tab. If he could get it perfect, just once when it really counted, then walking away from all of this would be worth it. Wouldn't it?

"Hey you," Anja said as she dropped a little tipsily into Rob's abandoned seat. "Thanks for being so nice to my kid. You're really great with him. He loved that clinic you did here in town last week, even if he was the oldest one there."

The seminar with the children in Missoula was good for Matty, just like Joanna predicted. "I wasn't sure if I'd enjoy it, but it was really fun. There were some great kids there. But honestly, none of them could hold a candle to Ben. He's got the pure talent you just have to be born with." Matty cleared his throat and let the necklace fall to rest against his shirt. "He's great. Talented, smart, and thoughtful." He motioned at his necklace. "Kind and creative. Really, I could go on and on."

"Please, I'm his mother. You're not boring me. Feel free."

Matty laughed. "Funny, generous, open-hearted, a hard worker, dedicated—"

Anja's wine glass shook with her shoulders. "I was kidding. You don't have to keep talking."

"Handsome, intelligent, ambitious, selfless, loving, warm, and a deeply good person."

Anja put up her hand, eyes shining as she smiled. "You had me at generous, and you won my heart at creative, and I was yours, body and soul, at hard worker."

"It's all true and all him. Well, and you and Rob. You've both done such an amazing job with him."

"Can you put that in writing? Just on a small little Post-It note or something so I can read it the twenty or forty times a day I wonder if I'm doing the right thing by him?"

"Sure. I'll call and leave a pep talk on your voicemail, and you can listen any time you want."

Anja faked a swoon, her hand to her forehead and her head falling back. "Rob, can I keep Matty?" she called out as Rob and Ben scooted the heavy, poinsettia-wrapped box over to the empty space on the floor in front of them.

"Sorry, no."

Ben looked to his mother eagerly, obviously waiting for her to give the go ahead for him to rip into the box.

158

"Go on," she said, but as soon as he started to tear, she exclaimed, "Wait! We need a camera!"

Rob dashed from the room and returned moments later with his phone. He took pictures as Ben demolished the wrapping paper, scrabbling eagerly at the box.

"A computer!"

"Yes, your grandparents thought you needed a laptop of your own. Something about papers and college and becoming a doctor one day."

"I'm going to skate. Like Matty."

"Great," Anja replied, looking genuinely pleased. "Let's all make a pact to never do anything my parents plan for us."

"I'm in," Rob said.

Ben rolled his eyes at his parents and then studied the box. "This is awesome. Check it out, Dad. It's got everything I could ever want."

Matty was surprised by how long Ben dragged the presents out given how excited he'd been to get to them. He took his time with his gifts, insisting that Matty, Anja, and Rob open presents in between his so it would take more time. Eventually Anja got up, fetched a gift, and handed it to Rob before returning to her original seat on the sofa.

Taking the large, rather squishy object that had been kind of haphazardly wrapped, Rob took the place next to Matty on the loveseat.

"It's for Lila," Anja said as Rob revealed a big dog sweater. "To keep her old bones warm."

Rob blew her a kiss, and Ben handed Anja a cream-and-gold-star package from the pile. Matty's stomach clenched. He had to bite back the ramble that formed on the tip of his tongue about how she could return it if she didn't like it, and he'd had to guess since he'd never met her, and she really could just say it wasn't her style, and he wouldn't mind at all. But he desperately wanted her to like it.

"This is beautiful!" Anja lifted out the silver and black houndstooth scarf he'd found in a small boutique in Whitefish. "I love it. You really didn't have to get me anything at all, Matty. This is very sweet."

"My pleasure. And if you don't like it—"

"I love it. Thank you."

She seemed sincere, so Matty let it drop, basking in the warm pleasure of successful gift giving.

Ben's next box was small and contained an envelope. He opened it with a frown of disappointment, but his eyes lit up when he read what was inside. "Really?"

"Of course," Rob said. "Matty's leaving and you've shown real commitment, so your mom and I decided you've definitely earned private lessons."

Matty knew Rob had taken a small loan from Bill in advance of selling the summer kids in order to pay for his half of the lessons.

Ben threw his arms around Anja first, and then Rob, and then Matty. Rob chuckled and nudged him toward another box.

"There's one more to make it complete."

Ben's eyes went wide as he tore open the package wrapped in Rob's plaid paper and pulled out shiny, new, perfect black boots with the blade already attached. Matty had helped Rob pick them out. They weren't the best of the best, but they'd serve Ben in good stead while his feet finished growing.

"This is amazing! Best Christmas ever!"

"Thank Matty too. He kicked in for them," Rob said.

Matty took the hug that was given and leaned back into the sofa, feeling tired but jolly.

In addition to the necklace, he received a set of glittery lotion and lip gloss from Ben—dollar store stuff, but still sweet. Anja gave him a scented candle and a set of nice handkerchiefs with his initials embroidered into them with a classy gray thread.

Rob's gift was a framed print of an illustration from a book of Russian fairy tales. The swan was beautifully rendered with its wings spread and ready for flight. Beneath the illustration Russian words were printed in gold font.

"See the Swan, the fair virgin—no, that's wrong. See the Swan, the fair maiden," Matty translated when Rob asked if he could read the words. "Let her body glint through her wings. Let her bones appear, and from bone to bone let the marrow run like a flowing string of pearls." He elbowed Rob playfully. "Is that more commentary on my eating habits?"

Rob shook his head. "I had no idea what it said when I bought it, but it seems to fit, doesn't it?"

"For God's sake, I eat!"

Anja's head tilted and she leaned forward to listen to their conversation.

Rob laughed. "No, you really don't eat enough."

Matty huffed, finding his irritation hard to hold on to in the face of such a beautiful present. He didn't know where he would hang it once training started with Valentina, mainly because he didn't know where he was going to stay in New York City yet, but for now he was going to replace the hen-scratching-at-feed picture in the Pages' guest room.

"But that's not what I meant." Rob's cheeks flushed a little. "Like it says, bone to bone, down to your marrow, you're beautifully made, like the swan. And like the string of pearls, you're precious, shining, and incredibly strong."

Anja made a soft noise and leaned back, calling Ben to her side as though she had suddenly realized she was listening to something private. Matty didn't know what she and Ben talked softly about as he looked at the picture, carefully running his fingers along the edge of the frame and studying the glinting words carefully.

"Thank you," he said, finally, pressing a kiss to Rob's mouth. "I love it."

While Ben and Anja cuddled and talked quietly on the sofa, Matty handed Rob the gift he'd managed to put together only the week before.

"I'm sorry," he said as Rob worked the wrapping off the box. "It's nothing special or beautiful like what you gave me. I couldn't find anything that was just right for you. I thought about getting you a miniature cow made out of brass, but it smacked oddly of false idols, which I don't even understand how I knew because it's not like I was really big on Sunday school back in the day. But, well, never mind." Matty bit his lip to stop the flow of words. He felt like a colossal gift-giving failure in the face of Rob's beautiful present.

Rob lifted the framed photo of Matty and Ben. It was a nice frame, silver and heavy, something that would fit well with the others Matty had seen around Rob's house. The picture was one Matty's mom had taken at Thanksgiving with her old, clunky film camera. It was Matty and Ben skating together on the pond in the morning. Both of them were laughing, their arms around each other as they took a turn around the edge of the pond. It wasn't particularly flattering for either of them, but they were genuinely happy.

"Thank you, Matty. I remember when your mom took this. Such a great morning."

"Like I said, it's not—"

"It's good. Thank you."

Rob's kiss was warm and short. Ben leaped from the sofa and declared that Rob simply had to go with him to take the new computer to his room and set it up. Rob obliged, leaving Matty alone with Anja for the first time all evening.

"So," Anja said, leaning back. "Rob's pretty great, isn't he?"

"He is. Truly."

"You care about him."

"Of course."

Anja's gaze turned thoughtful. "I can never repay you for the confidence and help you've given my son."

"Like I said before, it was all Ben. He's amazing."

"Thank you." Anja shifted forward. "So, do you mind me asking? Are you planning to continue this with Rob or is it all over when you leave?"

Matty's mouth went dry and he wished desperately for some of the wine Anja had been swilling all night. Why had he turned it down earlier? Calories were nothing compared to the sober-faced dread shooting through him now.

But he didn't have to answer because Anja saw it on his face. Her mouth puckered slightly, and she leaned back on the sofa and took another long sip of her drink. Matty thought about saying he was going to go check if they needed any help with the computer, but then Anja started talking.

"Rob wouldn't have made a very good doctor," she said, softly. "He wanted to be one, and he has a passion for helping people, for supporting them when they need someone to be strong because they can't." She looked at Matty with a piercing, knowing look.

Matty felt exposed under her gaze, like she knew how weak he'd been, and how strong Rob made him want to be. "I think he'd be a great doctor, actually."

"No." Anja shook her head. "He's not cut out for the drama of losing patients. But he isn't meant to be a rancher, either."

Matty stayed silent, remembering Rob walking the hills of the ranch. He tried to imagine Rob doing anything else, living anywhere else, and he just couldn't.

"What do you think he should do instead?"

Anja smiled. "I've always thought he'd be good with people. Something hands-on, of course. I think physical therapy would be a good fit."

"I think he'd be good at anything he put his mind to."

"That's because you're in love with him. I'm not, so I can see him a little more clearly. Physical therapy would be perfect for him."

Matty didn't appreciate his opinion being downplayed, but he didn't want to argue, so he asked about her job. The rest of their conversation was easier and superficial. Anja talked about her career, and how she preferred teaching second grade to kindergarten. She interrogated him a bit about his experience at the Olympics and about traveling the world, but especially Russia.

"My mother was fascinated by the whole story of Anastasia," Anja explained. "In fact, that's where she got my name. I've always thought I'd be doing myself a disservice not to get to Russia one day."

"Well, if Ben continues to improve, you never know. Cup of

Russia could be in his future."

She lifted her wine glass in a toast and drank a bit more of it. "I'm not usually this big of a lush, but I was nervous having you over tonight."

"You should've seen me in the truck. I was being a total bitch to Rob for the same reason."

Anja laughed softly. "But look. Here we are getting along like peas in a pod." She cocked her head. "It's too bad you're not sticking around. Rob hasn't looked this happy in a long time and, quite frankly, I think you could inspire him to do something more with his life."

Matty's skin felt tight. He took a long breath, trying to think of something to say in response.

"Don't panic. Life is what it is. I learned that lesson young. It doesn't stop for should've, would've, could've. It just chugs on ahead to the next station—some passengers get on, some get off, and then on it goes." Anja's cheeks were flushed and a flash of embarrassment crossed her face. "Now I'm babbling."

"I babble all the time. Usually about pissy things. Your babble is much more charming than mine. Feel free to continue."

Anja chuckled and stood up. "I think it's time to change to water. Can I get you anything from the kitchen?"

"No, thank you."

Ben appeared in the doorway, his eyes glittering. "Matty, come on! Dad got my computer set up and I want you see it."

Rob ran his hand down Matty's chest as they slid by each other in the hallway. "Getting a piece of pie. Want a slice?"

Matty's stomach rumbled, though he had no idea why since he'd eaten enough food already to satisfy a gluttonous pig for a week. He shook his head. "My ass grew ten sizes tonight, and unlike the Grinch's heart, it was never three sizes too small. Keep your delicious pie away from me. Devil be gone."

"You know it's all muscle," Rob said, continuing down the hallway to the kitchen.

"Could bounce a quarter off it," Matty agreed, following Ben into his room and shutting the door almost entirely to block off any thoughts of the kitchen and food that now seemed to be calling to him.

Matty sat down on Ben's bed so he had a good view of the screen and watched Ben play a video game with a warm glow in his chest. He'd had a good night, and Anja seemed to like him a lot, which was a hell of a relief.

He reclined a little, propping himself on Ben's pillows. His back had been aching this week, probably from the effort he'd put into quads and the number of spectacular falls he'd taken. He rubbed his lumbar with one hand while making encouraging noises as Ben played. It was turning out to be a very nice Christmas.

After about twenty minutes of watching Ben play the computer game, Matty started to miss Rob and excused himself to find him.

"You know what I'm saying, though, Rob." Anja's whisper traveled down the hallway. "It's time you moved on with your life. This guy is great, but he's leaving, so what then? Don't look at me like that. I've never seen you so in love before, and I lived through the drama of Daniel McKenzie, so please don't act like I'm an idiot."

"You pretend like you know what I should be doing, and we both know you don't."

"Look into it. That's all I'm saying. It's a great way back into medicine. Maybe not the doctor you wanted to be, but becoming a physical therapist could be something you would truly love. We can't put our lives on hold anymore, Rob. Both of us—all three of us—have to reach for our dreams."

"And what's your dream? To be the best grade school teacher you can be?"

Matty was surprised by Rob's cutting tone, and he pressed himself against the hallway wall to listen as quietly as possible.

"To be Ben's mother, and your best friend, and to do something I'm proud of. And yeah, fuck you, I'm proud of being a teacher."

"And I'm proud of being a rancher," Rob shot back.

"Tell that to your *daddy*, Rob, because I'm not buying it."

Anja stormed out of the kitchen, and Matty plastered a wide grin on his face as he was caught standing there against the wall listening. She stopped short and stared at him, and Matty didn't think she looked angry so much as surprised.

"Uh, this is...I'm sorry, I was looking for Rob. I didn't want to interrupt. This is really, um—"

"Awkward," Anja supplied. She sighed and rubbed her face. "Listen, I like you, but he deserves better than this. Not better than *you*, but better than this. His life is worth so much more than he gives it credit for, and he should be happy. I *love* him and I just want him to be happy. Do you understand?"

"Of course."

"I'm sorry. I've had too much to drink. But, it doesn't negate what I said. Okay? Just keep that in mind."

She swept further down the hallway and into her room. She didn't come out for nearly twenty minutes. When she did, Matty could see she had her game face on. Rob did too. He kissed her goodnight with a tension that even Ben seemed to notice, looking back and forth between them with a worried expression.

In the truck, driving back to the ranch, Matty said, "I didn't see hearts from her eyes, Rob."

"There were hearts," Rob replied, his voice sounding grim.

"When? Before the flames shot out and tried to burn me alive in anticipation of breaking your heart?"

"Yes, sometime before that there were hearts."

"See, I knew she'd hate me."

"She clearly doesn't hate you. She just doesn't want me to get hurt."

"So all of that in the kitchen was about me?"

Rob snorted. "No, sweetheart. You're not the center of the universe. It was about me."

"Oh." Matty reached out and took Rob's hand.

The night flashed by outside the window, and he hoped that Rob was awake enough for the drive. He was feeling sleepy and they still had hours to go. If only Rob were less conscientious of an employer, he could have pawned the Christmas morning chores off on the hands. Of course he'd never do that. So driving home late at night was the only option.

Tension vibrated off Rob, and Matty squeezed his hand. "Can I tell you something?"

"Yeah?"

"I really care about you. I want you to be happy."

"Join the club. Anja will make T-shirts."

"Seriously, does ranching make you happy? Really?"

Rob sighed. "No. Ranching doesn't make me happy. I like it well enough. It's familiar like a comfortable shoe, but it doesn't make me happy. Anja has my number on that front."

"Promise me something."

"I don't think I want to."

"Promise me that when I leave to pursue my dream, you'll do something to pursue yours."

Rob pulled his hand away and shook his head slowly. "I don't make promises I'm not sure I can keep."

"Yeah. I know."

The night flew by, and Matty rested his head back, falling asleep to the sound of cars passing by and Rob's fingers drumming on the steering wheel. He dreamed of flying, and Rob was there flying, too, but always just beyond his reach.

CHAPTER SIXTEEN

By New Year's Eve, Whitefish Lake and some of the bays of Flathead Lake had already frozen over thanks to the unusually early and cold winter. Matty decided it was the perfect time to skate on a real lake, and not just the Pages' shallow little pond.

"I just can't, sweetheart. Another day." Rob sipped his coffee, his eyes sliding over the newspaper before throwing it on the kitchen table.

"But I already arranged it with Bill! Come on. You've never been on ice with me."

"You're not missing much. I can get around, but I'm not you or Ben. I don't have any jumps to show off."

Matty sipped his hot water and bitters and pouted. "It's not about showing off. It's, I don't know, about you being part of *my* world for a change. Even going out on a lake like this is still part of your world. I've never skated on a lake. I'd love you to be there for my first time." Matty made sure the words "first time" sounded as flirty as possible.

Rob gazed at him thoughtfully before sighing and shaking out the paper again. "I'm sorry, but I've got to deal with the heat lamps in the chicken coop."

"How long does it take a hot rancher to change a light bulb?"

Rob smirked. "Longer than you'd think. It's not the bulb, it's the wiring."

"Is it even safe for you to mess with electrical wiring? If Bing and the others are up in the pastures, will anyone be around to call 911 if you barbeque yourself?"

"I'm not doing it myself. I'll be supervising a certified electrician. Normally, I'd just have Bing deal with that, but he's home with Candace because she's got the flu."

"You've got four employees."

"Dino, Terry, and Charlie have to fix that fence up on the north pasture, or we'll have to wrangle cattle again tomorrow, and I want to give them the holiday off. I'm sorry, Matty. It's supposed to get below zero again tonight, and the chickens need those lamps up and running."

"Fine. I understand." He knew he sounded bratty. "I guess I'll just spend New Year's Eve on a hot date with Bill." Of course he'd be back before evening, but that wasn't the point.

"Matty, this is life on a ranch. I've been working here long before you came around, and I'll be doing it long after you go."

"Okay. I said fine." Matty sighed and pressed a kiss to Rob's cheek. "See you tonight?"

"If the fence is done, yes. Have a great day on the lake, sweetheart."

During the drive to Whitefish to meet Bill, Matty stewed. He didn't want to think about Rob on the ranch, wrangling his small herd and doing God knows what dangerous things. He especially didn't want Rob doing it without him there to worry about him. Who was going to wait anxiously for him to come stumbling in with snow on his boots and a flush to his cheeks?

Bing and the ranch hands were great, but they weren't the same. They were employees, not a lover. Rob deserved to have someone who adored him watching out for him and waiting for his return every night.

Matty hated that it wasn't going to be him.

Bill's house was a little bungalow in a neighborhood of similar houses on Park Avenue in Whitefish. The outside was tidy, and Matty examined the small fire pit with remnants of charcoal left in it while he waited for Bill to answer the door.

"C'mon in," Bill said. Bags hung under his eyes, and he hadn't shaved at all. "'Scuse the mess."

Matty followed him through the short hallway, the scent of bacon and eggs hitting him hard, and making his stomach rumble. His breakfast of yogurt and fruit seemed hours ago, and he felt a little weak with longing for a crunchy piece of bacon. It had been forever since he'd had a taste.

He was just about to cave and ask Bill if he had any bacon left over when he saw the man sitting at the small kitchen table, sipping coffee and using a piece of toast to sop up runny egg yolk. The man was huge, with reddish hair, freckles, and a darker red beard. He wore a plaid shirt, jeans, and sported a crease along the side of his face from where he'd been sleeping.

"This is Angus," Bill said, motioning at him.

Angus lifted up the bread as a sort of hello and shoved more into his mouth.

"He's my roommate."

"Lover," Angus replied with his mouth full. "He doesn't want to claim me because he's a closeted dickwad."

"I own a gay bar. How can I be closeted?"

"You're closeted about us. About me being your lover."

"Bullshit," Bill growled.

Blinking, Matty looked between them. He really hoped they weren't going to have an all-out lover's spat. He just wanted to go skating on lake, not take one or both of them to the ER due to some

167

manly domestic violence or something crazy like that.

Bill shrugged into a coat he'd grabbed from a pegboard along the wall by the back door. "Screw a guy a few times and he wants you to call him something smarmy," Bill muttered. "I bet Rob, head-over-ass as he is for you, doesn't call you his lover."

"Boyfriend," Matty affirmed.

"See?" Bill said.

"So you'll call me your boyfriend?" Angus asked.

"Hell no."

Angus grinned at Matty and waggled his eyebrows. "He's gonna marry me one day."

Bill looked incredibly put out. "Finish your damn breakfast if you're coming with us. And stop lying to Rob's boyfriend before he gets the wrong idea about us."

Angus laughed and took his dishes to the sink. "What wrong idea? That we live together and fuck? I think he got that idea already."

"No, you made it sound like we're in *love* or some bullshit like that."

"Did I now?" Angus laughed a little more and pulled Bill into a hug before kissing the side of his face. "Gosh, I'd sure hate for him to think a thing like that."

Bill frowned and zipped up his parka. "Get your coat on. And don't forget your thick gloves. It's cold out there today."

Angus muttered under his breath to Matty as he sorted through the coats on the pegs. "Nope, doesn't care about me at all."

"Not even a little," Matty agreed, smiling. He wondered if Rob knew about Angus as he watched Angus and Bill argue about whether to bring extra socks. Then they both swung their hockey skates on their shoulders, and Bill nodded at Matty.

"We're going in my truck," Bill said. "You're small so you can ride on the hump."

Matty resisted making a lewd comment.

"So, how long have guys been, you know, not-lovers?" Matty said as they headed toward Whitefish Lake, Bill's truck bouncing roughly on the back roads. A few times Angus put his hand on Matty's knee in anticipation of a rough patch to hold him in place so he didn't slide into Bill despite the waist seat belt.

"A month," Angus said.

"We're just roommates."

"I answered his ad to rent a room last summer. I don't know about him, but I wanted him from the moment I saw him. He was all bruised up at the time because some dick he'd been seeing did what he seems to want them to do." Angus shook his head. "It's not like bruises are my thing. I don't know—there was just something about him that made my insides hum."

Bill made a soft snorting sound, but a glance at his face showed he wasn't displeased.

"I'm pretty sure he thought I was straight," Angus said.

"Worst disappointment in my life when I found out you're a cocksucker extraordinaire."

Angus rolled his eyes. "So sad, isn't it? That I'm gay and proud of it and good at it? So awfully sad."

"Really unfortunate," Matty concurred. "Me too. Guess we're pathetic together."

Bill snorted again.

"Anyway, because we're roommates and getting involved seemed like a terrible idea—"

"And I prefer straight guys," Bill added.

Angus laughed softly and went on, "We didn't act on the attraction until last month. Turns out that for a gay guy I can cook up some pretty smokin' sex."

"So you still wanted him even though he wasn't straight?" Matty had to keep himself from coughing after saying the word 'straight.' A guy who had sex with another guy, even if he loathed himself for it, even if he abused the guy afterward, was not straight. He was fucked up for sure, and possibly bi, but not straight. Not in Matty's book anyway.

"Yeah." Bill sounded disappointed in himself.

"So you really like it when assholes beat you up?"

Bill sighed. "No. I like the thrill of getting a straight guy to do something they think they don't want to do."

"So the fact that Angus wanted to do it was a turn off for you?"

"Not enough of one, I guess. Maybe the stupidity of screwing my roommate made up for his ongoing enthusiasm. I don't know." He glanced at Angus again, and Matty felt belatedly embarrassed to be between them. Bill's eyes were warm with affection and his cheeks a little flushed. It was clear that no matter what Bill said, he had feelings for Angus that went beyond the pleasure of making a bad decision.

Angus winked at Matty, and then said to Bill, "I haven't punched your face flat yet, so I'd say this bad choice is better than your last ten."

"Well, that's true." Bill glanced toward Angus, and Matty again saw the glimmer of affection under his resistance. His eyes were gentle and his lips softened as he turned back to the road. "You're the best mistake in a while."

Angus elbowed Matty but said nothing at all. His lips were twitching and he looked out the window, faking a cough. Matty realized he was trying not to laugh at what was probably the best declaration of love he was going to get from Bill anytime soon. Possibly ever.

"Such a sweet talker," Matty said.

"You should hear him when we're screwing. It's all kinds of sweetness then."

"N'aw, that's kinda cute."

Bill grunted. "Sure, sure, make fun, but you'll be sorry for teasing me."

"Promises, promises!"

Matty shook his head in amusement, staring out the windshield at the majesty of Montana. It struck him as surreal that he, Matty Marcus, was riding in a pickup truck between two burly, roughneck men, talking about sex. He was pretty sure he'd seen porn that started out just like this—twinky, effeminate guy and two mountain men. He knew he'd definitely jerked off to that once upon a time. Matty chuckled softly at the very idea of Bill or Angus fucking him. It was laughably never gonna happen.

They rode quietly for a while, and Matty decided to turn the conversation away from their relationship. "So, Angus, are you from around here?"

"No, I'm from over near Libby. Came to Whitefish to work up at the lodge. I'm a ski instructor some days, other days a bell boy."

"I haven't been up there. I've heard it's a nice place, but I don't ski."

"It's beautiful—if you don't work there. Like just about anything else in the world, it's better on the outside looking in. But, all in all, it isn't bad." He jerked his chin toward Bill. "Got this asshole from the whole thing, so it's okay. Just gotta learn how to deal with entitled tourists."

"Tourists bring in good money," Bill said. "Plenty of them find their way down to Bill's Place at night. They tip well too."

The rest of the ride was filled with horrifying and hilarious stories about Bill and Angus' experiences with tourists. Having traveled quite a lot, Matty felt half inclined to apologize for all the jerks, and half inclined to deride them even more than they did.

Eager to contribute his own story, Matty was telling them about his own experience traveling to Japan with some especially bratty world-renowned figure skaters he was kind enough to leave nameless when they pulled into the state park campground. The parking lot by the beach was mostly empty. There was no one on the ice.

Matty walked toward the frozen bay slowly, his heart in his throat. The mountains rose up over the ice, and the sky was a stretch of endless blue. He wished desperately that Rob was here to share it with him. He'd skated in outdoor rinks and he'd skated on the Pages' pond, but this was something else. This was the edge of paradise, and if anyone was going to skate with him there it should be Rob.

"Well, better hurry," Bill said as two trucks pulled up beside them and a posse of men tumbled out. "Don't you want to be the first one out there today? The first to cut through that fresh ice?"

"Was it that obvious?"

"Shit son, you looked like you just saw God."

"It's a common look around here," Angus confided. "That's how we're so good at recognizing the expression."

A third truck pulled up and a teenage boy jumped down, a pair of hockey skates in his hands.

Matty hustled to get his skates on as Angus tested the ice. Bill's eyes were on the teenager, and Matty spared a glance over at the kid, who was now talking to one of the men from the group that had arrived shortly before him.

"Don't worry. I'm way ahead of him. He won't get on the ice before me," Matty said.

"Not worried about that. He offered me a blow job for a shot of whiskey at the bar last night before I yanked him out by the ear. He's trouble."

Matty looked over at the kid and measured him up and down. He couldn't have been more than seventeen. He was scrawny, with wiry limbs and a shock of black hair that made his pasty skin look even starker. His mouth was nice, though, and Matty figured he'd grow into his nose. One day, he might even be borderline handsome. But right now he was just gawky as all hell.

Matty's own gawky period had been excruciating, and he resented that his mother even had pictures bearing witness to it. As for the films of competitions from that stage of his life, he tried to pretend they didn't exist.

"Did you take him up on it?" Matty asked.

Bill snorted. "Does he look like my type?"

"Not in the least."

"Even if he was, do I look like a man who belongs in jail? Don't answer that honestly," Bill warned.

"With a pretty face like yours? Hell no."

"Damn straight. Besides, apparently I've got a *lover* or some shit like that." Bill rolled his eyes and then gazed out to where Angus was testing the ice further out on the bay.

Matty grinned at Bill.

Angus gave a thumbs up and extended his investigation out a bit farther, moving back quickly from a point about six hundred feet out. He returned to where they sat on a bench and plopped down next to Matty before taking his hockey skates from Bill.

"Where I turned back it's only about four inches, and beyond that it looked dicey. Stay on this side of that area."

He called out the same information to the men who'd arrived. It looked as if they were considering some cross-country skiing on the lake, and they debated if the safe ice extended out far enough to make it worth their while.

The kid who'd tried his luck with Bill sat down on another bench a few feet away and started on his skates just as Matty finished with his. Matty left Bill and Angus behind so he could be first on the ice.

It was a little bumpy under his feet, but not bad. He swept out onto it and immediately built up speed, feeling the effervescent Montana air glide over him, tingling against his skin. Laughter bubbled up in his chest. He let go of his disappointment that Rob wasn't there and flew over the ice, sheer joy pulsing through him as he instinctively shifted into footwork from an old program, dancing across the lake. Then he pushed up and leaped, landing a perfect single Axel. Maybe he'd try for a triple once he was warmed up. A double at least.

Matty heard some loud voices and the echo of applause bouncing off the ice and mountains. He bowed and grinned before showing off a little more.

Bill and Angus were on the ice now, and so was the teenager. He circled around them, and every once in a while he'd say something, but Matty couldn't hear what. Angus and Bill looked annoyed, but they didn't pay the kid much attention either.

Matty drifted in his own world of snowy mountains, beautiful wide sky, and the strong, fresh ice under his feet.

After working up a good sweat, he skidded to a stop beside Bill and Angus, who were setting up a hockey goal on one side of the bay.

"Kevin over there is determined to woo Bill away from me," Angus said, nodding toward the teenager who was now thirty yards away watching them closely.

"You know him?" Matty asked Angus.

"Naw. He came over and introduced himself to Bill, though. He was all, 'Remember me, big stud?'"

Bill sent the puck flying into the net. "He literally said 'big stud.'"

"No, he didn't," Matty said.

"All right, no, he didn't," Angus confessed. "But he might as well have. What he did say is that he thinks Bill is handsome."

Bill snorted.

"And he was wondering if Bill wanted to have coffee or sex sometime."

"Wow, brazen," Matty said. He'd never been that aggressive when he was seventeen, especially not with an older man. Of course, he was only twenty-two now and he did nearly throw himself at Rob, so maybe he couldn't really judge Kevin.

"Ridiculous," Bill said. "I told him to take a few years to grow into his aspirations a little, and maybe he'd be lucky enough to break off a piece of me one day."

"He actually told him he should go home and hit on boys his own age," Angus noted. "And *I* told Kevin that Bill already had a boyfriend."

Matty gazed at Kevin, who was now skating around dramatically, swinging his arms and mimicking Matty's earlier movements. Matty cocked his head and remembered the first time he'd seen Ben on the ice—so much determination and potential. This kid had none of that.

"Look at him." Bill marveled. He spit on the ice as he watched Kevin do a ridiculous, clumsy jump and then blow a kiss his way. "I think that asshole is simultaneously flirting with me and making fun of you."

"It's a feat," Matty agreed, not sure how he felt about being mocked, but intrigued by the kid's audacity all the same.

"I almost feel sorry for him," Angus said, watching Bill skate around the net with the puck. "It's not easy being queer at his age. He's probably desperate for someone to pop his cherry. It'd almost be a kindness to make sure he doesn't get hurt."

"You can explain that to the judge." Bill snapped the puck into the net again. "He shoots—he scores."

Angus tapped his hockey stick against his thigh and contemplated Kevin. "I just mean the kid's probably pretty desperate."

"You must love the sound of a jail cell clinking shut."

Angus rolled his eyes. "I'm empathizing, not plotting."

"Here he comes again."

Kevin kicked up ice as he skid to a stop next to Matty. "Bill, wanna show me how to shoot the puck?"

"No."

"C'mon. I'm a really fast learner."

"Then you should know what the word scram means. Or beat it.

Or leave. Or go. Or you're not wanted here."

Kevin frowned and took off a glove to scratch at a pimple on his forehead. He then tried to cover it with his hair. "Maybe a little bit of two on two?" He glanced at Matty and then amended, "Or maybe two on one? I don't want him on my team."

Matty almost said something smart back, but shut his trap. As much time as he'd spent on the ice, he'd never even held a hockey stick. He wouldn't want himself on his team either.

"C'mon, kid. Shoo. Scram." Angus shook his stick at Kevin, who smirked and jerked it out of Angus' hands.

"Want it?" Kevin asked. "Come and get it."

Angus just crossed his arms over his chest and shook his head as Kevin skated away, unwilling to be goaded into a game of chase.

"Couldn't you have just called the police the other night? Had him arrested for being underage in your club? Saved us this trouble?"

"Done empathizing with the little shit, huh?"

"You could say that."

Matty saw someone approaching from the shoreline out of the corner of his eye. He glanced over, and his heart stuttered.

Rob skated toward them with long, sure strokes, wearing a thick green coat that brought out his eyes, and a big grin on his face.

"Hey you," Matty greeted him before grabbing his coat lapels and pulling them both into a slow circle. "I thought you couldn't get away from being a sexy rancher today."

"The wiring issue didn't take as long as I thought. And when I couldn't stop thinking about you and how hot you look in your skating clothes..." He skimmed his hand down the front of Matty's coat. "Which of course you're wearing beneath a parka."

"You can still see my leggings, and my legs are spectacular."

"That they are. Anyway, I called Terry down from mending fences to finish up the rest of the chores."

Matty gripped Rob's lapels tighter and pushed against the ice, increasing the velocity of their spin.

"Skating with you on this beautiful lake on this gorgeous day was something I couldn't miss."

Matty's stomach twisted up sweetly. He threw his arms around Rob's neck and breathed in the warm, familiar scent of him. He lifted his eyes to the mountains as they continued to spin slowly. Rob kissed him, and Matty's knees went weak.

"Now, see, that's what lovers look like," Bill said.

"Then I guess you'll be twirling me around like that in a few minutes."

Rob broke free of their embrace and, holding Matty's hand, skated over to where Bill was still putting the puck in the net, and Angus was waiting for Kevin to return his stick.

"My man, Angus." They exchanged high fives and manly clasps on the shoulder. "Have you managed to convince him yet?" Rob asked.

"Convince me of what?" Bill asked.

"That he's not just your roommate with benefits."

"Are you in on this too? I swear, you think someone's your friend—you think you know him and can trust him—and the next thing you know he's plotting with your boyfriend to—"

Angus let out a whoop and grabbed Bill around the waist, tackling him to the ice rather hard if the *ooph* Bill grunted was any indication.

"You said it!" Angus crowed as they rolled around and tussled. "You said boyfriend."

"Bullshit." Bill grappled with Angus' bigger form, but was trapped under him. "No way, no how. Never woulda or coulda." But Bill's lips were curved in a bright smile, and he laughed quietly.

When Angus kissed him, Bill gave up struggling. After a few seconds of holding Bill down on the ice, Angus pulled back, looking triumphant.

"Get a room!" Kevin called from across the ice. "With me!"

Angus shook his fist at him, but only in jest. Disgruntled and red-cheeked, Bill muttered under his breath. It sounded like more annoyed denials from where Matty stood, but Bill's eyes were soft when he looked at Angus.

Angus lent Bill a hand up, and once he was standing Bill grabbed him by the collar and pulled him in for a kiss again.

Rob took in the nearly empty lake. "Can't believe how quiet is out here today. I guess everyone's getting ready for the big night tonight."

"There were guys here earlier," Matty said. "But they left after Angus checked the ice and said it was only safe out about six hundred feet."

"That damn kid stuck around, though," Angus said, dusting the ice and snow off his butt and coat while Bill did the same.

Kevin still skated around on the pond with Angus' hockey stick, brandishing it occasionally and mocking Matty's leaps. Matty wished he'd try for a jump and get a spanking from the ice like he so obviously deserved.

"Come on." Rob pulled Matty away from Angus and Bill. "Skate with me." As they reached the middle of the area Angus had declared safe, Rob said, "Remember how I told you Anja and I used to pretend to be on Broadway out in the fields?"

"Mm-hmm."

"Well, on the ice we used to pretend to be some Russian couple she adored from the Olympics. They were in love and got married and—"

"Ekaterina Gordeeva and Sergei Grinkov?" Matty's hand flew to his chest. "Oh, I loved them. The heartbreak!"

"Yes, he died, right? That was sad. But this was years before that. Anyway, I was pretty good at sending Anja up for a throw loop jump. She was quite good back then, now that I think about it. So maybe Ben did come by some of it honestly."

Matty licked his lips, his heart kicking against his ribs. Had he just heard Rob correctly? He used to throw Anja for jumps? "How old was Anja then?"

"Oh, ten? Eleven? We were just kids."

Matty bit into his lip. "Oh."

"Why?"

"Nothing. I was just wondering."

"Just wondering what? Come on, that's not the face of idle curiosity. That's the face of Matty-has-a-bad-idea."

"Hey, my ideas are often astonishingly awesome."

"Tell that to someone who didn't have an orange for dessert last night. You ate it like an orphan at British Christmas or something. I had to pretend to love it, too, because you looked so ecstatic to be eating something sweet and juicy."

Matty shoved Rob playfully, and he slid sideways on the ice. "I never said you had to pretend to love it. And if the grumbles and moans and whining was you loving it, I'd hate to see the tears and wails when you get an actual dessert."

"Excuse me?" Rob cupped his ear. "You just admitted that oranges are not dessert."

Matty laughed and shrugged. "Don't tell my brain. I'm trying to fool it."

Rob grabbed hold of Matty's hand and put his arm around his waist, and Matty grinned as they glided together.

"Come on, out with it. There was something about me and Anja and Ben and skating that had the wheels in your head going pretty fast."

"It's just...do you think you could still throw someone? Like me for example?"

"Probably. It's not like you weigh anything since you've starved yourself to bones and feathers at this point."

Matty punched Rob's arm but didn't argue with him.

The food conversations were tiresome. He understood Rob worried about him and preferred him with more flesh, but his coach would not. Competition was his priority, and it was easier on his joints and muscles if he was at fighting weight. One day, when skating wasn't part of his life anymore, he'd stuff his face with brownies and pizza.

For now, he was going to train to be the best skater in America and then the world. Gold required sacrifice, and his sacrifice right now had to be eating junk food. And eventually Rob. But that wasn't today. Today he was skating on a lake in the middle of paradise, and his boyfriend had unexpected—albeit rusty—experience with throw jumps.

"It's just…I've always wanted to try one."

"But if you landed wrong? Couldn't you get hurt?"

"Maybe, but I won't land wrong."

Rob laughed. "Of course not."

"I won't. I mean, if you're not strong enough to throw me, I understand. You don't have to make up other excuses not to try it."

Rob's eyebrows went up, and Matty laughed softly.

"Okay, let's talk it through first. Anja and I just felt our way, and I never threw her very high."

"I don't have to go high. At first."

Rob shook his head, laughing under his breath. "So tell me, what do you know about throw jumps?"

"Oh, plenty. Basically, a throw is an assisted jump. You don't actually throw me so much as help me into the air."

"Right," Rob agreed.

"We'd start out skating together, holding hands, to get momentum. Then when I signal, you can pull me close to face you like we're dancing. Like this." Matty took hold of Rob's hand, and held it in his, and then placed Rob's other hand on the small of his back. "See?"

"Okay."

"I'll release you as I go into the jump, and you'll use your hand to propel me higher."

"Right, that's how we did it when we were kids," Rob said. "Is it like riding a bike? Will it come back to me?"

"Only way to know is to try it."

"C'mere, you. Let's do this thing. Hold on. I'll say one, two, three and then we'll go, okay?"

Matty tossed his coat aside and shivered. It was freezing, but he couldn't jump properly with it on. At Rob's disapproving look, he waved his hand dismissively. "Just for a little while since the wind died down. I still have all my accoutrements." He indicated his hat, scarf and gloves.

They skated together, holding hands for momentum, and when Rob counted off, Matty pulled toward him, assumed the position, and went into his double jump. Rob's hand sent him slightly higher than his solo loop, but his landing was rough. He had to squat down and touch the ice to keep from falling, but it wasn't a disaster.

"That wasn't bad," Matty said. "Let's do it again."

Rob grinned, and for the next twenty minutes they worked together. Matty noticed how much Rob was sweating, but he didn't want to stop, a look of determination coming over his face as he worked to give Matty what he wanted. Again and again, he threw Matty into the air until Matty landed perfectly.

Rob applauded, and Matty grinned. "Good. Now higher. I'm going for a triple."

It only took a few more tries until Matty was launched much farther into the air. The height and rush of wind over him was thrilling. He performed the triple and landed gracefully, arms spread, fingers lovely, and chin up. Pride and affection for Rob rushed over him, and he skated back to kiss him.

Angus and Bill clapped, but Kevin snorted and laughed before spreading his arms and mocking Matty as he skated in a dainty circle around Angus' stick. Just as Angus made a move to skate toward him, Kevin picked up the stick and darted off again.

Rob looked like he might say something to the kid, but Matty wasn't ready to give up the thrill of being thrown yet. "Got a few more in you?" he asked.

Rob shrugged and rotated his shoulders. "Three more."

"See, I'm heavier than I look."

"You're amazing."

The sky seemed to catch Matty and hold him up as he twirled in the air, and on the third throw, for just a moment, he felt as though he could come out of the loop, spread his arms, and fly. Then he sensed the approach of the ice and landed effortlessly.

Bill and Angus whistled, and Rob presented Matty with a sweep of his arm, indicating that Matty deserved all the applause.

Kevin continued to troll them from the edges of the lake.

"Ignore him," Matty said when Rob rolled his eyes and opened his mouth to yell something. "Don't let him ruin our fun." He took Rob's arm and guided him back toward Bill and Angus' hockey net.

"Who is that kid? A tourist?" Rob asked.

"Don't think so," Angus said. "He might have just moved here. I've seen him and his family around town a lot the last few weeks. I haven't ever seen them before, and they aren't staying up at the lodge."

"This is his idea of picking up men, I think," Matty said. "Or a man. Bill seems to be his main target, but based on his idiotic contributions to conversation, I suspect he might be up for a threesome."

Rob clicked his tongue against his teeth. "Shouldn't he be in school?"

"Wherever he should be, he *definitely* shouldn't be out that far," Angus said, interrupting. "Little bastard is gonna get himself hurt."

Matty, Angus, and Bill watched as Kevin skated way past the safe area. Kevin zipped farther out, and then a bit farther, shaking the hockey stick and jumping up in clownish imitations of Matty's leaps.

"Shit, he's going to go through the ice if he doesn't watch it," Bill said, shaking his head.

"Come back!" Angus yelled, cupping his hands around his mouth. "It's dangerous!"

Kevin smirked and flipped Angus the bird, skating even farther out.

"Someone's going to have to get him," Rob said.

Matty looked toward Rob, Angus and Bill. They were all a lot heavier than him. He didn't think Kevin could hear them from where he was and probably thought Angus was threatening him. He shoved off and skated toward Kevin, whipping over the ice.

He could hear Rob, Angus and Bill shouting at him as he went, but he ignored them. He was the lightest and fastest, and he was just going to get close enough to warn Kevin. As Matty put his hands up to his mouth and started to yell, a horrific sound echoed across the lake.

Crack.

He swore he felt the ice jolt under him. A sick feeling shot through him, along with cold terror, and he looked down at his feet. But the ice was solid, not a crack or edge to be seen. Then he heard a splash.

Kevin's arms flailed and the hockey stick struck the ice as he went in. Matty could hear Rob, Angus, and Bill shouting, but he couldn't make out their words over the pounding of his own pulse. He cautiously skated closer until he got near enough that he could lay flat on the ice. It shuddered beneath him as he scooted slowly toward the blackness of Kevin's hair bobbing up and down as he fought the shock of the icy water.

Kevin finally gasped, gurgling and terrified. "Help!" He barely got the word out as he hyperventilated.

Matty crept forward until he neared the place where the ice cracked and broke off into a frigid black pool. Kevin's pale skin was already blue and his hair was black as oil. "Here," Matty said, taking hold of the hockey stick. "Grab the end."

The water that splashed Matty's face and soaked into his clothes as Kevin struggled was so cold it burned. He shook the stick at him. "Grab it. You can do it!"

Gasping, Kevin shook his head.

"You can."

Kevin screamed brokenly, wild and disoriented fear in his eyes as he clutched the jagged ice.

"Grab the stick, you little shit, or I swear to God, I will let you drown," Matty said through gritted teeth. Kevin reached blindly for the hockey stick, and Matty guided it into his hands. "Don't let go."

Kevin went under, but he held onto the hockey stick that Matty yanked on with all his might. Kevin's head came back up, his dark eyes wide and scared, his mouth gaping.

"Hold on! Get your elbows up on the ice." Matty tugged again, and that's when he felt, more than saw, Rob behind him.

"Stay back," Matty called out. "The ice is going. You're too heavy. Stay back there or we'll both go in the lake with him."

Rob's frightened cursing reached his ears, but Matty concentrated on dragging Kevin out. "Kick your legs!"

He heard Rob's voice yelling behind him, but he couldn't focus on that. "Come on," he said. "You can do this." He didn't know if he was saying it to Kevin or himself.

As the ice creaked ominously, Matty heaved Kevin's upper body out of the hole. Then strong hands gripped his ankles and jerked him back, dragging him and Kevin, still clinging to the end of the hockey stick, away from the hole. Matty glanced behind and saw that Rob had his ankles, Angus had Rob's, and Bill had Angus'. At the end of the chain, Bill hauled him and Kevin to safety.

As soon as they were clear of danger, Rob had his arms around Matty before they could even stand up. Matty clung to him and looked over to where Bill and Angus were taking care of Kevin.

"Ambulance is on the way," Angus said as Bill hefted Kevin up into his arms.

Kevin's lips were blue, and his already-pale skin was now a terrifying white. "I knew I'd find a way to get you to hold me," he muttered, shaking all over as Bill hustled him over the ice.

"Asshole," Matty whispered, rubbing at his eyes, which had suddenly filled with burning tears. He wanted to blame it on the cutting pain of the wind and the ice-cold water that had soaked his entire chest, arms, and splashed his face, but the truth was he'd been really damn scared for a minute.

"C'mon, we need to get you warm too," Rob said, his lips against Matty's hair. His breath felt hot against Matty's scalp. "You're soaked and you didn't even have your coat on. Did you bring a change of clothes?"

Matty nodded but then shook his head, remembering he'd left his bigger bag in his car at Bill's house. He snuggled close to Rob, who unzipped his coat and invited Matty to burrow under it as they skated awkwardly toward shore.

"I've got some of my clothes in the truck," Rob said. "Never go out on a lake like this without a change of clothes. Anything can happen. The ice can be thick enough to hold your weight in one place, but two feet over thin enough that you could go through."

Angus skated on ahead of Bill, rushing to the truck and pulling a First Aid kit out from behind the seat. As he and Rob moved across the lake, Matty found he was shaking hard. Where the arms of his shirt had soaked felt like the winter wind was slicing through his skin.

Kevin seemed out of it as Bill and Angus worked to get him out of his clothes in the front of the truck. His head lolled back on the seat and his breath came in fast pants. Bill rubbed Kevin's bare skin vigorously before wrapping him in an emergency blanket and holding him close. Angus shut the door of the truck.

"Well, looks like that fucking brat got what he wanted," Angus said. "Just not the *way* he wanted it. Bill's in there crooning to him like he's a baby."

"Is he conscious?" Rob asked.

"Yeah. He's not that far gone."

Rob laughed. "Good. Bill's a softy."

"You're telling me."

Matty shivered in the wind as he pulled off his wet shirt and gratefully accepted a soft tee and a plaid flannel shirt from Rob. It was, without a doubt, a combination he'd never willingly wear otherwise. Rob handed him his parka and wrapped a blanket around Matty's chilled lower half. His legs weren't really wet, at least. He felt warm and snug in Rob's clothes, and he surreptitiously smelled the collar of the shirt. It smelled like Rob's shampoo and laundry detergent. It made Matty feel safe, taking the edge off his still-rushing adrenaline.

As the ambulance siren sounded in the distance, Angus patted Matty's shoulder. "Because of Mr. Fast Skates here, he'll be okay."

Rob threw his arms around Matty and drew him close, kissing his temple and then burying his face in Matty's hair. Then he pulled back. "Good work. You were so calm. I'm proud of you."

Warm pleasure suffused Matty at Rob's praise. It felt almost as good as winning a medal.

"How did you know what to do? Getting on your belly and keeping your distance with the hockey stick?"

"I watched a lot of Discovery Channel when I was laid up last winter."

Rob chuckled. "Still, you should've waited for us. There's protocol when things like that happen."

"Ignore him. He was just scared shitless you were going to go in too," Angus said. "You did a good job."

Rob nodded and kissed Matty's head again. "I'm glad you're safe."

Matty remembered how vulnerable he'd felt lying there on the ice as it crackled under him, desperately trying to haul Kevin up. "I don't know about you, but I don't feel like skating anymore today."

"Not even a little."

After one of the paramedics checked out Matty at Rob's insistence, they decided to leave Matty's car at Bill's until the next day and drove back to the ranch. Matty stared up at the blue Montana sky, the line of the mountains, and the lush of the evergreen trees. When he closed his eyes, he could still feel the jitter of ice under his feet and see the white chunks bobbing around Kevin's pale face and wet, black hair.

A nauseous roll of *so close* filled his mind and body with possibilities of what could have been. What if he hadn't been able to reach Kevin? What if he'd gone in too? What if he'd drowned? He wasn't a strong swimmer on the best of days, and in freezing water all bets were off.

If things had gone just a little differently, he'd never get to train with Valentina, or win another gold medal, or prove to himself he had what it took to make it. He'd never see his mother, or his dad, or Joey again. He'd never kiss Rob again.

He shuddered. Those things hadn't happened. He was Matty Marcus, and he'd once again rocked his performance on the ice. The hero performance. He deserved a medal. Or horse whips.

Yes, maybe now was the time to ask about those horse whips.

Matty glanced toward Rob and swallowed hard. He could see from the tension in Rob's grip, and the quiet, urgent way he gazed out the windshield that now was not the time to bring up a subject they'd quarreled about in the past. He put the wish aside and reached out to take one of Rob's hands in his.

"I love you," Matty said, because now that he understood how close he'd come to dying, it seemed like he should tell Rob again.

Rob kissed his fingers and whispered, "I love you too."

Chapter Seventeen

The fire was warm, and the occasional crackle reminded Matty, as he drowsed on the sofa with a mug of hot water and bitters in his hand, of the sound of the ice breaking. He woke blearily to find Rob at the other end of the sofa, head resting on his fist, staring at the flames.

"Bill called. Kevin's parents met them at the hospital. He's going to be fine. Bill said when he left Kevin was still trying to convince him, with his parents listening and everything, that he would make a good third if Bill insisted on keeping Angus in his life. Bill said his parents blamed it on the hypothermia, but I'm fairly sure aggressive come-ons are just that kid's get-laid plan."

"Someone needs to teach him some subtlety," Matty murmured into his cup before finishing his water.

"Not you."

Matty laughed softly. "Seriously, though, when I'm *not* the least subtle person in the room, it's time to reevaluate the possibility that the end times are coming."

Rob took the empty mug. "You seem tired."

"My shoulders are sore from pulling him out of the water."

"Mine are sore from all those throws."

Matty smiled, remembering the exhilaration of the height and speed. "Thank you for that. You made one of my dreams come true."

"My pleasure, sweetheart."

"Do you want a massage?"

Rob's voice was warm with something more than just affection when he answered. "No, I was thinking *you* might want a massage. And maybe something more. Upstairs. In my room."

Matty *was* tired and still a little sleepy, but the idea of Rob taking care of him, of possibly fucking his lingering uncomfortable thoughts away, was appealing. He reached up a hand and let Rob pull him to his feet. "Lead the way," he said, dreamily.

Upon entering Rob's bedroom, Matty saw that plans had been set into motion for the evening long before the skating incident. Apparently, Rob's excuse to stay home earlier had been, at least in part, to have time to prepare for what he'd hoped the evening would be.

The room was darkened, and Rob struck a match to light candles. As the comforting scent of jasmine and vanilla lifted from the candles around him, Matty took in the dark sheets on the bed—the ones Rob liked because they showed Matty's jizz better. A small table had been set up beside the bed, displaying lotion, lube, and rough-looking ropes

Rob had never used on him before.

And there, on a carefully folded towel, lay two braided leather whips coiled beautifully.

Matty's breath caught.

"Today didn't go the way I planned," Rob said. "If this isn't what you want tonight—"

"Whips to ring in the New Year? I have a safeword," Matty reminded him.

Rob nodded. "In that case, clothes off. Folded on the chair in the corner."

Matty's eyes didn't stray from the whips as he pulled off Rob's flannel shirt and tee and folded them as instructed. He glanced away long enough to get his tight skating leggings off and to straighten the pile of clothes, but then his eyes were back on the braided black and red leather.

One whip was a short-looking single-tail. The other was also short, but looked vicious, with three short laces dangling from the end, each with a sharp-pointed knot tied into it. He imagined those would bite. He shivered in the cool air of the bedroom and swallowed hard.

Rob crossed the room to him, still fully dressed in his sweater and blue jeans. He gripped Matty's hair and jerked his head back, and Matty whimpered into Rob's mouth as he took a rough kiss.

"I've been wanting this," Rob muttered, "ever since you asked for it the first time. But it needed to be safe and it needed to be when I wasn't angry with you, because I need you to understand very clearly why I'm doing it. It's because you need it, because you need to feel something hard and unfair and disconnected from any pointless or petty frustration I have with you. Understand?"

Matty felt a rush of arousal at the promise of Rob's words, followed by an urge to refute them, to rebel and claim he needed nothing of the sort. But the truth was there staring him in the face. He did need it and if he didn't get it from Rob, he'd end up punishing himself with crummy performances and lazy training. What was he going to do when he left here? He *needed* this.

Rob grabbed Matty's balls in a tight grip and squeezed. Matty felt himself flush red as he squealed in surprise and pain.

"Do you understand?" Rob asked again.

Sweat broke out all over Matty as he struggled not to beg for Rob to release his hold. "I understand." His voice was breathless and high.

Rob nodded. "Come with me." Leading Matty by the grip on his balls, he took him into the bathroom. "Get in the bathtub. On your hands and knees."

Matty balls ached a little as he knelt down in the tub. He looked up at Rob, whose expression was calm and impassive. He smiled softly at Matty after a moment's regard.

"Hands and knees."

Matty leaned forward, the hard tub hurt knees and felt cold on his palms.

"Relax. I'm in charge."

Matty took a deep breath and let it out slowly, then allowed his neck to relax so that his head hung down.

"Good boy," Rob said warmly, as his hand trailed down Matty's back. "Now I'll turn on the water and insert the enema tube."

Matty closed his eyes and took slow breaths. He'd used Rob's shower system before to get clean, but Rob had never done it for him. It seemed intimate and raw. He felt himself drop into a quiet place in his head, open, waiting, and receptive. The enema nozzle pressed against him, warm from the heat of the water, and Matty moaned as Rob loosened the valve and the familiar, hot rush flooded him.

"That's it, that's good," Rob said, rubbing his lower back and buttocks as the water filled Matty up. "There. That's about all you can take."

He pulled the head out of Matty's ass, and Matty reflexively clenched his anal muscles to hold the water inside. Rob sat down beside the tub and pulled his phone out from his pocket. "Timer is set for ten minutes. Think you can manage it?"

Matty nodded, though he was already feeling the urge to release.

"Good."

Rob looked at his phone some more, sent a few texts, and then put it aside. He turned his full attention back to Matty.

"Okay?"

Matty nodded and held his ass clenched tight.

Rob knelt beside the tub and pulled his sweater off to toss in the clothes hamper behind him. He unbuttoned and unzipped his pants, releasing his cock, and stroked it slowly.

"You are so hot," he muttered. "Here on your hands and knees for me, taking what I give you. Your body is amazing." He ran one hand down Matty's back, fingering the skin over his ribs and spine. "The way you're put together. Your muscles. Your bones."

Matty wanted desperately to snark about his weight and Rob's belief that he could put some on, but he found it difficult to speak. He'd already fallen so far into the quiet space in his head where there was only Rob's voice, a vague cramping in his gut, and the concentration it took to keep from releasing before he should.

"Your ass," Rob said, his voice deep and rough. "God, your *ass*."

Matty made a soft noise as Rob lifted him up to a standing position and turned on the shower. The warm water pelted down, and he hadn't realized he'd been so cold. He turned around so that he was facing Rob, the water sluicing down his back, over his buttocks and thighs. Standing made it more difficult to repress the urge to expel, but he managed it, taking a deep breath and controlling himself.

"How long has it been?" Matty asked softly.

Rob flicked a glance toward his phone. "Three minutes."

Matty nodded. In some ways it seemed longer and in others shorter. He closed his eyes and let the water slide over him.

He heard Rob flick open a shampoo bottle and he bent his head to give Rob better access to his hair.

"Bend your knees."

Matty did, and the shift made the pressure in his lower abdomen stronger.

"Good. Now hold that position until I tell you to move. Keep your eyes closed and breathe."

Matty shifted his feet and then stood as still as possible. Rob took his time soaping his hair, pulling the extra down over his shoulders and back, washing the sparse hairs on his chest, and then dragging the shampoo down to his treasure trail, using all of the suds.

"Straighten and rinse."

Matty rinsed off, and that was when the first strong cramp hit, the urge to push the enema water out of his ass nearly overwhelming. He took a long breath, bending over to grip his knees and breathe through it.

"That's my good boy," Rob said gently. "You can do this."

Matty nodded, inhaling slow and long, until he could stand straight again and finish rinsing his hair.

Then Rob uncapped the conditioner. After Matty had rinsed it out, Rob turned off the water, took his hand and led him out of the shower. He turned to the light switches and flipped on the one for the heat lamp, which warmed the room quickly given that it was already steamy from the shower. Matty shifted between his feet, the pressure building inside him, taking up more of his concentration.

"Here," Rob said, toweling him off gently before guiding him to the toilet. "You've got two minutes left. Sit here but keep it in."

The toilet seat felt cool against Matty's ass and slick from humidity. Rob crouched down in front of him and pushed the wet hair out of his face, studying him carefully.

Matty whispered, "You can leave now. I promise I'll wait the two minutes."

Rob smiled, a white flash that was kind and yet unrelenting. "Oh, I'm not leaving. You're doing this for me, Matty. All of it. Don't forget that."

Heat flashed through Matty's entire body, and sweat broke out all over him. Rob had seen him in so many states of vulnerability—even on the toilet before, but only in passing. He'd never had Rob sitting in front of him, holding his hands, and staring at his face as he held back the urge to let fouled enema water erupt from his ass. He'd never thought that Rob would want to see that, or that he'd be expected to share such a disgusting, private moment.

He wasn't hard, and he could see from Rob's exposed dick that he wasn't hard either. This wasn't about that, apparently. It was about something else.

"Why?" Matty asked, groaning and shifting on the toilet as he worked to hold back the rising pressure against his anus. His gut cramped again, and he gasped. By now, if he was alone, he'd have released. He'd never held it this long. He never really had to. With his diet, his colon was usually clean and easy to prepare, but that wasn't what this was about, either.

"Because I want it. That's all that matters right now. What I want. Not what you want or what you understand. What matters on the ice? What your coach wants. What the judges want. No one cares what Matty Marcus wants. Not on the ice and not right now. You're not in charge here, Matty. I am."

"Unless I use my safeword."

Rob nodded.

Matty closed his eyes and worked hard to hold the water inside. He thought about his safeword, rolled it around in his head, and suddenly he wondered what his safeword was for the ice. Did he have one? If his boyfriend Figure Skating was going to beat the hell out of him, didn't he have the right to a safeword? If he did, what would it be?

Rob.

"One minute," Rob said.

Matty whimpered, gripped Rob's hands, and bent over so his face was hidden.

"Uh-uh. Look up. Open your eyes. Look at me."

Matty didn't know if he could do that. He couldn't look at Rob while shit and water poured out of his ass into the toilet. It was too much—too humiliating. He swallowed hard and considered the whips on the bed, and how much he wanted them. He wondered if he'd get to use them if he safeworded out of this part of the night.

Matty lifted his chin and looked into Rob's green eyes, and took slow, long breaths, but he felt his face crumpling as he fought to hold on the last little bit.

"Sixteen, fifteen, fourteen..." Rob counted softly.

As soon as "one" left Rob's mouth, Matty released. He stared at Rob's face, a flood of hot embarrassment rolling through him as the water purged from his bowels. He felt a flicker of anger deep down wanting to roar into a flame, a rage and a rebelliousness that wanted to tear up into the moment, spit in Rob's face, and tell him to fuck off.

But Matty held it down, tamped it back, and concentrated on showing Rob whatever he wanted to see. If that was this moment, right now, vulnerable and gross on the toilet, then he'd let Rob have that, dammit. Fine. *Fuck him.* And just as soon as he surrendered the anger, he felt something inside himself break and heal.

Matty didn't know how much of his struggle showed on his own face. He was always an open book, so he knew it was probably most of it, but Rob's face remained steady, warm, and calm. There was little to no reaction from him, aside from a smile as Matty collapsed, sweaty and still cramping a little, against his shoulder, tucking his face against Rob's neck and shuddering on the toilet.

"You did a great job. I'm proud of you," Rob whispered.

He reached behind Matty and flushed the toilet, and let Matty rest against him for a few moments. "Now wipe and get back into the shower."

The shower this time was, for the most part, perfunctory. Rob handed him a washcloth and soap and watched intently as Matty washed everywhere. Only near the end did Rob reach into the shower, take the soap and washcloth away, and tell Matty to put his hands against the wall. Carefully, with a great deal of care, Rob washed Matty's buttocks, crack, and asshole, and then told him to turn around. The same amount of gentleness was applied to Matty's dick.

"Nice work," Rob murmured as he carefully dried Matty off after the shower. "Ready for that massage?"

Matty let Rob hold him close and kiss his neck and cheek before he nodded and followed Rob into the bedroom again.

* * *

After the massage, Matty was loose and warm. He lay on top of the sheets on his stomach, languidly rubbing his now definitely hard dick against the soft material beneath him. Rob hadn't told him he couldn't, so he took what he could get.

Every once in a while, as Rob had worked on his muscles, he'd been hit by a wave of excruciating embarrassment that Rob had watched him on the toilet as the enema had exploded out of him. It occurred to him that the humiliation and accompanying rage was like being in the Kiss and Cry, waiting for the scores he knew were going to be lower than he needed. Waiting for the proof that he really wasn't good enough. Was a disaster. A mess.

But Rob had been there for him in the bathroom. Matty had let him see those things because he'd demanded it, and Rob had somehow adored him through the ugliness of it all. Why couldn't it be like that with skating too? Why was it only here, in Rob's care, that he could feel safe enough to move past those feelings of shame into exquisite vulnerability? He could never trust his audience or his judges enough to give them that. Could he?

"On your back."

Matty rolled over, his eyes slitted dreamily. He watched Rob, who was now in just his boxer-briefs, lift up the lengths of rope he'd noted earlier. It wasn't soft rope, but rough, the kind of rope that Rob used in the barns. It wasn't thick, but it would rub against his wrists and hurt if he pulled.

Rob ran his fingers over it, a considering expression on his face. "This isn't going to be an easy night for you."

Matty's heart, which had settled into a slow *thump-thump* during the massage, now lurched. He felt a shot of heat rise up from his groin through his chest to burn in his cheeks. His cock took up the beat of his heart, thudding against his belly.

"You remember your safeword."

It wasn't really a question. Rob was simply reminding him that he could end the night at any point. Matty nodded. "I remember it."

"Good. Then we'll begin."

Rob bent Matty's left leg up to his chest and used his shoulder to hold it there as he tied Matty's left wrist to his ankle. The rope was itchy and dug into his skin. Rob shifted his bent leg out, and then used another rope behind Matty's knee to bind it to the headboard. Once Rob repeated these bindings on the right side, Matty was spread helplessly on the bed with his hard cock, balls, and ass open to whatever Rob wanted to do with them.

Rob ran his hand over Matty's legs, dragging the hairs backward—a small discomfort in comparison to the rough rope on this wrists and ankles. Matty's pulse beat fast with the rush of excitement and dread at being so vulnerably exposed.

"Pull on the ropes."

Matty did, and they dug into him but gave him almost no leeway with his body. He could hunch up a little or use his stomach muscles to lift his ass up a bit, but he was otherwise held in place.

"Good." Rob smiled as he ran his hand over Matty's body, lingering to rub the pads of his thumbs over Matty's nipples. Then he moved back to the small table he'd set up by the bed. He lifted the blindfold.

"I want you to be loud," Rob said as he placed it. "Don't hold back your noises. I want to hear them all."

Matty nodded. The darkness behind the blindfold was complete and Matty sank into it. He breathed in and out through his nose and waited for something to happen. In the quiet, he could hear Rob stroking his own cock. Matty could imagine how he looked to Rob, tied and naked, hard for him, blindfolded and completely at Rob's mercy. Matty remembered the tight coil of the whips on the table. Would they be next? Would he be able to deal with them?

Rob trailed his fingers over Matty's cock and then gripped his balls again. Matty went very still as Rob increased the pressure, and whimpers stole out of his throat. Then Rob slid thin, rough rope over Matty's balls. Matty's pulse throbbed in his ears as Rob circled it around his sac, separated his balls, and pulled the rope tight enough that Matty gasped. Then he crisscrossed the rope up Matty's aching cock, the almost straw-like texture rubbing and pricking into him.

He tied it off underneath the head of Matty's cock. Then a sharp pain rocked through Matty from the tip of his dick, shuddering through his abdomen and up to his throat. He yelled. It took him a moment to realize that Rob had flicked his cockhead with his finger—*hard*.

A shock of fear touched him. The flick was so unexpected, so unfair that it hurt him emotionally and he felt unsafe. Rob's hand gripping his restrained balls didn't take that fear away, especially not when Rob let go and flicked his balls, one after the other. Matty cried out, his muscles going taut and his asshole tightening up.

"Shh," Rob said near his ear. "You can handle it. I know you can."

Matty shivered, and when Rob kissed his mouth, licking gently at his lip and soothing him, his fingers tracing Matty's jawline and the slight stubble on this chin that had grown in since that morning, he wished he could wrap his arms around Rob and hold him tight until the pain went away. Instead, he tried to relax into his restraints, to show Rob he was right.

He could handle this.

Rob pulled away and came back with a slick hand on Matty's cock. He rubbed lotion up and down over the rope. Matty squirmed, the sensation weird and uncomfortable. The rope hurt as his cock expanded under Rob's ministrations, and the sharp threads dug into his tender skin. His balls drew tight and ached where they were restrained. Then Rob began to vigorously work a place right under his cockhead that felt amazing. Matty groaned, tossed his head, and squeezed his eyes shut hard under the blindfold.

The sensation built and built, riding through him until he was sure he was going to come. He shouted a warning to Rob, who kept on rubbing him until Matty was so close to the edge he wasn't going to be able to stop from going over it. He tensed and held on tight, ready for the bright, goodness of orgasm, when suddenly Rob let go of his cock and flicked his balls again.

Matty screamed. Rob grabbed a fistful of his hair and kissed him through it, swallowing all the noise Matty let loose. Taking in the pain, the disappointment, the relief—all of it. When Matty could breathe again, he felt Rob's fingers toying with his asshole and he pushed against them, wanting them inside. Rob laughed softly and pulled them away, but he kissed Matty's nose, cheekbones, and ears, and then kissed his lips again.

"That was the easy part," Rob said.

Matty swallowed and tried to laugh, but it came out all messy and tainted with fear. He heard a sound that could only be leather sliding on leather, and then he felt the cool braid against his stomach. Rob slid it over him slowly, giving him a chance to feel it and anticipate how it was going to hurt.

"This is a quirt. Back in the old days some men used it to train horses, but it was most commonly used to drive cattle. It's designed for thick skinned animals. It's got three long lashes at the end that sting, and there are knots at the end of those that bite. It'll mark your skin. It will hurt. You will scream and probably beg for me to stop. You remember your safeword?"

Matty was so deep into the darkness behind the mask, so inside himself in a place of terrified and thrilled expectation that he couldn't speak or move. It wasn't until Rob touched his face and asked again that he was able to summon his breath to say, "Yes. I remember."

"And you *will* use it if you need it."

"Yes."

"That's an order."

"Yes."

Matty didn't know how long he could stand the anticipation. He wanted to feel the whip against his skin, but not knowing where it would bite into him, not knowing where it would fall or how much it would hurt or *when* was agony. He shifted against the sheets, tugged

191

lightly on the rough restraints, and whispered, "Please do it."

Rob lifted the quirt from Matty's stomach and placed a hand on Matty's outstretched left knee. "Hold very still. Don't move."

The first lash was hard. Fire raced over his ass where it had landed along the line of his buttocks and thigh, just under his balls, close enough that the pain seemed to ricochet into them and rage up his entire body. Matty didn't know why he had thought Rob would build up to the pain, but the realization that Rob was going to actually *hurt* him with the whips rocked him down to his bones. He put up a struggle in earnest, pulling at the ropes, trying to kick with his feet, screaming his head off in an urgent need to fight his way out of the moment.

Rob let him struggle. There were no words of comfort, no soothing touches, just silence as Matty bucked and fought, his skin rubbing raw on the ropes.

Matty shuddered and heaved and finally collapsed. The ropes had won, and he surrendered to the panic and fear that flooded him. Rob touched his arm then, sliding down to secure the ropes a little tighter. Then there was the terrifying sound of wind and whip and the three biting knots tore across the back of Matty's right thigh, then his left, then across his ass again. Matty shook and fought the ropes, he cursed and yelled and screamed, and he had the safeword right there on this tongue but he swallowed it back.

Rob counted out the lashes, but Matty could barely hear the words over the sound of his own begging, sobs, and whimpers. His pulse rushed in his ears, his heart was loud and beating wildly, heat seared through his skin all over, and his ass burned like he'd never felt before. The most his father had ever given him was one fast whack with a belt on two occasions, and this was so far beyond that, so far beyond what Matty had expected that he didn't quite know what to do. He wanted to safeword, but he didn't. It felt like he had fallen so deep inside himself that that he didn't know if he ever wanted Rob to stop hitting him. It was awful, but it somehow felt right.

"Okay?" Rob's voice was breathless.

Matty whimpered and tried to nod his head. He thought he'd managed it, but then Rob touched his cheek.

"Okay, Matty?"

"Yes." He sounded drunk, the word was slurred and he laughed, deliriously adding, "Offisher," and then, "Yesh, offisher, I'm okay."

Rob rubbed a hand through his hair, which Matty realized was no longer wet from the shower, but wet with sweat. He felt Rob rub a tissue under his nose, wiping away snot from where he'd been crying.

"Good to hear it," Rob whispered. "You're so good at this. You're doing a great job."

Matty hiccupped on a small sob. "Am I?"

"Oh, sweetheart. You have no idea."

"Tell me."

"You are so beautiful and strong. You're doing a wonderful job."

Matty whispered, "Thank you."

"Now a little break, and then you'll take some more."

Matty trembled at the thought of more. He had never felt the kind of pain that the quirt had inflicted—so raw, nasty, and biting, and the sting had been overwhelming. He didn't think he could handle it.

Matty felt the bed dip and Rob settle below him. Rob's hands soothed over Matty's ass cheeks and he blew gently on Matty's hole. Shivering, Matty moaned at Rob's tongue dancing over his asshole, licking and tickling, shoving in and fucking into his ass. He squirmed on it and pushed to try to get Rob's tongue in deeper. But Rob pulled away and then he was pushing his cockhead into Matty in a sudden, surprising move.

Matty bore down to take him in, the sting of Rob's thick cock hard to take with just a little spit as lube. Rob pulled out and rubbed Matty's asshole with the pad of his thumb. Then the mattress shifted.

"Okay." Rob sounded excited and a little strained. "This is a short single tail. It's easy to control and lays a stingy thud. It's not as biting because it isn't knotted, but it's sharp. Especially on tender places like this."

Matty arched, cock pulsing against the harsh rope as Rob snapped the end of the single tail against Matty's anus. It was shocking and so painful that Matty couldn't breathe. Another snap landed across his hole, jerking him against the ropes.

"Here we go," Rob said. "This is the real thing."

Matty had no idea what that could mean when he was already lost in a world of hurt, and then the count began. He had never felt pain like that before. Sharp, burning, tearing into him until he was shaking and yet his cock was pulsing, his balls were aching, and his asshole trembled.

Sound filled the air: Rob's harsh breaths, Matty's screams, the whip hitting skin, and the keening howls of Lila from downstairs, reacting to Matty's cries of pain. The whole room was alive with the intensity and power between them. Matty felt the ropes cutting into his arms and legs, and only then understood that he was still struggling, trying to get away from the whip.

Rob took hold of his leg, and then a short, fast, tight strike landed against his bound balls. Matty felt sweat break over him followed by pure, roaring agony, and he couldn't breathe, couldn't move, couldn't do anything but try not to black out.

Then Rob was near his ear whispering, "Okay? Are you doing all right, sweetheart?"

Matty sobbed and shook his head no. He wasn't. He couldn't do this.

"Safeword?"

Matty gritted his teeth together, sweat stinging his eyes and running down his face. He shook his head.

Rob gently rubbed his hands over Matty's legs, down his arms, and then he lifted the blindfold off. Matty kept his eyes closed, his body shaking and his cock pounding painfully against the restraint of the rope. He hurt all over. He could barely find his own thoughts as far down as he was in his own body, aching and hurting, burning and stinging, and underneath it all a deep, welling urgent need for something to release— something to break.

Rob touched his cheek. "Look at me."

Matty's breath hitched and small sobs trembled through him as he fluttered his eyes open. His lashes stuck together with wetness. Rob dabbed his eyes with a soft tissue and wiped his nose again.

Rob's face was calm and deeply affectionate. "You've been amazing, sweetheart. You deserve a reward now."

Matty didn't understand, but some part of him was disappointed. It couldn't be over yet. He wasn't quite there. He could feel it, deep inside him, the place he needed to have cracked open, forced to the surface, and defeated under the whip. He *needed* it.

"No," he whispered. "More. Please, more."

Rob bent low and kissed him. He was gentle and loving, his tongue moving sweetly along Matty's lip and against his teeth. He kissed Matty's sweat-soaked neck and then down to his nipples, before kneeling on the bed at Matty's side and untying the ropes around his cock and balls.

Matty tensed and hissed, the release of his bound genitals hurting even more than the binding. His dick felt scraped and raw from the rope, and when Rob took it into his cool, lube-slick hand, Matty whimpered. It was pleasure mixed with pain, and he couldn't decide if he wanted Rob to let go or keep touching him.

It wasn't his choice anyway. Rob moved his hand, stroking and releasing, teasing the tip and smearing the pre-come that leaked from Matty's cock.

"Watch me," Rob said when Matty let his eyes drift shut. "Look at my face."

It was hard to keep his eyes on Rob when his ass and the backs of his thighs burned and ached, when his hamstrings were stretched and angry, when his balls were still thudding, and his asshole was hot with pain.

"Are you hurting, Matty?" Rob asked, his lashes shading his eyes.

"Yes," Matty whispered.

"Is it really bad?"

Matty choked on a small sob and nodded. He stared at Rob's face, the curve of his jaw, the flush in his cheeks. Matty's cock responded to the touch of Rob's fingers and hands, and he started to feel the needful rush of pleasure piggybacking on the pain.

"Have you ever hurt like this before?"

Matty shook his head, sweat sliding down his forehead and tickling his cheek.

"What about the Olympics? Did you hurt like this when you fucked it all up?"

Matty remembered the rage that had risen in him when he realized he wasn't going to win. How he'd purposely let himself fall rather than lose for anything less than a royal fuck-up. Because it would've hurt too much otherwise.

"No," Rob said. "You didn't let yourself hurt like this did you?"

Matty shook his head.

Rob let go of Matty's cock, the sweetness of pleasure ebbing as Rob sat calmly by Matty's ass, looking down at him and taking him in. Matty felt far away and close at the same time. He could see himself in his mind's eye, spread out, exposed, his balls and cock tight and straining, his ass and the backs of his thighs red from being struck, and his face a mess of tears and snot. He was helpless there, vulnerable, and so close, but so far, from what he needed.

Rob reached for lube, slicked his own cock, and then pressed into Matty's asshole. Groaning, Matty bit his lip and bore down to take him in all the way to the hilt. Rob's thighs and hips felt cool against the heat of Matty's whipped ass. Matty wished he could touch Rob—feel his chest or back under his palms—and he struggled against the ropes a little, feeling the dig of them into his skin, but almost oblivious now to the way it hurt.

Rob took Matty's mouth in a kiss and began thrusting. It hurt where his hips smacked against Matty's wounds, and Matty cried out into Rob's mouth with each thrust. Rob didn't slow. He fucked Matty hard and fast, grunting and pulling away enough to brush sweaty hair from Matty's forehead. Then he kissed him again. Matty whimpered and took Rob's cock, the pressure on his prostate sending up flares of pleasure mixed with the slap of pain as Rob rocked into him.

Rob whispered in his ear, "I love you, Matty. You are so strong and beautiful. You take my breath away." He groaned.

Matty felt the ratcheting up of tension in Rob's tight thrusts, in the way he dug into Matty, and then Rob's cock pulsed and thudded in him as Rob cried out his pleasure against Matty's cheek.

Rob kissed him again. "You're doing great. So proud of you. You're taking this so well."

Matty felt an odd sense of dissatisfaction, like he wanted to disagree with Rob. He wanted to tell him that he hadn't been good enough yet, that he hadn't broken through to where he needed to go. There was still pain and fear he needed to truly touch. It was there, like water under ice. It was cold and teeming and full of death, and Matty needed a hole cracked through to it. But Rob thought he'd done so well. He couldn't beg for more. He couldn't let Rob down.

If this was all he was going to get, then it was all he deserved.

Rob pulled out, and Matty gasped as his tender asshole stung and twitched. Rob kissed his inner thigh and cock, and then he took hold of it and met his eyes again.

"This is it. You're going to come now."

Matty nodded, keeping his eyes on Rob's face. Rob's hand worked him until he was straining up for more. His body ached distractingly, and he had to focus his mind again and again on the pleasure brought by Rob's fingers pressing into his ass, rubbing against his prostate, and on the up and down, slippery lubed slide of Rob's hand.

He tossed his head back, arching up, reaching for the beautiful oblivion of orgasm. He was suddenly urgently aware that he wanted to be untied, that he wanted to be in Rob's arms, comforted and loved, and to get there he needed to come.

"I love you," he whispered, staring up at Rob. "I love you. I love you so much."

Rob kissed the side of his knee and worked harder with his hands.

"Oh God, I'm almost...please, Rob, that's...yes, please!"

Rob's flushed face remained gentle and calm as he said, "Should I ruin it?"

Matty didn't understand for a moment, but then he felt Rob's fingers leave his ass, and Rob's grip on his cock go loose. His heart kicked hard. He'd hurt so much and Rob had said this was his reward. He deserved it, didn't he?

No.

But he wanted it. He wanted it now that he could feel the coil of pleasure in his gut and the thud of his need in every cell of his body.

Even if he didn't deserve it, he wanted it.

"I've been good!" Matty cried, tears stinging his eyes and the words surprising him. He sounded so young and desperate. He sounded terrified.

After all the pain he'd endured, what if Rob didn't let him come?

"Please, Rob, I've been so good."

"You *have* been good," Rob said. "You've been amazing."

"Thank you," Matty gasped, moving his hips desperately with Rob's tightening hand. "Thank you."

"But amazing isn't always enough."

With Rob's hand moving relentlessly on his freed cock, Matty spiraled into the beautiful, tense, aching place where there was no coming back. He strained for the orgasm, reached for it and cried out.

"And you don't get to decide." Rob slid his hand up—and let go.

Matty bellowed and twisted against the ropes, his orgasm sweeping over him. Then pain ripped through the pleasure as Rob slashed his ass with the quirt again and again, each throb of his cock punctuated with agony that took his breath away and choked him with tears—the pleasure stolen and the pain taking it all.

* * *

He didn't know how much time had passed, but he was untied in Rob's arms, safe and strong. He was still crying and shaking, and saying, "I'm sorry. I'm so sorry. I'm sorry," over and over though he didn't know exactly why.

He only knew that at the very end, Rob had done it. He'd broken through the ice, and the feelings under it were too strong for Matty to handle on his own. There was so *much* fear, so much guilt, sorrow, and humiliation. So much self-loathing, and a desperate, consuming need for forgiveness.

"It's okay, Matty, I've got you," Rob whispered, rubbing his back and kissing his temple.

Matty curled into Rob's arms and clung to him. "I'm so sorry," he whispered again. "I'm sorry."

"I know, sweetheart, I know."

Matty felt his heart break as another wave of emotion sloshed up, a swell of something small and needy, almost childlike in its bottomless fear.

As time passed in a haze, more swells of ugly feeling rose in him, breaking again and again, shuddering through his body and shivering across his skin. He cried like he had never cried before, and Rob held him, soothed him and whispered that he was okay. That nothing Matty

ever did or didn't do would make him anything less than okay—
anything less than amazing. That he was strong, brave, and beautiful.

"You're strong enough to let yourself hurt, Matty. That's the
strongest person there is." He kissed his again. "Happy New Year,
sweetheart."

It was a long time before Matty calmed enough to drink some
water, and even longer before Rob could smear thick aloe over Matty's
ass and the back of his thighs. He brought food, and Matty didn't say a
word about calories as he gobbled it up. He was too exhausted. He felt
scrubbed raw, inside and out—like everything dirty about him had
been flayed under Rob's whips and washed away in his own tears.

When Rob helped him to the shower to wash away the sweat,
Matty almost didn't recognize himself in the mirror. His face was puffy
from crying, his eyes red-rimmed, and when he turned for a glimpse of
his ass, he gasped at how red it was. But he was shocked that there were
no welts. The pain had been so intense, he was certain he'd have welts
or broken skin. Yet there were only sharp, red lines and some darkening
bruises.

"You'll still have some bruises tomorrow," Rob murmured. "But
they'll fade away completely in a few days."

Matty wanted to ask how Rob knew that. Had he used the whips
on someone before? Had someone used them on *him* when he was
experimenting with dominance and submission after his parents' death?
Why did that bother Matty? Rob needed to be practiced at these things
to be safe, and yet the idea that anyone else might have been as
vulnerable with Rob as Matty had just let himself be was somehow
terrifying. Matty wanted to be the only one Rob had ever taken that far.

After the shower, Rob applied more aloe and went downstairs to
make dinner. Matty distantly heard the sound of the back door opening
and then the *thump-thump-thump* of Lila's feet on the stairs. She
bounded up onto the bed and then approached him cautiously.

"Hey girl," Matty whispered. His voice sounded scratchy and
worn. "Come here."

She scooted across to him and rolled on her back next to his leg,
exposing her brown and white stomach. Matty rubbed the soft fur on
her chest. Her eyes closed, and Matty shut his own. The sounds of Rob
in the kitchen drifted up, all light clatters and the opening and closing
of cupboards, and Matty felt warm and tired. His body ached and his
soul felt worn, but he was filled with a sense of hard-won peace.

Eventually the scent of Rob's mother's Southwestern Chili Burger
and Bean Soup drifted up to him, and he fell asleep next to Lila with a
smile on his face and the memory of Rob watching him eat at the Pages'

house on that cold day in October filling his mind.

* * *

Training at the rink in Whitefish the next day, Matty rubbed his fingers over his chafed wrists and remembered Rob waking him that morning with kisses, soft words of praise, and a hot, slow, delicious blow job that left Matty feeling relaxed.

"Remember what we did last night," Rob had said as he sent Matty on his way to care for the horses. "Remember that you're brave enough to hurt. Don't let yourself give less than you're capable of giving."

Matty took several turns on the ice, getting accustomed to the way his bruised ass and thighs pulled and ached as he moved. Breathing through the discomfort, he executed several doubles and triples without much trouble. Then he went up for a quad.

The ice smacked his bruised ass hard and tears stung his eyes.

Amazing isn't good enough.

Quads had become the mark of champions in the time Matty had been away. He stood up, stuck his chin in the air, and tried again. This time in his mind he was competing against Alex and Vance at Nationals. He could imagine the crowd, the expectant hush and restrained applause, and when he fell again, he could almost hear the gasp of disappointment. He slapped his thigh as he stood up, recalling the pain of the whip.

His heart hammered as he circled the rink, went up, and fell again.

"Dammit," he cursed.

Why was he even doing this? He could just go home to Rob and eat soup until he got fat as a hog and roll around in Rob's love and affection. He could call out the safeword on this skating bullshit, walk out of the rink, and never come back. He could do that.

But he wouldn't.

You can't skate if you don't fall, he remembered telling Rob.

Memories of the night before flooded him and he ducked his head to hide his flushed cheeks. He'd put it all on the line for Rob, and even though he'd had his pleasure stripped from him at the last second, he wouldn't change what they'd done. Rob's arms around him, the struggle to express the wells of emotion the whips had opened up in him—all of it had been worth feeling, worth doing. Even the pain. Especially the pain.

He pushed around the ice, gaining momentum. "You can't win if you're not willing to lose, Matty," he whispered to himself.

It was all there somehow, tied up inside him—pain and reward, winning and losing, rage and joy, self-loathing and satisfaction. He had found them all the night before, teeming below the surface. He held the lessons close now, a strange set of new, inspiring friends, and he whispered, "Don't safeword, Matty. You can do this."

He tried again.

CHAPTER EIGHTEEN

February in Whitefish meant the Winter Carnival. Matty hadn't been sure what to expect, though he'd told Elliot he was sure there would be a bunch of roughnecks doing absurd things involving beer, cattle, and horses—and possibly clowns.

From the looks of things, he was mostly right. There were no clowns in sight, but plenty of people acting like them. There were events on skis and events with horses. He wasn't sure if they were going to all of them, but he'd already been told the skijoring competition was a must-see. Ben was especially excited about it and had spent most of a late breakfast at Loula's explaining to Matty how horses pulled the skiers at rapid speeds until they hurtled off a ski jump.

After breakfast, they'd joined most of the town, or so it seemed, at the edge of Whitefish Lake for another of the main events—a thing called the Penguin Plunge, which entailed clearly insane people voluntarily jumping through an opening in the ice on Whitefish Lake to raise money for the Special Olympics.

"Are they really going to do this?" Matty asked, staring at Bill and Angus, who were dressed in nothing but swim trunks and T-shirts bearing the Bill's Place logo. Angus had a red scuba mask over his face, and Bill wore a tiara, which, rumor had it, Angus had forced on him after losing a round of cards.

Rob and Matty stood leaning against a wooden picnic table guarding the small pile of clothes Ben had left there. Matty couldn't believe the number of people in the crowd. There were so many insane folks in the town that they'd actually been cordoned off into groups to take turns jumping in. Many of them were dressed far more outlandishly than Bill and Angus—he saw one man wearing a toga and another dressed as a pirate—and all of them were going to jump into the frigid, dark water.

"Yep," Rob said. "It's for a good cause." His eyes roamed the crowd restlessly, keeping an eye on Ben, who was in the second group.

Ben hadn't planned on going into the freezing water when they'd arrived, but when he'd seen Rebecca—the girl Matty knew only as his fan from the grocery—in a bikini and robe, shivering by the side of the crowd, he'd changed his mind.

"I've got my bag in the truck," Ben had argued when Rob had asked what he'd change into afterward. He'd spent two days in Libby with his mother while she interviewed for a slightly higher-paid position in a private elementary school there. "I've got plenty of clothes.

C'mon, Dad, please?"

He'd looked toward Rebecca, who was entirely too old for him, but it didn't seem to matter to Ben. Not when she wore a cheery smile and was looking very pretty in the cold morning air.

"Seriously, Dad, it's for a good cause. I'll pay you back even."

Rob had sighed heavily, looked at Rebecca and then at Matty, and eventually pulled cash from his wallet and handed it over. Now Ben orbited around Rebecca, along with three other boys who were much closer to her age.

"Does she have some kind of reputation or is she just the prettiest girl this town's got this year?" Matty asked.

"She's a sweet girl," Rob said. "Her parents are good people. She's pretty enough. Not every boy over there is thinking with just his dick."

"Your boy surely isn't."

Rob sighed. "Actually, he probably is. He's hit that age. Anja says he's spending a lot of time in the bedroom with the door locked."

"Oh yeah. I remember that. I got hard every time my dad had some kind of sport on the TV. Between football asses and the arms on basketball players, I was going out of my mind for the better part of several years."

Rob chuckled. "Well, that's her brother next to her now."

Matty looked him over. He was mature-looking with a nice chest and tight nipples raised in the winter air.

"I'm sure he'll keep the wolves at bay."

"Well, looky there," Matty said, indicating the surly-looking Kevin, who had approached from behind one of the stand-by emergency trucks.

Kevin was also staring in Ben's direction, though he seemed much more interested in checking out the boy Rob had referred to as Rebecca's brother.

"Our favorite little shit," Rob said.

"Yep." Then Matty's eye was back on Ben. "Oh bless him. He's going to stand on his head and sing the alphabet if she doesn't at least acknowledge him soon."

"Hormones. They make us do really stupid things."

Matty laughed, remembering the blow job he'd given Rob in the bathroom of the Amtrak station that morning while they'd been waiting for Ben's train. That'd certainly been a stupid thing to do, but Matty had felt inspired and Rob hadn't said no.

Even so, Matty still felt a little wary of the knees of his jeans now, and probably would until he'd washed them in scalding hot water. He'd been careful when eating his single egg for breakfast not to allow his napkin to brush across them, and he'd made Rob use hand sanitizer after he'd reached under the table to grip his knee. Who knew what all was on that bathroom floor? Other people's jizz, in all likelihood.

"She talked to him," Rob said, chuckling. "And now he's going to blow it."

Matty turned his attention back to Ben, who was positively luminescent as he gazed up at Rebecca. His lips moved very quickly and Matty had no idea what he might be saying. Kevin, who had moved closer, looked impressed, which couldn't be a good sign, since Kevin thought appropriate come-ons included stealing hockey sticks and falling through thin ice.

Rebecca ruffled Ben's hair and turned back to one of the older boys. For a moment, Ben's face was ecstatic, but then his shoulders dropped, as the realization seemed to hit that he'd been given the "you're a cute kid" brush-off.

"She used to babysit him while Anja studied, back during her BA. I think he was three," Rob said. "I bet he doesn't even remember."

"Bet *she* does," Matty said, chuckling.

"Yeah. And now he has to jump into freezing cold water all because he wanted to impress a girl who will never see him as more than the kid whose ass she wiped."

"There's a lesson here. I'm not sure just what, though."

"Don't commit to something that's going to hurt unless you're doing it for the right reasons."

"Well, it's for a good cause," Matty reiterated.

But as the minutes ticked by waiting for them to start the Penguin Plunge, he turned Rob's words over in his head. He considered the night Rob had committed to hurting him with the whips. What was Rob's reason for that? Matty was only just barely coming to understand his own reasons for wanting the pain, but Rob's reasons for giving it to him seemed a total mystery.

A horn sounded. Bill and Angus' group hit the water. Howls erupted and curses escaped into the open air as the cold water splashed and churned around a dozen bodies moving quickly to get out. Bill and Angus laughed together, slapping each other on the back, and raced toward the waiting hot tub that had been set up opposite to soak out the chill.

"What is the right reason?" Matty asked, thoughtfully. "What's a good reason to do something that hurts?"

Rob cleared his throat and looked down at the ground, scuffing his toe in the snow. "Why? Are you thinking of something in particular?"

The flush in Rob's cheeks let Matty know he was remembering the night with the whips, too, but Matty meant the question as so much more than that.

He turned his gaze away from Rob, unwilling to look at him as he asked. He watched Angus and Bill in the hot tub, splashing each other and chortling with the other men and women who'd shared their experience. Was there anyone in his or Rob's life who would understand what it was they'd done together and what kind of hurt walking away from each other now entailed?

"I guess I'm wondering why you're doing this. This thing with me."

"I ask myself that every damn day." Rob's voice was gruff, like it was hard for him to say the words but he was forcing them out anyway.

Matty stomach twisted. "You don't have to. We can quit."

The crowd teemed around them. Mrs. Guthries from the grocery store was in the next group to jump in the water, wearing a purple bathing suit and a tutu. Matty would never be able to wipe the image from his mind. Strangely, he wasn't sure he wanted to. Everything about Whitefish was somehow painful and yet precious.

"I've got a safeword, too, Matty," Rob whispered in his ear. "I haven't used it yet, now have I?"

Matty bit his lip and nodded. "Once. Whuffling. Remember?"

Rob laughed. "Okay, yeah, but not when it comes to us. It's going to hurt when you leave, but I can take it."

"It'll be too late to safeword then. You should do it now."

"Should I? You don't think I'm as tough as you?" Rob asked. He gazed down at Matty, his eyes going a darker shade of green. "Or is trying to get me to call it quits just another way for you to punish yourself?"

Pressure weighed on Matty's chest and he felt like he couldn't breathe. He didn't want Rob to break up with him. He wanted Rob to beg him to stay, to somehow make it okay for Matty to safeword out of skating, because it was so much easier to be with Rob than it was to pursue his dream. None of the judges would ever love one of his performances as much as Rob loved his performances in bed. Not unless he was so much better than he was now and worked so much harder, and he was afraid—terrified—that he couldn't do that.

Rob's expression settled into a sadness that hurt Matty's heart. "Well, I won't give you that out, Matty. I won't give you *any* out that doesn't involve you making the call for yourself. You should know that by now."

Matty swallowed around the tightness in his throat. The crowd, the carnival, and the Penguin Plunge seemed to fade away as he took in Rob's words. Even if he wanted to give up skating, even if he *could*, Rob expected more of him and he couldn't disappoint him. It would be worse, somehow, than disappointing his parents and himself. It would be the easy way out to give up now, to live with Rob and become something else. Someone else.

But that wasn't what Rob wanted. That wasn't the man he'd fallen in love with.

"Dad!" Ben's shout drew Matty's attention. It was his group's turn to go in and he stood with Rebecca, gripping her hand. How he'd managed that, Matty didn't know, but Ben's face was ecstatic, excited, and terrified. He was stripped down to just his jeans and his chest was already turning bright pink in the cold air. He reminded Matty of how he always felt just before skating at Nationals or Worlds.

Rob pulled out his phone and took a few pictures. Rebecca quaked, but she held Ben's hand firmly. As they plunged into the water together, she pulled Ben close to her, laughing and screeching.

"This shit is crazy," Kevin said, approaching from where he'd been lingering by the cordoned-off groups. "Being in that water is *not* fun." His eyes roamed over Rebecca's brother's chest and abs as he raced with Ben and Rebecca to the hot tub.

"How are you feeling?" Rob asked, clapping a hand on his shoulder. "Good as new?"

Kevin shrugged. He peeled his eyes away from the skin on display. "I guess. I'm not dead at least. Though if I keep on living in this town, I might want to be."

"Why's that?" Rob sounded genuinely concerned.

"I don't know. There are no gay kids here, are there? Just gay grown-ups and none of you will have sex with me." He flicked his eyes to Matty. "Not that I want to have sex with all of you. No offense. I mean, thanks for saving my life and all, but you're not my type."

"*Nyet problem.* Happy to oblige," Matty said, laughing softly. His stomach still churned a little from the conversation he'd been having with Rob, but he was willing to leave it behind. It changed nothing anyway. It just made him feel like puking.

"I don't know about that," Rob said. "There's a Gay-Straight Alliance at the high school, isn't there?"

Kevin frowned and shrugged. "Maybe. I haven't really heard anything about it."

"Well, there is, and you should look into that before you throw in the towel. Do your parents know you're feeling this way?"

"Yeah. I guess. I mean, we had to have a long talk about how going to Bill's Place wasn't okay and trying to get older men to have sex with me wasn't okay, and how I just need to calm down and give everything time to settle." Kevin looked uncomfortable. "But they told me it was all right that I was gay, and they want me to be happy. Whatever that means."

"It sounds like your parents are supportive. That's good," Rob said warmly. "Have some patience with life. Things don't always happen when you want them to. They happen when they should."

"Cue up some Mick Jagger," Kevin said in a surly tone, but Matty noticed his shoulders relax as if Rob's words had comforted him a little.

Patience. It seemed like an easy thing to buy into under a massive Montana sky while watching a bunch of lunatics jump into freezing cold water. It was easy to just forget about things like Champs Camp, competitors with amazing quads in their programs, and limited spots on the Olympic team. For a moment Matty wanted to scream *cowbell* at the sky and just safeword it all away, embrace this reality and life, throw away the pain of training, competing, and failing. Even the pain of winning.

Instead he took Rob's hand and watched Ben in the hot tub with Rebecca, chattering away to her, though she wasn't paying that much attention.

Patience came in all kinds of forms, and sometimes patience hurt worse than anything else.

But he could take it.

* * *

"And then the horse went flying—*whoosh* into the snow bank, and he was okay, but the rider totally did this flip through the air and—"

Matty felt a flash of sickness at the memory of the skijoring accident. The rider had been all right, but the moments before the emergency personnel had made it to him had been filled with images of snapped necks and broken spines.

Rob passed Matty a plastic cup of punch with a reassuring smile. Rebecca looked pretty interested in Ben's tale of horror, though the teenage boy next to her—her date, apparently—seemed ready to strangle Ben given the opportunity.

The Whitefish Winter Carnival Gala was pretty much exactly like Prom. Not that Matty would know since he didn't go. It had taken place at the same time as an ice show he'd been scheduled to perform in. He still wondered sometimes if he would have been daring enough to ask a male friend as his date. He liked to think he would have.

The gala was held in the school gymnasium and decorated with glitter-covered cardboard cutouts of palm trees and giant sea shells. The theme was Royal Beach Party—so half the attendees were dressed in courtly garb and the other half wore Hawaiian shirts, grass skirts, and fake coconut bras. So, perhaps it wasn't so much like Prom after all.

Matty wore black skinny jeans, a white blousy silk pirate shirt, and a tiara. He'd also slipped on a red princess sash that wrapped around his chest proclaiming him the first place winner of the Falling Leaves Figure Skating Competition in Tidewell. He had no idea what had possessed his mother to pack it—at times he was convinced she'd been drunk when filling the boxes she'd mailed to Montana—but it struck a vibrant chord with the rest of his outfit, and he thought he looked quite regal, if not very beachy.

Rob had chosen to be a fuddy-duddy and wore only a nice pair of black pants and a green button-up shirt that set off his eyes. At Ben's insistence, he also sported a *Hello, My Name Is...*sticker with "King Boring Pants" written underneath. Matty was amused by the designation but was fine with Rob's choice to remain low-key. He made a better backdrop for Matty that way.

As for Ben, he looked adorable in a Hawaiian shirt and some nice-looking board shorts. Though the truly adorable part was how he gazed at Rebecca in her clamshell-print 1950s-inspired dress. Matty decided she had rolled around in straight-boy nip before arriving, because she drew the eye of nearly every man under the age of twenty-five. He noticed three boys who seemed immune, and only one of them was Rebecca's brother. He thought it was too bad Kevin wasn't there to see he had a few comrades in arms at least.

"Rob, dear." Mrs. Guthries drifted up with a drink in hand, having apparently survived her dip into the freezing cold of Whitefish Lake. "Can we be expecting any announcements soon?" She looked at Matty with the glittering eyes of someone who'd had a bit too much to drink.

"About?" Rob sipped his Jack and Coke, his eyebrows creasing in confusion.

"About our friend the figure skater here," Mrs. Guthries said, nudging Matty with her elbow. She'd smeared some blue eye shadow on her crepe-paper eyelids and red lipstick over her lined mouth. She looked pretty for an elderly person. Or at least like she'd made an effort, and that was more than Matty could say for his own grandmothers, who had pretty much declined into decrepit old-ladyhood without a fight.

"Why don't you ask him, Mrs. Guthries?"

She turned to Matty expectantly. "Well? What do you have to say for yourself, young man?"

Matty smiled his media-smile. "I'll be returning to competition later this year. I'm pleased to say I've been taken on by a superb coach, and I believe she'll make all the difference in my future career. I'm cautiously optimistic that another Olympics is in my future."

Mrs. Guthries' lips twisted and her brows drew down. "That's wonderful, but what does that have to do with anything?"

Matty laughed in nervous confusion. "I'm sorry. I don't follow."

"I meant are the two of you going to make your relationship official? Or are you going to continue living in sin?" She clucked her tongue and then chuckled as though she was making a grand joke.

Matty blinked at her, astounded by her presumption. He said tartly, "I don't actually live with him. We just sleep together."

Rob made a strange choking noise as he swallowed his Jack and Coke. Matty patted his back.

Mrs. Guthries seemed torn between laughing and being scandalized by Matty's comment.

"Mrs. Guthries," Rob said hoarsely. "Matty will be returning to the East Coast soon. I'm sorry to disappoint you, but questions like yours are not only impertinent but very premature."

Matty rubbed his hand up and down Rob's back, feeling the fabric of his shirt underneath his fingertips and the strong, broad muscles beneath.

"Is that so?" Mrs. Guthries looked at Matty with suspicious disappointment, as though she had caught him red-handed stealing from the till and now expected him to lie about it.

"I'm afraid so," Matty said. "It's been wonderful living here—a much-needed break from the life I've led before—but it's time I got back to pursuing my dream."

"I see." Mrs. Guthries took a sip from her drink, a light-pink and frothy thing, and then made a sound that could only be described as a harrumph. "Well, I suppose commitment is too much to expect from young people these days." She swept away with her nose in the air.

"Wow. What the fuck?" Matty asked.

Rob sighed. "She's always been a little overprotective when it comes to me. I came out to her when I was still a teenager and she's made my happiness a personal mission. Which, in a way, is kind of sweet."

"And yet, in a way, it's kind of not."

"I've broken her heart many times over by refusing to go on a date with the gay son of her housekeeper or her dentist or her husband's Navy pal. But I know she just wants me to be happy, I suppose she thought you were it." Rob smiled sadly and placed his hand on the back of Matty's neck, dragged him closer, and gazed down into his face. "Can't blame her for thinking that. I mean, look at you."

Matty's stomach hurt. He wanted to kiss Rob and whisper his affection. He wanted to call Mrs. Guthries back and tell her that he *was* committed—to figure skating—and that it would be disloyal to himself and to his family if he threw it over now for the chance at some normal life as a "rancher's wife" here in Whitefish with Rob.

Then he wanted to do exactly the opposite of that and drop to one knee and ask Rob to marry him. He wanted to tell Mrs. Guthries and the room at large to get ready for the biggest, gayest wedding Whitefish had ever seen, because he wasn't going anywhere. He wanted to reverse time and never have been injured so he'd never had needed to come here at all. So he'd never know what it was he was going to lose.

Instead he said, "May I have this dance, Mr. Lovely? Or will a hate crime result from our bodies moving so close together so publicly?"

Rob looked over the crowed of gathered townspeople swaying slowly to some song that Matty remembered from the *Dirty Dancing* soundtrack. He thought Patrick Swayze had even sung the song himself. He wasn't sure. But it didn't matter because Rob took hold of his hand and pulled him toward the dance floor. Matty could feel eyes on them as Rob put his arms around Matty's waist and they began to rock back and forth with a half-foot of space between them—pushing the envelope, but chaste enough.

"I danced with Anja in this very same gym when I was fifteen," Rob said. "Mr. Charlo went around with a measuring tape and enforced the six-inch rule."

Matty laughed and moved a little closer. Rob dropped his forehead to Matty's and they swayed back and forth, eyes closed, while the townspeople of Whitefish thought whatever the fuck they wanted to think. They were amazing together, fabulous, and beautiful.

It was better than any Prom Matty had heard of in the history of ever.

* * *

"Hi, Mama," Matty whispered into the phone. He was in Rob's closet, sitting on the floor next to Rob's four pairs of nice, if incredibly common, shoes. He wrapped a fallen sweater around himself, and let the legs of two decent suits rub against his face. They smelled of old cologne, a scent he didn't recognize and that Rob never wore now, as far as Matty knew.

"Honey?" Donna's voice was sleep-blurred and confused. "Are you okay? Matty?"

Matty could hear his father rustling in the background, the soft rumble of his name on his father's lips.

"I'm okay," Matty said, closing his eyes and leaning his head back in the closet. "Physically, I'm okay."

"He's okay," his mother said, her voice a bit smudgy as though she'd put her hand over the mouthpiece to give Matty's dad the news. "So, physically you're okay, but emotionally...did you and Rob break up?"

"No. Nothing like that. It's just...Mama, tell me what's wrong with me."

"Honey, nothing is wrong with you. What's going on?"

Matty pressed his fingertips to his eyes. "I'm so in love with him, Mama. I feel like I might die. Like, just thinking about not being with him makes me ill. Truly ill. But I can't stay. I've got to go. I have to skate, and try for the Olympics again, and go on with my career. I can't quit. What's wrong with me? Why can't I just be *normal*?"

"Because you're Matty, that's why." His mother sighed. "You're Matty, and there's no one else like you in this world. What you bring to everything you do in your life is unique. Special. You love harder than other people, you hurt deeper, and you fight dirtier sometimes. But honey, there is nothing *wrong* with you."

"They won't give me medals," Matty said. "Not now. Not after everything. What's the point?"

"Valentina will change that. She's a powerhouse."

"She's a control freak." He'd heard rumors and, more than that, he'd read the contracts. He knew what he'd signed up for. What was required. Strict discipline.

"Matty..." Donna paused. "Do you want to come home? You don't have to stay there. We can find another way."

"No."

"All right. Is he good to you?"

"You know that he is, Mother."

They stayed silent on the phone for a moment, and Matty listened to her breathing.

"I miss you, Mom," Matty said, trying to sound stronger.

"I miss you, honey. We all do. Even the cats miss you." She paused again. "Honey, is there something else bothering you?"

Matty thought for a moment. "Yeah. I think I'm forgetting my Japanese."

"Oh for heaven's sake." Donna laughed. "Go to bed. Things will look better in the morning."

Matty hung up the phone and sat awhile in the den of Rob's closet, taking in the scents, feeling the fabrics, and wondering what Rob would look like in Versace or Lagerfeld. Probably incredibly fine.

Matty thought about calling Elliot, who probably would be even less tolerant of a middle of the night phone call during the work week, but he had no idea what Elliot could possibly tell him that would make the ache in his chest go away.

When he climbed into bed, Rob was asleep on his side, a pillow in his arms where Matty had stuffed it before he'd tiptoed off to call his mother. Matty curled next to him and watched his steady breath. He was exhausted, and his balls ached from coming too many times during the positively acrobatic sex they'd had after the gala. He had no idea how he was going to skate the next day, but he knew he would try.

If he didn't, then he wasn't Matty Marcus.

CHAPTER NINETEEN

The first time Matty saw Anja again after Christmas was when she drove up to get Ben at the ranch. Normally, Rob drove him back home, but his truck was in the shop. Matty could see that Rob and Anja had talked about what happened, or at least had moved on from it. He knew from experience with Elliot that when it came to old friends and bygones, drawn-out discussions weren't always necessary—the love between people who'd shared a lot together was usually enough to let the hurt go with a sincere "I love you and I'm sorry."

Matty leaned against the front door jamb, drinking hot water and bitters from a mug and watching Rob and Anja exchange a hug as Ben climbed into the backseat. Anja tucked her hair behind her ear and glanced toward Matty with a bashful expression. He lifted his steaming mug toward her and let his lips soften into a smile.

He wasn't angry about what she'd said to Rob or him at Christmas. It'd been the truth. He *was* leaving and Rob *did* deserve better—not only better than a guy who was on his way out the door, but better than a life that didn't fulfill his potential.

Matty cleared his throat as Anja's snow boots thudded on the steps to the porch. The media instincts in his brain clicked on, and he straightened up, put on a cheery smile and thought, *Charming-Matty activate in the shape of All-Is-Well and Never-You-Mind.*

"Matty, hi."

"Hello, Anja. You look lovely today. That blue coat is great on you. Brings out your eyes."

Her eyebrows flew up as if that was the last thing she expected him to say. Matty wasn't even sure why he'd defaulted to his usual compliments—true as they were—to deal with her. He didn't have the energy for a big talk or apology. Not when he was busy trying to live through the current state of anticipation he experienced twenty-four hours a day. It always lingered in the back of his mind—he was on his way out, but not yet. The living in-between was exhausting. He didn't need any additional emotional clutter in his life right now.

"I wanted to apologize to you for the way Christmas ended up. I had too much to drink and, while that's no excuse, it definitely doesn't bring out my best qualities. I don't take back what I said, but I do wish I hadn't said it at quite that time and in that particular state."

"You have nothing to worry about," Matty assured her, taking one of her gloved hands in his mug-hot fingers. "I promise. I'm not offended."

"Good. I'd hate to think that somewhere out in the world Matty Marcus was skating around with the opinion that Anja Lovely was bitch."

Matty laughed and shook his head before drawing her in for a hug. Her hair smelled like lavender, and he took a deep breath. "If I don't see you again before I leave…" His throat felt tight and his hand holding the mug shook a little. He hoped he didn't spill any on her as she hugged him back. "Just…take care of him," he whispered. "Take care of them both."

"I'll do my best," Anja whispered back. "Thank you for waking him up. He's been sleeping for too long now."

She pulled back and smiled at him, and Matty blinked away the sudden burn of tears as she clomped back down the stairs to the car. After another kiss to Rob's cheek, she was off, and Rob stood and waved as they drove away.

"Good talk?" Rob asked.

"She had nothing to apologize for."

"Oh, I think maybe she did." Rob joined him in the doorway. Snow started to fall, adding to the blankets already covering the fields, mountains, barn, and house. It was beautiful. Rob's arms around him were warm. Leaving this all seemed impossible, and yet not skating—not competing—wasn't even an option.

Valentina and his real life waited at the other side of the winter. This was a beautiful respite. And that was all it could ever be.

* * *

Margaret and George returned on a crisp morning in March. Matty and Rob waved to them from the front porch as they pulled up in the white hired car from the airport. Rob helped George with the luggage while Margaret chatted effusively to Matty about their travels.

As Rob took the heaviest suitcase out of George's hands, despite his protests, and hefted it up the stairs to the aired-out master bedroom that Matty had painstakingly vacuumed and dusted the night before, Margaret grabbed Matty's arm and tugged him down to the sofa next to her.

"I was hoping you and Rob would get along. He's wonderful, isn't he?" She smiled expectantly.

"He is," Matty agreed.

"So, you've become good friends?"

"Absolutely."

Margaret's eyes narrowed. "*Very* good friends?"

Matty's throat felt tight. Any other person would be happy to let

Margaret know that, yes, he and Rob were in love and were more than just good friends. But Matty was leaving tomorrow, and the love they shared was deep enough that he'd never ask Rob to wait for him. Rob deserved the freedom to discover and pursue his dream just like Matty needed freedom to pursue his.

"I suppose so."

Her face filled with delight. "Do tell."

Matty shook his head, feeling his cheeks heat up. He reached for the necklace around his neck, fingering the tab with a six-point-oh score on it, thinking of Christmas and Ben's faith in him, thinking of the corn maze, and of Rob's mother's soup. What could he possibly tell her that could sum up how he felt—what he'd gained by living here these months?

"I assume the horses are still alive?" George asked, leading Rob back downstairs, his cowboy boots clacking on the wood floor.

"Alive and kicking, sir. And I didn't burn the house down. Or bust my head open out on your pond. Not a single party was held here. It's all in order."

He didn't mention that early on he'd had reckless sex with a then-stranger on their kitchen floor, because they certainly didn't need to know about that. He still didn't look at the kitchen floor in quite the same way himself.

George harrumphed softly and then nodded his head. "Good work. The place looks nice. Neater than usual, I'll give you that."

Margaret rolled her eyes. "Now you've made me look bad, Matty." She laughed and looked at Rob speculatively before turning back to him. "Now tell me all about your training."

After a few minutes of listening to Matty's descriptions of the improvements his training had wrought, Margaret entreated Matty to drive to the Stumptown Ice Den and show her. Rob, having arranged for Bing and the hands to deal with the ranch duties for Matty's last day in town, tagged along. George remained behind, apparently disinterested in his hired house-sitter's figure skating prowess.

After Matty showed off for close to an hour, Margaret congratulated him on his improvement. As they left the building, Matty walked between Rob and Margaret. It was strange to think he'd probably never skate on that rink again. Or the Pages' pond. Yuliya Yasneyeva had officially retired.

"Do you still have packing left to do?" Margaret asked.

"Just a few things."

He'd mailed boxes of his things back to his mother in Virginia, and had left only enough clothing to get through the last week. Which, admittedly, was still two large suitcases of items, because he never knew just what he might feel like wearing. But except for the clothes on his back and an outfit for tomorrow, everything was packed. His flight left Missoula at noon, and it was nearly a three-hour drive. He'd be waking up very early.

"Well, let's get on back. You'll want to spend the night at Rob's, I imagine," she said. "I know he has a nice dinner planned for you. Something special he said."

Matty glanced at Rob, who smiled softly and reached to take hold of his hand.

Margaret chattered more about her trip as they drove back to the ranch. It was only as they pulled up to the house that she turned to Matty and said seriously, "I'm proud of you. You did everything you said you would and more. This time you'll be ready at the Olympics. I know you will."

Matty grabbed her in a hug. The gear shift stuck into his side, but he held on for a long time. "Thank you," he whispered vehemently in her ear.

He meant it for so many things. Thanks for the overpaid job that gave him a chance to compete again. Thanks for the time away from his usual life to re-focus and pull himself out of the self-pity he'd been wallowing in. Thanks for living next to Rob, who had shown him so much love and devotion. Thanks for her belief in him when so many others had lost it, and when maybe he'd started to lose it himself.

"Thank you. I won't let you down."

"Of course you won't. You're the amazing Matty Marcus."

* * *

Of course the special dinner Rob had planned was his mother's Southwestern Chili Burger and Bean Soup. They sat at the kitchen table and Matty ate like he was starving, which—given how little he'd eaten in the last week between his usual fastidiousness and his nerves about leaving—he might have been. Rob sat back and watched him eat with satisfaction and a touch of sadness in his eyes.

"I love watching you eat. You make everything that goes in your mouth look like it tastes so delicious."

"Everything?" Matty said, lowering his lashes. "Even your gorgeous dick?"

"Especially that."

Matty pushed the empty bowl away. "We don't have much time left. Just tonight. Take me upstairs now."

Rob shook his head. "First we need to talk."

"No," Matty said, his stomach tightening and his voice going rough. "I don't want to talk because then I'll cry, and I don't want to spend our last night together crying."

"Does it have to be our last night?"

Matty closed his eyes and held himself as still as possible, trying to take the pain as it smashed into him. Tears stung, and he waited for it to ease up. Pain always did, if only long enough for a person to breathe.

"We could call each other. Text and email."

Matty shook his head, feeling a tear slide down his cheek. "I won't have time for that. I won't have time for anything but skating."

Rob was quiet, but then he whispered, "I could wait. However long."

"No. You've got a dream to follow." Matty opened his eyes and met Rob's teary gaze. "You've got to find it and pursue it."

"But you're—"

"I'm not your dream. I can't be."

Rob's chin dropped down to his chest, and he went rigid, his breaths coming in short, difficult gasps. Matty felt a small well of anger. They were both crying, and this wasn't how Matty wanted their last night together to be. He wanted laughter and tenderness and sex that tore through his soul like a tornado. He wanted Rob to take him upstairs and make him forget that he wasn't going to be here tomorrow.

Then the anger ebbed away, and he was left with the desperate need to comfort Rob. He slid to the floor and walked on his knees to him, pushing himself between his legs and wrapping his arms around his quivering body.

"I love you. I'm so sorry. I'm so, so, so sorry."

Rob gripped him by the shoulders and lifted him into a searing kiss.

They didn't talk after that except for the usual words of pleasure and desire, affection and want. Upstairs in bed, Rob's body moved into him urgently again and again, stretching out their ecstasy for hours. As their emotions overwhelmed them, Matty loved and hated that they both cried more than once as they made love all night, knowing it was the last time.

* * *

The airport was bustling despite the early hour. Matty's eyes were swollen from crying and his lips were swollen for other reasons. His chin and cheek sported beard burn like none he'd ever had before. He hadn't even bothered to shave to keep from irritating it further.

Rob's own chin was red and rough from Matty's stubble. He was pale, and his hands shook whenever he took them out of his pocket. His eyes, which Matty kept searching out in an attempt to memorize everything about them, were brilliant green and red-rimmed, and Matty tried to recall how they'd looked that day on Whitefish Lake when he'd thrown Matty for jumps.

"The line for security is just up here." Rob's voice sounded weary.

"Is that a real stuffed bear in that case? Does PETA come throw blood on the glass?" Matty asked, but he didn't really care.

Rob ignored the question and pulled Matty to the side of the causeway. He held both of Matty's hands in his and gazed down at him. "I love you. You're going to be amazing. Train hard. Do what Valentina tells you. Don't decide that you don't deserve it. Let the judges do their job for themselves—don't throw the towel in and do it for them. Remember that I'm counting on you to believe in yourself."

"I promise," Matty whispered.

"Be happy, Matty. I just want you to be happy."

"Me too. For you." Dammit, the tears were starting up again. "I want you to be happy so much. Every day."

Rob nodded.

Matty wiped his face with the back of his hand and gave a wobbly smile. "By the way, that whole wooing with a chicken thing works pretty well. Next time you invite a guy for dinner, definitely kill a chicken for him. It's really flattering."

Rob shook his head and bent down to kiss Matty's lips softly. "I'll never kill a chicken to woo any guy but you."

"No, don't say that. There are so many chickens that need to be killed for so many guys. I want you to be happy, Rob."

"Shh. You sound ridiculous."

"I know, it's just…promise me you'll kill chickens."

Rob rolled his eyes, and yet his lips quirked into his first true smile Matty had seen since before their talk at dinner. "I promise to kill chickens."

"Okay. That's all I needed to hear."

The airport announced that Matty's flight would begin boarding shortly. There was no way to further delay going through security.

"I love you," Matty said as Rob led him to the line, gripping his hand.

"I know."

"Tell me."

"I love you, Matty."

Then it was Matty's turn to present his photo identification and boarding pass. The officer, a woman, looked at his picture and then at him, and broke into a smile.

"I know you. Matty Marcus. My daughter was rooting for you at the Olympics."

"Tell her thank you."

The woman lingered over his boarding pass and then asked shyly for an autograph. When Matty finished scrawling his name over a Post-it note the woman grabbed from her podium, he turned to say goodbye to Rob.

He was gone.

Matty almost burst into tears as a sharp, breathtaking pain tore into his stomach. He'd wanted one more kiss. One last goodbye.

Matty removed his shoes, put them in the bin, then removed the necklace Ben had made him, putting it in a small black plastic bowl. His heart beat so hard he felt like he was having a heart attack. His breaths came in short, sharp bursts, as he struggled not to cry.

Rob was gone.

It was time to face the real world. It was time to be a champion.

PART THREE

CHAPTER TWENTY

Seven Months Later

"*Nyet!*"

Matty thought he was going to slit his own throat if he heard that word one more time. Weren't there other ways of telling him he'd screwed up? Like, "Fuck you" or "You suck," or "Die, die, die"?

Apparently not. It was *nyet, nyet, nyet* all day, every day, and Matty hated it. Mainly because it meant he had to do it again— whatever it was—only better, and his entire body was sore from doing it so many times the wrong way.

"Quads are not for giggles and splits," Valentina shouted.

Matty bit the inside of his cheek so he didn't crack a smile. Valentina hated smiles only slightly less than she hated him.

"Quads are for champion!" She flexed her biceps. Her dark brown hair hung messily over half her face, grazing her shoulders. Her gray pantsuit looked as if it had been hand stitched in a Siberian work camp. She stood taller than Matty even in his skates, and she was thin like a whip. "Strong man. Be strong man, Matty. Not girly man."

Matty nodded and resigned himself to the bruises and pain he'd be dealing with that night. The entire afternoon had been devoted to quads, and his failure to achieve one. He ignored the pit of raging jealousy boiling in his gut at the knowledge that Alex Hampton was churning out quads like they were farts, all easy-peasy, lemon squeezy.

Dammit, he never should have let Joanna talk him into coaching that kid's seminar last weekend. He was still thinking like a nine-year-old.

"Tuck in tummy, lift from thighs and *go!*" Valentina raised her arms. "Then not to be screwing up. Understand?"

Matty nodded. He'd discovered when he'd first begun to skate with Valentina that it was best to keep his mouth shut. She didn't find much of what he had to say charming. Not even in Russian. *Especially* not in Russian.

"Again! Go!" Valentina said, crossing her arms over her chest and staring at him like he was gum on the bottom of her shoe.

Matty closed his eyes, touched the necklace Ben had made him, took a deep breath, and went.

Despite how tough she was, training with Valentina was the best choice he'd ever made as far as his skating career was concerned. He bowed under her command and excelled at her behest. He'd come in second at his Nebelhorn, his first competition. Skate America was in two weeks. He was ready.

Almost.

If he nailed the quad, he'd be set. Yes, if he could just get a consistent quad Salchow and toe, he'd strike fear in Alex Hampton's heart and every other contender he faced on the ice, because when it came to artistry and passion, he was just that good. Combined with a high technical mark, he could be unbeatable. Matty couldn't wait to see the look on Alex Hampton's stupid face when he finally bested him.

The practice ended on a high note when Matty landed two quad Sals successfully. He was still grinning to himself as he changed in the locker room, high from Valentina's enthusiastic words of praise: "Yes! *Da!*"

Technically Matty supposed it had just been one word of praise since "*da*" meant yes. He wondered if he'd ever hear the elusive "good" from her. Perhaps when he had a gold medal around his neck he'd get that great reward.

Rumor had it Julien Alban sometimes wrenched the word from her lips, but the French skater was basically made of flowers and purple ponies. Everyone loved him, and it was possible even Valentina wasn't immune to his charms.

Matty glanced over to where Julien was changing for his turn for a one-on-one torture session with their coach. His blond hair sat in long ringlets around his pretty-yet-masculine face. He looked like a porcelain doll—pale skin, blue eyes, and blond loveliness—until he took off his shirt. Then it was all *holy smoking body, Batman.* He was made like the beautiful naked men in Dali's less famous paintings—muscular, lean, and breathtaking.

Matty thought a fling with Julien, sometime after they'd both stolen medals from Vance and Alex, might be a fun way to celebrate. But he also knew better. Getting involved with another skater would be a huge mistake. He liked Julien, but they were competitors. Still, Julien's forearms were beautiful, and Matty sometimes thought of them as he was jerking off—before his mind's inevitable slide toward memories of Rob's hands and smile, his kisses, and his cock.

"Beautiful skate," Julien said, glancing Matty's way. "Finally, you are landing like, how does Valentina say it? Like a butterfly and not a hippopotamus. *Bon.*"

"Thanks," Matty said, tossing his dirty socks into his gym bag. "It felt pretty great. Now I just need to do it another thousand times."

"You're getting better and better." Julien smiled, his teeth gleaming like a toothpaste commercial. "You will do it. I know it in my heart."

Matty smiled back, pleased with Julien's generous praise and encouragement. He wasn't sure he'd be so nice himself. Julien was inspiring that way. It almost made Matty want to try to be sweet too. He took a deep breath and gave it a whirl. "How's it going? Last I heard, Valentina actually said you were good."

"No. She says I'm terrible. Yesterday she said, 'You are naughty and rotten as duck in a meat stack.'"

Matty cocked his head. "What does that even mean, Jules?"

"I don't know. She said it several times. It's a mystery."

Matty laughed.

"But it can't be a nice thing, no?"

"No."

"Yet she also says my Rippon Lutz is good. Twice even."

"Holy crap, man, give yourself a high five."

Julien held up both hands and slapped them together with a grin.

"Give *me* a high five." Matty zipped his jacket and held up his hand.

Julien slapped his palm and then grabbed his hand and squeezed it. "See you later, Matty. Don't be so self-defeating."

He wasn't sure what to say to that, but the assessment seemed pretty accurate. "Good luck," Matty said, the sensation of Julien's cool fingers lingering on his palm.

Matty watched Julien leave the locker room before pulling down his leggings. His legs and hips were mottled with bruises. He rubbed arnica over the worst places. No matter how badly his body ached, no matter how frustrated he got—it would be worth it to see Alex fail and him win. That was what Valentina was going to help him do, and that was why when she said go, he went, no matter how much he wanted to just collapse to the ice and cry instead. That was why the bruises didn't matter.

Sometimes when Matty submitted to Valentina's cruelty as a coach, he was assailed by thoughts of Rob, the whips, and of sinking into a stronger form of submission during truly intense sex. Instead of letting himself fall apart from missing Rob, he'd force himself to find that place inside for Valentina. Open himself to that abasement and let her push him further on the ice than he'd ever been pushed before. From that space of deep surrender, he'd brought home his first medal in two years.

He stared at the bruises and wondered what Rob was doing, how he was, and if he was happy. He wondered if Rob ever missed him.

Then he dressed in track pants and a thick sweater. It was time to go home to his tiny apartment in Chelsea and make dinner. If he was lucky, maybe he'd find the strength to read for a while as he soaked in a bath of Epsom salts. He was trying to get through the complete Sherlock Holmes and making terrible progress. He kept falling asleep before he made it more than a page or two.

Matty lifted his bag and shouldered his way past the hockey players making their way into the locker room. Snide remarks slid off their tongues, but Matty ignored them. It was the same old, same old. It couldn't touch him. Not when he was this tired. Exhaustion flooded him to the bone. He wouldn't read in the bath tonight. He'd be lucky not to fall asleep in the tub and drown.

The warmth of a late heat wave assailed him as he exited the cool sports complex. As he crossed Tenth Avenue, he pulled out his iPod. He wanted to listen to the new mix Elliot emailed him the other day. But he accidentally hit shuffle, and a random song started to play. Suddenly Matty was back in a dirty-looking bar in Montana, swaying back and forth with Rob's arms wrapped around him.

He stepped out of the middle of the sidewalk and leaned against a building. He closed his eyes as the song played on, allowing memories to flood him and sharpen in his mind—Ben's laughter, the effervescent sensation of Montana air against his skin, Rob's strong hands, and the warm, piney scent of Rob's neck.

Matty held very still, waiting for the song to end and the memories to let go. He wiped the back of his hand across his eyes as the last notes played and lifted his chin resolutely. He clicked on Elliot's playlist and rotated his shoulders, throwing off his reverie. When the first jarring notes of the power-pop song began, Matty opened his eyes again and started off again toward home, walking at a fast clip.

He was tired and he missed Rob, but this was his life and he was committed to it.

Still, the always painful questions lingered—had he made a mistake insisting that they go their separate ways? Could they have survived the distance, the lack of time together, and Matty's all-consuming commitment to the ice?

No. He hadn't and they couldn't.

Matty couldn't afford even the smallest distraction. Not now. Not when everything rode on the next couple years going exactly the way they needed to go for him to end up back on the Olympic team. It wouldn't have been fair to Rob or Ben or himself. It wouldn't have been fair to anyone at all.

As Christina sang his feelings, Matty wondered how long it would continue to hurt this badly. Would it be over when he walked in the

Olympic Opening Ceremony? When he brought home gold for the United States and showed everyone that Matty Marcus had what it took to win? Surely the pain and grief would finally wash away under the pride of finally achieving his goal.

He had to believe that was true.

* * *

Matty sat on the bench in the locker room, fingering the tabs of Ben's necklace as he stared at the YouTube video on his phone. It was his third time watching it, and he still felt as if the ground dropped out from under his feet when it reached its inevitable and triumphant conclusion. It was only a training video, so there was no roar of applause at the wildly glorious finish, but Matty could hear it in his head, explosive and insane, the sound of an audience leaping to its feet in overawed astonishment at a perfect performance.

Hank Babikov. A nineteen-year-old Canadian skater. No one had heard of him even a year ago, yet here he was. The technical aspects of the routine, clearly a long program intended for competition, were flawless, and the artistry was undeniable. But the aspect of Hank Babikov's performance that pierced Matty's heart with cold terror was something else entirely. Something uncontrollable. Something that no amount of practice was ever going to allow Matty to match.

Babikov's shoulders were wide and strong, waist narrow, and his legs were powerhouses of strength. His cheeks were dark with the shadow of a beard thick enough for the color to linger even after a fresh shave. Each move was certain and masculine, while retaining necessary grace. He was as rugged as a rancher, but he moved on the ice like he'd been born on it. If Matty was lovely and beautiful in his movements, Hank Babikov was powerful and strong. If Matty was like a bird, Hank was a lion. There was no doubt about it—this stranger was the international judges' dream. He was the manly man they'd wanted for years. He was the Patrick Swayze of ice.

He was perfection.

Matty wiped the back of his hand across his mouth and wondered how much it would cost to assassinate someone, and how one even found an assassin anyway. He closed his eyes and took a long, slow breath.

"Do you feel sick, Matty?" Julien's voice was gentle.

Matty felt him drop onto the bench beside him.

"You are really, how do you say? *Vert.*"

Green, Matty wanted to tell him. Green with envy and nausea. But he didn't trust his voice not to shake. After everything he'd given up, after leaving Rob and Montana, after training so hard, so *damn* hard, this kid—no, this man—could *not* just come in and steal his chance at Olympic gold. For the first time in his life, Matty felt perhaps he was a kindred spirit with Tonya Harding.

"Hank Babikov," Julien said, tapping the screen of Matty's phone. "We're fucked, aren't we? Let me guess, you're thinking, bye-bye gold medal, hello sadness? Don't be so ready to throw in the towel."

"You're going to be late," Matty said, standing up and shoving his phone in his bag. He didn't understand how Julien could sit there like everything in that video didn't render all of their effort wasted. Though Julien still stood a chance. He didn't have as much to prove. Julien hadn't screwed up his first Olympic opportunity with a bad attitude, laziness, and a deeply held belief that he didn't deserve a medal anyway. Not like Matty had.

Now he deserved a medal. He did. He knew it deep inside, and even if that was a lie, Rob had wanted him to believe in himself, and wasn't that close enough? Wasn't that what all of this was about anyway?

"Matty," Julien said, his voice tender. "Cheer up, friend. A practice video is not a competition. Even the best skater can fall apart under pressure. Our brains can steal medals right out of our hands, can't they? We don't know enough about Babikov to give up yet."

Matty cleared his throat and forced a media-smile. "Of course. I'm not giving up. I'm just tired."

"Good. Seriously, you get better every day. In my heart," he closed his eyes and took a deep breath and then broke into a big smile. "Yes, in my heart, I believe that, if you keep on working, you'll win satisfaction and happiness."

"And what do you win?" Matty asked.

"Gold," Julien said and winked.

"Julien! On ice!" Valentina's voice carried into the locker room like a crack of angry thunder. Matty shuddered and made an empathetic face.

"Sorry. I hope I didn't make you late."

"No worries. She often makes me cry, but that goes with the, what is the word? Territory. Go home and be happy, all right? You're my friend, sweet Matty, and I hate seeing you sad."

Matty watched Julien rush out the locker room door, a half-smile soft on his lips. If only Julien knew the murderous thoughts he'd been entertaining just before he'd come in. He wouldn't think Matty was so sweet then, would he?

Matty touched his necklace. He fingered through the most worn

226

tabs, the ones featuring the highest scores, and then let go. The Grand Prix season was starting. He couldn't let Hank Babikov do his head in. He wasn't out of the game when it hadn't even officially begun.

Matty resolved not to watch any more of Babikov's training videos. All that mattered was his own training and submitting to Valentina's coaching. He'd placed all his faith in her, and he had to hang on to that belief.

He remembered the strength he found in submission and surrender. He'd learned what it meant to give everything to his boyfriend Figure Skating. He remembered the pain of Rob's horse whips. He needed to close his eyes and find the place inside himself that was stronger than his fear.

Deep down, he was the man who could fight, take the pain, endure, and come out better. All he needed was to summon that strength and believe he was the man who deserved the ultimate reward.

CHAPTER TWENTY-ONE

Five Months Later

Matty watched the scores flash onto the boards at Worlds. Rage swept through him followed by a much more painful emotion, one he'd sworn he would never experience again. Humiliation. It was a feeling of nausea, burning shame, and deeply wounding *hurt*.

He hated knowing that his face revealed every swell of it. He hated the cameras he'd been waving and smiling at only moments before. They recorded every second of this shunning. Because that's what it was. There was no other explanation. He'd skated clean. His scores placed him firmly in fourth behind Babikov, Hampton and Alban—usually a fair, if disappointing, place to be ranked.

But he'd been perfect.

He'd been amazing, and Babikov had slipped up on landing his quad, Hampton had splatted twice, Julien had popped a triple Axel, and *was this really happening*?

"Scores are shit," Valentina whispered, rubbing a hand over his hair and smoothing it back from his sweaty forehead.

She smiled at him, the first time he'd ever properly seen her teeth, which were coffee stained. Her voice frightened him because it was warm and motherly.

"You my good boy. Scores baloney. I talk to judges. Find problem."

Good boy. He heard the words he'd longed for but it wasn't enough. Not nearly enough to wipe away the finality of the scores on the board.

In the locker room, he ignored the other skaters and found a toilet stall. He didn't remove his skates and he didn't give a damn about the fact that he was sitting on a toilet in his costume. Valentina had gone to ferret out some kind of answer to the question of why Matty's scores didn't reflect his performance.

Matty already knew. He was too gay for the judges. He'd been too lazy in the past and he'd disappointed them too badly with his prior screw-ups. The bar they wanted him to meet wasn't just out-performing Hank Babikov, but out-performing the impossible. Now that they had their macho man on the ice, if they could find any possible reason to count Matty down, they would. If Hank had been around before Matty was injured, Matty wouldn't have won a single medal. He knew it. The only reason he'd won any to begin with was the judges hadn't had a *choice.*

Matty felt the tightness in his throat, and he bit the inside of his cheek hard. He would not sit in the crowded locker room and cry in a toilet stall. He wouldn't give them that satisfaction.

Wiping his nose and eyes with the rough toilet paper, he stood up and flushed the toilet. He felt eyes on him when he walked out, but he didn't look at anyone. Instead, he headed directly to the locker he'd been assigned and worked to get it open. His fingers felt numb and clumsy, and at one point he punched the locker next to him, causing a brief quiet to descend and then dissipate.

"Great skate tonight, man."

Matty looked up to see Hank Babikov's bright hazel eyes shining down at him. "I know. Feel free to forfeit. Don't you have a medal ceremony to go to?"

Hank's face flushed. "Yeah."

Another skater shot Matty a dirty look and congratulated Hank on his first world championship. Matty quickly got changed, eager to get the hell out.

The thing that bothered him the most, what ate at him as he waited outside the locker room for Valentina to return from her fact-finding excursion, was how damn sincere Hank had sounded. It made his fantasies of hiring a hitman seem even more disgusting. It was a reflection of what a terrible human being he was that despite Hank's empathy, Matty still wanted nothing more than for him to walk out the door and be hit by a Mack truck. Or a Volvo. He wasn't sure he wanted Hank dead, but good and injured wouldn't be bad.

Christ, he was awful. Even Rob wouldn't love him anymore if he knew the kinds of things he was thinking about.

Tears filled his eyes and Matty bent his head, blinking rapidly. Deep breaths in and out finally put an end to the risk that he'd start to sob backstage, and when Valentina returned with an expression cold enough to make dinosaurs go extinct all over again, he simply followed her silently from the building. He didn't know where Julien was, but it didn't matter.

When they reached the waiting car, Valentina pulled him against her tall body and wrapped an arm around his waist. "You skate good today, Matty. Proud of you. You be proud too. Don't let the bastards shoot you down."

"Get you down," Matty murmured.

"When they have gun aimed at career of *my* figure skater, then I say shoot you down."

Matty's face crumpled, and Valentina wrapped both arms around him, drawing him close to her small bosom.

"Must make nice with the judges," she whispered in his ear. "Bronze, silver can be yours. Gold even, if Babikov make bad mistake. You must be more manly. Not so girly. Never give up. Proud of you." She pulled back and her clear brown eyes gazed down into his as her messy, dark hair swirled around her face. "Understand?"

"Yes."

"Tomorrow we skate. And next day. On we go. That is how we deal with it. My champion. Got it?"

"Yes."

He hugged her fiercely, and she kissed the top of his head.

Still, when Matty was finally alone in his hotel room, after a long, sobbing cry in the shower, he lay down in his bed and took out his phone. He ignored the calls and texts from his mother, brother, and Elliot.

Instead, he broke down and did something he'd sworn he would never do.

The email to Rob was a long, winding message that took him an hour to peck out on his phone. It explained the insult of his scores, the impossibility of ever coming out on top when going against a skater like Babikov, the politics that left him in a position little better than shit on the shoes of the judges, and the complete humiliation of being shunned by the judges.

He described his hurt and rage, and he questioned everything, including leaving Montana and Rob. For what? For this ruse? At the end he suggested he should quit and leave skating for good, because if he couldn't even hope to medal, what was the point?

He waited nine hours for an answer.

At first, he'd been full of excitement and hope, thinking that Rob would tell him to quit. To come home and forget the whole thing. Then he waited with *fear* that Rob would tell him to quit. Then he was devastated to think that Rob wasn't going to say anything at all.

He drove himself nearly wild with panic for several long hours, imagining Rob was dead, because that was the only excuse Matty could think of for Rob's lack of reply, forgetting the time difference between Sweden and Montana. Even if Rob had moved on and met someone else, he'd still reply in Matty's time of need, wouldn't he? Unless he was dead, right? It was the only explanation that made sense.

When the answer came, it was a single sentence. Matty stared at it for a long time. He hit reply and then canceled out. He looked at the message some more, and he imagined Rob's fingers putting in each letter of each word. It was a command, and Matty could feel it down to his bones.

Do what Valentina tells you.

That was all. Nothing more. Nothing less. But Matty read that sentence every day as the year went on, and it became his mantra. His marching orders. His battle cry. Sometimes he loved Valentina and sometimes he hated her, but as the months went by, he did what he was told.

* * *

"Mama," Matty whispered into the phone, burying his face into the pillow and pulling up the soft green and white comforter over his body.

"Matty? What's wrong, honey?" Donna asked, her voice sounding strong and stable.

"He has a boyfriend, Mama."

"Who? Elliot?"

"No."

Donna was silent for a few moments. "Oh honey. Rob?"

"Yeah," Matty whispered again, his throat aching and his eyes tearing up again.

"Matty..." Donna's sigh was sympathetic and also weary. "You knew this could happen. There were no promises. You were clear about that."

"I know."

"Did he...well, how do you know, honey? I thought you weren't in touch with each other."

"We're not. It's an email from Ben." Matty reached out from his cocoon of blankets, grabbed his phone and forwarded the message to his mother. "There," he said. "See for yourself."

"Ben sent you an email telling you that—"

"Just read it, Donna."

"Don't call me that," Donna murmured. "Let's see...'Matty, I hope you're training hard. Dad doesn't know I'm writing to you, but I had to because I won a medal! Gold! It's only the local summer pre-season, but it's still gold. I had to tell you. Please tell Yuliya. I hope you're both proud. Oh and here's a picture of us with the medal. I've grown since you saw me, can you tell? I miss you. Love always, Ben.' Okay, let me look at the picture. Oh...oh, I see. Honey, you don't know that—"

"He has to be. Look at him. He's Rob's type. Rob's got his arm around him. They look...happy." Matty felt as if he was going to vomit. "The guy has really ugly teeth. Did you see that? Has he never heard of an orthodontist? It's bad enough to be replaced, but to be replaced by someone ugly is such an insult."

Donna sighed and ignored his ungenerous comments. "Matty, it's a photo. For all you know, they're just friends."

"They aren't just friends."

"What makes you think that?"

Matty shrugged.

Because his mother knew him so well, she said, "I see. Okay. What are you going to do about it? Give up skating? Beg him to take you back? It doesn't change anything, honey. And don't you want him to be happy? He deserves that, don't you think? He's a good man, Matty. You're a good person, and I know, if you love him, then you want him to be happy."

"Yeah," Matty said, finding it so hard to breathe he couldn't say anything more. When the tears came hard and fast, he clung to the phone and listened to his mother say all kinds of ridiculous things about his future, his skating, and his happiness. He cried until he couldn't breathe.

"Oh Matty, honey, it's going to be okay."

One thing he knew for sure—when he had an Olympic medal around his neck, and he felt the certain surge of victorious joy race through his body, he would still miss Rob, and he would still know that being okay was completely relative. Because no matter what, there was part of him that was never okay. Part of him was always at war—always missing something, someone, and needing him badly. The only time that part of him had been satisfied was on a bed with ropes and a whip and Rob's steady hand. But now the ravenous need—the ruthless war—was back. Matty had to fight it for himself, and now he was so very *far* from okay.

The distance between New York City and Montana to be exact.

* * *

Matty could still feel Julien's cock jerking inside of him, and he already knew it was a mistake. It was a stupid, ridiculous mistake. Training had ended for the day, and he'd been fresh from the shower when, still swamped by jealousy, rage, and frustratingly uncontrollable tears, Matty had stood there naked for too long. Far longer than he should have.

Julien had been in the locker room, too, all French and beautiful. Matty wasn't even sure exactly how it had happened, but he'd dissolved into Julien's empathetic arms. Somewhere in the midst of Julien's attempts at sympathy and comfort, there had been kissing, and somehow Matty had shoved Julien onto his back. Julien had a good mouth, and it had been easy, so easy to grab the lubed condom he kept in his bag just in case, and climb on top of him and ride.

There hadn't been anyone since Rob, and it had felt so good to let himself go and have a dick inside him again. He'd closed his eyes and forgotten about everything else.

After they disentangled, Julien handed him a towel to wipe away the come on his stomach. "This was great, but...well, this wasn't anything more than feeling good together, right? Just friends having some orgasms, yes?"

Matty snorted and fought hysterical laughter. Friends having some orgasms—God, the absurdity of it all. If he wasn't completely a mess inside and out, covered with come and despair, he'd probably just give into it and roll on the floor laughing his ass off. But someone was bound to start banging on the locked door any minute now, and Valentina was going to know. She was going to look at them both and simply *know* and, Christ, they were going to pay for it.

Matty swallowed. "Just orgasms. I don't love you or anything like that."

"*Très bon. Dieu merci.*"

"Yeah," Matty said, feeling the awkwardness descend.

Julien unlocked the door to the locker room, and Matty was relieved no one immediately barged in and caught them looking filthy and fucked.

Julien started toward the showers. "We stink. If we take a shower now and scrub up well, so we smell clean as a field, Valentina will never know."

Matty thought of Montana and cows and shit patties in the snow. He smiled sadly. "Fields aren't clean, Julien."

As Julien scrubbed away the sex they'd just had in his shower stall, Matty turned on the water in the next one over. Julien's voice echoed oddly off the shower walls.

"Being loved by you wouldn't be a bad thing, would it? I bet your love is huge and strong. Bigger than you. Bigger than the sky, even."

Matty turned his face into the water, memories washing over him, and his tears lost in the rush.

"I think anyone would be proud to be loved by you."

Matty said nothing, thinking of the sky in Montana and knowing he could be flying in it right now if he had only wanted it more than ice.

* * *

Four Months Later

This was it.

Matty was in a precarious third after the Olympic short program. Hank Babikov and Akihito Tanaka were ranked first and second respectively. Julien was in fifth, and Alex Hampton rode hard on Matty's ass at fourth. Matty still had a chance for the gold if Hank and Akihito faltered under the pressure. It was unlikely, but possible, and even if they didn't, all he had to do was out-skate them both by a mile.

That was all. It was what he'd trained to do. It was imperative that right here, right now, Matty give the skate of his life.

Matty circled the rink as the crowd cheered for the long-program scores of the previous skater, a young Russian who wasn't in the medal hunt. As he shook his limbs to loosen up, his feathers rustled. The feathers and sequins on his chest were blue on his right side and black on his left, and his pant legs were blue and black as well.

One side represented sky and the other earth. In the interviews he'd done after his silver medal at Nationals, he'd explained that his piece was about the marriage of the two—the kiss of the horizon, the desperation of gravity, and the weightlessness of joy.

He returned to Valentina at the boards and she took his hands.

"You can do this. Believe it. Believe it, my good boy."

He could do this. He could.

The crowd roared when his name was called, and he smiled as he circled the rink one more time. The necklace Ben made for him was tucked into his costume, but he could feel it resting against his skin as he briefly closed his eyes. This was it. His moment. He was ready, unlike the last time he'd stood on Olympic ice and destroyed any chance he had for a medal.

This time he'd trained harder than he'd thought humanly possible. He'd fought against every impulse of laziness, overcome his insubordination, and sucked it up and kissed the ass of every judge who had ever docked points for any reason at all.

This was the moment he'd given everything for, and it was truly now or never.

Matty's heart throbbed so hard that the feathers of his costume trembled with each beat and he could see his chest rising in his peripheral vision as he took his position.

He brought his arms up, cradling the palm of one hand against his cheek, striking the tender opening pose his choreographer had chosen for him. Matty took a slow, deep breath and pulled up every beautiful memory he could from Montana.

He remembered the scent of horses, the sound of goats, and the white of snow. He recalled Rob's smile, Ben's old skates, and Yuliya's wig hanging on the peg in the Pages' guest room closet. He remembered cup after cup of hot water and bitters, and the scent of cow shit in the pasture. He brought to mind Rob's hands, laugh, and the tenderness in his eyes as he'd gazed at Matty for the last time in the airport. He recalled the promise Rob had asked Matty to make.

Here I am. I made it. I did it just like you said.

This time, I won't screw it up.

The rustling of the crowd was silenced by the roaring of his pulse.

The first delicate notes of a variation on Bach's Sonata No. 2, *Siciliana*, struck lightly, like a music box with Matty the ballerina in the center. Matty turned to it, a twirl that ended with a shift out from the center, moving with long, sure strokes of his blades over the ice, turning his back as he rounded the corner to push up into a triple Lutz, landing easily.

His body took over, his mind watching as though from a hazy distance as he moved with the music. His heart pounded in his chest as he gained speed, and vaguely he heard roars of approval from the audience as his body took him high, rotated four times, and landed cleanly.

Changing edges as he weaved and twisted was like breathing. The ice was the sky, the rink vanished and he was flight and motion, bright and pure. He danced through the circular step sequence and crouched into spin variations, rising again to skim across the ice effortlessly. Delicate footwork poured through him like the sparkling, tingling air of Montana, his arms floating like threads of clouds over mountaintops. Emotion flowed up through him, lending artistry, expression, and passion to every glance, turn, and jump.

He jumped, twisted, and landed combinations without a trace of strain, and reached the end of the required elements with a distant sense of unreality.

The pace of the music picked up as the program built to its climax, and he gave over to the sound. The practiced movements were more certain than his breath and he flew across the ice as graceful as a bird. The roar of the audience rattled through him like thunder. He bent left, then right, his body limber and loose as he did his final spin. Then he rose again, turning slowly, slowly until he returned to his opening stance, his hand cradled against his cheek.

The noise was deafening.

Matty's throat ached painfully as he blinked hard to hold back the tears of joy. He pumped his fists and waved, taking deep bows to each side of the rink, his eyes drawn up to the American flags and the signs bearing his name. He'd skated clean. He'd hit every point and aced it. It had been almost surreally effortless after all the years of training. It was impossible, wasn't it, that he was here now waving and smiling, bowing and crying, and hearing his fans chant his name?

He gave one last grin, his mouth trembling, and skated to the boards. Valentina was waiting for him, her eyes alight and her mouth turned up in a brilliantly toothy, happy smile.

Matty burst into tears, unable to hold them back a moment more. He'd given up Montana. He'd given up food and a normal life with friends. And he'd given up *Rob*. But he'd done it. The hard work and sacrifice had paid off. For this moment of joy—this moment of intense satisfaction and glory—it was all so very worth it. Now he just had to sit with his broadly smiling, terrifyingly happy coach and wait for the scores to come in to validate what he already knew to be true.

He was a beautiful bird and he *wasn't* too mucked up to fly clean.

PART FOUR

CHAPTER TWENTY-TWO

Five Months Later

Physical therapy was hell.

The injury to his hip was bad. His mother fretted, clucked, lifted her eyebrow speculatively, and said little. Matty could hear her unspoken questions echoing in his own head.

Is it time to walk away? Is it worth what you're doing to your body? Could he last another four long years?

Meredith, his physical therapist, pushed him hard, and he sometimes thought he would vomit from the pain. Still, he worked through it, determined to heal his body. He needed to get back to training. Back on the ice.

Not everyone agreed. Matty avoided talking to Elliot about his goal of returning to practice because he knew exactly what Elliot thought. Even if Elliot said nothing directly about the matter, it still lurked there in the tone of his voice and long sighs. He thought Matty should quit.

The Olympics had been the final straw for Elliot.

Matty couldn't blame him. It still hurt more than he could bear to remember how, despite giving the performance of his life, other skaters had somehow outperformed him. In the judges' estimation, at least, Matty had merited only fourth place at the Olympics.

A medal so close, but so far.

At least once a week Matty still dreamed of the joy and assurance he'd felt after his skate, and Valentina's prideful grin when the scores came in. Then the happy dream descended into a nightmare as he watched helplessly, horrified and crushed, as Hank Babikov, Alex Hampton, and Akihito Tanaka out-skated him. Just like reality.

Matty hated that nightmare.

For almost a month after the Games, he'd been in denial. At practice he'd forced himself to believe that the Olympics hadn't happened yet—that he still had a shot at the podium and he was still going to bring home Olympic gold.

It was astonishing how easy it had been to live, moment to moment, telling himself that lie. It worked as long as no one talked to him about the Games. He had vivid memories of the Olympic Village and the Opening Ceremony, and strong recollections of the media blitz both before and after his performances, and yet he was able to deny them all for the sake of his sanity.

He'd pushed on and trained hard, and when Valentina talked about Worlds, Matty heard it as Olympics. After how hard he'd worked and all he'd given up, it was impossible that he hadn't medaled. That just couldn't be true.

His mother had recommended grief counseling. Not that he'd admitted to her that he was getting by, day in and out, by pretending the Olympics hadn't happened yet. He knew how crazy that sounded. But his mother could tell he wasn't himself.

"You sound awful," she'd said over the phone. "The only other time you've ever sounded this way was when you left... You need help to deal with these feelings, Matty."

"I'm fine, Mama," he'd lied, and then ended their conversations as quickly as possible. Listening to his mother interfered with telling himself that he had to get up and train tomorrow because the Olympics were coming up. He honestly didn't know what he'd do if he couldn't believe that. He doubted he'd even be able to get out of bed.

Elliot had suggested grief counseling, too, probably at Donna's behest. But Matty ignored him. He knew the pain he was running from would catch him eventually. He remembered quite clearly the night with Rob and the whips. His first reaction had been to fight, deny, and escape. Eventually, he'd surrendered. He'd had no choice.

Matty knew pain always won.

Unfortunately, it didn't wait until after Worlds to have its victory. Three days before the March event, he woke up and couldn't move. Hell, it hurt so much, he couldn't cry. He didn't go to practice that day. He had no memory of telling Valentina he was sick, but the message was there in his text logs.

Matty didn't think his reaction was normal. He'd seen a lot of athletes fail to achieve their goals and, as far as he knew, none of them had lost their shit and stayed trapped in their bed, tortured by self-loathing thoughts that hurt like knives. He couldn't stop imagining all that might have been if only he'd done something differently. If only he'd chosen something else.

Montana. Rob. Love. Passion. Joy.

Why hadn't he chosen that? Why had he chosen his abusive boyfriend Figure Skating instead? Anger had flared. Why had his mother encouraged him? Why had Rob let him go? Was there no one who loved him enough to protect him from himself? He'd thrown himself back into the arms of a sport that would just as soon rape him as make love to him, and look what had come of it. How could his mother have failed to protect him from that? How could Rob have just let him walk into Figure Skating's crushing embrace?

Fuck them both!

But it wasn't long until Matty's anger shifted.

Was he like Bill? Had he chosen the abusive straight boyfriend who would yank the reward out from under his feet once he'd done everything asked of him? Where was his aftercare? Where were the arms wrapped around him, cuddling him through the pain and ruined joy?

What the *fuck* was wrong with him? He'd wanted to curl up and die. Instead, Matty had stared straight up at the ceiling. If he'd turned his head to the right he would see framed photos of himself wearing skating medals, and if he'd turned his head to the left he'd see the Russian fairy tale print Rob had bought for him. He wasn't the swan Rob thought he was. He wasn't even a bird. He couldn't fly even if he skated clean. He was too mucked up to win.

Early on the second day of Matty's collapse, Valentina had shown up at his door. She had no patience for his self pity, and the next thing Matty knew he was at the rink and on the ice.

"Worlds, Worlds, Worlds," she said to him.

Even though it had hurt, he didn't safeword. He practiced and practiced, and told himself that if he took gold at Worlds everything would all be all right. That's all he needed and he'd be fine.

Hank Babikov, Alex Hampton, and Akihito Tanaka had excused themselves from competition after the Olympics. Matty wouldn't be facing the best of the best, but the second-best of the best. He'd told himself it would be no sweat. He could beat them all with his hands behind his back and a blindfold on.

Valentina told him with confidence, "Everyone at Worlds is child. You are man. Here, you be champion."

So Matty competed like a man.

A man who stood on the ice, pasted on his media smile, and waved to his fans. A man who bowed his head, struck his opening pose, and skated because his body didn't know how to do anything else. A man whose heart was broken, but who could still fake a steady beat.

A man who stood on the podium with a medal.

Bronze.

Not a champion.

And instead of doing ice shows in Asia and making money, now he was in the middle of a sweltering New York summer with what his doctor called a "slight" labral tear complicated by femoroacetabular impingement due to the wear and tear years of skating and jumping had put on his body. This was in addition to the lesser problem of chondromalacia patellae resulting from the misalignment of one of his knee caps secondary to the fall. The doctor told him he was lucky to have not torn his ACL too.

Lucky.

All thanks to the stupid quad. He hadn't even needed to do one in the exhibition shows, but he'd been determined to keep his form. This was what he got in return. He'd come down hard on an under-rotated quad toe, and the white-hot pain had been blinding.

Matty sure didn't feel lucky. In the end, the surgery had been successful enough. He would probably be able to skate again, if he gave it enough time to heal and went to physical therapy.

Matty tried to stay positive, but he was furious with himself for falling and getting hurt. He desperately needed the income the summer shows would provide. He had an exorbitant rent to pay for his small studio apartment in Chelsea, and it was looking more and more likely he'd need to move to New Jersey. Elliot had offered to let him move in with him, but Matty didn't think sharing a place with his party-animal BFF was a good idea.

Money was such a problem though. He didn't even want to think about his medical bills. His mother had anticipated using some of his summer show earnings toward supporting the household and helping with Joey's college. She'd even been planning to quit her second job. It broke Matty's heart to think of her working so hard.

Then there was his competitive skating career. Valentina had told him she'd always have a place for him if and when he recovered, but he hadn't been able to earn the money at shows to pay her fee. Even if he miraculously came into the money, there was no way he'd be ready to register for Nationals by the deadline. Healing took much too long and at twenty-four, he wasn't a spring chicken. He didn't have a ton of time left to skate at the highest levels of the sport.

The next four years were, without a doubt, his absolute last chance for winning Worlds and medaling at the Olympics. He just had to be better, stronger, smarter, and possibly less gay.

* * *

The rink in New Jersey smelled like every rink Matty had ever been in—the mix of sweat and ice, hockey equipment, leather, and more ice. He inhaled deeply, taking in the added scent of soft pretzels and bad coffee. The arena was nothing fancy, but it was close to the apartment building he was considering. He headed in to have a look at the ice itself. It would be months before he could train again, but he wanted a place where he could glide around without pressure and expectations.

He grinned as he pulled open the door separating the comparative warmth of the lobby from the cold air of the rink. He could see three male skaters in training with their coach, all in black, taking turns around the ice. He climbed up the bleachers, careful of his hip, and took a seat, watching carefully.

One after another, their coach drilled them through a series of jumps. Matty studied their form and, suddenly, watching the tallest one in the back go up for a triple, he just *knew*. It was in the complete commitment to the jump, the arms, and the energy of the landing.

Ben.

Matty's hand came up to cover his heart like something sharp had hit him there, and he bit his lower lip. *His* Ben—so tall, so strong, and better than Matty had even believed possible, and he'd believed a whole hell of a lot. But what was he doing here? Had he and Anja moved away from Rob? He couldn't imagine Ben without his father.

Matty watched silently, feasting his eyes on Ben. He didn't mean to draw attention to himself, but he was Matty Marcus after all. Before long, Ben spotted him in the stands. His face cracked into a wide smile.

"Matty!"

His coach scolded him, but Ben broke off practice and skated directly for him with his hands outstretched and a grin the size of Montana. He banged out of the rink and Matty gingerly made his way down the stands and into the arms of a kid who was taller than him now.

"Oh my God, you've gotten so short!"

Matty smacked his arm. "No, you've become a giant in two years!"

Ben laughed. "What are you doing here?"

Matty's throat was tight but he managed to say, "I was going to ask you the same thing."

"Oh man, it's a long story." Ben's eyes darted back to his coach, who was glaring at them both with his hands on his hips. "Can you stick around? Please? I've only got another half hour."

"Of course." Matty wasn't going *anywhere*. Not until he'd talked to Ben and held him close and ferreted out every detail of what was happening in his life...and Rob's.

"Get your ass back on the ice, Lovely," Ben's coach barked, his face turning red.

"But it's Matty Marcus, Coach," Ben said.

"It could be Alex Hampton or Hank Babikov and I wouldn't give a damn. Skate or go home."

Ben groaned. "He's pissed. Crap."

Matty shook off the sting of hearing Alex Hampton's name held above his own. "Go on, go. Show Yuliya what you can do."

Ben's smile was his father's—wide, easy, and bright. Matty's heart clenched.

"Okay, but promise that you'll stay?"

"I swear."

Ben kissed Matty's cheek and hurried back.

Matty made a note to look up more about Ben's coach. He knew his name was Greg Simon, and the manager of the rink had said he'd been making a name for himself among the junior skaters, but Matty wanted to be certain Ben was with the best.

Ben was stunning on the ice. He had artistry and skill, but moved with strength and raw masculinity that Matty knew would go over well with judges. He smiled, feeling a little sad for himself. He'd always been too fey, too feminine, and too gay for the political atmosphere. Then there had been his own failings, his laziness, and his inability to tough out the hard times. Though he'd tried. God, had he ever tried. After Rob, he'd given it his all.

But sometimes, as Rob had once tried to explain to him in an especially memorable way, amazing wasn't good enough.

Deep down he knew that in the end, being too gay hadn't been the reason he'd failed to make the podium at the Olympics. He'd simply been outskated. End of story.

The other skaters on the ice were good, too, but Matty only had eyes for Ben. He was hungry to look at him, trying to ferret out the curves of the child he'd been somewhere in the angles of his new adolescent face. Matty wanted to see his father in him too. He wasn't disappointed. Ben was so like Rob in some of his movements—the way he used his hands, the tilt of his head. His smile.

After practice, Matty waited for Ben to emerge from the locker room. Greg Simon exited with him and, with his hand on Ben's shoulder and a frown on his face, he guided him toward Matty.

"Mr. Marcus, it's a pleasure," Greg said.

Matty shook his hand despite the sense that Greg was not, in fact, feeling pleasured by his making his acquaintance.

"Let's just get one thing straight. Ben is my finest skater. Rumor has it you're looking to get into coaching, and if you want to do that, more power to you, but you can't have Ben."

"You can rest assured, Greg," Matty said, calling him by his first name to show that he wasn't intimidated. "I have no plans to take up coaching. I'm not sure where that rumor comes from since I'm going to be training again soon for—"

"We all know you're out, Marcus," Greg said. "You know it too. Better accept it now before you do real damage to your body."

Ben looked embarrassed, angry, and worried.

Matty crossed his arms over his chest but said nothing as Greg walked away. It wasn't like he'd said anything Matty hadn't heard before or thought himself, but it was one thing to overhear hushed murmurs, and another to have a person straight up tell him he was washed up.

"He's an ass," Ben said. "Mom says that's why he's good."

"Well, your mom is probably right." Matty cleared his throat and tried to swallow down the bitterness in his mouth. He put his arms around Ben and hugged him again, feeling the strength in his arms and shoulders. "How is she, by the way?"

Ben stepped back ran a hand through his hair. "Great. Fine. Holy shit, I can't believe you're here with me."

Matty couldn't believe it either. He felt lightheaded with joy and nauseous with anxiety. He wanted to ask about Rob, but he didn't know how. He stuck to Anja instead. "She's here in New Jersey with you?"

"Of course," Ben said. "We moved here earlier this year."

"And...your dad? How is he?"

"Great." Ben's expression shuttered.

His smile was no less genuine when he spoke again, but it had a new edge to it, like he really didn't want Matty to ask that question again.

"But, what about you, Matty?" Ben guided him over to the concession stand, pulled out a wad of money, and gestured to a pretzel, a bag of chips, and a bottle of water. "How are you? Are you really going to train again? After everything? Isn't that kind of...bananas?"

"Well, you know better than most that I'm stark-raving *bananas*," Matty said, following Ben to the table in the corner.

"Mom comes in fifteen minutes, but I'm all yours until then," Ben said, tossing his phone in his bag. "So, come on. What's up? You're really going to try to skate again?"

"Of course," Matty said. It was a reflex. He was going to skate. That was what he did. It was who he was. He was Matty Marcus and he was a competitive figure skater. He trained and he medaled when he could, and that was his life.

"Oh." Ben sounded disappointed.

"Why? Afraid you'll have to go up against me in a few years?" Matty asked.

Ben chuckled. "Oh yeah. You just wait, old fart. You'll be eating all my ice while I'm winning all your medals."

Matty laughed softly at the joke but coldness crept through him. It was truth. And it was terrifying.

"You're amazing, Ben," Matty said. "Yuliya and I watched you out there and you took our breath away."

Ben's face scrunched with pleasure, and then a loud noise sounded from the phone in his bag. It was the sound of a cow mooing. Matty hadn't heard that particular noise in a very long time and wanted to ask about it, but Ben ignored it.

"So what are you doing here at my rink?" Ben asked.

"I'm thinking of moving to Jersey. I was checking out the digs in case I need a local rink."

He didn't admit that by even considering the move he was making a concession to a future without competitive skating. Valentina worked exclusively in the city and if he trained with her, he'd need to stay where he was or make the crappy commute, which he didn't want to do. This entire excursion into New Jersey was an admission that he was a failure.

"That would be so cool," Ben said. "I could see you all the time."

"I'd love that."

He'd missed Ben so much that he felt weak seeing him now, like his limbs were made of pasta. His heart thrummed as he worked up the nerve to ask about Rob again. Ben had clammed up quick the last time. Still, Matty had to know.

"How did Rob handle the two of you moving away?" Matty asked. "I bet that was hard for him."

Ben frowned and ran his hand through his hair. "Well, he moved too."

"He did?" Matty's pulse raced in his ears. "To New Jersey?"

Ben shrugged. He looked uncomfortable. "He's in the city, actually. He works there."

"He works in the city?" Matty imagined him in a suit on Wall Street and then in a pair of jeans loading and unloading from a truck. Neither of those were occupations he could imagine Rob enjoying. "Doing what?"

"He went back to school," Ben said. "He's training to be a physical therapist. He just started his internship."

"Wow. That's amazing." Matty could easily imagine Rob in scrubs like his own physical therapist wore, easing people through painful exercises, using his calm authority to challenge and comfort them.

"Yeah. Life didn't stop because you left."

Matty swallowed hard. There was a slight note of bitterness in

246

Ben's tone. "Of course not. I'm glad. Is he happy? Does he like it?" He couldn't bring himself to pump Ben for information on Rob's love life, but he desperately wanted to ask if Rob was seeing anyone.

"Hold on," Ben said, digging around until he pulled out his phone. "Crap. Mom's here early. I really wanted to talk with you more, I swear, but I have to go. I'm sorry."

"I could come out with you. I'd love to see her."

Ben made another strange face. "Another time. She's in a hurry today."

He'd always been a bad liar. There had never been hearts from Anja's eyes after all.

"I'll see you then," Matty said, disappointment welling in him. He wanted to spend more time with Ben. He wanted to talk choreography and costumes, and plans for the year. He wanted to ask him more about Rob and if Rob had a boyfriend. He wanted to somehow be right back in Ben's life like he hadn't been gone for two years.

Ben poked at his phone. "Can we exchange numbers? I want to text and keep in touch."

That was something at least. Matty smiled. "Here, I'll message you."

Ben told him his number as he hauled his bag over his shoulder. He hugged Matty hard. "I've missed you, Matty. I'm glad we can talk now."

"Me too."

"Um, so, I'll text you?"

"Sure."

"And you'll text me back?"

"I will."

Ben released him and walked out, looking back to wave a few times. There were whispers in the room. Matty could hear the murmur of his name and the glances his way. One woman stared outright, and he smiled at her, blinking back tears as he gave a jaunty wave before collecting his purse and leaving too.

* * *

"Mama, everyone thinks I'm washed up."

Matty could hear the sound of typing and the clatter of voices. He knew better than to call his mother at work to have this kind of conversation, but he was desperate. He'd almost called Elliot, but he needed wisdom, not snark and an *I told you so.*

"Who's everyone, Matty?"

"People. Coaches. Probably Valentina in Russian when she thinks

I'm not listening."

Donna's breath was soft on the phone but she didn't say anything for a beat too long. Matty's throat spasmed and he rolled over in the bed, clutching the sheet to his mouth to try to hold back the sob.

"Matty…" She trailed off.

"I love it, Mama. I love skating so much."

"I know, baby, and it's hurt you so much too."

Matty cried hard, opening all the boxes inside him where he'd tried to contain the pain, humiliation, and failure. He let it all spill out.

"Matty, figure skating has always been your dream."

"Yes," he whispered.

"But part of life is figuring out that sometimes dreams have to change. Part of being a grown-up is accepting that no matter how hard we work, sometimes our dreams just don't look like we thought they would. Sometimes we have to change our dreams. You accomplished so much in your career. Two national titles. A bronze at Worlds. Countless medals at the Grand Prix events. Just going to the Olympics twice is more than most skaters ever get. You have nothing to be ashamed of. You left it all out on the ice, and we're all so proud of you. You have nothing left to prove."

Matty cried for a long time while his mother breathed softly and made the occasional sound of support. When he finally stopped sobbing, transitioning into snotty sniffles, she didn't say anything else about his career.

He didn't either. Instead, he took a deep breath. "Mama, I have to tell you something."

"Okay."

"It's really important."

"All right, baby."

He could hear the fear in her voice and it occurred to him that drawing it out would be cruel. She was probably imagining all kinds of awful things. "I saw Ben today."

"Ben?"

"Rob's Ben."

She inhaled sharply and then laughed a little under her breath. "Oh!"

"Yeah. He's here. Well, in New Jersey. He's training there."

"Well, I can't say I'm not surprised, because I am. Very surprised. At the same time, I'm not. He certainly had talent."

"Yeah," Matty agreed.

"How long have you known?"

"I didn't." Matty explained how he came to be at the rink in New

Jersey.

"Tell me what you're thinking."

Matty grabbed the pillow on the opposite side of the bed and replaced his now damp one. The fabric was soft and dry. He rubbed his face against it. "Rob's here too, Mama. Right this minute he's in the same city as me. He's breathing and eating and living here somewhere. Now that I know I can almost feel him."

"And what are you planning to do about that?"

"I'm pretty sure he has a boyfriend. Or else he would have called me when he moved here. Wouldn't he?" Or maybe he didn't want anything to do with Matty anymore.

"Did Ben say that?"

"No, it's just…how could he not have a boyfriend? He's incredible. What if it's the same guy? What if it's serious?"

"Oh Matty."

"What do I do, Mama?"

Donna was quiet for some time. Finally, she said, "You have to listen to your heart. When it comes to skating and when it comes to Rob, you've got to really listen and figure out what you truly want. Then—and this is just as important—you have to figure out what you can realistically have. Can your body skate competitively for another year? For four?"

"I don't know. Other skaters do it, but we both know most of them are built physically stronger than I am."

"You need to figure that out. You can keep on training and hope for the best, and I'll support you in that. Or you can say enough is enough, cut your losses, and start to look at the rest of your life."

"And what is that? I mean, what do I have if I don't compete?"

"You have love for one thing."

"No, I don't. I lost that when I left him."

"First off, you don't know that for sure. And even if there's nothing there, or he's committed to someone else, Rob isn't the only man who will love you, Matty. Or the only person. We all love you and support you."

"I know. But what if he's the only man I can love?"

"Well, that's something you need to find out."

"I'm not signing up for Match-dot-com, Donna."

Donna laughed. "Where do you even come up with these things? Baby, I just want you to be happy. You've worked so hard. You're so young to have worked so hard."

But not hard enough. Matty knew that. He'd always been too lazy, too rebellious, and he'd never had the discipline of Alex Hampton or even stupid Vance Jones. But in the end, when he'd given it his all, had truly given up everything in his life except for training and skating—it still hadn't been enough.

Life was nothing like those fairy tales he read as a kid. Life wasn't even like *Ice Castles*. He was no Lexie and Rob wasn't Nick. Reality was an endless string of failure and disappointment as far as he could see.

"Honey, can you commit yourself to finding happiness in whatever form it might take? Even if it's not with Rob?"

"I don't know. I doubt it. Maybe."

"When you figure it out, let me know. There's one last thing, honey."

"Yeah, Mama?"

"When you know what you want, I expect you to fight for it with all the fire you've put into skating, because that's who you are. That's what Matty Marcus does. Even when he fails, he fails with flair."

Matty snorted and wiped at his eyes. "I will, Mama."

That night he stared at the ceiling, his mother's words echoing in his mind. There was only one way to find out if he had any hope of a future with Rob. What did he have to lose? The wheels started turning, and he formulated a plan. It was over the top and a little insane, but that was what Matty Marcus did best.

He was going to get Rob back.

Though he was sure his mother hadn't intended her advice to be taken in quite the way Matty was now planning, he was certain of one thing. To win, he had to be all in.

CHAPTER TWENTY-THREE

Matty sat down on the massage table to wait.

The clinic had a different color scheme than the one he usually went to for his appointments—green and taupe cabinets, instead of blue and white. Other than that, it was almost the same. It would have been comforting if Matty wasn't about to crawl out of his skin.

His heart pounded. He was surprised the receptionist had even led him back without a drug test. He knew he'd probably come across as a nutcase given how he'd been shaking and twitching as he'd signed in and filled out the paperwork. Of course he might in fact be a nutcase. At that moment he wasn't entirely sure if he was okay with that.

It had only taken a dozen phone calls to Manhattan clinics to discover Rob was completing his internship at a practice not even twelve blocks from where Matty lived. It blew his mind to think that Rob had been so close and yet, in the hustle of the city, they'd never run into each other. But now they were going to run into each other for sure.

Any second now.

Oh *God.*

Matty fiddled with his necklace, touching the tabs Ben had etched. He shook and felt cold, so he pulled the carefully folded green blanket over his lap. It wasn't any better quality than the blankets in Meredith's office.

Minutes passed.

He was still fully dressed in track pants and a tee, but he'd taken off his socks and sneakers. He stared down at his toes. He needed a pedicure, but beyond that his feet looked a disaster—beaten up and wounded. They had nothing on his knees, which were bruised from an unfortunate fall doing a simple waltz jump.

He'd secretly taken the subway to a rink in Queens since he shouldn't have even been on the ice at this stage of healing. But he hadn't been able to keep himself away. At least he'd landed on his hands and knees to avoid smashing his hip directly. Even so, it had hurt so badly he'd almost vomited on the ice.

He wondered what Rob would think of him. What would he say? Matty's pulse raced. This was a *terrible* idea. He should go. He should put his shoes on and just leave.

But no. He'd already canceled with Meredith.

Before he was ready, Matty heard the sound of his patient file being removed from the plastic container on the back of the door.

Sweat broke out over his body. The door opened and a tall, blond man in blue scrubs walked in with a wide, welcoming smile and glittering, green eyes. Matty's heart stopped, his stomach rolled, and he felt as though he couldn't breathe.

"Good morning," Rob said, and then stopped short with his hand on the knob of the now-closed door. "Holy shit."

Holy shit was right. Matty didn't know if he was going to cry or be a massive drama queen and pass out. Rob looked amazing. He was beautiful. And real. And *right there in front of him*. What the fuck was he supposed to *say*? Why hadn't he planned this out better? Had he really thought he should wing it? He was insane. This was insane.

Rob.

"Matty," Rob whispered. He cleared his throat. "I...wow, it's been a long time."

Matty heard himself replying, but he didn't know what he was saying. It was the same part of himself that took over after competitions, talking to the press, filling in the silence with sound. Afterwards, watching himself on video, he was always impressed at how he held it together, how he managed to make sense, but it was all second-hand to him because he had no recollection of it.

Rob took a deep breath. "Ben told me—I knew you were in the city—and he told me, and when I saw the name Matthew Marcus on my schedule I ho—wondered, but—you look..." Rob trailed off.

"Rough?"

"You look good." Rob blinked, an expression of hurt dropping over his features, and then, with a shake of his head, he cleared it away. "So, did you realize you were making an appointment with me? Or...?"

"I knew. I wanted to see you."

"I see." Rob swallowed hard and opened Matty's file. He shook his head, rubbed a hand over his eyes, and sighed.

"That bad?" Matty asked.

"A Type 2 labral tear requiring hip arthroscopy and shaving, on top of chondromalacia patellae from a misaligned knee cap, followed by additional injuries from a stubborn refusal to rest and recuperate on the part of the patient? Let's just say it's not the prettiest thing I've read this week."

Meredith scolded him sometimes, but Rob sounded like Matty had really let him down. It made his stomach hurt. *What the fuck am I doing here anyway? What was I thinking?*

"Okay, I'll step out of the room and you get undressed to your underwear. We'll start with massage to get your muscles loose, and then move on to the weights and machines."

Matty carefully folded his clothes and placed them on the chair, staring at the door Rob had just closed behind him. He was terrified that when the knock came, it would be someone else. He lay down on the table and covered himself with the blanket, his eyes on the ceiling tiles while his mind raced madly.

"Aren't you going to ask why I wanted to see you?" Matty blurted out as Rob stepped back into the room. Relief at the fact that Rob hadn't sent another therapist to deal with him made him ask without thinking.

"This is my place of business. As far as I'm concerned, you're here for treatment," Rob said, lifting the blanket off Matty's leg to start working on his calf. "I see you've got some fresh bruising here on your knees. I'm guessing you still aren't following doctor's orders about going out on the ice. Is this disregard endorsed by your coach?"

Matty cleared his throat. "Valentina would probably kill me with her bare hands."

"Mm-hmm," Rob murmured. "I'd like to witness her technique. Sell tickets. I'll attend."

"It can be my final show." Matty yelped as Rob's fingers hit a tender area. "Ow! Are you sure you know what you're doing?"

Rob smiled tightly. "I may not have my certification yet, but yes, I know what I'm doing."

"I'm sorry. I didn't mean—"

"Maybe I should get another therapist in here for you." He said it like it had only just occurred to him that he might do that.

"No. I don't want another therapist. I only want to see you."

Rob went back to massaging. "Okay. Then you need to stay calm."

Matty widened his eyes. Had Rob gone insane? How was he supposed to stay calm? Rob was acting like he was going to treat Matty as a *patient*. Was Matty going to have to just spell out what was going on here?

"Can't you talk to me?" Matty said. "Please?"

"What do you want me to say?"

"I don't know. Tell me things, like how you decided to become a physical therapist, and what happened to the ranch. Just…please talk to me. I've missed you."

Rob's mouth worked for a moment, and Matty's stomach twisted. He just knew that Rob was going to refuse or possibly even leave the room.

"I sold the ranch. Bing bought me out."

"Right. Bing." Matty hadn't thought of Bing in a long time.

"That gave me enough money to go back to school. Anja was right, of course. She usually is, and it turned out that physical therapy *is* a good fit."

"That's great. Right?"

"Yeah, of course. I find my work very rewarding."

"And Ben?"

Rob's expression turned a bit skeptical. "As you well know, Ben is still skating and has a new coach in New Jersey, so I relocated with them."

"You live in Jersey? I'm thinking of moving there."

"No. I live in Brooklyn."

Matty smiled, trying to keep Rob engaged with him. "Brooklyn's good. What part?"

Rob frowned and was silent for a long moment. "Park Slope."

"Quality."

"Yeah, it's a nice place. Anyway, I'm sure Ben's told you but his goal is Junior Worlds this year. They think he'll make it." He smiled softly at Matty and then turned his focus back to his work. "It's hard to sum up almost two and a half years in a few sentences, but that about does it."

Rob shifted the blanket down over Matty's left leg and moved on to his right, which was the injured side of his body. Matty shut up because it hurt a hell of a lot, and he had to concentrate on not yelling from the pain. Rob grew very quiet as well, very intense and focused on his work. Matty glanced up at him occasionally, and then forced himself to look away because it was too much. Too close to something this wasn't.

"Okay, I'm going to stretch your leg now. Take a deep breath, and as you let it out, I'm going to push your leg up, okay? It's going to hurt but—"

"I fucking know, okay?" Matty gritted out as his hands clenched on the edge of the table.

Rob ran his hands soothingly down Matty's leg, and then reached up to Matty's fingers, prying them loose. "Relax."

Matty felt a small quiver run through him. He recognized the voice—warm and commanding. It brought back so many memories and none of them were appropriate for the therapy room.

Rob came around the table and moved his hands over Matty's shoulders, pressing the tension down his arms to his fingertips. "Stay relaxed. Close your eyes. Good."

Rob's hands felt so big and warm, and Matty could almost believe he was back in Rob's bedroom at the ranch. His stomach flip-flopped.

"Now breathe in the sky. Take in the entire sky and let it out."

"Ridiculous," Matty muttered.

"Do it."

His voice was the one Matty obeyed—the voice that took him places he was afraid to go and brought him back whole. Matty breathed deeply, the sky moving into his lungs. He blew it back out, blue and expanding and huge.

"Again," Rob said. "Now I'll lift your leg when you exhale."

Matty whimpered a little but he handled the pain better than usual. His body stayed relaxed, and Rob took the stretch farther than Meredith managed, pushing Matty's leg up, then using his arm to adjust Matty's hip and bring it into alignment.

"Good," Rob said.

He felt so rewarded. He wanted to do it again and hear Rob say it just like that.

Matty opened his eyes on the fourth repetition, and his entire body jerked, a shock of hot pain arcing through him. He met Rob's gaze, intimate and raw, focused on Matty in a way that was so familiar that it made Matty feel like he'd come home after a really fucking brutal trip.

"Hey," Matty said, his voice small.

"All right?"

"Yeah," Matty whispered.

Swallowing hard, Rob lowered Matty's leg and stepped back from the table, making notes in the chart. "Range of motion is better than last week, according to the file your former therapist sent over, and—"

"Are you seeing anyone?" Matty asked, his heart hammering in his chest and his mouth dry. The fierce wings of hope beat in his stomach, and he looked up at Rob through his lashes.

"Yes. I am."

"Oh." It was more of an involuntary reaction than anything else, as if the wind was knocked out of him.

"For a while now. And you?"

Matty stared at him, licked his lips and said, "Yeah, me too."

Rob's eyebrows lifted and he sat down on the small chair beside the massage table with a bottle of IcyHot in his hand. He lifted the blanket from Matty's legs again and began to rub it into Matty's muscles. "Is his name Figure Skating?"

Matty stared at the ceiling, his throat tight. "Of course."

"He's as abusive as ever it seems," Rob said. "Still fucking you without any lube."

"Something like that." The ceiling tiles were white with black holes, and he began to count them silently, trying to hold onto something tangible before the tears took over.

"Okay, we'll move to the exercise room now," Rob said, patting Matty's leg. "Get dressed and we'll see how you do with the weights."

Half an hour later, Matty was sweating and hurting, wanting to go home, take a Motrin, cry for a month, and then sleep for a year. He was going to have to take a cab back to his apartment because walking was out of the question, as were the steps down to the subway.

"Well, Matty," Rob said as he guided him toward the front waiting room. "It was good to see you."

"You too."

"So now that you've satisfied your curiosity, you can go back to your former therapist, and this will be the end."

Matty narrowed his eyes. "Is that what you think this was about? Curiosity?"

After a long moment, Rob shrugged. "Go back to your former therapist." He walked away.

As Matty wrote a check for his co-pay, he watched Sylvia, the receptionist, peck at the keyboard. "Sylvia, can you schedule me with Rob for next week?"

"But I thought he just said..." She trailed off and put a long, French-manicured nail between her teeth.

"He's got much stronger hands than my previous therapist and I thought we had a better rapport."

Sylvia looked even more confused.

"We got along well," Matty clarified.

"Let me check Rob's schedule," Sylvia said, uncertainly. "He's got...well, the only open slots he has right now are Tuesdays and Thursdays at ten in the morning?"

"I'll take them both."

* * *

The elegant curving line of Murano-glass bubbles swept along above Matty and Elliot in the Saks Fifth Avenue shoe department. Elliot stood before one of the full-length mirrors with one slim hip jutted out. The B Brian Atwood ankle boots encasing his narrow feet were stunning four-inch heels with tops made of iridescent canvas and suede and cut with peep-toes. The purple and turquoise feather print matched his purple skinny jeans and pink button-up nicely.

"I look amazing in these, bitch."

Matty took in Elliot's tall, skinny frame—all pointy elbows and sharp corners—and his soft blond hair, wide, innocent-looking brown eyes, and full lips. His best friend did indeed look amazing. He even tried to infuse his voice with enthusiasm when he said, "Buy them, then."

"They're five hundred and twenty-five bucks. Are you crazy?

That's like a fourth of my rent."

Still Elliot looked thoughtful as he considered the shoes a few more moments. Then he turned to Matty and indicated the metallic and snakeskin three-inch heels Matty had requested. "Aren't you going to try those on? Or did you scandalize the salesgirl for nothing?"

"She wasn't scandalized. This is Saks. No one's ever scandalized here."

"Not that they let on anyway."

"And I don't think we're allowed to call them salesgirls. I think that's sexist or something. We probably have to call them shoe specialists." Matty put the shoes aside with a sigh.

Elliot's brows lowered and he sat down next to Matty, taking his hands in his own. "Oh my God, what's wrong? Is it your mother? Does she have cancer or something?"

"What are you talking about?"

"We are on a girls' day out together and you *won't even try on your shoes!* Something awful has to have happened."

"She's fine. I mean, as far as I know, she's fine." He hadn't actually talked to her in a while since he was avoiding telling her about Rob. He was also avoiding telling Elliot about Rob, so he had to tread carefully now. Still, he could use his best friend's advice, even if he already knew what it was going to be.

"Are you sick? Is it your hip? Or your knee? Is something not healing right?" He gasped. "Did you get tested and you're positive?"

Matty ripped his hands out of Elliot's grasp. "That's not even funny."

"I'm not trying to be funny, bitch, I'm trying to figure out why you're broken. *Shoes*, Matty. There are shiny shoes right in front of you but they aren't on your feet!"

Matty rubbed his hands over his face, and Elliot softly cursed.

"And now you've smeared your mascara," he said, reaching over to rub his thumb under Matty's eyes.

Glancing in the mirror, he saw that Elliot had only made it worse. Instead of looking like he'd smeared his mascara, he now had really dark circles under his eyes, like maybe he was actually sick.

"It's about my skating career," Matty said, bending over to put on the shoes so Elliot would stop imagining the worst. He didn't need to look up to know Elliot was rolling his eyes. It was evident in the slight bend of his body away from Matty and his exasperated huff of breath.

"You know what I think about that," Elliot said, standing up to examine his feet in the B Brian Atwoods again.

"I know." Matty strapped the shoes on, noting that he definitely needed a pedicure before he saw Rob again, and stood gingerly, putting the weight on his good leg. The heels made him almost as tall as Elliot was normally. "These are only three hundred and seventy-five," Matty said. "A bargain price."

"If you quit skating, you might actually have some money to spend on some extravagances, baby. No more coaches to pay. No more costumes. No more choreographers or travel expenses or fees."

He said it slow and enticing, like Matty had always imagined a drug pusher would sound when offering him heroin or steroids. "You have a good point."

The shoes lifted his already gargantuan skater's ass up in the air, and he turned to study his reflection. His strong, thin legs were wrapped up in dark gray skinny jeans, and his shapely arms looked good coming out of the open sleeves of the long, purple, clinging Phillip Lim silk T-shirt dress he wore. Still, no matter how good the shoes looked, or how well they complemented his outfit, there was no way he was going to drop that much for them. It wasn't even a temptation.

"Don't you love living in the city?" Elliot asked. "Remember back home in Virginia when we risked getting punched just for wearing lip gloss? Well, baby, look at us now. Alive and well in the Big Apple and both of us pretty as princesses."

Matty smiled and put his arm around Elliot's waist. He remembered their childhood in Virginia well. From the very first moment he'd passed Elliot that glitter crayon, it had been the two of them against a world bent on humiliating and hurting them for being too obviously gay.

"Remember gym class?" Matty asked.

"Who could forget Jim and Sam Mayfield? Twin closet cases, I bet you anything."

"Yeah, probably. They were a nightmare, but at least we had each other." Matty remembered how nervously they'd waited for the thuggish twins to come through the locker room after P.E. class.

"Nothing like the comfort of knowing that if we had to be tortured, we'd be tortured together."

Matty almost mentioned physical therapy, since torture had come to mind during the weight session with Rob. But he wasn't going to chance bringing that up with Elliot just yet. He needed it to play out first. It'd be less humiliating when it all came crashing down around his head if he was the only one who knew what he had done.

Elliot murmured, "You should totally buy those. Quit skating and buy them."

Matty wondered what Rob would think of him in the shiny

metallic heels. In Montana, he'd never worn his most outrageous shoes. There'd been too much snow and his mother hadn't sent them anyway. Would Rob think he looked hot? Matty bit his lip and stared at himself in the mirror. His eyes were dark and tired, his skin was pale and clear, but he was still sexy, in a world-weary sort of way, wasn't he? The shoes *did* make his ass look like it was served up on a platter. How could Rob resist that?

He has a boyfriend. He's a loyal, good man who will respect his partner. That's how.

"Seriously, they look so hot on you. Be crazy. Buy them."

"I think I might," Matty said, staring at the way the metallic leather caught the light reflecting from the cascading bubbles above. "Quit competing, that is."

Elliot clucked his tongue. "Oh, bitch, don't lie to me."

Matty lifted his gaze and locked it on Elliot. "I'm not." The certainly washed over him. His skin tingled, and his breath caught.

He was going to quit competing. It was the right thing. He was ready to move on.

His throat was dry, and he swallowed thickly. "Will you be honest with me, Elliot?"

"You know I will."

"Will you think less of me if I throw in the towel and stop competing?"

"Are you being serious right now?"

"Yes."

Elliot's face flushed, and he grabbed Matty's hands. "No. A world of no, baby. I swear on my soul, Matty. No one *could* think less of you, not if they know what you've given up and what you've gone through for this sport."

"Really?"

"Matty, I'm so proud of you. I've always been so proud of you. I tell everyone I know what an amazing person you are because I love you—for *you*. Not because you're some world-famous figure skater, okay? To be honest, that's not got a lot of street cred attached it, if you know what I mean? I mean, you're no NBA quarterback."

Matty chuckled. "You know nothing about sports."

"Like you do?"

"I'm a world-class athlete! And it's *NFL* quarterback."

"Sure. Well, are we done being sincere now? It makes me look pale."

Matty squeezed Elliot's hand and took a deep breath. "I think this is it, Elliot. This is the right time for me to hang up the skates. I'm

21222324

getting a little old for all this bullshit."

Elliot's long lashes fluttered and a hand came up to his chest. For a moment, he looked like he was going to break into a grin, and Matty's heart lifted in anticipation of that familiar, loved expression. But then he narrowed his eyes and his lips straightened tightly at the edges.

"Why?"

Matty closed his eyes. How could he sum up everything? It was the way Hank Babikov skated, it was the pain of surgery, and the agony of physical therapy. It was the way Rob smiled and the hope that even if he couldn't have Rob—but he wanted Rob, dammit—that maybe he'd find someone to have a life with.

It was the fact that he had only kept training because that was all he knew how to do. It was because he didn't know what life looked like without figure skating controlling every aspect of it, and he thought he really should find out.

"Because I'm done. I just need to figure how to do it and when. I could send Joanna a text right now, but I should give her the respect of saying it to her face. Valentina probably knows, but I should talk to her too. Man to man, so to speak. She'll think it's for the best. If she's one thing, it's practical."

"When? Because I won't believe it until I see it."

"I'll talk to Valentina tomorrow, and Joanna next week. She'll need to market my career in a whole new way if I'm not competing. There could be other opportunities now that I don't even know about."

"Totally. This could be a great thing, Matty."

"Yeah. She'll know better than I do what I might do next. She's guided other skaters through the transition."

"Matty Marcus, you are my hero," Elliot whispered, his brown eyes filling with tears.

"What the fuck, Elliot?" Matty cupped Elliot's cheek. "You're going to mess up your make-up and I don't even know why."

"Because you're amazing. You're strong and smart, and you're so fucking brave. I know you're scared to make this choice, but this is going to be the best thing you ever did. Wait and see."

Matty refrained from reminding Elliot that once he'd promised that Matty was going to be the next Olympic champion with very nearly the same words. Instead, he let Elliot pull him into a fierce embrace.

"You're going to buy those shoes," Elliot said. "Understand me, bitch? You'll buy those fucking shoes and we'll celebrate your profound and very adult decision by spending shit tons of money on frivolous items. Got it?"

"I'll buy those for you too," Matty said. "As my promise to you.

I'm done with figure skating."

"Holy shit, are you serious? You don't have to do that. Besides, you don't have that kind of money."

"No, I don't. But hey, when's the last time I did something incredibly stupid?"

"Uh, how about when you admitted that you didn't think that Anna Wintour was the finest bitch of high fashion? That was stupid."

"I don't get your obsession with her. She's just a fifty-something, uptight, rich lady with access to good clothes."

"Don't make me cut you."

"Whatever. Buying these shoes is stupider than not worshipping at the altar of Vogue's elderly editor...and I earned it."

"You totally earned it with blood, sweat, and tears."

Matty paid for their shoes, and the very un-scandalized shoe specialist smiled winningly as he handed her the credit card. He pulled Elliot close and wrapped his arm around his waist. "No matter what, it's you and me against the world, right? I can count on you? Together forever?"

"Together forever," Elliot answered and kissed his cheek solemnly.

* * *

Matty didn't know what he expected from Rob, but some kind of acknowledgment that Matty had rather defiantly returned the next week was definitely on that list. Yet Rob didn't say a thing.

He worked with Matty twice a week, and kept it strictly professional. It took a lot of effort to get him to open up about anything aside from Matty's hip and his therapy, but eventually Rob chatted about Ben and his skating goals, and about the leaky faucet in his apartment in Brooklyn. But he never said anything like, *"So, what the fuck are you up to, Matty? Why are you here?"*

Matty didn't tell him, but he thought Rob was a better therapist than Meredith anyway. Matty always wanted to impress people, but when it came to Rob it went beyond that. Hearing Rob say the word "good" made Matty shiver and relax at the same time. It made him want to do whatever it was again, only *better*, and maybe with an orgasm at the end.

He missed being with Rob so much it ached, and though he had no intention of backing out, Matty asked himself nearly every day what it was he was doing. He'd never been good at keeping secrets from his mother, and yet he didn't tell her about Rob. Nor did he tell Rob that he'd broken up with his boyfriend, Figure Skating.

One night, he pulled up the picture of Ben and Rob with the guy with the terrible teeth. Matty stared at it, wondering if *he* was the man in Rob's life. If he'd moved from Montana with Rob because he'd been smart enough to not let a good thing get away, or if they were carrying on a long-distance thing.

He closed the file and bit the inside of his cheek until he tasted blood.

The next day at therapy, Matty swallowed back a yelp of pain during the weight training session. With his eyes still closed in effort, he asked, "How long have you been seeing your boyfriend now?"

Rob's voice was casual when he answered, "Hmm. I guess for about two years. Maybe a little longer. It's hard to say. I should keep better track of those things."

Matty gritted his teeth together, his gut burning as he opened his eyes. He couldn't stop himself from spitting out, "Why do I always get replaced by someone uglier than me?"

Rob blinked at him for a moment and looked as though he might laugh. "I have no idea."

"I mean, it's called an orthodontist. Look into it. And that's all I have to say about that."

Rob seemed flummoxed, and Matty wanted to punch him. Then Matty wanted to punch *himself* for having given so much away in just a few seconds. Sometimes he hated his mouth.

"All right," Rob said, and Matty heard the quiver of repressed laughter in his voice. "Let's add some additional weight and see how you tolerate it."

"Bitch," Matty said. "Fine, that teeth thing was low. I apologize."

Rob shrugged. "It's got nothing to do with your random comment on teeth, Matty. It's just my job."

"Professional sadist at my service," Matty murmured, surprised at the venom in his voice.

"Ten reps. If you can do it," Rob said, cheerfully.

After that, Matty listened every day for some kind of mention of the guy Rob was seeing. He strained to come up with questions that might elicit a response from Rob that included the guy's name, or, more importantly, if Rob was in love with him. Matty thought not. Surely Rob would talk about him a lot more if he was in love with him. Or was Rob just being polite and sparing Matty's feelings?

"So, does your boyfriend enjoy restraints?" Matty practiced asking the mirror one night as he moisturized. He attempted to look incredibly innocent while saying the words, but he had to admit, there was just no way he was going to ask that. Well, not yet anyway.

"Is it as good with him as it was with me?" Matty tried. Again, it just wasn't happening.

Still it pricked at his mind like those horrible garden weeds his mother used to make him pull—the ones that just irritated the surface of his skin at first, a slight annoyance, but over time became a fire of itchy madness that couldn't be scratched enough or entirely washed away with soap.

Did the mystery guy suck cock well? Did he beg for it like Matty had? Was he *better* at...anything? Because seriously, Matty didn't know how it could be better than what they'd had together. But maybe Rob didn't feel the same. Maybe in-need-of-an-orthodontist guy had a magic ass and made Rob shoot glitter or something.

Maybe Matty needed to accept that he could never turn back time. That he and Rob were over for good.

"I'm glad we can be friends," Rob said one day at the very end of their next session, right after he'd let Matty know he'd improved enough to drop to only one visit a week. Earlier, while Matty had worked his way almost easily through the weight training, Rob had revealed to Matty some of Ben's issues with his coach, and Matty had given him earnest and hard-won advice to pass on.

"Me too," Matty lied, and he endured Rob's friendly clap on the shoulder with a smile.

"Listen, I hope this isn't asking too much, but this entire conversation reminded me of a favor I've wanted to ask you."

"Anything." Matty hoped this favor didn't include something horrible like picking Rob's boyfriend up at the airport, because Matty might shove him out of the moving car before he could stop himself.

"Would you be willing to meet with Ben on the ice and give him some pointers to work on his artistry?"

"I'm pretty sure that would piss off his coach."

"Well, it might, but I'd like to think that Greg would know when he has a good opportunity right in front of him. You'd be amazing for Ben, and I know he'd love to work with you again. You could be so good for him right now. If you have the time, of course. I'm sure you'll be busy soon with full-time training again and—"

"I'll always have the time for him." Maybe this was the opportunity to tell Rob that Matty had time for him too. Yet somehow the words wouldn't come. If he told Rob he'd quit skating then Rob might think of him as a failure. That would be devastating. At least if Rob didn't know, it seemed like Matty had *something*.

"Great. I'll let Ben know to expect a text from you about it." Rob checked his watch. "I have to get to my next patient. Have a good day."

As Matty left the clinic, the world looked strange. It seemed like someone had turned New York City into a lifeless puppet show. Ambling blindly down the street, barely paying attention to where he was going and lost in the weirdness inside his mind, there were two things Matty Marcus knew for sure.

First—regardless of anything else, he wanted to work with Ben. The thought excited him and broke his heart at the same time. He wanted to help Ben skate up to his potential. Maybe he could even look into choreographing for him. Somewhere in his soul where she'd been resting for a long time, Yuliya Yasneyeva was ready to make a comeback.

Second—he absolutely did *not* want to be friends with Rob Lovely.

Chapter Twenty-four

The day the doctor deemed Matty healed enough to stop physical therapy entirely, he stood outside the clinic doors waiting and hoping that he'd chosen the right side of the building by which to loiter.

If Rob was going to take the subway to Brooklyn, he'd exit this side for sure. But what if Rob wasn't going home straight away? What if he was meeting up with Anja and Ben somewhere? Or his boyfriend? Matty needed to talk to Rob before he had a chance to get the news from anyone else, and he needed to tell him how he felt.

Matty pushed up his sunglasses on his nose and noticed some paparazzi taking photos of him as he leaned against the clinic building. Good to know that a fresh retirement announcement was enough to make him fodder for the gossip columns. Head high and fabulous scarf around his neck, he breathed slowly, letting the energy of the city writhe around him as he pulled strength from it.

"Matty, what are you doing out here?"

Matty pushed off from the wall and breathlessly gazed at Rob for a moment before blurting out, "I don't want to be friends."

Rob's lips quirked, but he said nothing. He looked *amused*, which infuriated Matty, whose heart was hammering so hard his hand was pressed to his chest to help hold it in. He hadn't been this nervous since the Olympics. He thought he might puke.

Rob cleared his throat. "You want my bad romance?"

Matty punched him lightly in the chest. "Shut up." Matty wanted to smile, but he couldn't. He was shaking so hard he didn't think he could fake his way out of it. "What the fuck are you talking about?"

"Come on, Matty, there's no way you don't like Gaga."

Matty stared at him, the urge to smile vanished. "I'm being serious and you're making a joke out of this?"

"I'm not making a joke out of whatever you're trying to say, swee—Matty." He shifted his bag on his shoulder and leaned against the building. "You don't want to be friends with me. I can deal with that. Being around each other was probably a bad idea to begin with. But it was your idea, not mine."

Matty narrowed his eyes. Rob was purposely misinterpreting him. He supposed it was a kind thing to do, rather than humiliate him with a reminder of his boyfriend, but Matty was putting it all out and Rob was going to have to acknowledge it. "You know that's not what I meant."

Rob shrugged and nodded. He leaned his head up and squinted into the sun as it slotted through the tall buildings. "Listen, Matty, you know that..." Rob trailed off and glanced across the street at the paparazzi. He frowned. "Do they follow you everywhere now?"

"Ha! No. I'm not *that* amazing. Though for some reason I get more press than Hank Babikov."

Rob looked like he was going to say something else but thought better of it. Instead, he said, "I was headed home."

He took a step, and Matty grabbed hold of his arm. "Please, Rob, don't go. Talk to me. Say something. Anything at all. Just don't walk away now."

"Matty—"

His heart pounded. "Do you miss Montana?"

Rob was silent for a long time. He studied his shoes like they held the answer to whether or not he should reply. He shifted slightly and then met Matty's eye, but he said nothing.

Matty's throat went tight and he whispered, "I miss it. A lot. Tell me you do too."

Rob hadn't changed that much had he? He wasn't citified yet. Matty could see his roots in his every step and hear them in every word. Montana would always hold a place in Rob's heart.

Finally, Rob licked his lips. "Sure."

"So many times I was about to give up and I'd remember something you said or something we did, and I found the strength to keep going."

Rob put his hands in his pockets and gazed at Matty from under his lashes, a flush on the top of his cheekbones.

"Please. Say something, Rob."

After a long moment, Rob said, "You can't see the stars in the city at night. I used to look up in Montana, see the North Star, and I'd remember. Can't see it much now. But I still remember."

"Me too."

Matty reached out, his hand coming close to Rob's face, but Rob grabbed his fingers and gently lowered his hand.

"Don't want to give the tabloids dirt for their gossip columns," Rob whispered.

"Of course I do," Matty said, but he felt too vulnerable, too hopeful and needy to sound half as pompous as he knew he should.

Rob sighed. "Are you coming to my place?"

"Your place?"

"So we can finally talk in private."

Matty wanted to say yes. He was dying to know where Rob lived—if only so he could stalk the address when Rob rejected him for his buck-toothed, blond, ugly boyfriend. Speaking of...

"Will your boyfriend be there?"

"Oh, my boyfriend." Rob waved his hand dismissively. "His name is Physical Therapy, and he's not nearly so demanding as Figure Skating. He has a regular schedule that's easy to plan around. Nine to five—what a way to make a living. Three weeks vacation, and a retirement plan. He's pretty cool. I'm in love with him."

Matty blinked. "You mean—I've been—oh my God. I hate you."

Rob chuckled softly, but there was sadness under it. "I don't think you hate me at all."

"No...no, I don't think I ever could."

Rob glanced over toward the paparazzi again. "Are you coming to my place? Or do I need to pick you up and carry you there?"

Joy, raw and unexpected, leapt in Matty's heart. "Carry me. Give the photographers something fantastic to print about me in their ridiculous paper."

Rob laughed and swooped him up into his arms. Matty had only just caught a whiff of Rob's familiar scent when Rob promptly set him down again. "Apparently, I need to work out more often."

"I ate some pizza. And some cake," Matty confessed. "There was an apple pie once. And steak. Several hamburgers. More than one bag of frozen french fries. Actual ice cream for dessert. Doughnuts."

Rob grinned. "Good for you."

"I blame the steroid injections and pills the doctors gave me for my hip. They made me so hungry."

"That's what they're supposed to do, so you'll eat and have fuel to heal."

"Now I'm fatter than ever and—"

"Shh," Rob said. "Your body is amazing."

"Amazing isn't good enough."

Rob's eyes flickered with recognition, and he bit his lip. He squinted up at the sun again. "We can talk more easily at my place," Rob said. "Come on." He tugged Matty toward the subway.

Rob's apartment was on the ground floor of a Brooklyn townhouse. It had a single bedroom and a small bathroom, a combined kitchen and sitting area featuring a fold-out sofa for Ben. There was also a tiny patio with a small garden in the back.

The apartment was clean and well-appointed, though there were almost no items from the house in Montana, as far as Matty could tell. Everything was new except for a few knick-knacks of sentimental value, the photo of Matty and Ben, which hung on a wall underneath a photo of Ben and Anja, and Rob's bed, which Matty saw as they passed through the bedroom on their way out to the patio.

"So," Rob said, sitting down in a lawn chair. It was plastic and bucket-seated, like the kind Matty's mom had kept around for backyard barbeques when he was a kid. He had a bottle of wine in one hand and two brightly colored plastic wine glasses in the other. "I know it's not much. Not like the ranch. But it's home."

"It's nice. Much bigger than my tiny apartment," Matty said, perching on the more solid wooden chair that Rob indicated for him. "I never imagined you'd fit in here, but look at you. You really do."

Rob handed him one of the plastic wine glasses filled halfway with a Pinot noir. "I'm pretty sure it's not very New York to serve wine in these, but screw it. They work." Rob studied his—a turquoise green. "They were a moving gift from Bill and Angus. I think Angus picked them out."

"They're still together?"

"Married."

Matty gasped happily. "No way."

"Well, not legally—not yet—Montana is behind the times on that front, but they stood up in front of everyone and said words, exchanged rings, and bought a new house together."

"When I left, Bill wouldn't even admit he loved him."

"His vows were hilarious. He said, 'By now, everyone here knows I like you some.'"

Matty laughed and took a very unladylike gulp of wine, overwhelmed with nervous excitement and happiness to be sitting and talking with Rob again.

"Then he said, 'I guess I promise to keep on liking you until I die. Seems probable that I will anyway.'"

Matty could barely catch his breath, wiping at his eyes as he laughed.

Rob gazed fondly at his wine glass. "Man, I miss him. I need to call him. It's been a month or so." He met Matty's gaze. "After you started coming to the clinic, I didn't dare call him. I knew what he'd say and I didn't want him to be right."

Matty's heart skipped a beat. "What would he have been right about?"

"That I shouldn't let you keep coming to see me. That you'd get the wrong idea. Or he'd suggest that I should definitely give you the wrong idea, because it was actually the right idea. Or something like that."

"Was it the right idea?"

"I don't know." Rob looked troubled.

Matty took another sip of wine and let it slide over his tongue.

Suddenly he remembered something else Rob hadn't brought from Montana. "I guess Lila didn't make the trip?" Matty asked, a little tentatively, knowing the answer. She hadn't been well when they were together. He was sure she was long gone now.

"She didn't even make the next year. She was gone about three months after you left."

Matty felt somehow responsible, as though if only he'd stayed then Lila would have stuck around. "I'm sorry."

Rob snorted. "Control freak. She would have died anyway. And last time I checked, you are a very good figure skater, not the messiah."

"I was the messiah once when I was sixteen for an Easter show in Russia. It was loosely based on *Jesus Christ Superstar*, and they made me skate around with a cross on my back. It was very weird, and it wasn't a good look on me."

"You can say that again. I remember when I first saw those online," Rob laughed. "It's kind of horrifying that those photos will always be in the public domain. Do you suffer nightmares from it? Dreams that you're back in school for some reason and you look down to find yourself in front of the class in that awful costume?"

Matty laughed again. It wasn't even that funny, but he was shot through with nerves and it broke the tension. After all, he knew things had changed, but he didn't want *this*, this thing between them, to be one of them.

"I missed you," Rob said, thoughtfully. "I missed hearing you laugh."

Matty swallowed hard and took another steadying sip of the wine. He wasn't sure he was ready for this part of the conversation. This was the part where anything could happen. It had been so good so far. Matty didn't want whatever Rob had to say next to destroy the beautiful, buoyant hope that was growing in his heart.

"You know, it pretty much destroyed me when you left," Rob said, his eyes focused on the garden. "I could barely get out of bed for a week after you were gone. I'd say it took me a couple of months to get it together even a little bit. Bing, Bill, Anja—even Ben—were pretty damn worried about me. Eventually I realized that, aside from Ben, I had nothing to lose after I lost you. When Bing asked about buying the ranch, I sold it to him and I started to build a new life."

Rob smiled with a sad, sweet look in his eyes. "In that way, leaving me like you did was a good thing. It shook me up hard. Bing said it nearly killed me, but in the end, I got a better life than the one I had before. Phoenix from the flame, as some would say."

Matty put his hand on Rob's knee as if he could absorb the pain from Rob's past and take away anything he'd ever suffered on Matty's account.

"I'm happier now, though sometimes I miss the open spaces. Even the damn cattle. But all in all, this is a better life for me. And I wouldn't miss Ben growing up for the world. So it's all good."

"I'm glad." Matty's voice was gruff, and he cleared his throat softly. "I never wanted to hurt you."

Rob didn't respond to that. Instead he said, "I dated around a little when I first got here. It was surprisingly easy to find men who wanted a dominant top."

Matty took his hand away and clenched his teeth as a shot of jealousy struck him to the quick. As always, he couldn't bear to think of Rob taking anyone but him to such raw, vulnerable places.

"Though there was no one that meant anything."

"Me too," Matty said. "I mean, there was no one that meant anything. There was pretty much no one at all, except Julien, but...he's just a friend. It was a weird, fucked-up friendship thing. Julien was empathetic, and I had just found out about that guy you were dating in Montana—"

"You don't have to confess anything to me, Matty. Frankly, I don't want to think about it. But I'm confused—what guy that I was dating in Montana? I didn't date anyone in Montana."

"Blond, messed up teeth. He was in the photo Ben sent me. His first medal at some summer competition?"

Rob's laughter was warm and deep, rumbling inside his body, and Matty wanted to press himself against Rob's chest to feel it on his skin.

"Barry? You thought I was dating Barry? He'll get a kick out of that."

Matty waited for the punch line, for the reason the jealousy he'd endured was so funny, but Rob just shook his head, still laughing, and took a sip of his wine.

"What? He's small, effeminate, and aside from his teeth, he is exactly your type."

"What do you know about my type? I've dated all kinds of men. I'll have you know that you're the first and only guy I've dated who regularly wears make-up, and—" Rob motioned at Matty's Chanel sweater "—women's clothing. Not that I have a problem with it. It's just that, in general, I date guys who aren't Matty Marcus."

"In general. But there are exceptions."

"Once there was an exception, yes. Just once. Matty Marcuses are hard to come by." Rob smiled fondly. "Anyway, Barry was one of Ben's coaches, and he's very much taken...by an incredibly beautiful *woman*, sweetheart."

Matty's stomach fluttered. He sat down his wine glass on the patio, and he leaned forward, elbows on his knees and his heart in his throat. "For fuck's sake, when are you going to kiss me?"

Rob's gaze moved from Matty's eyes to his lips and lingered there. Then he stared down at his wine glass. When Rob cleared his throat, Matty's stomach twisted. He tried so hard to keep his face from showing how he was feeling, knowing that he completely failed.

"I hadn't planned on kissing you, actually."

"But why not?"

Rob's lips twisted, and for the first time he looked as if he was losing his composure. "Don't you think I know exactly what's going on with you right now? I watched the Olympics, Matty, and I saw the outcome of Worlds. As you might imagine, given what I sacrificed for it, I've been kind of invested in your career." His voice lowered to a tight whisper. "I know exactly what's going on with you."

Matty didn't know why it hadn't occurred to him before, but it suddenly hit him. Rob had *seen him fail*. There was a rush of adrenaline in his veins, a tight feeling of panic in his chest, and a hot splash of raw, awful humiliation.

Of course he had. Of course he'd watched—even if he hadn't cared for Matty, he'd have watched with Ben, *for* Ben, and he saw it all. He'd seen Matty's joy when he thought he'd flown and he'd witnessed his crushing devastation when the other skaters' scores came in. For a moment, hateful rage flashed through Matty, and then it faded into the dull, ever-present ache in his chest, the one he hadn't found a way to fully cope with yet.

Why would Rob want him? He was a pain in the ass, selfish, egomaniacal, and he didn't even have an Olympic medal to show for it.

Rob went on, "You're hurt, you're angry, and you're injured. I don't want to be your rebound relationship, Matty. I also *really* don't want to be the person you use to punish yourself for what happened."

"I don't want that." Matty's voice was barely audible even to himself. He wasn't sure Rob heard.

"I let you believe I had a boyfriend. I told myself that if I put that barrier between us, if I kept you at a distance, then I could pretend you were just a patient. Just an old friend. But that's not the reality. I should never have let you stay on with me. I should have made you go back to your old clinic. But...I couldn't. I wanted to be near you."

"I'm so glad you didn't. I want to be near you too. I've never stopped loving you, Rob. I'd never use you." Rob's eyebrows went up in a challenge and Matty sucked in a breath. "Please don't tell me that's how you see our time together in Montana?" He felt as though he would be crushed under a great weight if Rob said he did.

"No. Of course not. It's just...last time...Matty, I can't do that again. When you left—"

Matty fell to his knees and took Rob's free hand in both of his own. "Me too. I swear. When I left, I didn't handle it well. Valentina is the only reason I made it. She kept me focused. She's the only reason I even got on the Olympic team at all."

Rob put his wine down and took Matty's chin in his hand. "Matty, Valentina didn't get you to the Olympics. *You* did that."

"And I failed."

Rob released his chin. "You were amazing. Your performance was stunning. It was so beautiful that it broke my heart."

"But amazing isn't always enough."

Rob swallowed hard and whispered, "Exactly."

Matty gazed up at Rob, watching his eyes shift through emotions, seeing things there that he'd missed before—vulnerability, fear, and boundless affection. "Kiss me."

Rob's eyes crinkled as he smiled. "Are you bossing me around?"

"Yeah." Matty shifted up and put his mouth within striking distance. "Maybe it won't be the same. Maybe we'll kiss and—"

Rob's mouth tasted of wine, and it was so right—so perfect and slick. Matty grasped Rob's shirt and clung. He felt as though he were tumbling, falling through space and time, and it was everything he needed. Matty caught Rob's noises, and fed them back to him, and the kiss went on and on, hands grappling. Rob lifted Matty from the ground onto his lap, and it was fucking perfect.

"Shh," Rob said, pulling away, pressing his hand to Matty's lips to prevent Matty from leaning in to begin the kiss again. "This needs to stop right now."

"Why?" Matty panted.

"Because," Rob said, pushing Matty from his lap and standing. "I don't want it."

Matty felt punched in the gut. The kiss had been so passionate. The rush had been so real. He'd felt so much between them in those moments. How could he have been wrong?

"You don't want it," Matty repeated back slowly. His legs quivered.

"No, I don't." Rob closed his eyes and wiped his hand over his mouth. "It's too much."

Matty sucked in a breath. He was *too much*. He was always over the top, always too flamboyant for judges—too gay for *figure skating* for

God's sake—and now he was too much for Rob?

"I'm sorry," Rob said, pacing the length of the patio. "I shouldn't have let you get close to me again. I shouldn't have invited you here and I should've stopped you when I realized what you were doing."

"And what am I doing?"

"Trying to start something with me again."

"*Obviously*. But when did you know that, Rob? Have you been just toying with me?"

Rob rubbed a hand over his hair. "I knew when you came back after I told you to go. I should've refused you. I should have told them to reschedule you with someone else."

"But you didn't. Part of you must have wanted—"

"Yes, of course I *wanted*." He looked at Matty with wild eyes, his hands shaking. Matty had never seen him lose control of his body that way. "I still *want* you, Matty."

"But you just said you *didn't* want me."

Rob laughed bitterly, his face contorting with pain. "Don't be a brat. Hell, you know I'm attracted to you. I have feelings for you. But I don't want *it*."

Matty rushed over and clung to Rob's forearms. Rob didn't push him away. "What does that mean? I don't understand."

"I can't start any kind of relationship with you. Got it?"

"No! I really don't."

"The last time, Matty, I was a disaster. It was like you were a drug and when you left I was alone for a pretty harrowing detox. I said I was a mess earlier, but it was so much worse."

"I'm sorry. I never wanted that."

"I know you didn't, but I can't go through it again."

"You wouldn't have to! You're here now and I'm here now. We can be together."

"We can't, Matty. You're still committed to something else."

"Are you saying I can't have you and my career?"

"I'm saying you can't have me and *compete*. Not because I don't want you to win, or because I don't believe in you, or because I'm too selfish to let you do what you love, but because I can't watch you starve yourself, bruise yourself, and break yourself for a something that is *never* going to reward you for your pain, Matty. Do you have any idea how it hurts to watch you give your entire self to something that isn't me, and then watch that thing kick you in the nuts? It doesn't even hold you afterward and tell you that you did a good job. It just hurts you and then hurts you some more."

"That's how sports work. Unless you're four, not everyone gets a trophy. And if that *was* how it worked, I wouldn't want one. I want to be the best."

"I know, and I want you to have what you want, I truly do, but I need someone whose dream lines up with reality."

Denial flared in Matty. He wanted to bring up every skater who had medaled at an older age, and every skater who had somehow carried on a relationship, too, but he knew it was so much more than that. Those people weren't Matty Marcus—they didn't have his build, his past injuries, or his broken heart. And they certainly hadn't sent out a retirement announcement to the press that afternoon.

Rob was talking on, looking up at the sky, and Matty studied the underside of his chin as the words rolled out of him in a kind of purge.

"I need to know that whoever I'm with is in it for the long haul, and that he's not going to take off across the country or around the world chasing a coach, or some self-abusive dream. I always supported your choices, but you take it too far and break yourself in the process. I'm going to be honest. Skating isn't good for you. You might love it, but it doesn't love you. It hurts you, it breaks your body, your heart, and your soul, and it makes you miserable. I can't watch that. I especially can't watch you give it everything you have, and then—"

"Shh," Matty said, stroking his hands up and down Rob's trembling arms. "I know, I know."

"I'm selfish. Fine. I'll admit that. I'm listening to myself right now and all signs point to me being a controlling dickwad."

"No."

"I want to pretend I'm not, but I am. I can't watch someone I care about do that to themselves. Not when I'm not in charge of the outcome and I can't control if you're rewarded or not."

Matty had never heard Rob talk so much, and it was amazing and terrifying. He made soft noises, hoping to keep Rob going. He needed to hear all of it so he could know Rob's darkest hesitations. That way he could fight them.

"I'm already scared for Ben. I see how hard he tries, but somehow it's different for him than it is for you. He's macho and the judges like him. I don't understand it and it's not fair, but it's there all the same. I already know he's going to have it easier than you, but I'm *still* scared for him. He loves it, but he doesn't love it like you do. He's competitive but he doesn't break himself trying to win. I have hope for him, but it's still so much pressure for a kid of his age."

"I understand," Matty soothed.

Rob jerked his head in a nod, and seemed to try to force himself back together. "Good. Then I think we need to just end this."

"But it doesn't have to be this way."

"It does. I'm not a masochist, Matty. I don't like to hurt. Last time, I wasn't the only one in pain. Ben was hurt when you left too."

"I'm so sorry."

"I know you are, and so am I." Rob closed his eyes. "I was as much to blame for it as you."

"But now—"

"Matty, please, I can't just do it again."

"You won't have to. I promise."

Rob opened his eyes, and they glistened. "You won't give up skating. Ben said you told his coach—"

"It was all bravado. You know how I am. Rob, I promise you now—right here and right now—I'm through."

"Since when?"

"Since I realized I want more from my life than some medals as passing proof that I was once spectacularly good at something. I want to be spectacularly good at living my *life*. I want to be good for you." Matty squeezed Rob's hand. "I mean that in so many ways, Rob. I want to be good *for* you, and I want to be good *because* of you. I want to show you how good I can be. I want to make *your* life good because of me."

"Stop. You won't actually quit. You don't mean this."

"I mean every word."

"You're really done?"

"I really am. I'm kicking my boyfriend Figure Skating to the curb."

Rob made a soft sound and rubbed a hand over his eyes. "So what now? I can't just throw you on the bed and do the things I want to do with you."

"Why the fuck not?" Matty demanded.

"Because I'm still *in love with you* and I'm scared. Christ, is that what you wanted to hear?"

Matty breathed out long and slow, a purr of a reply on his lips. "Oooh, oooh, yes, that is exactly what I wanted to hear. *Exactly*."

The kiss was rough, almost angry, and Matty submitted to it, letting Rob lift and carry him inside.

By the bed, Rob put him down and tore at Matty's sweater and tight-fitting jeans. "You better not be fucking with me, Matty."

"I'm not. I'm absolutely not, and be careful! This sweater is really expen—oh, my God...fuck..."

Rob's mouth was hot on his neck as he yanked him close. His hands grabbed at Matty's back and ass, roughly moving up to cup the back of his head as they kissed and fought together to get Matty's clothes off.

Naked, Matty fell to his knees, ripping off Rob's shoes and then scrabbling at the fastenings of Rob's jeans, pulling them down as Rob tossed his own sweater aside. He'd just grabbed hold of the waistband of Rob's underwear when Rob gripped his hands. He stared down at Matty, his chest heaving and his cock pushing hard against his boxer-briefs. His eyes were raw, vulnerable, and desperate. Matty's heart clenched. He'd never meant to hurt Rob so deeply and he needed to make him understand—he'd *never* hurt him like that again.

"I told Valentina I was quitting a few weeks ago, and the press release announcing my retirement went out today," Matty whispered, licking his lips. "I swear, Rob, it's over."

Rob hauled him to his feet and backed him up to the bed. "You couldn't have just told me that to begin with?"

"I didn't know that's what you needed to hear."

Rob grunted, a noise between disapproval and relief, and pushed Matty back onto the soft mattress. Rob seemed to hold himself back as he stared at Matty, his eyes greedily taking in his body. "Show me," he demanded. "I want to see you."

Since he was completely naked, Matty wasn't sure what else there was to see, but he planted his feet on the bed. He brought his hands down to cup his balls and grip his hard cock, the beat of his pulse rushing against his palm as he held it.

Rob's nostrils flared and his breath quickened. "What else do you have?"

Matty licked his lips and rolled over onto his hands and knees, flexing his back to serve up his ass. With his forehead and shoulders down against the matress, he reached back with both hands to spread his ass cheeks and gently rub the pads of his fingers over his hole. He heard Rob hiss, and then the bed dipped.

Kneeling beside him, Rob grabbed Matty's arms around the wrists and held them crossed at Matty's back in one hand. Matty panted into the fresh-smelling duvet as Rob rubbed his free hand over Matty's ass cheeks and dipped fingers into his crack, sliding against his asshole.

"You are such a brat. Making an appointment and coming to my office instead of calling me like a normal person," Rob said.

Matty jerked as Rob's hand swept down and slapped his ass hard. He grunted, rubbing his face against the duvet, as tears he'd managed to keep at bay while they talked welled in his eyes, and the sharp sting in the shape of Rob's hand roared through him.

"Coming back after I told you not to." Rob's hand connected again, and Matty writhed and whimpered. It'd been so long, so damn long since he'd had this and he needed it so badly. He wanted it more than anything. He pressed back, lifting his ass for more.

"Making me miss you again and fuck, Matty, making me want you so bad." And Rob slapped a palm roughly against his other ass cheek

The pain burned through him, and Matty cried out.

"That's it. Make some noise." Rob spanked him in a rapid fire of three fast hits.

Matty struggled slightly against the grip on his wrists, but not hard enough to break free. He knew the upstairs neighbors had to be able to hear him, but he didn't care—he just let his feelings out in cries and grunts that filled the room around him.

"Waiting for me today. Making me confess everything to you. Holding back the most important information until you've already got your way."

Matty arched as Rob's hand landed harder than before, and his thighs started to shake, his cock hard and leaking precum onto the soft duvet.

"Goddammit, Matty," Rob whispered, and his hand fell again. "I love you and you make me crazy."

Matty pulled his wrists free and flipped over, grabbing Rob around the neck and kissing him hard. Rob wrestled him down to the bed and Matty loved being under Rob's heavy weight, legs around his lower back, as their cocks rutting against each other while they rocked. Rob's mouth and hands were everywhere, and Matty couldn't get enough of Rob's skin. He licked and touched, smoothing his hands down Rob's back and gripping his ass.

Rob kissed his way down Matty's body, licking the lines of his muscles, the small scars from his hip surgery, and finally sucking Matty's dick into his mouth.

"I'm going to come so fast," Matty whispered, the hot suction around his dick and the burning from his freshly spanked ass combining with Rob's touch and scent to put him right at the edge, his balls drawing tight and his toes curling as need raked through him.

Rob popped off his cock and sucked hard kisses into his thighs, making him gasp. Matty spread his legs to accommodate the sweet, wet tickle of Rob's tongue against his asshole.

"Oh fuck," Matty whimpered, covering his mouth with one hand, his body shaking and jerking spasmodically on the bed as Rob held his legs firmly up and out, eating Matty's hole urgently.

"Come on. Open up for me."

Matty shivered as Rob's tongue forced its way past his sphincter and gripped Rob's hair in a fist, holding him in place while he rode

Rob's stabbing tongue. He cried out when Rob pulled away and opened a side drawer beside the bed. Matty trembled and quaked, hot joy spreading through his chest and stomach as Rob drizzled lube onto his asshole.

He was here. He'd made it.

As Rob rolled on the condom and pushed Matty's knees up, taking aim, Matty kept his eyes open, watching Rob's face intently as he pushed against him. The look of urgency and awe in Rob's eyes as his cock breached Matty's hole was too much, and Matty struggled to take Rob's thickness and his raw vulnerability at once.

"I love you," Matty whispered.

Rob ducked down to capture Matty's mouth in a brutal kiss as his cock forced Matty open, fucking him with strong, quick strokes.

"I love you too," Rob muttered, his mouth barely leaving Matty's as he spoke. Rob was unrelenting, plowing into him again and again, stroking over his prostate, and leaving him clinging to Rob's hunching body with arms and legs.

Matty gasped for breath around Rob's demanding kiss. "Show me," he whispered in Rob's ear. "Give me more. I want to see what else you have."

Rob groaned and reared back, his hand coming up to Matty's throat and pressing there lightly, holding Matty in place as he fucked him. Matty's cock pulsed and thudded between them, precome sliding against their stomachs. Rob's hand on his throat was dizzyingly good. "More," Matty gasped.

"Three snaps."

"Yes, my safeword," Matty confirmed.

Rob collapsed against him, his hips rolling and digging, moving his cock hard into Matty's body as he slid his hand up from Matty's throat to cover his mouth and pinch off his nose. Matty convulsed, and his ass grabbed around Rob's cock, making Rob curse and slam into him roughly.

"Come for me like this," Rob whispered. "Come now."

Matty tried to keep his gaze on Rob's face, but his eyes rolled up and he shook as Rob fucked him, grinding into him. He brought up his hands to hold Rob's in place, while his cock ached and throbbed between them.

He was so close, so close, and his lungs burned for air as he climbed like a rocket into a dark, starry night. As Rob gripped his face harder, reminding him who commanded his breath, his body, and his future, Matty came. His orgasm was an explosion—convulsing joy, love, and pleasure, cresting wonder, need, and hope—and he dug his heels into Rob's still hunching back. He surrendered. He was safe. He was loved.

He was home.

EPILOGUE

Matty glanced at Rob, seated beside him at the packed Thanksgiving dinner table, listening to Donna hold forth about the importance of being yourself and not caving to the political nature of the sport. Ben nodded earnestly. He hadn't won any medals during his first junior season, but he'd been damn close.

"So, Matty," Ben said, breaking off the conversation with Donna. "Are you sharing a room with Julien on the Skate Skate tour?"

Matty felt Rob stiffen next to him.

"I doubt it," Matty said, rubbing Rob's thigh reassuringly. Rob could be adorably jealous sometimes, although he'd never admit it. "Why?"

"A friend of mine has a crush on him."

"And?"

"Well, I kind of told her that if you room with Julien, then when I come visit you, I might, maybe, *possibly* steal some of his underwear for her."

Matty blinked and fought to keep from laughing. "Tell your friend that's not going to happen for so many reasons."

"*I* could probably get some of his underwear," Elliot said. "All I'd have to do is get Matty to introduce us and we'd be lovers instantly."

Matty snorted.

"You know it's true, bitch." Then he asked Ben earnestly, "How much would you pay me to sleep with him?"

"Uh, I wouldn't. That would make you a prostitute," Ben said. "And, seriously, no one pays to sleep with Julien Alban. I'm straight and even I can see how pretty he is."

"Julien's a nice guy and I'll be happy to introduce your friend if she comes to a show, but there'll be no underwear stealing. That's just weird."

"Is this really the conversation we want to have over Thanksgiving dinner?" Matty's mother asked, passing around a dish of green bean casserole.

"No!" Joey and Randy replied in unison.

Anja just laughed and shook her head. "Donna, I'd like to pick your brain later about what to do about Ben's travels while I work. I hate sending him around the world with just his coach. How did you deal with that when it came to Matty?"

"Mom, I don't need a babysitter." Ben sighed, frowning at her. "Coach takes good care of us."

Donna winked at Anja and said, "Sounds like the perfect conversation for a post-dinner walk while the men clean up the kitchen."

Anja lifted her glass of wine in a toast of agreement.

Rob spooned beans onto his plate before handing the dish to Matty. He gamely changed the subject. "Has Matty told you all about his coaching plans?"

He had, actually, a dozen times, but his mother encouraged him to tell them again as they passed the food around and shoveled heaps of sweet potatoes and slices of turkey onto their plates.

"I like kids, and Joanna's right, kids like me."

"It's true," Ben agreed, already over being annoyed with his mom. "You're awesome with kids."

"I figure if I start with nine or ten-year-olds, that will give me and the skating world time to move on before I ever have to worry about dragging my own baggage into a student's competition."

"Will Yuliya do any coaching?" Ben asked, taking the tray of turkey from Elliot.

"Sure. Assuming she ever wants to dust off her red wig." Matty had a feeling she would. She kept things interesting for everyone.

"Since you're so great with kids, do you think I might get a little brother or sister?" Ben asked pointedly.

"*Ben.*" Anja gave him a warning glance before winking at Matty. "Give them a few years."

She smiled, and there were definitely hearts in her eyes. Matty smiled back, despite the fact that he would never be interested in changing dirty diapers.

"Donna, did you put him up to that?" Matty asked.

His mother smiled sweetly and shrugged.

Rob cleared his throat. "Son, I'm fairly sure I taught you about the birds and the bees, but just in case you got confused, let me clarify. There has to be a man and a *woman* to make a baby—and even though Matty is currently wearing more make-up than the two women in this room, he is, in fact, a man. And yes, we know there's adoption and surrogacy, but there will be no babies."

"Just students," Matty added, frowning at his mother. "Leave the babies to your other son, okay?"

"I might not be wearing make-up, but I don't even have a girlfriend, so don't look at me for any babies," Joey said, spooning homemade applesauce onto his plate.

"What about marriage, then?" Donna asked, looking at Rob.

Matty was getting ready to strangle her when Elliot saved the day.

"Speaking of make-up," Elliot said, leaning toward Ben.

"Stop," Ben said, batting at Elliot's hand. "Leave it."

"But you smeared the mascara. All my hard work is defeated by your inability to keep your hands off your face."

"You put too much glitter on me anyway. Girls like eyeliner. Not glitter. Boys like glitter. Don't think I don't know these things."

Elliot turned to Matty. "Matty, make him fix it. It looks so trashy."

"He's fifteen and straight, Elliot. I don't think he gives a fuck about smearing his mascara. I can't believe he even let you put it on him."

"I know but..."

Rob leaned over and rubbed the wayward make-up from Ben's face. "There. Happy now?"

Elliot smiled and lowered his lashes flirtatiously. "Quite. Rob, darling, I think I have a little on my face too. Can you get it?"

Matty rolled his eyes. "Give up on the threesome idea."

"Really, Matty, there are mothers and children in the room." Donna threw up her hands.

"And brothers," Joey added.

"Dads too," Randy said gruffly from the head of the table.

"I wonder what it would be like to have a threesome?" Matty mused.

"I've offered," Elliot said.

"Yeah, but I've seen your dick and it's really not impressive enough to make it worthwhile."

"My dick is amazing!"

"Amazingly average. Besides, Rob's a little possessive."

"Matty!" Donna said. "Rob, can you control him?"

"We're already being reprimanded for excessive sexual content at the table, Donna. I don't think you really want me to control him here." Rob's voice was casual as he squeezed Matty's knee under the table, their signal for "shut up now and I'll reward you later."

"It's time to pray." Matty's dad interrupted before anything else could be said to escalate the inappropriate jokes.

Everyone put down their forks and spoons, having already dug in before grace, just like always.

"Dear God, whom I only believe in sometimes," Matty began, and his dad threw a dinner roll at him. "Okay, okay, you do it."

Matty closed his eyes, twining his fingers with Rob's, as his father began to speak.

"Heavenly Father, thank you for the food before us and the company around us. Thank you for the blessings of this past year. But most of all, thank you for the failures and heartbreaks, because they are our best teachers. Thank you for this day, this hour, and the joy we have as a family. Amen." Randy cleared his throat. "And now I'll shut up for another twelve months."

Matty looked around the table. Everyone important to him was here. These were the people who had his back no matter what. No matter how often he failed, or what stupid things he said or did. They loved him. They endured glittery make-up attacks from his best friend and sexual innuendos from his boyfriend. They let him try to fly even when he was too mucked up to make it.

When he fell, they held him, and helped him find a new way to soar.

"Happy Thanksgiving," Rob whispered in his ear. "Now eat your food."

"But it smells so divine. Eating would ruin it."

It had been a while now since he'd weighed anything close to competitive lows, but he was happy with his body, and the strength of it. He was especially happy with how nice it felt to not be hungry anymore. To not be starving for food—or for anything else.

Letting go wasn't easy. He missed Valentina and her drill sergeant ways, and he missed knowing that his body was trained—that it would do whatever he wanted or needed it to do on the ice all on its own without conscious effort.

But he was happier. He was content to have walked away when he did. At night, underneath Rob's body, in his strong arms, Matty didn't even miss his ex-boyfriend Figure Skating at all. One day, he hoped that feeling would translate into the daytime as well. As it was, nighttime was enough.

That night, he woke from a dream of Montana. He left Rob sleeping, and tiptoed into his parents' backyard to search the sky for the North Star. He thought of bouquets of roses, shouts from the crowd, and scores that broke his heart, and he let the wave of sadness wash over him. Then he remembered winter fields, cows, horses, and a frozen-over pond. Reverence and joy descended upon him and drove away the sadness.

Even when he couldn't find it, lost behind city-shine or cloud cover, the North Star was still there. It shone brighter than any medal. It was forever and constant—and no one could take it away.

THE END

Author's Note

First, I'd like to apologize to the residents of Whitefish, MT, for the portrayal of their Whitefish Winter Carnival Gala. In reality, it is a lovely event held at the country club. For my purposes, I wanted it set it in the high school gymnasium. Forgive me.

Second, I'd like to apologize for the indulgent thank yous that follow. For those who don't wish to read all my gooeyness, they can be summed up as follows: thank you to my readers, my family, and my friends for supporting me in this writing endeavor.

Now, for specifics!

Thank you to Adam Rippon, Max Aaron, Denis Ten, and many other skaters for their performances and for inspiration. Thank you to Johnny Weir for inspiration and for being himself.

Thank you to my best friend, Jed, who goes above and beyond for me always and ever. There's no quantifying my love for her and my gratitude to her. She makes me a better writer and I have no idea what I'd do without her. One day, we will find just the right old folks' home to grow senile in together and then hopefully die on the same day.

Thank you to Keira Andrews for a wonderful, amazing editing job and for her dedicated friendship.

Thank you to Amelia Gormley for the encouragement and help with regards to self-publishing, and for being a wonderful, giving friend.

Thank you to Tracy for an incredibly helpful and smart beta reading and her astute assessment that no athlete should eat like Matty. Seriously, kids, eat your food!

Thank you to Cindy for beta reading an earlier version. Her opinions and input set me on the right path to write about 50,000 more words than what she originally saw.

Thank you to Sharon for her quick read when I needed some advice. Thank you to Anne-Marie for the wonderful help and the kind notes! Thank you to Alice, Aimee, and Brigid for read throughs of a very, very early version, and for being such wonderful friends. Thank you to Beth for the many years of supportive friendship.

Thank you to Kim for the girls' nights out and for always supporting me by listening and cheering me on! Thank you to Liza for the pep talks and for being the sister-of-my-heart.

Thank you to Jacyn and Rachel for their never-ending love and support, and for their deep and true friendship—SO MUCH LOVE!

Thank you to my parents and in-laws for their love and support.

And thank you to my daughter for being so understanding when imaginary people demand Mommy's attention. Thank you to my husband for his love, faith, and unfailing encouragement.

Thank you to any and all readers of this work. No book is complete without a reader and all of you hold a dear place in my heart.

All my best,

Leta Blake

ABOUT THE AUTHOR

While Leta Blake would love to tell you that writing transports her to worlds of magic and wonder and then safely returns her to a home of sparkling cleanliness and carefully folded laundry, the reality is a bit different.

For as long as Leta can recall, stories have hijacked her mind, abducting her to other lands, and forcing her to bend to the will of imaginary people. All returns to reality are accompanied by piles of laundry and forgotten appointments. But with her faithful friends and family by her side, the fall-out isn't usually too severe, and the joy of writing and the thrill of finishing a book makes it all worth it.

At her home in the Southern U.S., Leta works hard at achieving balance between her day job, her writing, and her family.

You can find out more about her by following her at the following places:

letablake.wordpress.com

facebook.com/letablake

twitter/letablake

Other Books by Leta Blake

Free Read
Stalking Dreams

Tempting Tales with Keira Andrews
Earthly Desires
Ascending Hearts
Love's Nest

Made in the USA
Monee, IL
05 July 2020